The Lady of
the Shroud

The Lady of the Shroud

Bram Stoker

MINT EDITIONS

The Lady of the Shroud was first published in 1909.

This edition published by Mint Editions 2021.

ISBN 9781513271507 | E-ISBN 9781513276502

Published by Mint Editions®

 **MINT EDITIONS**

minteditionbooks.com

Publishing Director: Jennifer Newens
Design & Production: Rachel Lopez Metzger
Project Manager: Micaela Clark
Typesetting: Westchester Publishing Services

Contents

Book I

The Will of Roger Melton

The Reading of the Will of Roger Melton and all that Followed

Record made by Ernest Roger Halbard Melton, law-student of the Inner Temple, eldest son of Ernest Halbard Melton, eldest son of Ernest Melton, elder brother of the said Roger Melton and his next of kin.

I consider it at least useful—perhaps necessary—to have a complete and accurate record of all pertaining to the Will of my late grand-uncle Roger Melton.

To which end let me put down the various members of his family, and explain some of their occupations and idiosyncrasies. My father, Ernest Halbard Melton, was the only son of Ernest Melton, eldest son of Sir Geoffrey Halbard Melton of Humcroft, in the shire of Salop, a Justice of the Peace, and at one time Sheriff. My great-grandfather, Sir Geoffrey, had inherited a small estate from his father, Roger Melton. In his time, by the way, the name was spelled Milton; but my great-great-grandfather changed the spelling to the later form, as he was a practical man not given to sentiment, and feared lest he should in the public eye be confused with others belonging to the family of a Radical person called Milton, who wrote poetry and was some sort of official in the time of Cromwell, whilst we are Conservatives. The same practical spirit which originated the change in the spelling of the family name inclined him to go into business. So he became, whilst still young, a tanner and leather-dresser. He utilized for the purpose the ponds and streams, and also the oak-woods on his estate—Torraby in Suffolk. He made a fine business, and accumulated a considerable fortune, with a part of which he purchased the Shropshire estate, which he entailed, and to which I am therefore heir-apparent.

Sir Geoffrey had, in addition to my grandfather, three sons and a daughter, the latter being born twenty years after her youngest brother. These sons were: Geoffrey, who died without issue, having been killed in the Indian Mutiny at Meerut in 1857, at which he took up a sword, though a civilian, to fight for his life; Roger (to whom I shall refer presently); and John—the latter, like Geoffrey, dying unmarried. Out of

Sir Geoffrey's family of five, therefore, only three have to be considered: My grandfather, who had three children, two of whom, a son and a daughter, died young, leaving only my father, Roger and Patience. Patience, who was born in 1858, married an Irishman of the name of Sellenger—which was the usual way of pronouncing the name of St. Leger, or, as they spelled it, Sent Leger—restored by later generations to the still older form. He was a reckless, dare-devil sort of fellow, then a Captain in the Lancers, a man not without the quality of bravery—he won the Victoria Cross at the Battle of Amoaful in the Ashantee Campaign. But I fear he lacked the seriousness and steadfast strenuous purpose which my father always says marks the character of our own family. He ran through nearly all of his patrimony—never a very large one; and had it not been for my grand-aunt's little fortune, his days, had he lived, must have ended in comparative poverty. Comparative, not actual; for the Meltons, who are persons of considerable pride, would not have tolerated a poverty-stricken branch of the family. We don't think much of that lot—any of us.

Fortunately, my great-aunt Patience had only one child, and the premature decease of Captain St. Leger (as I prefer to call the name) did not allow of the possibility of her having more. She did not marry again, though my grandmother tried several times to arrange an alliance for her. She was, I am told, always a stiff, uppish person, who would not yield herself to the wisdom of her superiors. Her own child was a son, who seemed to take his character rather from his father's family than from my own. He was a wastrel and a rolling stone, always in scrapes at school, and always wanting to do ridiculous things. My father, as Head of the House and his own senior by eighteen years, tried often to admonish him; but his perversity of spirit and his truculence were such that he had to desist. Indeed, I have heard my father say that he sometimes threatened his life. A desperate character he was, and almost devoid of reverence. No one, not even my father, had any influence—good influence, of course, I mean—over him, except his mother, who was of my family; and also a woman who lived with her—a sort of governess—aunt, he called her. The way of it was this: Captain St. Leger had a younger brother, who made an improvident marriage with a Scotch girl when they were both very young. They had nothing to live on except what the reckless Lancer gave them, for he had next to nothing himself, and she was "bare"—which is, I understand, the indelicate Scottish way of expressing lack of fortune.

She was, however, I understand, of an old and somewhat good family, though broken in fortune—to use an expression which, however, could hardly be used precisely in regard to a family or a person who never had fortune to be broken in! It was so far well that the MacKelpies—that was the maiden name of Mrs. St. Leger—were reputable—so far as fighting was concerned. It would have been too humiliating to have allied to our family, even on the distaff side, a family both poor and of no account. Fighting alone does not make a family, I think. Soldiers are not everything, though they think they are. We have had in our family men who fought; but I never heard of any of them who fought because they *wanted* to. Mrs. St. Leger had a sister; fortunately there were only those two children in the family, or else they would all have had to be supported by the money of my family.

Mr. St. Leger, who was only a subaltern, was killed at Maiwand; and his wife was left a beggar. Fortunately, however, she died—her sister spread a story that it was from the shock and grief—before the child which she expected was born. This all happened when my cousin—or, rather, my father's cousin, my first-cousin-once-removed, to be accurate—was still a very small child. His mother then sent for Miss MacKelpie, her brother-in-law's sister-in-law, to come and live with her, which she did—beggars can't be choosers; and she helped to bring up young St. Leger.

I remember once my father giving me a sovereign for making a witty remark about her. I was quite a boy then, not more than thirteen; but our family were always clever from the very beginning of life, and father was telling me about the St. Leger family. My family hadn't, of course, seen anything of them since Captain St. Leger died—the circle to which we belong don't care for poor relations—and was explaining where Miss MacKelpie came in. She must have been a sort of nursery governess, for Mrs. St. Leger once told him that she helped her to educate the child.

"Then, father," I said, "if she helped to educate the child she ought to have been called Miss MacSkelpie!"

When my first-cousin-once-removed, Rupert, was twelve years old, his mother died, and he was in the dolefuls about it for more than a year. Miss MacKelpie kept on living with him all the same. Catch her quitting! That sort don't go into the poor-house when they can keep out! My father, being Head of the Family, was, of course, one of the trustees, and his uncle Roger, brother of the testator, another. The third was General MacKelpie, a poverty-stricken Scotch laird who had a lot of valueless land at Croom, in Ross-shire. I remember father gave me a new ten-pound note when I interrupted him whilst he was telling me of the incident of young St. Leger's improvidence by remarking that he was in error as to the land. From what I had heard of MacKelpie's estate, it was productive of one thing; when he asked me "What?" I answered "Mortgages!" Father, I knew, had bought, not long before, a lot of them at what a college friend of mine from Chicago used to call "cut-throat" price. When I remonstrated with my father for buying them at all, and so injuring the family estate which I was to inherit, he gave me an answer, the astuteness of which I have never forgotten.

"I did it so that I might keep my hand on the bold General, in case he should ever prove troublesome. And if the worst should ever come to the worst, Croom is a good country for grouse and stags!" My father can see as far as most men!

When my cousin—I shall call him cousin henceforth in this record, lest it might seem to any unkind person who might hereafter read it that I wished to taunt Rupert St. Leger with his somewhat obscure position, in reiterating his real distance in kinship with my family—when my cousin, Rupert St. Leger, wished to commit a certain idiotic act of financial folly, he approached my father on the subject, arriving at our estate, Humcroft, at an inconvenient time, without permission, not having had even the decent courtesy to say he was coming. I was then a little chap of six years old, but I could not help noticing his mean appearance. He was all dusty and dishevelled. When my father saw him—I came into the study with him—he said in a horrified voice:

"Good God!" He was further shocked when the boy brusquely acknowledged, in reply to my father's greeting, that he had travelled third class. Of course, none of my family ever go anything but first class; even the servants go second. My father was really angry when he said he had walked up from the station.

"A nice spectacle for my tenants and my tradesmen! To see my—my—a kinsman of my house, howsoever remote, trudging like a tramp on the road to my estate! Why, my avenue is two miles and a perch! No wonder you are filthy and insolent!" Rupert—really, I cannot call him cousin here—was exceedingly impertinent to my father.

"I walked, sir, because I had no money; but I assure you I did not mean to be insolent. I simply came here because I wished to ask your advice and assistance, not because you are an important person, and have a long avenue—as I know to my cost—but simply because you are one of my trustees."

"*Your* trustees, sirrah!" said my father, interrupting him. "Your trustees?"

"I beg your pardon, sir," he said, quite quietly. "I meant the trustees of my dear mother's will."

"And what, may I ask you," said father, "do you want in the way of advice from one of the trustees of your dear mother's will?" Rupert got very red, and was going to say something rude—I knew it from his look—but he stopped, and said in the same gentle way:

"I want your advice, sir, as to the best way of doing something which I wish to do, and, as I am under age, cannot do myself. It must be done through the trustees of my mother's will."

"And the assistance for which you wish?" said father, putting his hand in his pocket. I know what that action means when I am talking to him.

"The assistance I want," said Rupert, getting redder than ever, "is from my—the trustee also. To carry out what I want to do."

"And what may that be?" asked my father. "I would like, sir, to make over to my Aunt Janet—" My father interrupted him by asking—he had evidently remembered my jest:

"Miss MacSkelpie?" Rupert got still redder, and I turned away; I didn't quite wish that he should see me laughing. He went on quietly:

"*MacKelpie*, sir! Miss Janet MacKelpie, my aunt, who has always been so kind to me, and whom my mother loved—I want to have made over to her the money which my dear mother left to me." Father doubtless wished to have the matter take a less serious turn, for Rupert's eyes were all shiny with tears which had not fallen; so after a little pause he said, with indignation, which I knew was simulated:

"Have you forgotten your mother so soon, Rupert, that you wish to give away the very last gift which she bestowed on you?" Rupert was sitting, but he jumped up and stood opposite my father with his fist clenched. He was quite pale now, and his eyes looked so fierce that I thought he would do my father an injury. He spoke in a voice which did not seem like his own, it was so strong and deep.

"Sir!" he roared out. I suppose, if I was a writer, which, thank God, I am not—I have no need to follow a menial occupation—I would call it "thundered." "Thundered" is a longer word than "roared," and would, of course, help to gain the penny which a writer gets for a line. Father got pale too, and stood quite still. Rupert looked at him steadily for quite half a minute—it seemed longer at the time—and suddenly smiled and said, as he sat down again:

"Sorry. But, of course, you don't understand such things." Then he went on talking before father had time to say a word.

"Let us get back to business. As you do not seem to follow me, let me explain that it is *because* I do not forget that I wish to do this. I remember my dear mother's wish to make Aunt Janet happy, and would like to do as she did."

"*Aunt* Janet?" said father, very properly sneering at his ignorance. "She is not your aunt. Why, even her sister, who was married to your uncle, was only your aunt by courtesy." I could not help feeling that Rupert meant to be rude to my father, though his words were quite polite. If I had been as much bigger than him as he was than me, I should have flown at him; but he was a very big boy for his age. I am myself rather thin. Mother says thinness is an "appanage of birth."

"My Aunt Janet, sir, is an aunt by love. Courtesy is a small word to use in connection with such devotion as she has given to us. But I needn't trouble you with such things, sir. I take it that my relations on the side of my own house do not affect you. I am a Sent Leger!" Father looked quite taken aback. He sat quite still before he spoke.

"Well, Mr. St. Leger, I shall think over the matter for a while, and shall presently let you know my decision. In the meantime, would you like something to eat? I take it that as you must have started very early, you have not had any breakfast?" Rupert smiled quite genially:

"That is true, sir. I haven't broken bread since dinner last night, and I am ravenously hungry." Father rang the bell, and told the footman who answered it to send the housekeeper. When she came, father said to her:

"Mrs. Martindale, take this boy to your room and give him some breakfast." Rupert stood very still for some seconds. His face had got red again after his paleness. Then he bowed to my father, and followed Mrs. Martindale, who had moved to the door.

Nearly an hour afterwards my father sent a servant to tell him to come to the study. My mother was there, too, and I had gone back with her. The man came back and said:

"Mrs. Martindale, sir, wishes to know, with her respectful service, if she may have a word with you." Before father could reply mother told him to bring her. The housekeeper could not have been far off—that kind are generally near a keyhole—for she came at once. When she came in, she stood at the door curtseying and looking pale. Father said:

"Well?"

"I thought, sir and ma'am, that I had better come and tell you about Master Sent Leger. I would have come at once, but I feared to disturb you."

"Well?" Father had a stern way with servants. When I'm head of the family I'll tread them under my feet. That's the way to get real devotion from servants!

"If you please, sir, I took the young gentleman into my room and ordered a nice breakfast for him, for I could see he was half famished—a growing boy like him, and so tall! Presently it came along. It was a good breakfast, too! The very smell of it made even me hungry. There were eggs and frizzled ham, and grilled kidneys, and coffee, and buttered toast, and bloater-paste—"

"That will do as to the menu," said mother. "Go on!"

"When it was all ready, and the maid had gone, I put a chair to the table and said, 'Now, sir, your breakfast is ready!' He stood up and said, 'Thank you, madam; you are very kind!' and he bowed to me quite nicely, just as if I was a lady, ma'am!"

"Go on," said mother.

"Then, sir, he held out his hand and said, 'Good-bye, and thank you,' and he took up his cap.

"'But aren't you going to have any breakfast, sir?' I says.

"'No, thank you, madam,' he said; 'I couldn't eat here. . . in this house, I mean!' Well, ma'am, he looked so lonely that I felt my heart melting, and I ventured to ask him if there was any mortal thing I could do for him. 'Do tell me, dear,' I ventured to say. 'I am an old woman, and you, sir, are only a boy, though it's a fine man you will be—like your dear, splendid father, which I remember so well, and gentle like your poor dear mother.'

"'You're a dear!' he says; and with that I took up his hand and kissed it, for I remember his poor dear mother so well, that was dead only a year. Well, with that he turned his head away, and when I took him by the shoulders and turned him round—he is only a young boy, ma'am, for all he is so big—I saw that the tears were rolling down his cheeks. With that I laid his head on my breast—I've had children of my own, ma'am, as you know, though they're all gone. He came willing enough, and sobbed for a little bit. Then he straightened himself up, and I stood respectfully beside him.

"'Tell Mr. Melton,' he said, 'that I shall not trouble him about the trustee business.'

"'But won't you tell him yourself, sir, when you see him?' I says.

"'I shall not see him again,' he says; 'I am going back now!'

"Well, ma'am, I knew he'd had no breakfast, though he was hungry, and that he would walk as he come, so I ventured to say: 'If you won't take it a liberty, sir, may I do anything to make your going easier? Have you sufficient money, sir? If not, may I give, or lend, you some? I shall be very proud if you will allow me to.'

"'Yes,' he says quite hearty. 'If you will, you might lend me a shilling, as I have no money. I shall not forget it.' He said, as he took the coin: 'I shall return the amount, though I never can the kindness. I shall keep the coin.' He took the shilling, sir—he wouldn't take any more—and then he said good-bye. At the door he turned and walked back to me, and put his arms round me like a real boy does, and gave me a hug, and says he:

"'Thank you a thousand times, Mrs. Martindale, for your goodness to me, for your sympathy, and for the way you have spoken of my father and mother. You have seen me cry, Mrs. Martindale,' he said; 'I don't often cry: the last time was when I came back to the lonely house after my poor dear was laid to rest. But you nor any other shall ever see a tear of mine again.' And with that he straightened out his big back and held up his fine proud head, and walked out. I saw him from the window striding down the avenue. My! but he is a proud boy, sir—an honour to your family, sir, say I respectfully. And there, the proud child has gone away hungry, and he won't, I know, ever use that shilling to buy food!"

Father was not going to have that, you know, so he said to her:

"He does not belong to my family, I would have you to know. True, he is allied to us through the female side; but we do not count him or his in my family." He turned away and began to read a book. It was a decided snub to her.

But mother had a word to say before Mrs. Martindale was done with. Mother has a pride of her own, and doesn't brook insolence from inferiors; and the housekeeper's conduct seemed to be rather presuming. Mother, of course, isn't quite our class, though her folk are quite worthy and enormously rich. She is one of the Dalmallingtons, the salt people, one of whom got a peerage when the Conservatives went out. She said to the housekeeper:

"I think, Mrs. Martindale, that I shall not require your services after this day month! And as I don't keep servants in my employment when I dismiss them, here is your month's wages due on the 25th of this month, and another month in lieu of notice. Sign this receipt." She was writing a receipt as she spoke. The other signed it without a word, and handed it to her. She seemed quite flabbergasted. Mother got up and sailed—that is the way that mother moves when she is in a wax—out of the room.

Lest I should forget it, let me say here that the dismissed housekeeper was engaged the very next day by the Countess of Salop. I may say in explanation that the Earl of Salop, K.G., who is Lord-Lieutenant of the County, is jealous of father's position and his growing influence. Father is going to contest the next election on the Conservative side, and is sure to be made a Baronet before long.

Letter from Major-General Sir Colin Alexander MacKelpie, V.C., K.C.B., of Croom, Ross, N.B., to Rupert Sent Leger, Esq., 14, Newland Park, Dulwich, London, S.E.

July 4, 1892

MY DEAR GODSON,

I am truly sorry I am unable to agree with your request that I should acquiesce in your desire to transfer to Miss Janet MacKelpie the property bequeathed to you by your mother, of which property I am a trustee. Let me say at once that, had it been possible to me to do so, I should have held it a privilege to further such a wish—not because the beneficiare whom you would create is a near kinswoman of my own. That, in truth, is my real difficulty. I have undertaken a trust made by an honourable lady on behalf of her only son—son of a man of stainless honour, and a dear friend of my own, and whose son has a rich heritage of honour from both parents, and who will, I am sure, like to look back on his whole life as worthy of his parents, and of those whom his parents trusted. You will see, I am sure, that whatsoever I might grant regarding anyone else, my hands are tied in this matter.

And now let me say, my dear boy, that your letter has given me the most intense pleasure. It is an unspeakable delight to me to find in the son of your father—a man whom I loved, and a boy whom I love—the same generosity of spirit which endeared your father to all his comrades, old as well as young. Come what may, I shall always be proud of you; and if the sword of an old soldier—it is all I have—can ever serve you in any way, it and its master's life are, and shall be, whilst life remains to him, yours.

It grieves me to think that Janet cannot, through my act, be given that ease and tranquillity of spirit which come from competence. But, my dear Rupert, you will be of full age in seven years more. Then, if you are in the same mind—and I am sure you will not change—you, being your own master, can do freely as you will. In the meantime, to secure, so far as I can, my dear Janet against any malign stroke of fortune, I have given orders to my factor to remit semi-annually to Janet one full half of such income as may be derived in any form from my estate of Croom. It is, I am sorry to say, heavily mortgaged; but of such as is—or may be, free from such charge as the mortgage entails— something at least will, I trust, remain to her. And, my dear boy, I can frankly say that it is to me a real pleasure that you and I can be linked in one more bond in this association of purpose. I have always held you in my heart as though you were my own son. Let me tell you now that you have acted as I should have liked a son of my own, had I been blessed with one, to have acted. God bless you, my dear.

Yours ever,
COLIN ALEX. MACKELPIE

Letter from Roger Melton, of Openshaw Grange, to Rupert Sent Leger, Esq., 14, Newland Park, Dulwich, London, S.E.

July 1, 1892

MY DEAR NEPHEW,

Your letter of the 30th ult. received. Have carefully considered matter stated, and have come to the conclusion that my duty as a trustee would not allow me to give full consent, as you wish. Let me explain. The testator, in making her will, intended that such fortune as she had at disposal should be used to supply to you her son such benefits as its annual product should procure. To this end, and to provide against wastefulness or foolishness on your part, or, indeed, against any generosity, howsoever worthy, which might impoverish you and so defeat her benevolent intentions regarding your education, comfort, and future good, she did not place the estate directly in your hands, leaving you to do as you might feel inclined about it. But, on the contrary, she entrusted the corpus of it in the hands of men whom she believed should be resolute enough and strong enough to carry out her intent, even against any cajolements or pressure which might be employed to the contrary. It being her intention, then, that such trustees as she appointed would use for your benefit the interest accruing annually from the capital at command, *and that only* (as specifically directed in the will), so that on your arriving at full age the capital entrusted to us should be handed over to you intact, I find a hard-and-fast duty in the matter of adhering exactly to the directions given. I have no doubt that my co-trustees regard the matter in exactly the same light. Under the circumstances, therefore, we, the trustees, have not only a single and united duty towards you as the object of the testator's wishes, but towards each other as regards the manner of the carrying out of that duty. I take it, therefore, that it would not be consonant with the spirit of the trust or of our own ideas in accepting it that any of us should take a course pleasant to himself which would or might involve a stern opposition on the part of other of the co-trustees. We have each of us to do the unpleasant part of this duty without fear or favour. You understand, of course, that the time which must elapse before you come into absolute possession of your estate is a limited one. As by the terms of the will we are to hand over our trust when you have reached the age of twenty-one, there are only seven years to expire. But till then, though I should gladly meet your wishes if I could, I must adhere to the duty which I have undertaken. At the expiration of that period you will be quite free to divest yourself of your estate without protest or comment of any man.

Having now expressed as clearly as I can the limitations by which I am bound with regard to the corpus of your estate, let me say that in any other way which is in my power or discretion I shall be most happy to see your wishes carried out so far as rests with me. Indeed, I shall undertake to use what influence I may possess with my co-trustees to induce them to take a similar view of your wishes. In my own thinking you are quite free to use your own property in your own way. But as, until you shall have attained your majority, you have only life-user in your mother's bequest, you are only at liberty to deal with the annual increment. On our part as trustees we have a first charge on that increment to be used for purposes of your maintenance, clothes, and education. As to what may remain over each half-year, you will be free to deal with it as you choose. On receiving from you a written authorization to your trustees, if you desire the whole sum or any part of it to be paid over to Miss Janet MacKelpie, I shall see that it is effected. Believe me, that our duty is to protect the corpus of the estate, and to this end we may not act on any instruction to imperil it. But there our warranty stops. We can deal during our trusteeship with the corpus only. Further, lest there should arise any error on your part, we can deal with any general instruction for only so long as it may remain unrevoked. You are, and must be, free to alter your instructions or authorizations at any time. Thus your latest document must be used for our guidance.

As to the general principle involved in your wish I make no comment. You are at liberty to deal with your own how you will. I quite understand that your impulse is a generous one, and I fully believe that it is in consonance with what had always been the wishes of my sister. Had she been happily alive and had to give judgment of your intent, I am convinced that she would have approved. Therefore, my dear nephew, should you so wish, I shall be happy for her sake as well as your own to pay over on your account (as a confidential matter between you and me), but from my own pocket, a sum equal to that which you wish transferred to Miss Janet MacKelpie. On hearing from you I shall know how to act in the matter. With all good wishes,

Believe me to be,
Your affectionate uncle,
ROGER MELTON

To Rupert Sent Leger, Esq.

Letter from Rupert Sent Leger to Roger Melton,

July 5, 1892

My Dear Uncle,

Thank you heartily for your kind letter. I quite understand, and now see that I should not have asked you as a trustee, such a thing. I see your duty clearly, and agree with your view of it. I enclose a letter directed to my trustees, asking them to pay over annually till further direction to Miss Janet MacKelpie at this address whatever sum may remain over from the interest of my mother's bequest after deduction of such expenses as you may deem fit for my maintenance, clothing, and education, together with a sum of one pound sterling per month, which was the amount my dear mother always gave me for my personal use—"pocket-money," she called it.

With regard to your most kind and generous offer to give to my dear Aunt Janet the sum which I would have given myself, had such been in my power, I thank you most truly and sincerely, both for my dear aunt (to whom, of course, I shall not mention the matter unless you specially authorize me) and myself. But, indeed, I think it will be better not to offer it. Aunt Janet is very proud, and would not accept any benefit. With me, of course, it is different, for since I was a wee child she has been like another mother to me, and I love her very much. Since my mother died—and she, of course, was all-in-all to me—there has been no other. And in such a love as ours pride has no place. Thank you again, dear uncle, and God bless you.

Your loving nephew,
Rupert Sent Leger

Ernest Roger Halbard Melton's Record—*Continued*

And now *re* the remaining one of Sir Geoffrey's children, Roger. He was the third child and third son, the only daughter, Patience, having been born twenty years after the last of the four sons. Concerning Roger,

I shall put down all I have heard of him from my father and grandfather. From my grand-aunt I heard nothing, I was a very small kid when she died; but I remember seeing her, but only once. A very tall, handsome woman of a little over thirty, with very dark hair and light-coloured eyes. I think they were either grey or blue, but I can't remember which. She looked very proud and haughty, but I am bound to say that she was very nice to me. I remember feeling very jealous of Rupert because his mother looked so distinguished. Rupert was eight years older than me, and I was afraid he would beat me if I said anything he did not like. So I was silent except when I forgot to be, and Rupert said very unkindly, and I think very unfairly, that I was "A sulky little beast." I haven't forgot that, and I don't mean to. However, it doesn't matter much what he said or thought. There he is—if he is at all—where no one can find him, with no money or nothing, for what little he had he settled when he came of age, on the MacSkelpie. He wanted to give it to her when his mother died, but father, who was a trustee, refused; and Uncle Roger, as I call him, who is another, thought the trustees had no power to allow Rupert to throw away his matrimony, as I called it, making a joke to father when he called it patrimony. Old Sir Colin MacSkelpie, who is the third, said he couldn't take any part in such a permission, as the MacSkelpie was his niece. He is a rude old man, that. I remember when, not remembering his relationship, I spoke of the MacSkelpie, he caught me a clip on the ear that sent me across the room. His Scotch is very broad. I can hear him say, "Hae some attempt at even Soothern manners, and dinna misca' yer betters, ye young puddock, or I'll wring yer snoot!" Father was, I could see, very much offended, but he didn't say anything. He remembered, I think, that the General is a V.C. man, and was fond of fighting duels. But to show that the fault was not his, *he* wrung *my* ear— and the same ear too! I suppose he thought that was justice! But it's only right to say that he made up for it afterwards. When the General had gone he gave me a five-pound note.

I don't think Uncle Roger was very pleased with the way Rupert behaved about the legacy, for I don't think he ever saw him from that day to this. Perhaps, of course, it was because Rupert ran away shortly afterwards; but I shall tell about that when I come to him. After all, why should my uncle bother about him? He is not a Melton at all, and I am to be Head of the House—of course, when the Lord thinks right to take father to Himself! Uncle Roger has tons of money, and he never married, so if he wants to leave it in the right direction he needn't have any trouble. He made his money in what he calls "the Eastern Trade." This, so far as I can gather, takes in the Levant and all east of it. I know he has what they call in trade "houses" in all sorts of places—Turkey, and Greece, and all round them, Morocco, Egypt, and Southern Russia, and the Holy Land; then on to Persia, India, and all round it; the Chersonese, China, Japan, and the Pacific Islands. It is not to be expected that we landowners can know much about trade, but my uncle covers—or alas! I must say "covered"—a lot of ground, I can tell you. Uncle Roger was a very grim sort of man, and only that I was brought up to try and be kind to him I shouldn't ever have dared to speak to him. But when was a child father and mother—especially mother—forced me to go and see him and be affectionate to him. He wasn't ever even civil to me, that I can remember—grumpy old bear! But, then, he never saw Rupert at all, so that I take it Master R—is out of the running altogether for testamentary honours. The last time I saw him myself he was distinctly rude. He treated me as a boy, though I was getting on for eighteen years of age. I came into his office without knocking; and without looking up from his desk, where he was writing, he said: "Get out! Why do you venture to disturb me when I'm busy? Get out, and be damned to you!" I waited where I was, ready to transfix him with my eye when he should look up, for I cannot forget that when my father dies I shall be Head of my House. But when he did there was no transfixing possible. He said quite coolly:

"Oh, it's you, is it? I thought it was one of my office boys. Sit down, if you want to see me, and wait till I am ready." So I sat down and waited. Father always said that I should try to conciliate and please my uncle. Father is a very shrewd man, and Uncle Roger is a very rich one.

But I don't think Uncle R—is as shrewd as he thinks he is. He sometimes makes awful mistakes in business. For instance, some years ago he bought an enormous estate on the Adriatic, in the country they call the "Land of Blue Mountains." At least, he says he bought it. He told father so in confidence. But he didn't show any title-deeds, and I'm greatly afraid he was "had." A bad job for me that he was, for father believes he paid an enormous sum for it, and as I am his natural heir, it reduces his available estate to so much less.

And now about Rupert. As I have said, he ran away when he was about fourteen, and we did not hear about him for years. When we—or, rather, my father—did hear of him, it was no good that he heard. He had gone as a cabin-boy on a sailing ship round the Horn. Then he joined an exploring party through the centre of Patagonia, and then another up in Alaska, and a third to the Aleutian Islands. After that he went through Central America, and then to Western Africa, the Pacific Islands, India, and a lot of places. We all know the wisdom of the adage that "A rolling stone gathers no moss"; and certainly, if there be any value in moss, Cousin Rupert will die a poor man. Indeed, nothing will stand his idiotic, boastful wastefulness. Look at the way in which, when he came of age, he made over all his mother's little fortune to the MacSkelpie! I am sure that, though Uncle Roger made no comment to my father, who, as Head of our House, should, of course, have been informed, he was not pleased. My mother, who has a good fortune in her own right, and has had the sense to keep it in her own control—as I am to inherit it, and it is not in the entail, I am therefore quite impartial—I can approve of her spirited conduct in the matter. We never did think much of Rupert, anyhow; but now, since he is in the way to be a pauper, and therefore a dangerous nuisance, we look on him as quite an outsider. We know what he really is. For my own part, I loathe and despise him. Just now we are irritated with him, for we are all kept on tenterhooks regarding my dear Uncle Roger's Will. For Mr. Trent, the attorney who regulated my dear uncle's affairs and has possession of the Will, says it is necessary to know where every possible beneficiary is to be found before making the Will public, so we all have to wait. It is especially hard on me, who am the natural heir. It is very thoughtless indeed of Rupert to keep away like that. I wrote to old MacSkelpie about it, but he didn't seem to understand or to be at all anxious—he is not the heir! He said that probably Rupert Sent Leger—he, too, keeps to the old spelling—did not know of his uncle's death, or he would have taken steps to relieve our anxiety. Our anxiety, forsooth! We are not anxious; we only wish to *know*. And if we—and especially me—who have all the annoyance of thinking of the detestable and unfair death-duties, are anxious, we should be so. Well, anyhow, he'll get a properly bitter disappointment and set down when he does turn up and discovers that he is a pauper without hope!

To-day we (father and I) had letters from Mr. Trent, telling us that the whereabouts of "Mr. Rupert Sent Leger" had been discovered, and that a letter disclosing the fact of poor Uncle Roger's death had been sent to him. He was at Titicaca when last heard of. So goodness only knows when he may get the letter, which "asks him to come home at once, but only gives to him such information about the Will as has already been given to every member of the testator's family." And that is nil. I dare say we shall be kept waiting for months before we get hold of the estate which is ours. It is too bad!

Letter from Edward Bingham Trent to Ernest Roger Halbard Melton.

176, LINCOLN'S INN FIELDS,
December 28, 1906

DEAR SIR,

I am glad to be able to inform you that I have just heard by letter from Mr. Rupert St. Leger that he intended leaving Rio de Janeiro by the S.S. *Amazon*, of the Royal Mail Company, on December 15. He further stated that he would cable just before leaving Rio de Janeiro, to say on what day the ship was expected to arrive in London. As all the others possibly interested in the Will of the late Roger Melton, and whose names are given to me in his instructions regarding the reading of the Will, have been advised, and have expressed their intention of being present at that event on being apprised of the time and place, I now beg to inform you that by cable message received the date scheduled for arrival at the Port of London was January 1 prox. I therefore beg to notify you, subject to postponement due to the non-arrival of the *Amazon*, the reading of the Will of the late Roger Melton, Esq., will take place in my office on Thursday, January 3 prox., at eleven o'clock A.M.

I have the honour to be, sir,
Yours faithfully,
EDWARD BINGHAM TRENT

To ERNEST ROGER HALBARD MELTON, ESQ.,
HUMCROFT,
SALOP

Cable: *Rupert Sent Leger to Edward Bingham Trent.*
Amazon arrives London January 1. SENT LEGER.

Telegram (per Lloyd's): Rupert Sent Leger to Edward Bingham Trent.

THE LIZARD,
December 31

Amazon arrives London to-morrow morning. All well.—
Leger.

Telegram: *Edward Bingham Trent to Ernest Roger Halbard Mellon*.

Rupert Sent Leger arrived. Reading Will takes place as arranged.—Trent.

Ernest Roger Halbard Melton's Record

January 4, 1907

The reading of Uncle Roger's Will is over. Father got a duplicate of Mr. Trent's letter to me, and of the cable and two telegrams pasted into this Record. We both waited patiently till the third—that is, we did not say anything. The only impatient member of our family was my mother. She *did* say things, and if old Trent had been here his ears would have been red. She said what ridiculous nonsense it was delaying the reading of the Will, and keeping the Heir waiting for the arrival of an obscure person who wasn't even a member of the family, inasmuch as he didn't bear the name. I don't think it's quite respectful to one who is some day to be Head of the House! I thought father was weakening in his patience when he said: "True, my dear—true!" and got up and left the room. Some time afterwards when I passed the library I heard him walking up and down.

Father and I went up to town on the afternoon of Wednesday, January 2. We stayed, of course, at Claridge's, where we always stay when we go to town. Mother wanted to come, too, but father thought it better not. She would not agree to stay at home till we both promised to send her separate telegrams after the reading.

At five minutes to eleven we entered Mr. Trent's office. Father would not go a moment earlier, as he said it was bad form to seem eager at any time, but most of all at the reading of a will. It was a rotten grind, for we had to be walking all over the neighbourhood for half an hour before it was time, not to be too early.

When we went into the room we found there General Sir Colin MacKelpie and a big man, very bronzed, whom I took to be Rupert St. Leger—not a very creditable connection to look at, I thought! He and old MacKelpie took care to be in time! Rather low, I thought it. Mr. St. Leger was reading a letter. He had evidently come in but lately, for though he seemed to be eager about it, he was only at the first page, and I could see that there were many sheets. He did not look up when we came in, or till he had finished the letter; and you may be sure that neither I nor my father (who, as Head of the House, should have had more respect from him) took the trouble to go to him. After all, he is a pauper and a wastrel, and he has not the honour of bearing our Name. The General, however, came forward and greeted us both cordially. He evidently had forgotten—or pretended to have—the discourteous way he once treated me, for he spoke to me quite in a friendly way—I thought more warmly than he did to father. I was pleased to be spoken to so nicely, for, after all, whatever his manners may be, he is a distinguished man—has won the V.C. and a Baronetcy. He got the latter not long ago, after the Frontier War in India. I was not, however, led away into cordiality myself. I had not forgotten his rudeness, and I thought that he might be sucking up to me. I knew that when I had my dear Uncle Roger's many millions I should be a rather important person; and, of course, he knew it too. So I got even with him for his former impudence. When he held out his hand I put one finger in it, and said, "How do?" He got very red and turned away. Father and he had ended by glaring at each other, so neither of us was sorry to be done with him. All the time Mr. St. Leger did not seem to see or hear anything, but went on reading his letter. I thought the old MacSkelpie was going to bring him into the matter between us, for as he turned away I heard him say something under his breath. It sounded like "Help!" but Mr. S—did not hear. He certainly no notice of it.

As the MacS—and Mr. S—sat quite silent, neither looking at us, and as father was sitting on the other side of the room with his chin in his hand, and as I wanted to show that I was indifferent to the two S's, I took out this notebook, and went on with the Record, bringing it up to this moment.

THE RECORD—*Continued*

When I had finished writing I looked over at Rupert.

When he saw us, he jumped up and went over to father and shook his hand quite warmly. Father took him very coolly. Rupert, however, did not seem to see it, but came towards me heartily. I happened to be doing something else at the moment, and at first I did not see his hand; but just as I was looking at it the clock struck eleven. Whilst it was striking Mr. Trent came into the room. Close behind him came his clerk, carrying a locked tin box. There were two other men also. He bowed to us all in turn, beginning with me. I was standing opposite the door; the others were scattered about. Father sat still, but Sir Colin and Mr. St. Leger rose. Mr. Trent not did shake hands with any of us—not even me. Nothing but his respectful bow. That is the etiquette for an attorney, I understand, on such formal occasions.

He sat down at the end of the big table in the centre of the room, and asked us to sit round. Father, of course, as Head of the Family, took the seat at his right hand. Sir Colin and St. Leger went to the other side, the former taking the seat next to the attorney. The General knows, of course, that a Baronet takes precedence at a ceremony. I may be a Baronet some day myself, and have to know these things.

The clerk took the key which his master handed to him, opened the tin box, and took from it a bundle of papers tied with red tape. This he placed before the attorney, and put the empty box behind him on the floor. Then he and the other man sat at the far end of the table; the latter took out a big notebook and several pencils, and put them before him. He was evidently a shorthand-writer. Mr. Trent removed the tape from the bundle of papers, which he placed a little distance in front of him. He took a sealed envelope from the top, broke the seal, opened the envelope, and from it took a parchment, in the folds of which were some sealed envelopes, which he laid in a heap in front of the other paper. Then he unfolded the parchment, and laid it before him with the outside page up. He fixed his glasses, and said:

"Gentlemen, the sealed envelope which you have seen me open is endorsed 'My Last Will and Testament—ROGER MELTON, *June*, 1906.' This document"—holding it up—"is as follows:

"I Roger Melton of Openshaw Grange in the County of Dorset; of number one hundred and twenty-three Berkeley Square London; and of the Castle of Vissarion in the Land of the Blue Mountains, being of sound mind do make this my Last Will and Testament on this day Monday the eleventh day of the month of June in the year of Our Lord one thousand nine hundred and six at the office of my old friend and Attorney Edward Bingham Trent in number one hundred and seventy-six Lincoln's Inn Fields London hereby revoking all other wills that I may have formerly made and giving this as my sole and last Will making dispositions of my property as follows:

"1. To my kinsman and nephew Ernest Halbard Melton Esquire, justice of the Peace, Humcroft the County of Salop, for his sole use and benefit the sum of twenty thousand pounds sterling free of all Duties Taxes and charges whatever to be paid out of my Five per centum Bonds of the City of Montreal, Canada.

"2. To my respected friend and colleague as co-trustee to the Will of my late sister Patience late widow of the late Captain Rupert Sent Leger who predeceased her, Major-General Sir Colin Alexander MacKelpie, Baronet, holder of the Victoria Cross, Knight Commander of the Order of the Bath, of Croom in the county of Ross Scotland a sum of Twenty thousand pounds sterling free of all Taxes and charges whatsoever; to be paid out of my Five per centum Bonds of the City of Toronto, Canada.

"3. To Miss Janet MacKelpie presently residing at Croom in the County of Ross Scotland the sum of Twenty thousand pounds sterling free of all Duties Taxes and Charges whatsoever, to be paid out of my Five per centum Bonds of the London County Council.

"4. To the various persons charities and Trustees named in the schedule attached to this Will and marked A. the various sums mentioned therein, all free of Duties and Taxes and charges whatsoever.'"

Here Mr. Trent read out the list here following, and announced for our immediate understanding of the situation the total amount as two hundred and fifty thousand pounds. Many of the beneficiaries were old friends, comrades, dependents, and servants, some of them being left quite large sums of money and specific objects, such as curios and pictures.

"5. To my kinsman and nephew Ernest Roger Halbard Melton presently living in the house of his father at Humcroft Salop the sum of Ten thousand pounds sterling.

"6. To my old and valued friend Edward Bingham Trent of one hundred and seventy-six Lincoln's Inn Fields sum of Twenty thousand pounds sterling free from all Duties Taxes and Charges whatsoever to be paid out of my Five per centum Bonds of the city of Manchester England.

"'7. To my dear nephew Rupert Sent Leger only son of my dear sister Patience Melton by her marriage with Captain Rupert Sent Leger the sum of one thousand pounds sterling. I also bequeath to the said Rupert Sent Leger a further sum conditional upon his acceptance of the terms of a letter addressed to him marked B, and left in the custody of the above Edward Bingham Trent and which letter is an integral part of this my Will. In case of the non-acceptance of the conditions of such letter, I devise and bequeath the whole of the sums and properties reserved therein to the executors herein appointed Colin Alexander MacKelpie and Edward Bingham Trent in trust to distribute the same in accordance with the terms of the letter in the present custody of Edward Bingham Trent marked C, and now deposited sealed with my seal in the sealed envelope containing my last Will to be kept in the custody of the said Edward Bingham Trent and which said letter C is also an integral part of my Will. And in case any doubt should arise as to my ultimate intention as to the disposal of my property the above-mentioned Executors are to have full power to arrange and dispose all such matters as may seem best to them without further appeal. And if any beneficiary under this Will shall challenge the same or any part of it, or dispute the validity thereof, he shall forfeit to the general estate the bequest made herein to him, and any such bequest shall cease and be void to all intents and purposes whatsoever.

"'8. For proper compliance with laws and duties connected with testamentary proceedings and to keep my secret trusts secret I direct my Executors to pay all Death, Estate, Settlement, Legacy, Succession, or other duties charges impositions and assessments whatever on the residue of my estate beyond the bequests already named, at the scale charged in the case of most distant relatives or strangers in blood.

"'9. I hereby appoint as my Executors Major-General Sir Colin Alexander MacKelpie, Baronet, of Croom in the County of

Ross, and Edward Bingham Trent Attorney at Law of one hundred and seventy-six Lincoln's Inn Fields London West Central with full power to exercise their discretion in any circumstance which may arise in the carrying out my wishes as expressed in this Will. As reward for their services in this capacity as Executors they are to receive each out of the general estate a sum of one hundred thousand pounds sterling free of all Duties and impositions whatsoever.

"12. The two Memoranda contained in the letters marked B and C are Integral Parts of this my Last Will are ultimately at the Probate of the Will to be taken as Clauses 10 and 11 of it. The envelopes are marked B and C on both envelope and contents and the contents of each is headed thus: B to be read as Clause 10 of my Will and the other C to be read as Clause 11 of my Will.

"13. Should either of the above-mentioned Executors die before the completion of the above year and a half from the date of the Reading of my Will or before the Conditions rehearsed in Letter C the remaining Executor shall have all and several the Rights and Duties entrusted by my Will to both. And if both Executors should die then the matter of interpretation and execution of all matters in connection with this my Last Will shall rest with the Lord Chancellor of England for the time being or with whomsoever he may appoint for the purpose.

"'This my Last Will is given by me on the first day of January in the year of Our Lord one thousand nine hundred and seven.

"'ROGER MELTON

"We Andrew Rossiter and John Colson here in the presence of each other and of the Testator have seen the Testator Roger Melton sign and seal this document. In witness thereof we hereby set our names

"'ANDREW ROSSITER clerk of 9 Primrose Avenue London W.C.

"'JOHN COLSON caretaker of 176 Lincoln's Inn Fields and Verger of St. Tabitha's Church Clerkenwell London.'"

When Mr. Trent had finished the reading he put all the papers together, and tied them up in a bundle again with the red tape. Holding the bundle in his hand, he stood up, saying as he did so:

"That is all, gentlemen, unless any of you wish to ask me any questions; in which case I shall answer, of course, to the best of my power. I shall ask you, Sir Colin, to remain with me, as we have to deal with some matters, or to arrange a time when we may meet to do so. And you also, Mr. Sent Leger, as there is this letter to submit to you. It is necessary that you should open it in the presence of the executors, but there is no necessity that anyone else should be present."

The first to speak was my father. Of course, as a county gentleman of position and estate, who is sometimes asked to take the chair at Sessions—of course, when there is not anyone with a title present—he found himself under the duty of expressing himself first. Old MacKelpie has superior rank; but this was a family affair, in which my father is Head of the House, whilst old MacKelpie is only an outsider brought into it—and then only to the distaff side, by the wife of a younger brother of the man who married into our family. Father spoke with the same look on his face as when he asks important questions of witnesses at Quarter Sessions.

"I should like some points elucidated." The attorney bowed (he gets his 120 thou', any way, so he can afford to be oily—suave, I suppose he would call it); so father looked at a slip of paper in his hand and asked:

"How much is the amount of the whole estate?"

The attorney answered quickly, and I thought rather rudely. He was red in the face, and didn't bow this time; I suppose a man of his class hasn't more than a very limited stock of manners:

"That, sir, I am not at liberty to tell you. And I may say that I would not if I could."

"Is it a million?" said father again. He was angry this time, and even redder than the old attorney. The attorney said in answer, very quietly this time:

"Ah, that's cross-examining. Let me say, sir, that no one can know that until the accountants to be appointed for the purpose have examined the affairs of the testator up to date."

Mr. Rupert St. Leger, who was looking all this time angrier than even the attorney or my father—though at what he had to be angry about I can't imagine—struck his fist on the table and rose up as if to speak, but as he caught sight of both old MacKelpie and the attorney he sat down again. *Mem.*—Those three seem to agree too well. I must keep a sharp eye on them. I didn't think of this part any more at the time, for father asked another question which interested me much:

"May I ask why the other matters of the Will are not shown to us?" The attorney wiped his spectacles carefully with a big silk bandanna handkerchief before he answered:

"Simply because each of the two letters marked 'B' and 'C' is enclosed with instructions regarding their opening and the keeping secret of their contents. I shall call your attention to the fact that both envelopes are sealed, and that the testator and both witnesses have signed their names across the flap of each envelope. I shall read them. The letter marked 'B,' directed to 'Rupert Sent Leger,' is thus endorsed:

"'This letter is to be given to Rupert Sent Leger by the Trustees and is to be opened by him in their presence. He is to take such copy or make such notes as he may wish and is then to hand the letter with envelope to the Executors who are at once to read it, each of them being entitled to make copy or notes if desirous of so doing. The letter is then to be replaced in its envelope and letter and envelope are to be placed in another envelope to be endorsed on outside as to its contents and to be signed across the flap by both the Executors and by the said Rupert Sent Leger.

(Signed) Roger Melton 1/6/'06

"The letter marked 'C,' directed to 'Edward Bingham Trent,' is thus endorsed:

"'This letter directed to Edward Bingham Trent is to be kept by him unopened for a term of two years after the reading of my Last Will unless said period is earlier terminated by either the acceptance or refusal of Rupert Sent Leger to accept the conditions mentioned in my letter to him marked 'b' which he is to receive and read in the presence of my Executors at the same meeting as but subsequent to the Reading of the clauses (except those to be ultimately numbers ten and eleven) of my Last Will. This letter contains instructions as to what both the Executors and the said Rupert Sent Leger are to do when such acceptance or refusal of the said Rupert

Sent Leger has been made known, or if he omit or refuse to make any such acceptance or refusal, at the end of two years next after my decease.

(Signed) ROGER MELTON 1/6/'06

When the attorney had finished reading the last letter he put it carefully in his pocket. Then he took the other letter in his hand, and stood up. "Mr. Rupert Sent Leger," he said, "please to open this letter, and in such a way that all present may see that the memorandum at top of the contents is given as—

"'B. To be read as clause ten of my Will.'"

St. Leger rolled up his sleeves and cuffs just as if he was going to perform some sort of prestidigitation—it was very theatrical and ridiculous—then, his wrists being quite bare, he opened the envelope and took out the letter. We all saw it quite well. It was folded with the first page outward, and on the top was written a line just as the attorney said. In obedience to a request from the attorney, he laid both letter and envelope on the table in front of him. The clerk then rose up, and, after handing a piece of paper to the attorney, went back to his seat. Mr. Trent, having written something on the paper, asked us all who were present, even the clerk and the shorthand man, to look at the memorandum on the letter and what was written on the envelope, and to sign the paper, which ran:

"We the signatories of this paper hereby declare that we have seen the sealed letter marked B and enclosed in the Will of Roger Melton opened in the presence of us all including Mr. Edward Bingham Trent and Sir Colin Alexander MacKelpie and we declare that the paper therein contained was headed 'B. To be read as clause ten of my Will' and that there were no other contents in the envelope. In attestation of which we in the presence of each other append our signatures."

The attorney motioned to my father to begin. Father is a cautious man, and he asked for a magnifying-glass, which was shortly brought to him by a clerk for whom the clerk in the room called. Father examined the envelope all over very carefully, and also the memorandum at top of the paper. Then, without a word, he signed the paper. Father is a just man. Then we all signed. The attorney folded the paper and put it in an envelope. Before closing it he passed it round, and we all saw that it had not been tampered with. Father took it out and read it, and then put it back. Then the attorney asked us all to sign it across the flap, which we did. Then he put the sealing-wax on it and asked father to seal it with his own seal. He did so. Then he and MacKelpie sealed it also with their own seals, Then he put it in another envelope, which he sealed himself, and he and MacKelpie signed it across the flap.

Then father stood up, and so did I. So did the two men—the clerk and the shorthand writer. Father did not say a word till we got out into the street. We walked along, and presently we passed an open gate into the fields. He turned back, saying to me:

"Come in here. There is no one about, and we can be quiet. I want to speak to you." When we sat down on a seat with none other near it, father said:

"You are a student of the law. What does all that mean?" I thought it a good occasion for an epigram, so I said one word:

"Bilk!"

"H'm!" said father; "that is so far as you and I are concerned. You with a beggarly ten thousand, and I with twenty. But what is, or will be, the effect of those secret trusts?"

"Oh, that," I said, "will, I dare say, be all right. Uncle Roger evidently did not intend the older generation to benefit too much by his death. But he only gave Rupert St. Leger one thousand pounds, whilst he gave me ten. That looks as if he had more regard for the direct line. Of course—" Father interrupted me:

"But what was the meaning of a further sum?"

"I don't know, father. There was evidently some condition which he was to fulfil; but he evidently didn't expect that he would. Why, otherwise, did he leave a second trust to Mr. Trent?"

"True!" said father. Then he went on: "I wonder why he left those enormous sums to Trent and old MacKelpie. They seem out of all proportion as executors' fees, unless—"

"Unless what, father?"

"Unless the fortune he has left is an enormous one. That is why I asked."

"And that," I laughed, "is why he refused to answer."

"Why, Ernest, it must run into big figures."

"Right-ho, father. The death-duties will be annoying. What a beastly swindle the death-duties are! Why, I shall suffer even on your own little estate. . ."

"That will do!" he said curtly. Father is so ridiculously touchy. One would think he expects to live for ever. Presently he spoke again:

"I wonder what are the conditions of that trust. They are as important—almost—as the amount of the bequest—whatever it is. By the way, there seems to be no mention in the will of a residuary legatee. Ernest, my boy, we may have to fight over that."

"How do you make that out, father?" I asked. He had been very rude over the matter of the death-duties of his own estate, though it is entailed and I *must* inherit. So I determined to let him see that I know a good deal more than he does—of law, at any rate. "I fear that when we come to look into it closely that dog won't fight. In the first place, that may be all arranged in the letter to St. Leger, which is a part of the Will. And if that letter should be inoperative by his refusal of the conditions (whatever they may be), then the letter to the attorney begins to work. What it is we don't know, and perhaps even he doesn't—I looked at it as well as I could—and we law men are trained to observation. But even if the instructions mentioned as being in Letter C fail, then the corpus of the Will gives full power to Trent to act just as he darn pleases. He can give the whole thing to himself if he likes, and no one can say a word. In fact, he is himself the final court of appeal."

"H'm!" said father to himself. "It is a queer kind of will, I take it, that can override the Court of Chancery. We shall perhaps have to try it before we are done with this!" With that he rose, and we walked home together—without saying another word.

My mother was very inquisitive about the whole thing—women always are. Father and I between us told her all it was necessary for her to know. I think we were both afraid that, woman-like, she would make trouble for us by saying or doing something injudicious. Indeed, she manifested such hostility towards Rupert St. Leger that it is quite on the cards that she may try to injure him in some way. So when father said that he would have to go out shortly again, as he wished to consult his solicitor, I jumped up and said I would go with him, as I, too, should take advice as to how I stood in the matter.

The Contents of Letter marked "B" attached as an Integral Part to the Last Will of Roger Melton.

June 11, 1907

"This letter an integral part of my Last Will regards the entire residue of my estate beyond the specific bequests made in the body of my Will. It is to appoint as Residuary Legatee of such Will—in case he may accept in due form the Conditions herein laid down—my dear Nephew Rupert Sent Leger only son of my sister Patience Melton now deceased by her marriage with Captain Rupert Sent Leger also now deceased. On his acceptance of the Conditions and the fulfilment of the first of them the Entire residue of my estate after payments of all specific Legacies and of all my debts and other obligations is to become his absolute property to be dealt with or disposed of as he may desire. The following are the conditions.

"1. He is to accept provisionally by letter addressed to my Executors a sum of nine hundred and ninety-nine thousand pounds sterling free of all Duties Taxes or other imposts. This he will hold for a period of six months from the date of the Reading of my Last Will and have user of the accruements thereto calculated at the rate of ten per centum per annum which amount he shall under no circumstances be required to replace. At the end of said six months he must express in writing directed to the Executors of my Will his acceptance or refusal of the other conditions herein to follow. But if he may so choose he shall be free to declare in writing to the Executors within one week from the time of the Reading of the Will his wish to accept or to withdraw altogether from the responsibility of this Trust. In case of withdrawal he is to retain absolutely and for his own use the above-mentioned sum of nine hundred and ninety-nine thousand pounds sterling free of all Duties Taxes and imposts whatsoever making with the specific bequest of one thousand pounds a clear sum of one million pounds sterling free of all imposts. And he will from the moment of the delivery of such written withdrawal cease to have any right or interest whatsoever in the further disposition of my estate under this instrument. Should such written withdrawal be received by my Executors they shall have possession of such residue of my estate as shall remain after the payment of the above sum of nine hundred and ninety-nine thousand pounds sterling and the payment of all Duties Taxes assessments or Imposts as may be entailed by law by its conveyance to the said Rupert Sent Leger and these my Executors shall hold the same for the further disposal of it according to the instructions given in the letter marked C and which is also an integral part of my Last Will and Testament.

"2. If at or before the expiration of the six months above-mentioned the said Rupert Sent Leger shall have accepted the further conditions herein stated, he is to have user of the entire income produced by such residue of my estate the said income being paid to him Quarterly on the usual Quarter Days by the aforesaid Executors to wit Major General Sir Colin Alexander MacKelpie Bart. and Edward Bingham Trent to be used by him in accordance with the terms and conditions hereinafter mentioned.

"3. The said Rupert Sent Leger is to reside for a period of at least six months to begin not later than three months from the reading of my Will in the Castle of Vissarion in the Land of the Blue Mountains. And if he fulfil the Conditions imposed on him and shall thereby become possessed of the residue of my estate he is to continue to reside there in part for a period of one year. He is not to change his British Nationality except by a formal consent of the Privy Council of Great Britain.

"At the end of a year and a half from the Reading of my Will he is to report in person to my Executors of the expenditure of amounts paid or due by him in the carrying out of the Trust and if they are satisfied that same are in general accord with the conditions named in above-mentioned letter marked C and which is an integral part of my Will they are to record their approval on such Will which can then go for final Probate and Taxation. On the Completion of which the said Rupert Sent Leger shall become possessed absolutely and without further act or need of the entire residue of my estate. In witness whereof, etc.

(Signed) ROGER MELTON

This document is attested by the witnesses to the Will on the same date.

(*Personal and Confidential*)
MEMORANDA MADE BY EDWARD BINGHAM TRENT IN
CONNECTION WITH THE WILL OF ROGER MELTON

The interests and issues of all concerned in the Will and estate of the late Roger Melton of Openshaw Grange are so vast that in case any litigation should take place regarding the same, I, as the solicitor, having the carriage of the testator's wishes, think it well to make certain memoranda of events, conversations, etc., not covered by documentary evidence. I make the first memorandum immediately after the event, whilst every detail of act and conversation is still fresh in my mind. I shall also try to make such comments thereon as may serve to refresh my memory hereafter, and which in case of my death may perhaps afford as opinions contemporaneously recorded some guiding light to other or others who may later on have to continue and complete the tasks entrusted to me.

I

Concerning the Reading of the will of Roger Melton

When, beginning at 11 o'clock a.m. on this the forenoon of Thursday, the 3rd day of January, 1907, I opened the Will and read it in full, except the clauses contained in the letters marked "B" and "C"; there were present in addition to myself, the following:

1. Ernest Halbard Melton, J.P, nephew of the testator.
2. Ernest Roger Halbard Melton, son of the above.
3. Rupert Sent Leger, nephew of the testator.
4. Major-General Sir Colin Alexander MacKelpie, Bart., co-executor with myself of the Will.
5. Andrew Rossiter, my clerk, one of the witnesses of the testator's Will.
6. Alfred Nugent, stenographer (of Messrs. Castle's office, 21, Bream's Buildings, W.C.).

When the Will had been read, Mr. E. H. Melton asked the value of the estate left by the testator, which query I did not feel empowered or otherwise able to answer; and a further query, as to why those present were not shown the secret clauses of the Will. I answered by reading the instructions endorsed on the envelopes of the two letters marked "B" and "C," which were sufficiently explanatory.

But, lest any question should hereafter arise as to the fact that the memoranda in letters marked "B" and "C," which were to be read as clauses 10 and 11 of the Will, I caused Rupert Sent Leger to open the envelope marked "B" in the presence of all in the room. These all signed a paper which I had already prepared, to the effect that they had seen the envelope opened, and that the memorandum marked "B. To be read as clause ten of my Will," was contained in the envelope, of which it was to be the sole contents. Mr. Ernest Halbard Melton, J.P., before signing, carefully examined with a magnifying-glass, for which he had asked, both the envelope and the heading of the memorandum enclosed in the letter. He was about to turn the folded paper which was lying on the table over, by which he might have been able to read the matter of the memorandum had he so desired. I at once advised him that the memorandum he was to sign dealt only with the heading of the page, and not with the matter. He looked very angry, but said nothing, and after a second scrutiny signed. I put the memorandum in an envelope, which we all signed across the flap. Before signing, Mr Ernest Halbard Melton took out the paper and verified it. I then asked him to close it, which he did, and when the sealing-wax was on it he sealed it with his own seal. Sir Colin A. MacKelpie and I also appended our own seals. I put the envelope in another, which I sealed with my own seal, and my co-executor and I signed it across the flap and added the date. I took charge of this. When the others present had taken their departure, my co-executor and I, together with Mr. Rupert Sent Leger, who had remained at my request, went into my private room.

Here Mr. Rupert Sent Leger read the memorandum marked "B," which is to be read as clause 10 of the Will. He is evidently a man of considerable nerve, for his face was quite impassive as he read the document, which conveyed to him (subject to the conditions laid down) a fortune which has no equal in amount in Europe, even, so far as I know, amongst the crowned heads. When he had read it over a second time he stood up and said:

"I wish I had known my uncle better. He must have had the heart of a king. I never heard of such generosity as he has shown me. Mr. Trent, I see, from the conditions of this memorandum, or codicil, or whatever it is, that I am to declare within a week as to whether I accept the conditions imposed on me. Now, I want you to tell me this: must I wait a week to declare?" In answer, I told him that the testator's intention was manifestly to see that he had full time to consider fully every point before making formal decision and declaration. But, in answer to the specific question, I could answer that he might make declaration when he would, provided it was *within*, or rather not after, the week named. I added:

"But I strongly advise you not to act hurriedly. So enormous a sum is involved that you may be sure that all possible efforts will be made by someone or other to dispossess you of your inheritance, and it will be well that everything shall be done, not only in perfect order, but with such manifest care and deliberation that there can be no question as to your intention."

"Thank you, sir," he answered; "I shall do as you shall kindly advise me in this as in other things. But I may tell you now—and you, too, my dear Sir Colin—that I not only accept my Uncle Roger's conditions in this, but that when the time comes in the other matters I shall accept every condition that he had in his mind—and that I may know of—in everything." He looked exceedingly in earnest, and it gave me much pleasure to see and hear him. It was just what a young man should do who had seen so generously treated. As the time had now come, I gave him the bulky letter addressed to him, marked "D" which I had in my safe. As I fulfilled my obligation in the matter, I said:

"You need not read the letter here. You can take it away with you, and read it by yourself at leisure. It is your own property, without any obligation whatever attached to it. By the way, perhaps it would be well if you knew. I have a copy sealed up in an envelope, and endorsed, 'To be opened if occasion should arise,' but not otherwise. Will you see me to-morrow, or, better still, dine with me alone here to-night? I should like to have a talk with you, and you may wish to ask me some questions." He answered me cordially. I actually felt touched by the way he said good-bye before he went away. Sir Colin MacKelpie went with him, as Sent Leger was to drop him at the Reform.

Letter from Roger Melton to Rupert Sent Leger, endorsed "D. re Rupert Sent Leger. To be given to him by Edward Bingham Trent if and as soon as he has declared (formally or informally) his intention of accepting the conditions named in Letter B., forming Clause 10 in my Will. R. M., 1/1/'07.

"*Mem.*—Copy (sealed) left in custody of E. B. Trent, to be opened if necessary, as directed."

June 11, 1906

My Dear Nephew,

When (if ever) you receive this you will know that (with the exception of some definite bequests) I have left to you, under certain conditions, the entire bulk of my fortune—a fortune so great that by its aid as a help, a man of courage and ability may carve out for himself a name and place in history. The specific conditions contained in Clause 10 of my Will have to be observed, for such I deem to be of service to your own fortune; but herein I give my advice, which you are at liberty to follow or not as you will, and my wishes, which I shall try to explain fully and clearly, so that you may be in possession of my views in case you should desire to carry them out, or, at least, to so endeavour that the results I hope for may be ultimately achieved. First let me explain—for your understanding and your guidance—that the power, or perhaps it had better be called the pressure, behind the accumulation of my fortune has been ambition. In obedience to its compulsion, I toiled early and late until I had so arranged matters that, subject to broad supervision, my ideas could be carried out by men whom I had selected and tested, and not found wanting. This was for years to the satisfaction, and ultimately to the accumulation by these men of fortune commensurate in some measure to their own worth and their importance to my designs. Thus I had accumulated, whilst still a young man, a considerable fortune. This I have for over forty years used sparingly as regards my personal needs, daringly with regard to speculative investments. With the latter I took such very great care, studying the conditions surrounding them so thoroughly, that even now my schedule of bad debts or unsuccessful investments is almost a blank. Perhaps by such means things flourished with me, and wealth piled in so fast that at times I could hardly use it to advantage. This was all done as the forerunner of ambition, but I was over fifty years of age when the horizon of ambition itself opened up to me. I speak thus freely, my dear Rupert, as when you read it I shall have passed away, and not ambition nor the fear of misunderstanding, nor even of scorn can touch me. My ventures in commerce and finance covered not only the Far East, but every foot of the way to it, so that the Mediterranean and all its opening seas were familiar to me. In my journeyings up and down the Adriatic I was always struck by the great beauty and seeming richness—native richness—of the Land of the Blue Mountains. At last Chance took me into that delectable region. When the "Balkan Struggle" of '90 was on, one of the great Voivodes came to me in secret to arrange a large loan for national purposes. It was known in financial circles of both Europe and Asia that I took an active part in the *haute politique* of national treasuries, and the Voivode Vissarion came to me as to one able and willing to carry out his wishes. After confidential pour-parlers, he explained to me that his nation was in the throes of a great crisis. As you perhaps know, the gallant little Nation in the Land of the Blue Mountains has had a strange history. For more than a thousand years—ever since its settlement after the disaster of Rossoro—it had maintained its national independence under several forms of Government. At first it had a King whose successors became so despotic that they were dethroned. Then it was governed by its Voivodes, with the combining influence of a Vladika somewhat similar in power and function to the Prince-Bishops of Montenegro; afterwards by a Prince; or, as at present, by an irregular elective Council, influenced in a modified form by the Vladika, who was then supposed to exercise a purely spiritual function. Such a Council in a small, poor nation did not have sufficient funds for armaments, which were not immediately and imperatively necessary; and therefore the Voivode Vissarion, who had vast estates in his own possession, and who was the present representative a family which of old had been leaders in the land, found it a duty to do on his own account that which the State could not do. For security as to the loan which he wished to get, and which was indeed a vast one, he offered to sell me his whole estate if I would secure to him a right to repurchase it within a given time (a time which I may say has some time ago expired). He made it a condition that the sale and agreement should remain a strict secret between us, as a widespread knowledge that his estate had changed hands would in all probability result in my death and his own at the hands of the mountaineers, who are beyond everything loyal, and were jealous to the last degree. An attack by Turkey was feared, and new armaments were required; and the patriotic Voivode was sacrificing his own great fortune for the public good. What a sacrifice this was he well knew, for in all discussions regarding a possible change in the Constitution of the Blue Mountains it was always taken for granted that if the principles of the Constitution should change to a more personal rule, his own family should be regarded as the Most Noble. It had ever been on the side of freedom in olden time; before the establishment of the Council, or even during the rule of the Voivodes, the Vissarion had every now and again stood out against the King or challenged the Princedom. The very name stood for freedom, for nationality, against foreign oppression; and the bold mountaineers were devoted to it, as in other free countries men follow the flag.

Such loyalty was a power and a help in the land, for it knew danger in every form; and anything which aided the cohesion of its integers was a natural asset. On every side other powers, great and small, pressed the land, anxious to acquire its suzerainty by any means—fraud or force. Greece, Turkey, Austria, Russia, Italy, France, had all tried in vain. Russia, often hurled back, was waiting an opportunity to attack. Austria and Greece, although united by no common purpose or design, were ready to throw in their forces with whomsoever might seem most likely to be victor. Other Balkan States, too, were not lacking in desire to add the little territory of the Blue Mountains to their more ample possessions. Albania, Dalmatia, Herzegovina, Servia, Bulgaria, looked with lustful eyes on the land, which was in itself a vast natural fortress, having close under its shelter perhaps the finest harbour between Gibraltar and the Dardanelles.

But the fierce, hardy mountaineers were unconquerable. For centuries they had fought, with a fervour and fury that nothing could withstand or abate, attacks on their independence. Time after time, century after century, they had opposed with dauntless front invading armies sent against them. This unquenchable fire of freedom had had its effect. One and all, the great Powers knew that to conquer that little nation would be no mean task, but rather that of a tireless giant. Over and over again had they fought with units against hundreds, never ceasing until they had either wiped out their foes entirely or seen them retreat across the frontier in diminished numbers.

For many years past, however, the Land of the Blue Mountains had remained unassailable, for all the Powers and States had feared lest the others should unite against the one who should begin the attack.

At the time I speak of there was a feeling throughout the Blue Mountains—and, indeed, elsewhere—that Turkey was preparing for a war of offence. The objective of her attack was not known anywhere, but here there was evidence that the Turkish "Bureau of Spies" was in active exercise towards their sturdy little neighbour. To prepare for this, the Voivode Peter Vissarion approached me in order to obtain the necessary "sinews of war."

The situation was complicated by the fact that the Elective Council was at present largely held together by the old Greek Church, which was the religion of the people, and which had had since the beginning its destinies linked in a large degree with theirs. Thus it was possible that if a war should break out, it might easily become—whatever might have been its cause or beginnings—a war of creeds. This in the Balkans must be largely one of races, the end of which no mind could diagnose or even guess at.

I had now for some time had knowledge of the country and its people, and had come to love them both. The nobility of Vissarion's self-sacrifice at once appealed to me, and I felt that I, too, should like to have a hand in the upholding of such a land and such a people. They both deserved freedom. When Vissarion handed me the completed deed of sale I was going to tear it up; but he somehow recognized my intention, and forestalled it. He held up his hand arrestingly as he said:

"I recognize your purpose, and, believe me, I honour you for it from the very depths of my soul. But, my friend, it must not be. Our mountaineers are proud beyond belief. Though they would allow me—who am one of themselves, and whose fathers have been in some way leaders and spokesmen amongst them for many centuries—to do all that is in my power to do—and what, each and all, they would be glad to do were the call to them—they would not accept aid from one outside themselves. My good friend, they would resent it, and might show to you, who wish us all so well, active hostility, which might end in danger, or even death. That was why, my friend, I asked to put a clause in our agreement, that I might have right to repurchase my estate, regarding which you would fain act so generously."

Thus it is, my dear nephew Rupert, only son of my dear sister, that I hereby charge you solemnly as you value me—as you value yourself—as you value honour, that, should it ever become known that that noble Voivode, Peter Vissarion, imperilled himself for his country's good, and if it be of danger or evil repute to him that even for such a purpose he sold his heritage, you shall at once and to the knowledge of the mountaineers—though not necessarily to others—reconvey to him or his heirs the freehold that he was willing to part with—and that he has *de facto* parted with by the effluxion of the time during which his right of repurchase existed. This is a secret trust and duty which is between thee and me alone in the first instance; a duty which I have undertaken on behalf of my heirs, and which must be carried out, at whatsoever cost may ensue. You must not take it that it is from any mistrust of you or belief that you will fail that I have taken another measure to insure that this my cherished idea is borne out. Indeed, it is that the law may, in case of need—for no man can know what may happen after his own hand be taken from the plough—be complied with, that I have in another letter written for the guidance of others, directed that in case of any failure to carry out this trust—death or other—the direction become a clause or codicil to my Will. But in the meantime I wish that this be kept a secret between us two. To show you the full extent of my confidence, let me here tell you that the letter alluded to above is marked "C," and directed to my solicitor and co-executor, Edward Bingham Trent, which is finally to be regarded as clause eleven of my Will. To which end he has my instructions and also a copy of this letter, which is, in case of need, and that only, to be opened, and is to be a guide to my wishes as to the carrying out by you of the conditions on which you inherit.

And now, my dear nephew, let me change to another subject more dear to me—yourself. When you read this I shall have passed away, so that I need not be hampered now by that reserve which I feel has grown upon me through a long and self-contained life. Your mother was very dear to me. As you know, she was twenty years younger than her youngest brother, who was two years younger than me. So we were all young men when she was a baby, and, I need not say, a pet amongst us—almost like our own child to each of us, as well as our sister. You knew her sweetness and high quality, so I need say nothing of these; but I should like you to understand that she was very dear to me. When she and your father came to know and love each other I was far away, opening up a new branch of business in the interior of China, and it was not for several months that I got home news. When I first heard of him they had already been married. I was delighted to find that they were very happy. They needed nothing that I could give. When he died so suddenly I tried to comfort her, and all I had was at her disposal, did she want it. She was a proud woman—though not with me. She had come to understand that, though I seemed cold and hard (and perhaps was so generally), I was not so to her. But she would not have help of any kind. When I pressed her, she told me that she had enough for your keep and education and her own sustenance for the time she must still live; that your father and she had agreed that you should be brought up to a healthy and strenuous life rather than to one of luxury; and she thought that it would be better for the development of your character that you should learn to be self-reliant and to be content with what your dear father had left you. She had always been a wise and thoughtful girl, and now all her wisdom and thought were for you, your father's and her child. When she spoke of you and your future, she said many things which I thought memorable. One of them I remember to this day. It was apropos of my saying that there is a danger of its own kind in extreme poverty. A young man might know too much want. She answered me: "True! That is so! But there is a danger that overrides it;" and after a time went on:

"It is better not to know wants than not to know want!" I tell you, boy, that is a great truth, and I hope you will remember it for yourself as well as a part of the wisdom of your mother. And here let me say something else which is a sort of corollary of that wise utterance:

I dare say you thought me very hard and unsympathetic that time I would not, as one of your trustees, agree to your transferring your little fortune to Miss MacKelpie. I dare say you bear a grudge towards me about it up to this day. Well, if you have any of that remaining, put it aside when you know the truth. That request of yours was an unspeakable delight to me. It was like your mother coming back from the dead. That little letter of yours made me wish for the first time that I had a son—and that he should be like you. I fell into a sort of reverie, thinking if I were yet too old to marry, so that a son might be with me in my declining years—if such were to ever be for me. But I concluded that this might not be. There was no woman whom I knew or had ever met with that I could love as your mother loved your father and as he loved her. So I resigned myself to my fate. I must go my lonely road on to the end. And then came a ray of light into my darkness: there was you. Though you might not feel like a son to me—I could not expect it when the memory of that sweet relationship was more worthily filled. But I could feel like a father to you. Nothing could prevent that or interfere with it, for I would keep it as my secret in the very holy of holies of my heart, where had been for thirty years the image of a sweet little child—your mother. My boy, when in your future life you shall have happiness and honour and power, I hope you will sometimes give a thought to the lonely old man whose later years your very existence seemed to brighten.

The thought of your mother recalled me to my duty. I had undertaken for her a sacred task: to carry out her wishes regarding her son. I knew how she would have acted. It might—would—have been to her a struggle of inclination and duty; and duty would have won. And so I carried out my duty, though I tell you it was a harsh and bitter task to me at the time. But I may tell you that I have since been glad when I think of the result. I tried, as you may perhaps remember, to carry out your wishes in another way, but your letter put the difficulty of doing so so clearly before me that I had to give it up. And let me tell you that that letter endeared you to me more than ever.

I need not tell you that thenceforth I followed your life very closely. When you ran away to sea, I used in secret every part of the mechanism of commerce to find out what had become of you. Then, until you had reached your majority, I had a constant watch kept upon you—not to interfere with you in any way, but so that I might be able to find you should need arise. When in due course I heard of your first act on coming of age I was satisfied. I had to know of the carrying out of your original intention towards Janet Mac Kelpie, for the securities had to be transferred.

From that time on I watched—of course through other eyes—your chief doings. It would have been a pleasure to me to have been able to help in carrying out any hope or ambition of yours, but I realized that in the years intervening between your coming of age and the present moment you were fulfilling your ideas and ambitions in your own way, and, as I shall try to explain to you presently, my ambitions also. You were of so adventurous a nature that even my own widely-spread machinery of acquiring information—what I may call my private "intelligence department"—was inadequate. My machinery was fairly adequate for the East—in great part, at all events. But you went North and South, and West also, and, in addition, you essayed realms where commerce and purely real affairs have no foothold—worlds of thought, of spiritual import, of psychic phenomena—speaking generally, of mysteries. As now and again I was baffled in my inquiries, I had to enlarge my mechanism, and to this end started—not in my own name, of course—some new magazines devoted to certain branches of inquiry and adventure. Should you ever care to know more of these things, Mr. Trent, in whose name the stock is left, will be delighted to give you all details. Indeed, these stocks, like all else I have, shall be yours when the time comes, if you care to ask for them. By means of *The Journal of Adventure*, *The Magazine of Mystery*, *Occultism*, *Balloon and Aeroplane*, *The Submarine*, *Jungle and Pampas*, *The Ghost World*, *The Explorer*, *Forest and Island*, *Ocean and Creek*, I was often kept informed when I should otherwise have been ignorant of your whereabouts and designs. For instance, when you had disappeared into the Forest of the Incas, I got the first whisper of your strange adventures and discoveries in the buried cities of Eudori from a correspondent of *The Journal of Adventure* long before the details given in *The Times* of the rock-temple of the primeval savages, where only remained the little dragon serpents, whose giant ancestors were rudely sculptured on the sacrificial altar. I well remember how I thrilled at even that meagre account of your going in alone into that veritable hell. It was from *Occultism* that I learned how you had made a stay alone in the haunted catacombs of Elora, in the far recesses of the Himalayas, and of the fearful experiences which, when you came out shuddering and ghastly, overcame to almost epileptic fear those who had banded themselves together to go as far as the rock-cut approach to the hidden temple.

All such things I read with rejoicing. You were shaping yourself for a wider and loftier adventure, which would crown more worthily your matured manhood. When I read of you in a description of Mihask, in Madagascar, and the devil-worship there rarely held, I felt I had only to wait for your home-coming in order to broach the enterprise I had so long contemplated. This was what I read:

"He is a man to whom no adventure is too wild or too daring. His reckless bravery is a byword amongst many savage peoples and amongst many others not savages, whose fears are not of material things, but of the world of mysteries in and beyond the grave. He dares not only wild animals and savage men; but has tackled African magic and Indian mysticism. The Psychical Research Society has long exploited his deeds of valiance, and looked upon him as perhaps their most trusted agent or source of discovery. He is in the very prime of life, of almost giant stature and strength, trained to the use of all arms of all countries, inured to every kind of hardship, subtle-minded and resourceful, understanding human nature from its elemental form up. To say that he is fearless would be inadequate. In a word, he is a man whose strength and daring fit him for any enterprise of any kind. He would dare and do anything in the world or out of it, on the earth or under it, in the sea or—in the air, fearing nothing material or unseen, not man or ghost, nor God nor Devil."

If you ever care to think of it, I carried that cutting in my pocket-book from that hour I read it till now.

Remember, again, I say, that I never interfered in the slightest way in any of your adventures. I wanted you to "dree your own weird," as the Scotch say; and I wanted to know of it—that was all. Now, as I hold you fully equipped for greater enterprise, I want to set your feet on the road and to provide you with the most potent weapon—beyond personal qualities—for the winning of great honour—a gain, my dear nephew, which, I am right sure, does and will appeal to you as it has ever done to me. I have worked for it for more than fifty years; but now that the time has come when the torch is slipping from my old hands, I look to you, my dearest kinsman, to lift it and carry it on.

The little nation of the Blue Mountains has from the first appealed to me. It is poor and proud and brave. Its people are well worth winning, and I would advise you to throw in your lot with them. You may find them hard to win, for when peoples, like individuals, are poor and proud, these qualities are apt to react on each other to an endless degree. These men are untamable, and no one can ever succeed with them unless he is with them in all-in-all, and is a leader recognized. But if you can win them they are loyal to death. If you are ambitious—and I know you are—there may be a field for you in such a country. With your qualifications, fortified by the fortune which I am happy enough to be able to leave you, you may dare much and go far. Should I be alive when you return from your exploration in Northern South America, I may have the happiness of helping you to this or any other ambition, and I shall deem it a privilege to share it with you; but time is going on. I am in my seventy-second year. . . the years of man are three-score and ten—I suppose you understand; I do. . . Let me point out this: For ambitious projects the great nationalities are impossible to a stranger—and in our own we are limited by loyalty (and common-sense). It is only in a small nation that great ambitions can be achieved. If you share my own views and wishes, the Blue Mountains is your ground. I hoped at one time that I might yet become a Voivode—even a great one. But age has dulled my personal ambitions as it has cramped my powers. I no longer dream of such honour for myself, though I do look on it as a possibility for you if you care for it. Through my Will you will have a great position and a great estate, and though you may have to yield up the latter in accordance with my wish, as already expressed in this letter, the very doing so will give you an even greater hold than this possession in the hearts of the mountaineers, should they ever come to know it. Should it be that at the time you inherit from me the Voivode Vissarion should not be alive, it may serve or aid you to know that in such case you would be absolved from any conditions of mine, though I trust you would in that, as in all other matters, hold obligation enforced by your own honour as to my wishes. Therefore the matter stands thus: If Vissarion lives, you will relinquish the estates. Should such not be the case, you will act as you believe that I would wish you to. In either case the mountaineers should not know from you in any way of the secret contracts between Vissarion and myself. Enlightenment of the many should (if ever) come from others than yourself. And unless such take place, you would leave the estates without any *quid pro quo* whatever. This you need not mind, for the fortune you will inherit will leave you free and able to purchase other estates in the Blue Mountains or elsewhere that you may select in the world.

If others attack, attack them, and quicker and harder than they can, if such be a possibility. Should it ever be that you inherit the Castle of Vissarion on the Spear of Ivan, remember that I had it secretly fortified and armed against attack. There are not only massive grilles, but doors of chilled bronze where such be needed. My adherent Rooke, who has faithfully served me for nearly forty years, and has gone on my behalf on many perilous expeditions, will, I trust, serve you in the same way. Treat him well for my sake, if not for your own. I have left him provision for a life of ease; but he would rather take a part in dangerous enterprises. He is silent as the grave and as bold as a lion. He knows every detail of the fortification and of the secret means of defence. A word in your ear—he was once a pirate. He was then in his extreme youth, and long since changed his ways in this respect; but from this fact you can understand his nature. You will find him useful should occasion ever arise. Should you accept the conditions of my letter, you are to make the Blue Mountains—in part, at least—your home, living there a part of the year, if only for a week, as in England men of many estates share the time amongst them. To this you are not bound, and no one shall have power to compel you or interfere with you. I only express a hope. But one thing I do more than hope—I desire, if you will honour my wishes, that, come what may, you are to keep your British nationality, unless by special arrangement with and consent of the Privy Council. Such arrangement to be formally made by my friend, Edward Bingham Trent, or whomsoever he may appoint by deed or will to act in the matter, and made in such a way that no act save that alone of Parliament in all its estates, and endorsed by the King, may or can prevail against it.

My last word to you is, Be bold and honest, and fear not. Most things—even kingship—*somewhere* may now and again be won by the sword. A brave heart and a strong arm may go far. But whatever is so won cannot be held merely by the sword. Justice alone can hold in the long run. Where men trust they will follow, and the rank and file of people want to follow, not to lead. If it be your fortune to lead, be bold. Be wary, if you will; exercise any other faculties that may aid or guard. Shrink from nothing. Avoid nothing that is honourable in itself. Take responsibility when such presents itself. What others shrink from, accept. That is to be great in what world, little or big, you move. Fear nothing, no matter of what kind danger may be or whence it come. The only real way to meet danger is to despise it—except with your brains. Meet it in the gate, not the hall.

My kinsman, the name of my race and your own, worthily mingled in your own person, now rests with you!

Letter from Rupert Sent Leger, 32 *Bodmin Street, Victoria, S.W., to Miss Janet MacKelpie, Croom, Ross-shire.*

January 3, 1907

My Dearest Aunt Janet,

You will, I know, be rejoiced to hear of the great good-fortune which has come to me through the Will of Uncle Roger. Perhaps Sir Colin will have written to you, as he is one of the executors, and there is a bequest to you, so I must not spoil his pleasure of telling you of that part himself. Unfortunately, I am not free to speak fully of my own legacy yet, but I want you to know that at worst I am to receive an amount many times more than I ever dreamt of possessing through any possible stroke of fortune. So soon as I can leave London—where, of course, I must remain until things are settled—I am coming up to Croom to see you, and I hope I shall by then be able to let you know so much that you will be able to guess at the extraordinary change that has come to my circumstances. It is all like an impossible dream: there is nothing like it in the "Arabian Nights." However, the details must wait, I am pledged to secrecy for the present. And you must be pledged too. You won't mind, dear, will you? What I want to do at present is merely to tell you of my own good-fortune, and that I shall be going presently to live for a while at Vissarion. Won't you come with me, Aunt Janet? We shall talk more of this when I come to Croom; but I want you to keep the subject in your mind.

Your loving
Rupert

From Rupert Sent Leger's Journal.

January 4, 1907

Things have been humming about me so fast that I have had
hardly time to think. But some of the things have been so
important, and have so changed my entire outlook on life,
that it may be well to keep some personal record of them. I
may some day want to remember some detail—perhaps the
sequence of events, or something like that—and it may be
useful. It ought to be, if there is any justice in things, for it
will be an awful swot to write it when I have so many things
to think of now. Aunt Janet, I suppose, will like to keep it
locked up for me, as she does with all my journals and papers.
That is one good thing about Aunt Janet amongst many: she
has no curiosity, or else she has some other quality which
keeps her from prying as other women would. It would seem
that she has not so much as opened the cover of one of my
journals ever in her life, and that she would not without
my permission. So this can in time go to her also.

I dined last night with Mr. Trent, by his special desire.
The dinner was in his own rooms. Dinner sent in from the
hotel. He would not have any waiters at all, but made them
send in the dinner all at once, and we helped ourselves. As we
were quite alone, we could talk freely, and we got over a lot
of ground while we were dining. He began to tell me about
Uncle Roger. I was glad of that, for, of course, I wanted to
know all I could of him, and the fact was I had seen very little
of him. Of course, when I was a small kid he was often in our
house, for he was very fond of mother, and she of him. But I
fancy that a small boy was rather a nuisance to him. And then
I was at school, and he was away in the East. And then poor
mother died while he was living in the Blue Mountains, and I
never saw him again. When I wrote to him about Aunt Janet
he answered me very kindly but he was so very just in the
matter that I got afraid of him. And after that I ran away, and
have been roaming ever since; so there was never a chance
of our meeting. But that letter of his has opened my eyes.
To think of him following me that way all over the world,
waiting to hold out a helping hand if I should want it, I only

wish I had known, or even suspected, the sort of man he was, and how he cared for me, and I would sometimes have come back to see him, if I had to come half round the world. Well, all I can do now is to carry out his wishes; that will be my expiation for my neglect. He knew what he wanted exactly, and I suppose I shall come in time to know it all and understand it, too.

I was thinking something like this when Mr. Trent began to talk, so that all he said fitted exactly into my own thought. The two men were evidently great friends—I should have gathered that, anyhow, from the Will—and the letters—so I was not surprised when Mr. Trent told me that they had been to school together, Uncle Roger being a senior when he was a junior; and had then and ever after shared each other's confidence. Mr. Trent, I gathered, had from the very first been in love with my mother, even when she was a little girl; but he was poor and shy, and did not like to speak. When he had made up his mind to do so, he found that she had by then met my father, and could not help seeing that they loved each other. So he was silent. He told me he had never said a word about it to anyone—not even to my Uncle Roger, though he knew from one thing and another, though he never spoke of it, that he would like it. I could not help seeing that the dear old man regarded me in a sort of parental way—I have heard of such romantic attachments being transferred to the later generation. I was not displeased with it; on the contrary, I liked him better for it. I love my mother so much—I always think of her in the present—that I cannot think of her as dead. There is a tie between anyone else who loved her and myself. I tried to let Mr. Trent see that I liked him, and it pleased him so much that I could see his liking for me growing greater. Before we parted he told me that he was going to give up business. He must have understood how disappointed I was—for how could I ever get along at all without him?—for he said, as he laid a hand quite affectionately, I thought—on my shoulder:

"I shall have one client, though, whose business I always hope to keep, and for whom I shall be always whilst I live glad to act—if he will have me." I did not care to speak as I took his hand. He squeezed mine, too, and said very earnestly:

"I served your uncle's interests to the very best of my ability for nearly fifty years. He had full confidence in me, and I was proud of his trust. I can honestly say, Rupert—you won't mind me using that familiarity, will you?—that, though the interests which I guarded were so vast that without abusing my trust I could often have used my knowledge to my personal advantage, I never once, in little matters or big, abused that trust—no, not even rubbed the bloom off it. And now that he has remembered me in his Will so generously that I need work no more, it will be a very genuine pleasure and pride to me to carry out as well as I can the wishes that I partly knew, and now realize more fully towards you, his nephew."

In the long chat which we had, and which lasted till midnight, he told me many very interesting things about Uncle Roger. When, in the course of conversation, he mentioned that the fortune Uncle Roger left must be well over a hundred millions, I was so surprised that I said out loud—I did not mean to ask a question:

"How on earth could a man beginning with nothing realize such a gigantic fortune?"

"By all honest ways," he answered, "and his clever human insight. He knew one half of the world, and so kept abreast of all public and national movements that he knew the critical moment to advance money required. He was always generous, and always on the side of freedom. There are nations at this moment only now entering on the consolidation of their liberty, who owe all to him, who knew when and how to help. No wonder that in some lands they will drink to his memory on great occasions as they used to drink his health."

"As you and I shall do now, sir!" I said, as I filled my glass and stood up. We drank it in bumpers. We did not say a word, either of us; but the old gentleman held out his hand, and I took it. And so, holding hands, we drank in silence. It made me feel quite choky; and I could see that he, too, was moved.

January 4, 1907

I asked Mr. Rupert Sent Leger to dine with me at my office alone, as I wished to have a chat with him. To-morrow Sir Colin and I will have a formal meeting with him for the settlement of affairs, but I thought it best to have an informal talk with him alone first, as I wished to tell him certain matters which will make our meeting to-morrow more productive of utility, as he can now have more full understanding of the subjects which we have to discuss. Sir Colin is all that can be in manhood, and I could wish no better colleague in the executorship of this phenomenal Will; but he has not had the privilege of a lifelong friendship with the testator as I have had. And as Rupert Sent Leger had to learn intimate details regarding his uncle, I could best make my confidences alone. To-morrow we shall have plenty of formality. I was delighted with Rupert. He is just what I could have wished his mother's boy to be—or a son of my own to be, had I had the good-fortune to have been a father. But this is not for me. I remember long, long ago reading a passage in Lamb's Essays which hangs in my mind: "The children of Alice call Bartrum father." Some of my old friends would laugh to see *me* write this, but these memoranda are for my eyes alone, and no one shall see them till after my death, unless by my own permission. The boy takes some qualities after his father; he has a daring that is disturbing to an old dryasdust lawyer like me. But somehow I like him more than I ever liked anyone—any man—in my life—more even than his uncle, my old friend, Roger Melton; and Lord knows I had much cause to like him. I have more than ever now. It was quite delightful to see the way the young adventurer was touched by his uncle's thought of him. He is a truly gallant fellow, but venturesome exploits have not affected the goodness of heart. It is a pleasure to me to think that Roger and Colin came together apropos of the boy's thoughtful generosity towards Miss MacKelpie. The old soldier will be a good friend to him, or I am much mistaken. With an old lawyer like me, and an old soldier like him, and a real old gentlewoman like Miss MacKelpie, who loves the very ground he walks on, to look after him, together with all his own fine qualities and his marvellous experience of the world, and the gigantic wealth that will surely be his, that young man will go far.

Letter from Rupert Sent Leger to Miss Janet MacKelpie, Croom.

January 5, 1907

MY DEAREST AUNT JANET,

It is all over—the first stage of it; and that is as far as I can get at present. I shall have to wait for a few days—or it may be weeks—in London for the doing of certain things now necessitated by my acceptance of Uncle Roger's bequest. But as soon as I can, dear, I shall come down to Croom and spend with you as many days as possible. I shall then tell you all I am at liberty to tell, and I shall thank you personally for your consent to come with me to Vissarion. Oh, how I wish my dear mother had lived to be with us! It would have made her happy, I know, to have come; and then we three who shared together the old dear, hard days would have shared in the same way the new splendour. I would try to show all my love and gratitude to you both. . . You must take the whole burden of it now, dear, for you and I are alone. No, not alone, as we used to be, for I have now two old friends who are already dear to me. One is so to you already. Sir Colin is simply splendid, and so, in his own way, is Mr. Trent. I am lucky, Aunt Janet, to have two such men to think of affairs for me. Am I not? I shall send you a wire as soon as ever I can see my way to get through my work; and I want you to think over all the things you ever wished for in your life, so that I may—if there is any mortal way of doing so—get them for you. You will not stand in the way of my having this great pleasure, will you, dear? Good-bye.

Your loving
RUPERT

January 6, 1907

The formal meeting of Sir Colin and myself with Rupert Sent Leger went off quite satisfactorily. From what he had said yesterday, and again last night, I had almost come to expect an unreserved acceptance of everything stated or implied in Roger Melton's Will; but when we had sat round the table—this appeared, by the way, to be a formality for which we were all prepared, for we sat down as if by instinct—the very first words he said were:

"As I suppose I must go through this formality, I may as well say at once that I accept every possible condition which was in the mind of Uncle Roger; and to this end I am prepared to sign, seal, and deliver—or whatever is the ritual—whatever document you, sir"—turning to me—"may think necessary or advisable, and of which you both approve." He stood up and walked about the room for a few moments, Sir Colin and I sitting quite still, silent. He came back to his seat, and after a few seconds of nervousness—a rare thing with him, I fancy—said: "I hope you both understand—of course, I know you do; I only speak because this is an occasion for formality—that I am willing to accept, and at once! I do so, believe me, not to get possession of this vast fortune, but because of him who has given it. The man who was fond of me, and who trusted me, and yet had strength to keep his own feelings in check—who followed me in spirit to far lands and desperate adventures, and who, though he might be across the world from me, was ready to put out a hand to save or help me, was no common man; and his care of my mother's son meant no common love for my dear mother. And so she and I together accept his trust, come of it what may. I have been thinking it over all night, and all the time I could not get out of the idea that mother was somewhere near me. The only thought that could debar me from doing as I wished to do—and intend to do—would be that she would not approve. Now that I am satisfied she would approve, I accept. Whatever may result or happen, I shall go on following the course that he has set for me. So help me, God!" Sir Colin stood up, and I must say a more martial figure I never saw. He was in full uniform, for he was going on to the King's levee after our business. He drew his sword from the scabbard and laid it naked on the table before Rupert, and said:

"You are going, sir, into a strange and danger country—I have been reading about it since we met—and you will be largely alone amongst fierce mountaineers who resent the very presence of a stranger, and to whom you are, and must be, one. If you should ever be in any trouble and want a man to stand back to back with you, I hope you will give me the honour!" As he said this pointed to his sword. Rupert and I were also standing now—one cannot sit down in the presence of such an act as that. "You are, I am proud to say, allied with my family: and I only wish to God it was closer to myself." Rupert took him by the hand and bent his head before him as answered:

"The honour is mine, Sir Colin; and no greater can come to any man than that which you have just done me. The best way I can show how I value it will be to call on you if I am ever in such a tight place. By Jove, sir, this is history repeating itself. Aunt Janet used to tell me when I was a youngster how MacKelpie of Croom laid his sword before Prince Charlie. I hope I may tell her of this; it would make her so proud and happy. Don't imagine, sir, that I am thinking myself a Charles Edward. It is only that Aunt Janet is so good to me that I might well think I was."

Sir Colin bowed grandly:

"Rupert Sent Leger, my dear niece is a woman of great discretion and discernment. And, moreover, I am thinking she has in her some of the gift of Second Sight that has been a heritage of our blood. And I am one with my niece—in everything!" The whole thing was quite regal in manner; it seemed to take me back to the days of the Pretender.

It was not, however, a time for sentiment, but for action— we had met regarding the future, not the past; so I produced the short document I had already prepared. On the strength of his steadfast declaration that he would accept the terms of the Will and the secret letters, I had got ready a formal acceptance. When I had once again formally asked Mr. Sent

Leger's wishes, and he had declared his wish to accept, I got in a couple of my clerks as witnesses.

Then, having again asked him in their presence if it was his wish to declare acceptance of the conditions, the document was signed and witnessed, Sir Colin and I both appending our signatures to the Attestation.

And so the first stage of Rupert Sent Leger's inheritance is completed. The next step will not have to be undertaken on my part until the expiration of six months from his entry on his estate at Vissarion. As he announces his intention of going within a fortnight, this will mean practically a little over six months from now.

Book II

Vissarion

Letter from Rupert Sent Leger, Castle of Vissarion, the Spear of Ivan, Land of the Blue Mountains, to Miss Janet MacKelpie, Croom Castle, Ross-shire, N.B.

January 23, 1907

My Dearest Aunt Janet,

As you see, I am here at last. Having got my formal duty done, as you made me promise—my letters reporting arrival to Sir Colin and Mr. Trent are lying sealed in front of me ready to post (for nothing shall go before yours)—I am free to speak to you.

This is a most lovely place, and I hope you will like it. I am quite sure you will. We passed it in the steamer coming from Trieste to Durazzo. I knew the locality from the chart, and it was pointed out to me by one of the officers with whom I had become quite friendly, and who kindly showed me interesting places whenever we got within sight of shore. The Spear of Ivan, on which the Castle stands, is a headland running well out into the sea. It is quite a peculiar place—a sort of headland on a headland, jutting out into a deep, wide bay, so that, though it is a promontory, it is as far away from the traffic of coast life as anything you can conceive. The main promontory is the end of a range of mountains, and looms up vast, towering over everything, a mass of sapphire blue. I can well understand how the country came to be called the "Land of the Blue Mountains," for it is all mountains, and they are all blue! The coast-line is magnificent—what is called "iron-bound"—being all rocky; sometimes great frowning precipices; sometimes jutting spurs of rock; again little rocky islets, now and again clad with trees and verdure, at other places stark and bare. Elsewhere are little rocky bays and indentations—always rock, and often with long, interesting caves. Some of the shores of the bays are sandy, or else ridges of beautiful pebbles, where the waves make endless murmur.

But of all the places I have seen—in this land or any other—the most absolutely beautiful is Vissarion. It stands at the ultimate point of the promontory—I mean the little, or, rather, lesser promontory—that continues on the spur of the mountain range. For the lesser promontory or extension of the mountain is in reality vast; the lowest bit of cliff along the sea-front is not less than a couple of hundred feet high. That point of rock is really very peculiar. I think Dame Nature must, in the early days of her housekeeping—or, rather, house-*building*—have intended to give her little child, man, a rudimentary lesson in self-protection. It is just a natural bastion such as a titanic Vauban might have designed in primeval times. So far as the Castle is concerned, it is alone visible from the sea. Any enemy approaching could see only that frowning wall of black rock, of vast height and perpendicular steepness. Even the old fortifications which crown it are not built, but cut in the solid rock. A long narrow creek of very deep water, walled in by high, steep cliffs, runs in behind the Castle, bending north and west, making safe and secret anchorage. Into the creek falls over a precipice a mountain-stream, which never fails in volume of water. On the western shore of that creek is the Castle, a huge pile of buildings of every style of architecture, from the Twelfth century to where such things seemed to stop in this dear old-world land—about the time of Queen Elizabeth. So it is pretty picturesque. I can tell you. When we got the first glimpse of the place from the steamer the officer, with whom I was on the bridge, pointed towards it and said:

"That is where we saw the dead woman floating in a coffin." That was rather interesting, so I asked him all about it. He took from his pocket-book a cutting from an Italian paper, which he handed to me. As I can read and speak Italian fairly well, it was all right; but as you, my dear Aunt Janet, are not skilled in languages, and as I doubt if there is any assistance of the kind to be had at Croom, I do not send it. But as I have heard that the item has been produced in the last number of *The Journal of Occultism*, you will be easily able to get it. As he handed me the cutting he said: "I am Destilia!" His story was so strange that I asked him a good many questions about it. He answered me quite frankly on every point, but always adhering stoutly to the main point—namely, that it was no phantom or mirage, no dream or imperfect vision in a fog. "We were four in all who saw it," he said—"three from the bridge and the Englishman, Caulfield—from the bows—whose account exactly agreed with what we saw. Captain Mirolani and Falamano and I were all awake and in good trim. We looked with our night-glasses, which are more than usually powerful. You know, we need good glasses for the east shore of the Adriatic and for among the islands to the south. There was a full moon and a brilliant light. Of course we were a little way off, for though the Spear of Ivan is in deep water, one has to be careful of currents, for it is in just such places that the dangerous currents run." The agent of Lloyd's told me only a few weeks ago that it was only after a prolonged investigation of the tidal and sea currents that the house decided to except from ordinary sea risks losses due to a too close course by the Spear of Ivan. When I tried to get a little more definite account of the coffin-boat and the dead lady that is given in *The Journal of Occultism* he simply shrugged his shoulders. "Signor, it is all," he said. "That Englishman wrote everything after endless questioning."

So you see, my dear, that our new home is not without superstitious interests of its own. It is rather a nice idea, is it not, to have a dead woman cruising round our promontory in a coffin? I doubt if even at Croom you can beat that. "Makes the place kind of homey," as an American would say. When you come, Aunt Janet, you will not feel lonesome, at any rate, and it will save us the trouble of importing some of your Highland ghosts to make you feel at home in the new land. I don't know, but we might ask the stiff to come to tea with us. Of course, it would be a late tea. Somewhere between midnight and cock-crow would be about the etiquette of the thing, I fancy!

But I must tell you all the realities of the Castle and around it. So I will write again within a day or two, and try to let you know enough to prepare you for coming here. Till then adieu, my dear.

Your loving
RUPERT

From Rupert Sent Leger, Vissarion, to Janet MacKelpie, Croom.

January 25, 1907

I hope I did not frighten you, dear Aunt Janet, by the yarn of the lady in the coffin. But I know you are not afraid; you have told me too many weird stories for me to dread that. Besides, you have Second Sight—latent, at all events. However, there won't be any more ghosts, or about ghosts, in this letter. I want to tell you all about our new home. I am so glad you are coming out so soon; I am beginning to feel so lonesome—I walk about sometimes aimlessly, and find my thoughts drifting in such an odd way. If I didn't know better, I might begin to think I was in love! There is no one here to be in love with; so make your mind easy, Aunt Janet. Not that you would be unhappy, I know, dear, if I *did* fall in love. I suppose I must marry some day. It is a duty now, I know, when there is such an estate as Uncle Roger has left me. And I know this: I shall never marry any woman unless I love her. And I am right sure that if I do love her you will love her, too, Aunt Janet! Won't you, dear? It wouldn't be half a delight if you didn't. It won't if you don't. There, now!

But before I begin to describe Vissarion I shall throw a sop to you as a chatelaine; that may give you patience to read the rest. The Castle needs a lot of things to make it comfortable—as you would consider it. In fact, it is absolutely destitute of everything of a domestic nature. Uncle Roger had it vetted on the defence side, and so far it could stand a siege. But it couldn't cook a dinner or go through a spring-cleaning! As you know, I am not much up in domestic matters, and so I cannot give you details; but you may take it that it wants everything. I don't mean furniture, or silver, or even gold-plate, or works of art, for it is full of the most magnificent old things that you can imagine. I think Uncle Roger must have been a collector, and gathered a lot of good things in all sorts of places, stored them for years, and then sent them here. But as to glass, china, delft, all sorts of crockery, linen, household appliances and machinery, cooking utensils—except of the simplest—there are none. I don't think Uncle Roger could have lived here more than on a temporary picnic. So far as I only am concerned, I am all right; a gridiron and a saucepan are all *I* want—and I can use them myself. But, dear Aunt Janet, I don't want you to pig it. I would like you to have everything you can imagine, and all of the very best. Cost doesn't count now for us, thanks to Uncle Roger; and so I want you to order all. I know you, dear—being a woman—won't object to shopping. But it will have to be wholesale. This is an enormous place, and will swallow up all you can buy—like a quicksand. Do as you like about choosing, but get all the help you can. Don't be afraid of getting too much. You can't, or of being idle when you are here. I assure you that when you come there will be so much to do and so many things to think of that you will want to get away from it all. And, besides, Aunt Janet, I hope you won't be too long. Indeed, I don't wish to be selfish, but your boy is lonely, and wants you. And when you get here you will be an EMPRESS. I don't altogether like doing so, lest I should offend a millionairess like you; but it may facilitate matters, and the way's of commerce are strict, though devious. So I send you a cheque for 1,000 pounds for the little things: and a letter to the bank to honour your own cheques for any amount I have got.

I think, by the way, I should, if I were you, take or send out a few servants—not too many at first, only just enough to attend on our two selves. You can arrange to send for any more you may want later. Engage them, and arrange for their being paid—when they are in our service we must treat them well—and then they can be at our call as you find that we want them. I think you should secure, say, fifty or a hundred—'tis an awfu' big place, Aunt Janet! And in the same way will you secure—and, of course, arrange for pay similarly—a hundred men, exclusive of any servants you think it well to have. I should like the General, if he can give the time, to choose or pass them. I want clansmen that I can depend on, if need be. We are going to live in a country which is at present strange to us, and it is well to look things in the face. I know Sir Colin will only have men who are a credit to Scotland and to Ross and to Croom—men who will impress the Blue Mountaineers. I know they will take them to their hearts—certainly if any of them are bachelors the girls will! Forgive me! But if we are to settle here, our followers will probably want to settle also. Moreover, the Blue Mountaineers may want followers also! And will want them to settle, too, and have successors!

Now for the description of the place. Well, I simply can't just now. It is all so wonderful and so beautiful. The Castle—I have written so much already about other things that I really must keep the Castle for another letter! Love to Sir Colin if he is at Croom. And oh, dear Aunt Janet, how I wish that my dear mother was coming out! It all seems so dark and empty without her. How she would have enjoyed it! How proud she would have been! And, my dear, if she could be with us again, how grateful she would have been to you for all you have done for her boy! As I am, believe me, most truly and sincerely and affectionately grateful.

Your loving
RUPERT

Rupert Sent Leger, Vissarion, to Janet MacKelpie, Croom.

January 26, 1907

MY DEAR AUNT JANET,

Please read this as if it was a part of the letter I wrote yesterday.

The Castle itself is so vast that I really can't describe it in detail. So I am waiting till you come; and then you and I will go over it together and learn all that we can about it. We shall take Rooke with us, and, as he is supposed to know every part of it, from the keep to the torture-chamber, we can spend a few days over it. Of course, I have been over most of it, since I came—that, is, I went at various times to see different portions—the battlements, the bastions, the old guard-room, the hall, the chapel, the walls, the roof. And I have been through some of the network of rock passages. Uncle Roger must have spent a mint of money on it, so far as I can see; and though I am not a soldier, I have been in so many places fortified in different ways that I am not entirely ignorant of the subject. He has restored it in such an up-to-date way that it is practically impregnable to anything under big guns or a siege-train. He has gone so far as to have certain outworks and the keep covered with armoured plating of what looks like harveyized steel. You will wonder when you see it. But as yet I really know only a few rooms, and am familiar with only one—my own room. The drawing-room—not the great hall, which is a vast place; the library—a magnificent one, but in sad disorder—we must get a librarian some day to put it in trim; and the drawing-room and boudoir and bedroom suite which I have selected for you, are all fine. But my own room is what suits me best, though I do not think you would care for it for yourself. If you do, you shall have it. It was Uncle Roger's own room when he stayed here; living in it for a few days served to give me more insight to his character—or rather to his mind—than I could have otherwise had. It is just the kind of place I like myself; so, naturally, I understand the other chap who liked it too. It is a fine big room, not quite within the Castle, but an outlying part of it. It is not detached, or anything of that sort, but is a sort of garden-room built on to it. There seems to have been always some sort of place where it is, for the passages and openings inside seem to accept or recognize it. It can be shut off if necessary—it would be in case of attack—by a great slab of steel, just like the door of a safe, which slides from inside the wall, and can be operated from either inside or outside—if you know how. That is from my room or from within the keep. The mechanism is a secret, and no one but Rooke and I know it. The room opens out through a great French window—the French window is modern, I take it, and was arranged by or for Uncle Roger; I think there must have been always a large opening there, for centuries at least—which opens on a wide terrace or balcony of white marble, extending right and left. From this a white marble stair lies straight in front of the window, and leads down to the garden. The balcony and staircase are quite ancient—of old Italian work, beautifully carved, and, of course, weather-worn through centuries. There is just that little tinging of green here and there which makes all outdoor marble so charming. It is hard to believe at times that it is a part of a fortified castle, it is so elegant and free and open. The first glance of it would make a burglar's heart glad. He would say to himself: "Here is the sort of crib I like when I'm on the job. You can just walk in and out as you choose." But, Aunt Janet, old Roger was cuter than any burglar. He had the place so guarded that the burglar would have been a baffled burglar. There are two steel shields which can slide out from the wall and lock into the other side right across the whole big window. One is a grille of steel bands that open out into diamond-shaped lozenges. Nothing bigger than a kitten could get through; and yet you can see the garden and the mountains and the whole view—much the same as you ladies can see through your veils. The other is a great sheet of steel, which slides out in a similar way in different grooves. It is not, of course, so heavy and strong as the safe-door which covers the little opening in the main wall, but Rooke tells me it is proof against the heaviest rifle-ball.

Having told you this, I must tell you, too, Aunt Janet, lest you should be made anxious by the *arriere-pensee* of all these warlike measures of defence, that I always sleep at night with one of these iron screens across the window. Of course, when I am awake I leave it open. As yet I have tried only, but not used, the grille; and I don't think I shall ever use anything else, for it is a perfect guard. If it should be tampered with from outside it would sound an alarm at the head of the bed, and the pressing of a button would roll out the solid steel screen in front of it. As a matter of fact, I have been so used to the open that I don't feel comfortable shut in. I only close windows against cold or rain. The weather here is delightful—as yet, at all events—but they tell me that the rainy season will be on us before very long.

I think you will like my den, aunty dear, though it will doubtless be a worry to you to see it so untidy. But that can't be helped. I must be untidy *somewhere*; and it is best in my own den!

Again I find my letter so long that I must cut it off now and go on again to-night. So this must go as it stands. I shall not cause you to wait to hear all I can tell you about our new home.

Your loving
RUPERT

From Rupert Sent Leger, Vissarion, to Janet MacKelpie, Croom.

January 29, 1907

MY DEAR AUNT JANET,

My den looks out, as I told you in my last letter, on the garden, or, to speak more accurately, on *one* of the gardens, for there are acres of them. This is the old one, which must be almost as old as the Castle itself, for it was within the defences in the old days of bows. The wall that surrounds the inner portion of it has long ago been levelled, but sufficient remains at either end where it joined the outer defences to show the long casemates for the bowmen to shoot through and the raised stone gallery where they stood. It is just the same kind of building as the stone-work of the sentry's walk on the roof and of the great old guard-room under it.

But whatever the garden may have been, and no matter how it was guarded, it is a most lovely place. There are whole sections of garden here of various styles—Greek, Italian, French, German, Dutch, British, Spanish, African, Moorish—all the older nationalities. I am going to have a new one laid out for you—a Japanese garden. I have sent to the great gardener of Japan, Minaro, to make the plans for it, and to come over with workmen to carry it out. He is to bring trees and shrubs and flowers and stone-work, and everything that can be required; and you shall superintend the finishing, if not the doing, of it yourself. We have such a fine head of water here, and the climate is, they tell me, usually so lovely that we can do anything in the gardening way. If it should ever turn out that the climate does not suit, we shall put a great high glass roof over it, and *make* a suitable climate.

This garden in front of my room is the old Italian garden. It must have been done with extraordinary taste and care, for there is not a bit of it which is not rarely beautiful. Sir Thomas Browne himself, for all his *Quincunx*, would have been delighted with it, and have found material for another "Garden of Cyrus." It is so big that there are endless "episodes" of garden beauty I think all Italy must have been ransacked in old times for garden stone-work of exceptional beauty; and these treasures have been put together by some master-hand. Even the formal borders of the walks are of old porous stone, which takes the weather-staining so beautifully, and are carved in endless variety. Now that the gardens have been so long neglected or left in abeyance, the green staining has become perfect. Though the stone-work is itself intact, it has all the picturesque effect of the wear and ruin wrought by many centuries. I am having it kept for you just as it is, except that I have had the weeds and undergrowth cleared away so that its beauties might be visible.

But it is not merely the architect work of the garden that is so beautiful, nor is the assembling there of the manifold wealth of floral beauty—there is the beauty that Nature creates by the hand of her servant, Time. You see, Aunt Janet, how the beautiful garden inspires a danger-hardened old tramp like me to high-grade sentiments of poetic fancy! Not only have limestone and sandstone, and even marble, grown green in time, but even the shrubs planted and then neglected have developed new kinds of beauty of their own. In some far-distant time some master-gardener of the Vissarions has tried to realize an idea—that of tiny plants that would grow just a little higher than the flowers, so that the effect of an uneven floral surface would be achieved without any hiding of anything in the garden seen from anywhere. This is only my reading of what has been from the effect of what is! In the long period of neglect the shrubs have outlived the flowers. Nature has been doing her own work all the time in enforcing the survival of the fittest. The shrubs have grown and grown, and have overtopped flower and weed, according to their inherent varieties of stature; to the effect that now you see irregularly scattered through the garden quite a number—for it is a big place—of vegetable products which from a landscape standpoint have something of the general effect of statues without the cramping feeling of detail. Whoever it was that laid out that part of the garden or made the choice of items, must have taken pains to get strange specimens, for all those taller shrubs are in special colours, mostly yellow or white—white cypress, white holly, yellow yew, grey-golden box, silver juniper, variegated maple, spiraea, and numbers of dwarf shrubs whose names I don't know. I only know that when the moon shines—and this, my dear Aunt Janet, is the very land of moonlight itself!—they all look ghastly pale. The effect is weird to the last degree, and I am sure that you will enjoy it. For myself, as you know, uncanny things hold no fear. I suppose it is that I have been up against so many different kinds of fears, or, rather, of things which for most people have terrors of their own, that I have come to have a contempt—not an active contempt, you know, but a tolerative contempt—for the whole family of them. And you, too, will enjoy yourself here famously, I know. You'll have to collect all the stories of such matters in our new world and make a new book of facts for the Psychical Research Society. It will be nice to see your own name on a title-page, won't it, Aunt Janet?

From Rupert Sent Leger, Vissarion, to Janet MacKelpie, Croom.

January 30, 1907

My Dear Aunt Janet,

I stopped writing last night—do you know why? Because I wanted to write more! This sounds a paradox, but it is true. The fact is that, as I go on telling you of this delightful place, I keep finding out new beauties myself. Broadly speaking, it *is all* beautiful. In the long view or the little view—as the telescope or the microscope directs—it is all the same. Your eye can turn on nothing that does not entrance you. I was yesterday roaming about the upper part of time Castle, and came across some delightful nooks, which at once I became fond of, and already like them as if I had known them all my life. I felt at first a sense of greediness when I had appropriated to myself several rooms in different places—I who have never in my life had more than one room which I could call my own—and that only for a time! But when I slept on it the feeling changed, and its aspect is now not half bad. It is now under another classification—under a much more important label—*proprietorship*. If I were writing philosophy, I should here put in a cynical remark:

"Selfishness is an appanage of poverty. It might appear in the stud-book as by 'Morals' out of 'Wants.'"

I have now three bedrooms arranged as my own particular dens. One of the other two was also a choice of Uncle Roger's. It is at the top of one of the towers to the extreme east, and from it I can catch the first ray of light over the mountains. I slept in it last night, and when I woke, as in my travelling I was accustomed to do, at dawn, I saw from my bed through an open window—a small window, for it is in a fortress tower— the whole great expanse to the east. Not far off, and springing from the summit of a great ruin, where long ago a seed had fallen, rose a great silver-birch, and the half-transparent, drooping branches and hanging clusters of leaf broke the outline of the grey hills beyond, for the hills were, for a wonder, grey instead of blue. There was a mackerel sky, with the clouds dropping on the mountain-tops till you could hardly say which was which. It was a mackerel sky of a very bold and extraordinary kind—not a dish of mackerel, but a world of mackerel! The mountains are certainly most lovely. In this clear air they usually seem close at hand. It was only this morning, with the faint glimpse of the dawn whilst the night clouds were still unpierced by the sunlight, that I seemed to realize their greatness. I have seen the same enlightening effect of aerial perspective a few times before—in Colorado, in Upper India, in Thibet, and in the uplands amongst the Andes.

There is certainly something in looking at things from above which tends to raise one's own self-esteem. From the height, inequalities simply disappear. This I have often felt on a big scale when ballooning, or, better still, from an aeroplane.

Even here from the tower the outlook is somehow quite different from below. One realizes the place and all around it, not in detail, but as a whole. I shall certainly sleep up here occasionally, when you have come and we have settled down to our life as it is to be. I shall live in my own room downstairs, where I can have the intimacy of the garden. But I shall appreciate it all the more from now and again losing the sense of intimacy for a while, and surveying it without the sense of one's own self-importance.

I hope you have started on that matter of the servants. For myself, I don't care a button whether or not there are any servants at all; but I know well that you won't come till you have made your arrangements regarding them! Another thing, Aunt Janet. You must not be killed with work here, and it is all so vast. . . Why can't you get some sort of secretary who will write your letters and do all that sort of thing for you? I know you won't have a man secretary; but there are lots of women now who can write shorthand and typewrite. You could doubtless get one in the clan—someone with a desire to better herself. I know you would make her happy here. If she is not too young, all the better; she will have learned to hold her tongue and mind her own business, and not be too inquisitive. That would be a nuisance when we are finding our way about in a new country and trying to reconcile all sorts of opposites in a whole new country with new people, whom at first we shan't understand, and who certainly won't understand us; where every man carries a gun with as little thought of it as he has of buttons! Good-bye for a while.

Your loving
Rupert

From Rupert Sent Leger, Vissarion, to Janet MacKelpie, Croom.

February 3, 1907

I am back in my own room again. Already it seems to me that to get here again is like coming home. I have been going about for the last few days amongst the mountaineers and trying to make their acquaintance. It is a tough job; and I can see that there will be nothing but to stick to it. They are in reality the most primitive people I ever met—the most fixed to their own ideas, which belong to centuries back. I can understand now what people were like in England—not in Queen Elizabeth's time, for that was civilized time, but in the time of Coeur-de-Lion, or even earlier—and all the time with the most absolute mastery of weapons of precision. Every man carries a rifle—and knows how to use it, too. I do believe they would rather go without their clothes than their guns if they had to choose between them. They also carry a handjar, which used to be their national weapon. It is a sort of heavy, straight cutlass, and they are so expert with it as well as so strong that it is as facile in the hands of a Blue Mountaineer as is a foil in the hands of a Persian *maitre d'armes*. They are so proud and reserved that they make one feel quite small, and an "outsider" as well. I can see quite well that they rather resent my being here at all. It is not personal, for when alone with me they are genial, almost brotherly; but the moment a few of them get together they are like a sort of jury, with me as the criminal before them. It is an odd situation, and quite new to me. I am pretty well accustomed to all sorts of people, from cannibals to Mahatmas, but I'm blessed if I ever struck such a type as this—so proud, so haughty, so reserved, so distant, so absolutely fearless, so honourable, so hospitable. Uncle Roger's head was level when he chose them out as a people to live amongst. Do you know, Aunt Janet, I can't help feeling that they are very much like your own Highlanders—only more so. I'm sure of one thing: that in the end we shall get on capitally together. But it will be a slow job, and will need a lot of patience. I have a feeling in my bones that when they know me better they will be very loyal and very true; and I am not a hair's-breadth afraid of them or anything they shall or might do. That is, of course, if I live long enough for them to have time to know me. Anything may happen with such an indomitable, proud people to whom pride is more than victuals. After all, it only needs one man out of a crowd to have a wrong idea or to make a mistake as to one's motive—and there you are. But it will be all right that way, I am sure. I am come here to stay, as Uncle Roger wished. And stay I shall even if it has to be in a little bed of my own beyond the garden—seven feet odd long, and not too narrow—or else a stone-box of equal proportions in the vaults of St. Sava's Church across the Creek—the old burial-place of the Vissarions and other noble people for a good many centuries back. . .

I have been reading over this letter, dear Aunt Janet, and I am afraid the record is rather an alarming one. But don't you go building up superstitious horrors or fears on it. Honestly, I am only joking about death—a thing to which I have been rather prone for a good many years back. Not in very good taste, I suppose, but certainly very useful when the old man with the black wings goes flying about you day and night in strange places, sometimes visible and at others invisible. But you can always hear wings, especially in the dark, when you cannot see them. *You* know that, Aunt Janet, who come of a race of warriors, and who have special sight behind or through the black curtain.

Honestly, I am in no whit afraid of the Blue Mountaineers, nor have I a doubt of them. I love them already for their splendid qualities, and I am prepared to love them for themselves. I feel, too, that they will love me (and incidentally they are sure to love you). I have a sort of undercurrent of thought that there is something in their minds concerning me—something not painful, but disturbing; something that has a base in the past; something that has hope in it and possible pride, and not a little respect. As yet they can have had no opportunity of forming such impression from seeing me or from any thing I have done. Of course, it may be that, although they are fine, tall, stalwart men, I am still a head and shoulders over the tallest of them that I have yet seen. I catch their eyes looking up at me as though they were measuring me, even when they are keeping away from me, or, rather, keeping me from them at arm's length. I suppose I shall understand what it all means some day. In the meantime there is nothing to do but to go on my own way—which is Uncle Roger's—and wait and be patient and just. I have learned the value of that, any way, in my life amongst strange peoples. Good-night.

Your loving
RUPERT

February 24, 1907

MY DEAR AUNT JANET,

I am more than rejoiced to hear that you are coming here so soon. This isolation is, I think, getting on my nerves. I thought for a while last night that I was getting on, but the reaction came all too soon. I was in my room in the east turret, the room on the *corbeille*, and saw here and there men passing silently and swiftly between the trees as though in secret. By-and-by I located their meeting-place, which was in a hollow in the midst of the wood just outside the "natural" garden, as the map or plan of the castle calls it. I stalked that place for all I was worth, and suddenly walked straight into the midst of them. There were perhaps two or three hundred gathered, about the very finest lot of men I ever saw in my life. It was in its way quite an experience, and one not likely to be repeated, for, as I told you, in this country every man carries a rifle, and knows how to use it. I do not think I have seen a single man (or married man either) without his rifle since I came here. I wonder if they take them with them to bed! Well, the instant after I stood amongst them every rifle in the place was aimed straight at me. Don't be alarmed, Aunt Janet; they did not fire at me. If they had I should not be writing to you now. I should be in that little bit of real estate or the stone box, and about as full of lead as I could hold. Ordinarily, I take it, they would have fired on the instant; that is the etiquette here. But this time they—all separately but all together—made a new rule. No one said a word or, so far as I could see, made a movement. Here came in my own experience. I had been more than once in a tight place of something of the same kind, so I simply behaved in the most natural way I could. I felt conscious—it was all in a flash, remember—that if I showed fear or cause for fear, or even acknowledged danger by so much as even holding up my hands, I should have drawn all the fire. They all remained stock-still, as though they had been turned into stone, for several seconds. Then a queer kind of look flashed round them like wind over corn—something like the surprise one shows unconsciously on waking in a strange place. A second after they each dropped the rifle to the hollow of his arm and stood ready for anything. It was all as regular and quick and simultaneous as a salute at St. James's Palace.

Happily I had no arms of any kind with me, so that there could be no complication. I am rather a quick hand myself when there is any shooting to be done. However, there was no trouble here, but the contrary; the Blue Mountaineers—it sounds like a new sort of Bond Street band, doesn't it?—treated me in quite a different way than they did when I first met them. They were amazingly civil, almost deferential. But, all time same, they were more distant than ever, and all the time I was there I could get not a whit closer to them. They seemed in a sort of way to be afraid or in awe of me. No doubt that will soon pass away, and when we know one another better we shall become close friends. They are too fine fellows not to be worth a little waiting for. (That sentence, by the way, is a pretty bad sentence! In old days you would have slippered me for it!) Your journey is all arranged, and I hope you will be comfortable. Rooke will meet you at Liverpool Street and look after everything.

I shan't write again, but when we meet at Fiume I shall begin to tell you all the rest. Till then, good-bye. A good journey to you, and a happy meeting to us both.

RUPERT

Letter from Janet MacKelpie, Vissarion, to Sir Colin MacKelpie, United Service Club, London.

February 28, 1907

DEAREST UNCLE,

I had a very comfortable journey all across Europe. Rupert wrote to me some time ago to say that when I got to Vissarion I should be an Empress, and he certainly took care that on the way here I should be treated like one. Rooke, who seems a wonderful old man, was in the next compartment to that reserved for me. At Harwich he had everything arranged perfectly, and so right on to Fiume. Everywhere there were attentive officials waiting. I had a carriage all to myself, which I joined at Antwerp—a whole carriage with a suite of rooms, dining-room, drawing-room, bedroom, even bath-room. There was a cook with a kitchen of his own on board, a real chef like a French nobleman in disguise. There were also a waiter and a servant-maid. My own maid Maggie was quite awed at first. We were as far as Cologne before she summoned up courage to order them about. Whenever we stopped Rooke was on the platform with local officials, and kept the door of my carriage like a sentry on duty.

At Fiume, when the train slowed down, I saw Rupert waiting on the platform. He looked magnificent, towering over everybody there like a giant. He is in perfect health, and seemed glad to see me. He took me off at once on an automobile to a quay where an electric launch was waiting. This took us on board a beautiful big steam-yacht, which was waiting with full steam up and—how he got there I don't know—Rooke waiting at the gangway.

I had another suite all to myself. Rupert and I had dinner together—I think the finest dinner I ever sat down to. This was very nice of Rupert, for it was all for me. He himself only ate a piece of steak and drank a glass of water. I went to bed early, for, despite the luxury of the journey, I was very tired.

I awoke in the grey of the morning, and came on deck. We were close to the coast. Rupert was on the bridge with the Captain, and Rooke was acting as pilot. When Rupert saw me, he ran down the ladder and took me up on the bridge. He left me there while he ran down again and brought me up a lovely fur cloak which I had never seen. He put it on me and kissed me. He is the tenderest-hearted boy in the world, as well as the best and bravest! He made me take his arm whilst he pointed out Vissarion, towards which we were steering. It is the most lovely place I ever saw. I won't stop to describe it now, for it will be better that you see it for yourself and enjoy it all fresh as I did.

The Castle is an immense place. You had better ship off, as soon as all is ready here and you can arrange it, the servants whom I engaged; and I am not sure that we shall not want as many more. There has hardly been a mop or broom on the place for centuries, and I doubt if it ever had a thorough good cleaning all over since it was built. And, do you know, Uncle, that it might be well to double that little army of yours that you are arranging for Rupert? Indeed, the boy told me himself that he was going to write to you about it. I think old Lachlan and his wife, Sandy's Mary, had better be in charge of the maids when they come over. A lot of lassies like yon will be iller to keep together than a flock of sheep. So it will be wise to have authority over them, especially as none of them speaks a word of foreign tongues. Rooke—you saw him at the station at Liverpool Street—will, if he be available, go over to bring the whole body here. He has offered to do it if I should wish. And, by the way, I think it will be well, when the time comes for their departure, if not only the lassies, but Lachlan and Sandy's Mary, too, will call him *Mister* Rooke. He is a very important person indeed here. He is, in fact, a sort of Master of the Castle, and though he is very self-suppressing, is a man of rarely fine qualities. Also it will be well to keep authority. When your clansmen come over, he will have charge of them, too. Dear me! I find I have written such a long letter, I must stop and get to work. I shall write again.

Your very affectionate
JANET

From the Same to the Same.

March 3, 1907

DEAREST UNCLE,

All goes well here, and as there is no news, I only write because you are a dear, and I want to thank you for all the trouble you have taken for me—and for Rupert. I think we had better wait awhile before bringing out the servants. Rooke is away on some business for Rupert, and will not be back for some time; Rupert thinks it may be a couple of months. There is no one else that he could send to take charge of the party from home, and I don't like the idea of all those lassies coming out without an escort. Even Lachlan and Sandy's Mary are ignorant of foreign languages and foreign ways. But as soon as Rooke returns we can have them all out. I dare say you will have some of your clansmen ready by then, and I think the poor girls, who may feel a bit strange in a new country like this, where the ways are so different from ours, will feel easier when they know that there are some of their own mankind near them. Perhaps it might be well that those of them who are engaged to each other—I know there are some—should marry before they come out here. It will be more convenient in many ways, and will save lodgment, and, besides, these Blue Mountaineers are very handsome men. Good-night.

JANET

Sir Colin MacKelpie, Croom, to Janet MacKelpie, Vissarion.

March 9, 1907

MY DEAR JANET,

I have duly received both your letters, and am delighted to find you are so well pleased with your new home. It must certainly be a very lovely and unique place, and I am myself longing to see it. I came up here three days ago, and am, as usual, feeling all the better for a breath of my native air. Time goes on, my dear, and I am beginning to feel not so young as I was. Tell Rupert that the men are all fit, and longing to get out to him. They are certainly a fine lot of men. I don't think I ever saw a finer. I have had them drilled and trained as soldiers, and, in addition, have had them taught a lot of trades just as they selected themselves. So he shall have nigh him men who can turn their hands to anything—not, of course, that they all know every trade, but amongst them there is someone who can do whatever may be required. There are blacksmiths, carpenters, farriers, saddle-makers, gardeners, plumbers, cutlers, gunsmiths, so, as they all are farmers by origin and sportsmen by practice, they will make a rare household body of men. They are nearly all first-class shots, and I am having them practise with revolvers. They are being taught fencing and broadsword and ju-jitsu; I have organized them in military form, with their own sergeants and corporals. This morning I had an inspection, and I assure you, my dear, they could give points to the Household troop in matters of drill. I tell you I am proud of my clansmen!

I think you are quite wise about waiting to bring out the lassies, and wiser still about the marrying. I dare say there will be more marrying when they all get settled in a foreign country. I shall be glad of it, for as Rupert is going to settle there, it will be good for him to have round him a little colony of his own people. And it will be good for them, too, for I know he will be good to them—as you will, my dear. The hills are barren here, and life is hard, and each year there is more and more demand for crofts, and sooner or later our people must thin out. And mayhap our little settlement of MacKelpie clan away beyond the frontiers of the Empire may be some service to the nation and the King. But this is a dream! I see that here I am beginning to realise in myself one part of Isaiah's prophecy:

"Your young men shall see visions, and your old men shall dream dreams."

By the way, my dear, talking about dreams, I am sending you out some boxes of books which were in your rooms. They are nearly all on odd subjects that *we* understand—Second Sight, Ghosts, Dreams (that was what brought the matter to my mind just now), superstitions, Vampires, Wehr-Wolves, and all such uncanny folk and things. I looked over some of these books, and found your marks and underlining and comments, so I fancy you will miss them in your new home. You will, I am sure, feel more at ease with such old friends close to you. I have taken the names and sent the list to London, so that when you pay me a visit again you will be at home in all ways. If you come to me altogether, you will be more welcome still—if possible. But I am sure that Rupert, who I know loves you very much, will try to make you so happy that you will not want to leave him. So I will have to come out often to see you both, even at the cost of leaving Croom for so long. Strange, is it not? that now, when, through Roger Melton's more than kind remembrance of me, I am able to go where I will and do what I will, I want more and more to remain at home by my own ingle. I don't think that anyone but you or Rupert could get me away from it. I am working very hard at my little regiment, as I call it. They are simply fine, and will, I am sure, do us credit. The uniforms are all made, and well made, too. There is not a man of them that does not look like an officer. I tell you, Janet, that when we turn out the Vissarion Guard we shall feel proud of them. I dare say that a couple of months will do all that can be done here. I shall come out with them myself. Rupert writes me that he thinks it will be more comfortable to come out direct in a ship of our own. So when I go up to London in a few weeks' time I shall see about chartering a suitable vessel. It will certainly save a lot of trouble to us and anxiety to our people. Would it not be well when I am getting the ship, if I charter one big enough to take out all your lassies, too? It is not as if they were strangers. After all, my dear, soldiers are soldiers and lassies are lassies. But these are all kinsfolk, as well as clansmen and clanswomen, and I, their Chief, shall be there. Let me know your views and wishes in this respect. Mr. Trent, whom I saw before leaving London, asked me to "convey to you his most respectful remembrances"—these were his very words, and here they are. Trent is a nice fellow, and I like him. He has promised to pay me a visit here before the month is up, and I look forward to our both enjoying ourselves.

Good-bye, my dear, and the Lord watch over you and our dear boy.

Your affectionate Uncle,
COLIN ALEXANDER MACKELPIE

Book III

The Coming of the Lady

Rupert Sent Leger's Journal

April 3, 1907

I have waited till now—well into midday—before beginning to set down the details of the strange episode of last night. I have spoken with persons whom I know to be of normal type. I have breakfasted, as usual heartily, and have every reason to consider myself in perfect health and sanity. So that the record following may be regarded as not only true in substance, but exact as to details. I have investigated and reported on too many cases for the Psychical Research Society to be ignorant of the necessity for absolute accuracy in such matters of even the minutest detail.

Yesterday was Tuesday, the second day of April, 1907. I passed a day of interest, with its fair amount of work of varying kinds. Aunt Janet and I lunched together, had a stroll round the gardens after tea—especially examining the site for the new Japanese garden, which we shall call "Janet's Garden." We went in mackintoshes, for the rainy season is in its full, the only sign of its not being a repetition of the Deluge being that breaks in the continuance are beginning. They are short at present but will doubtless enlarge themselves as the season comes towards an end. We dined together at seven. After dinner I had a cigar, and then joined Aunt Janet for an hour in her drawing-room. I left her at half-past ten, when I went to my own room and wrote some letters. At ten minutes past eleven I wound my watch, so I know the time accurately. Having prepared for bed, I drew back the heavy curtain in front of my window, which opens on the marble steps into the Italian garden. I had put out my light before drawing back the curtain, for I wanted to have a look at the scene before turning in. Aunt Janet has always had an old-fashioned idea of the need (or propriety, I hardly know which) of keeping windows closed and curtains drawn. I am gradually getting her to leave my room alone in this respect, but at present the change is in its fitful stage, and of course I must not hurry matters or be too persistent, as it would hurt her feelings. This night was one of those under the old regime. It was a delight to look out, for the scene was perfect of its own kind. The long spell of rain—the ceaseless downpour which had for the time flooded everywhere—had passed, and water in abnormal places rather trickled than ran. We were now beginning to be in the sloppy rather than the deluged stage. There was plenty of light to see by, for the moon had begun to show out fitfully through the masses of flying clouds. The uncertain light made weird shadows with the shrubs and statues in the garden. The long straight walk which leads from the marble steps is strewn with fine sand white from the quartz strand in the nook to the south of the Castle. Tall shrubs of white holly, yew, juniper, cypress, and variegated maple and spiraea, which stood at intervals along the walk and its branches, appeared ghost-like in the fitful moonlight. The many vases and statues and urns, always like phantoms in a half-light, were more than ever weird. Last night the moonlight was unusually effective, and showed not only the gardens down to the defending wall, but the deep gloom of the great forest-trees beyond; and beyond that, again, to where the mountain chain began, the forest running up their silvered slopes flamelike in form, deviated here and there by great crags and the outcropping rocky sinews of the vast mountains.

Whilst I was looking at this lovely prospect, I thought I saw something white flit, like a modified white flash, at odd moments from one to another of the shrubs or statues—anything which would afford cover from observation. At first I was not sure whether I really saw anything or did not. This was in itself a little disturbing to me, for I have been so long trained to minute observation of facts surrounding me, on which often depend not only my own life, but the lives of others, that I have become accustomed to trust my eyes; and anything creating the faintest doubt in this respect is a cause of more or less anxiety to me. Now, however, that my attention was called to myself, I looked more keenly, and in a very short time was satisfied that something was moving—something clad in white. It was natural enough that my thoughts should tend towards something uncanny—the belief that this place is haunted, conveyed in a thousand ways of speech and inference. Aunt Janet's eerie beliefs, fortified by her books on occult subjects—and of late, in our isolation from the rest of the world, the subject of daily conversations—helped to this end. No wonder, then, that, fully awake and with senses all on edge, I waited for some further manifestation from this ghostly visitor—as in my mind I took it to be. It must surely be a ghost or spiritual manifestation of some kind which moved in this silent way. In order to see and hear better, I softly moved back the folding grille, opened the French window, and stepped out, barefooted and pyjama-clad as I was, on the marble terrace. How cold the wet marble was! How heavy smelled the rain-laden garden! It was as though the night and the damp, and even the moonlight, were drawing the aroma from all the flowers that blossomed. The whole night seemed to exhale heavy, half-intoxicating odours! I stood at the head of the marble steps, and all immediately before me was ghostly in the extreme—the white marble terrace and steps, the white walks of quartz-sand glistening under the fitful moonlight; the shrubs of white or pale green or yellow,—all looking dim and ghostly in the glamorous light; the white statues and vases. And amongst them, still flitting noiselessly, that mysterious elusive figure which I could not say was based on fact or imagination. I held my breath, listening intently for every sound; but sound there was none, save those of the night and its denizens. Owls hooted in the forest; bats, taking advantage of the cessation of the rain, flitted about silently, like shadows in the air. But there was no more sign of moving ghost or phantom, or whatever I had seen might have been—if, indeed, there had been anything except imagination.

So, after waiting awhile, I returned to my room, closed the window, drew the grille across again, and dragged the heavy curtain before the opening; then, having extinguished my candles, went to bed in the dark. In a few minutes I must have been asleep.

"What was that?" I almost heard the words of my own thought as I sat up in bed wide awake. To memory rather than present hearing the disturbing sound had seemed like the faint tapping at the window. For some seconds I listened, mechanically but intently, with bated breath and that quick beating of the heart which in a timorous person speaks for fear, and for expectation in another. In the stillness the sound came again—this time a very, very faint but unmistakable tapping at the glass door.

I jumped up, drew back the curtain, and for a moment stood appalled.

There, outside on the balcony, in the now brilliant moonlight, stood a woman, wrapped in white grave-clothes saturated with water, which dripped on the marble floor, making a pool which trickled slowly down the wet steps. Attitude and dress and circumstance all conveyed the idea that, though she moved and spoke, she was not quick, but dead. She was young and very beautiful, but pale, like the grey pallor of death. Through the still white of her face, which made her look as cold as the wet marble she stood on, her dark eyes seemed to gleam with a strange but enticing lustre. Even in the unsearching moonlight, which is after all rather deceptive than illuminative, I could not but notice one rare quality of her eyes. Each had some quality of refraction which made it look as though it contained a star. At every movement she made, the stars exhibited new beauties, of more rare and radiant force. She looked at me imploringly as the heavy curtain rolled back, and in eloquent gestures implored me to admit her. Instinctively I obeyed; I rolled back the steel grille, and threw open the French window. I noticed that she shivered and trembled as the glass door fell open. Indeed, she seemed so overcome with cold as to seem almost unable to move. In the sense of her helplessness all idea of the strangeness of the situation entirely disappeared. It was not as if my first idea of death taken from her cerements was negatived. It was simply that I did not think of it at all; I was content to accept things as they were—she was a woman, and in some dreadful trouble; that was enough.

I am thus particular about my own emotions, as I may have to refer to them again in matters of comprehension or comparison. The whole thing is so vastly strange and abnormal that the least thing may afterwards give some guiding light or clue to something otherwise not understandable. I have always found that in recondite matters first impressions are of more real value than later conclusions. We humans place far too little reliance on instinct as against reason; and yet instinct is the great gift of Nature to all animals for their protection and the fulfilment of their functions generally.

When I stepped out on the balcony, not thinking of my costume, I found that the woman was benumbed and hardly able to move. Even when I asked her to enter, and supplemented my words with gestures in case she should not understand my language, she stood stock-still, only rocking slightly to and fro as though she had just strength enough left to balance herself on her feet. I was afraid, from the condition in which she was, that she might drop down dead at any moment. So I took her by the hand to lead her in. But she seemed too weak to even make the attempt. When I pulled her slightly forward, thinking to help her, she tottered, and would have fallen had I not caught her in my arms. Then, half lifting her, I moved her forwards. Her feet, relieved of her weight, now seemed able to make the necessary effort; and so, I almost carrying her, we moved into the room. She was at the very end of her strength; I had to lift her over the sill. In obedience to her motion, I closed the French window and bolted it. I supposed the warmth of the room—though cool, it was warmer than the damp air without—affected her quickly, for on the instant she seemed to begin to recover herself. In a few seconds, as though she had reacquired her strength, she herself pulled the heavy curtain across the window. This left us in darkness, through which I heard her say in English:

"Light. Get a light!"

I found matches, and at once lit a candle. As the wick flared, she moved over to the door of the room, and tried if the lock and bolt were fastened. Satisfied as to this, she moved towards me, her wet shroud leaving a trail of moisture on the green carpet. By this time the wax of the candle had melted sufficiently to let me see her clearly. She was shaking and quivering as though in an ague; she drew the wet shroud around her piteously. Instinctively I spoke:

"Can I do anything for you?"

She answered, still in English, and in a voice of thrilling, almost piercing sweetness, which seemed somehow to go straight to my heart, and affected me strangely: "Give me warmth."

I hurried to the fireplace. It was empty; there was no fire laid. I turned to her, and said:

"Wait just a few minutes here. I shall call someone, and get help— and fire."

Her voice seemed to ring with intensity as she answered without a pause:

"No, no! Rather would I be"—here she hesitated for an instant, but as she caught sight of her cerements went on hurriedly—"as I am. I trust you—not others; and you must not betray my trust." Almost instantly she fell into a frightful fit of shivering, drawing again her death-clothes close to her, so piteously that it wrung my heart. I suppose I am a practical man. At any rate, I am accustomed to action. I took from its place beside my bed a thick Jaeger dressing-gown of dark brown—it was, of course, of extra length—and held it out to her as I said:

"Put that on. It is the only warm thing here which would be suitable. Stay; you must remove that wet—wet"—I stumbled about for a word that would not be offensive—"that frock—dress—costume—whatever it is." I pointed to where, in the corner of the room, stood a chintz-covered folding-screen which fences in my cold sponge bath, which is laid ready for me overnight, as I am an early riser.

She bowed gravely, and taking the dressing-gown in a long, white, finely-shaped hand, bore it behind the screen. There was a slight rustle, and then a hollow "flop" as the wet garment fell on the floor; more rustling and rubbing, and a minute later she emerged wrapped from head to foot in the long Jaeger garment, which trailed on the floor behind her, though she was a tall woman. She was still shivering painfully, however. I took a flask of brandy and a glass from a cupboard, and offered her some; but with a motion of her hand she refused it, though she moaned grievously.

"Oh, I am so cold—so cold!" Her teeth were chattering. I was pained at her sad condition, and said despairingly, for I was at my wits' end to know what to do:

"Tell me anything that I can do to help you, and I will do it. I may not call help; there is no fire—nothing to make it with; you will not take some brandy. What on earth can I do to give you warmth?"

Her answer certainly surprised me when it came, though it was practical enough—so practical that I should not have dared to say it. She looked me straight in the face for a few seconds before speaking. Then, with an air of girlish innocence which disarmed suspicion and convinced me at once of her simple faith, she said in a voice that at once thrilled me and evoked all my pity:

"Let me rest for a while, and cover me up with rugs. That may give me warmth. I am dying of cold. And I have a deadly fear upon me—a deadly fear. Sit by me, and let me hold your hand. You are big and strong, and you look brave. It will reassure me. I am not myself a coward, but to-night fear has got me by the throat. I can hardly breathe. Do let me stay till I am warm. If you only knew what I have gone through, and have to go through still, I am sure you would pity me and help me."

To say that I was astonished would be a mild description of my feelings. I was not shocked. The life which I have led was not one which makes for prudery. To travel in strange places amongst strange peoples with strange views of their own is to have odd experiences and peculiar adventures now and again; a man without human passions is not the type necessary for an adventurous life, such as I myself have had. But even a man of passions and experiences can, when he respects a woman, be shocked—even prudish—where his own opinion of her is concerned. Such must bring to her guarding any generosity which he has, and any self-restraint also. Even should she place herself in a doubtful position, her honour calls to his honour. This is a call which may not be—*must* not be—unanswered. Even passion must pause for at least a while at sound of such a trumpet-call.

This woman I did respect—much respect. Her youth and beauty; her manifest ignorance of evil; her superb disdain of convention, which could only come through hereditary dignity; her terrible fear and suffering—for there must be more in her unhappy condition than meets the eye—would all demand respect, even if one did not hasten to yield it. Nevertheless, I thought it necessary to enter a protest against her embarrassing suggestion. I certainly did feel a fool when making it, also a cad. I can truly say it was made only for her good, and out of the best of me, such as I am. I felt impossibly awkward; and stuttered and stumbled before I spoke:

"But surely—the convenances! Your being here alone at night! Mrs. Grundy—convention—the—"

She interrupted me with an incomparable dignity—a dignity which had the effect of shutting me up like a clasp-knife and making me feel a decided inferior—and a poor show at that. There was such a gracious simplicity and honesty in it, too, such self-respecting knowledge of herself and her position, that I could be neither angry nor hurt. I could only feel ashamed of myself, and of my own littleness of mind and morals. She seemed in her icy coldness—now spiritual as well as bodily—like an incarnate figure of Pride as she answered:

"What are convenances or conventions to me! If you only knew where I have come from—the existence (if it can be called so) which I have had—the loneliness—the horror! And besides, it is for me to *make* conventions, not to yield my personal freedom of action to them. Even as I am—even here and in this garb—I am above convention. Convenances do not trouble me or hamper me. That, at least, I have won by what I have gone through, even if it had never come to me through any other way. Let me stay." She said the last words, in spite of all her pride, appealingly. But still, there was a note of high pride in all this— in all she said and did, in her attitude and movement, in the tones of her voice, in the loftiness of her carriage and the steadfast look of her open, starlit eyes. Altogether, there was something so rarely lofty in herself and all that clad her that, face to face with it and with her, my feeble attempt at moral precaution seemed puny, ridiculous, and out of place. Without a word in the doing, I took from an old chiffonier chest an armful of blankets, several of which I threw over her as she lay, for in the meantime, having replaced the coverlet, she had lain down at length on the bed. I took a chair, and sat down beside her. When she stretched out her hand from beneath the pile of wraps, I took it in mine, saying:

"Get warm and rest. Sleep if you can. You need not fear; I shall guard you with my life."

She looked at me gratefully, her starry eyes taking a new light more full of illumination than was afforded by the wax candle, which was shaded from her by my body. . . She was horribly cold, and her teeth chattered so violently that I feared lest she should have incurred some dangerous evil from her wetting and the cold that followed it. I felt, however, so awkward that I could find no words to express my fears; moreover, I hardly dared say anything at all regarding herself after the haughty way in which she had received my well-meant protest. Manifestly I was but to her as a sort of refuge and provider of heat, altogether impersonal, and not to be regarded in any degree as an individual. In these humiliating circumstances what could I do but sit quiet—and wait developments?

Little by little the fierce chattering of her teeth began to abate as the warmth of her surroundings stole through her. I also felt, even in this strangely awakening position, the influence of the quiet; and sleep began to steal over me. Several times I tried to fend it off, but, as I could not make any overt movement without alarming my strange and beautiful companion, I had to yield myself to drowsiness. I was still in such an overwhelming stupor of surprise that I could not even think freely. There was nothing for me but to control myself and wait. Before I could well fix my thoughts I was asleep.

I was recalled to consciousness by hearing, even through the pall of sleep that bound me, the crowing of a cock in some of the out-offices of the castle. At the same instant the figure, lying deathly still but for the gentle heaving of her bosom, began to struggle wildly. The sound had won through the gates of her sleep also. With a swift, gliding motion she slipped from the bed to the floor, saying in a fierce whisper as she pulled herself up to her full height:

"Let me out! I must go! I must go!"

By this time I was fully awake, and the whole position of things came to me in an instant which I shall never—can never—forget: the dim light of the candle, now nearly burned down to the socket, all the dimmer from the fact that the first grey gleam of morning was stealing in round the edges of the heavy curtain; the tall, slim figure in the brown dressing-gown whose over-length trailed on the floor, the black hair showing glossy in the light, and increasing by contrast the marble whiteness of the face, in which the black eyes sent through their stars fiery gleams. She appeared quite in a frenzy of haste; her eagerness was simply irresistible.

I was so stupefied with amazement, as well as with sleep, that I did not attempt to stop her, but began instinctively to help her by furthering her wishes. As she ran behind the screen, and, as far as sound could inform me,—began frantically to disrobe herself of the warm dressing-gown and to don again the ice-cold wet shroud, I pulled back the curtain from the window, and drew the bolt of the glass door. As I did so she was already behind me, shivering. As I threw open the door she glided out with a swift silent movement, but trembling in an agonized way. As she passed me, she murmured in a low voice, which was almost lost in the chattering of her teeth:

"Oh, thank you—thank you a thousand times! But I must go. I *must*! I *must*! I shall come again, and try to show my gratitude. Do not condemn me as ungrateful—till then." And she was gone.

I watched her pass the length of the white path, flitting from shrub to shrub or statue as she had come. In the cold grey light of the undeveloped dawn she seemed even more ghostly than she had done in the black shadow of the night.

When she disappeared from sight in the shadow of the wood, I stood on the terrace for a long time watching, in case I should be afforded another glimpse of her, for there was now no doubt in my mind that she had for me some strange attraction. I felt even then that the look in those glorious starry eyes would be with me always so long as I might live. There was some fascination which went deeper than my eyes or my flesh or my heart—down deep into the very depths of my soul. My mind was all in a whirl, so that I could hardly think coherently. It all was like a dream; the reality seemed far away. It was not possible to doubt that the phantom figure which had been so close to me during the dark hours of the night was actual flesh and blood. Yet she was so cold, so cold! Altogether I could not fix my mind to either proposition: that it was a living woman who had held my hand, or a dead body reanimated for the time or the occasion in some strange manner.

The difficulty was too great for me to make up my mind upon it, even had I wanted to. But, in any case, I did not want to. This would, no doubt, come in time. But till then I wished to dream on, as anyone does in a dream which can still be blissful though there be pauses of pain, or ghastliness, or doubt, or terror.

So I closed the window and drew the curtain again, feeling for the first time the cold in which I had stood on the wet marble floor of the terrace when my bare feet began to get warm on the soft carpet. To get rid of the chill feeling I got into the bed on which *she* had lain, and as the warmth restored me tried to think coherently. For a short while I was going over the facts of the night—or what seemed as facts to my remembrance. But as I continued to think, the possibilities of any result seemed to get less, and I found myself vainly trying to reconcile with the logic of life the grim episode of the night. The effort proved to be too much for such concentration as was left to me; moreover, interrupted sleep was clamant, and would not be denied. What I dreamt of—if I dreamt at all—I know not. I only know that I was ready for waking when the time came. It came with a violent knocking at my door. I sprang from bed, fully awake in a second, drew the bolt, and slipped back to bed. With a hurried "May I come in?" Aunt Janet entered. She seemed relieved when she saw me, and gave without my asking an explanation of her perturbation:

"Oh, laddie, I hae been so uneasy aboot ye all the nicht. I hae had dreams an' veesions an' a' sorts o' uncanny fancies. I fear that—" She was by now drawing back the curtain, and as her eyes took in the marks of wet all over the floor the current of her thoughts changed:

"Why, laddie, whativer hae ye been doin' wi' yer baith? Oh, the mess ye hae made! 'Tis sinful to gie sic trouble an' waste. . ." And so she went on. I was glad to hear the tirade, which was only what a good housewife, outraged in her sentiments of order, would have made. I listened in patience—with pleasure when I thought of what she would have thought (and said) had she known the real facts. I was well pleased to have got off so easily.

RUPERT'S JOURNAL—*Continued*

April 10, 1907

For some days after what I call "the episode" I was in a strange condition of mind. I did not take anyone—not even Aunt Janet—into confidence. Even she dear, and open-hearted and liberal-minded as she is, might not have understood well enough to be just and tolerant; and I did not care to hear any adverse comment on my strange visitor. Somehow

I could not bear the thought of anyone finding fault with her or in her, though, strangely enough, I was eternally defending her to myself; for, despite my wishes, embarrassing thoughts *would* come again and again, and again in all sorts and variants of queries difficult to answer. I found myself defending her, sometimes as a woman hard pressed by spiritual fear and physical suffering, sometimes as not being amenable to laws that govern the Living. Indeed, I could not make up my mind whether I looked on her as a living human being or as one with some strange existence in another world, and having only a chance foothold in our own. In such doubt imagination began to work, and thoughts of evil, of danger, of doubt, even of fear, began to crowd on me with such persistence and in such varied forms that I found my instinct of reticence growing into a settled purpose. The value of this instinctive precaution was promptly shown by Aunt Janet's state of mind, with consequent revelation of it. She became full of gloomy prognostications and what I thought were morbid fears. For the first time in my life I discovered that Aunt Janet had nerves! I had long had a secret belief that she was gifted, to some degree at any rate, with Second Sight, which quality, or whatever it is, skilled in the powers if not the lore of superstition, manages to keep at stretch not only the mind of its immediate pathic, but of others relevant to it. Perhaps this natural quality had received a fresh impetus from the arrival of some cases of her books sent on by Sir Colin. She appeared to read and reread these works, which were chiefly on occult subjects, day and night, except when she was imparting to me choice excerpts of the most baleful and fearsome kind. Indeed, before a week was over I found myself to be an expert in the history of the cult, as well as in its manifestations, which latter I had been versed in for a good many years.

The result of all this was that it set me brooding. Such, at least, I gathered was the fact when Aunt Janet took me to task for it. She always speaks out according to her convictions, so that her thinking I brooded was to me a proof that I did; and after a personal examination I came—reluctantly—to the conclusion that she was right, so far, at any rate, as my outer conduct was concerned. The state of mind I was in, however, kept me from making any acknowledgment of it—the real cause of my keeping so much to myself and of being so *distrait*. And so I went on, torturing myself as before with introspective questioning; and she, with her mind set on my actions, and endeavouring to find a cause for them, continued and expounded her beliefs and fears.

Her nightly chats with me when we were alone after dinner—for I had come to avoid her questioning at other times—kept my imagination at high pressure. Despite myself, I could not but find new cause for concern in the perennial founts of her superstition. I had thought, years ago, that I had then sounded the depths of this branch of psychicism; but this new phase of thought, founded on the really deep hold which the existence of my beautiful visitor and her sad and dreadful circumstances had taken upon me, brought me a new concern in the matter of self-importance. I came to think that I must reconstruct my self-values, and begin a fresh understanding of ethical beliefs. Do what I would, my mind would keep turning on the uncanny subjects brought before it. I began to apply them one by one to my own late experience, and unconsciously to try to fit them in turn to the present case.

The effect of this brooding was that I was, despite my own will, struck by the similarity of circumstances bearing on my visitor, and the conditions apportioned by tradition and superstition to such strange survivals from earlier ages as these partial existences which are rather Undead than Living—still walking the earth, though claimed by the world of the Dead. Amongst them are the Vampire, or the Wehr-Wolf. To this class also might belong in a measure the Doppelganger—one of whose dual existences commonly belongs to the actual world around it. So, too, the denizens of the world of Astralism. In any of these named worlds there is a material presence—which must be created, if only for a single or periodic purpose. It matters not whether a material presence already created can be receptive of a disembodied soul, or a soul unattached can have a body built up for it or around it; or, again, whether the body of a dead person can be made seeming quick through some diabolic influence manifested in the present, or an inheritance or result of some baleful use of malefic power in the past. The result is the same in each case, though the ways be widely different: a soul and a body which are not in unity but brought together for strange purposes through stranger means and by powers still more strange.

Through much thought and a process of exclusions the eerie form which seemed to be most in correspondence with my adventure, and most suitable to my fascinating visitor, appeared to be the Vampire. Doppelganger, Astral creations, and all such-like, did not comply with the conditions of my night experience. The Wehr-Wolf is but a variant of the Vampire, and so needed not to be classed or examined at all. Then it was that, thus focussed, the Lady of the Shroud (for so I came to hold her in my mind) began to assume a new force. Aunt Janet's library afforded me clues which I followed with avidity. In my secret heart I hated the quest, and did not wish to go on with it. But in this I was not my own master. Do what I would—brush away doubts never so often, new doubts and imaginings came in their stead. The circumstance almost repeated the parable of the Seven Devils who took the place of the exorcised one. Doubts I could stand. Imaginings I could stand. But doubts and imaginings together made a force so fell that I was driven to accept any reading of the mystery which might presumably afford a foothold for satisfying thought. And so I came to accept tentatively the Vampire theory—accept it, at least, so far as to examine it as judicially as was given me to do. As the days wore on, so the conviction grew. The more I read on the subject, the more directly the evidences pointed towards this view. The more I thought, the more obstinate became the conviction. I ransacked Aunt Janet's volumes again and again to find anything to the contrary; but in vain. Again, no matter how obstinate were my convictions at any given time, unsettlement came with fresh thinking over the argument, so that I was kept in a harassing state of uncertainty.

Briefly, the evidence in favour of accord between the facts of the case and the Vampire theory were:

Her coming was at night—the time the Vampire is according to the theory, free to move at will.

She wore her shroud—a necessity of coming fresh from grave or tomb; for there is nothing occult about clothing which is not subject to astral or other influences.

She had to be helped into my room—in strict accordance with what one sceptical critic of occultism has called "the Vampire etiquette."

She made violent haste in getting away at cock-crow.

She seemed preternaturally cold; her sleep was almost abnormal in intensity, and yet the sound of the cock-crowing came through it.

These things showed her to be subject to *some* laws, though not in exact accord within those which govern human beings. Under the stress of such circumstances as she must have gone through, her vitality seemed more than human—the quality of vitality which could outlive ordinary burial. Again, such purpose as she had shown in donning, under stress of some compelling direction, her ice-cold wet shroud, and, wrapt in it, going out again into the night, was hardly normal for a woman.

But if so, and if she was indeed a Vampire, might not whatever it may be that holds such beings in thrall be by some means or other exorcised? To find the means must be my next task. I am actually pining to see her again. Never before have I been stirred to my depths by anyone. Come it from Heaven or Hell, from the Earth or the Grave, it does not matter; I shall make it my task to win her back to life and peace. If she be indeed a Vampire, the task may be hard and long; if she be not so, and if it be merely that circumstances have so gathered round her as to produce that impression, the task may be simpler and the result more sweet. No, not more sweet; for what can be more sweet than to restore the lost or seemingly lost soul of the woman you love! There, the truth is out at last! I suppose that I have fallen in love with her. If so, it is too late for me to fight against it. I can only wait with what patience I can till I see her again. But to that end I can do nothing. I know absolutely nothing about her—not even her name. Patience!

Rupert's Journal—*Continued*

April 16, 1907

The only relief I have had from the haunting anxiety regarding the Lady of the Shroud has been in the troubled state of my adopted country. There has evidently been something up which I have not been allowed to know. The mountaineers are troubled and restless; are wandering about, singly and in parties, and holding meetings in strange places. This is what I gather used to be in old days when intrigues were on foot with Turks, Greeks, Austrians, Italians, Russians. This concerns me vitally, for my mind has long been made up to share the fortunes of the Land of the Blue Mountains. For good or ill I mean to stay here: *J'y suis, j'y reste*. I share henceforth the lot of the Blue Mountaineers; and not Turkey, nor Greece, nor Austria, nor Italy, nor Russia—no, not France nor Germany either; not man nor God nor Devil shall drive me from my purpose. With these patriots I throw in my lot! My only difficulty seemed at first to be with the men themselves. They are so proud that at the beginning I feared they would not even accord me the honour of being one of them! However, things always move on somehow, no matter what difficulties there be at the beginning. Never mind! When one looks back at an accomplished fact the beginning is not to be seen—and if it were it would not matter. It is not of any account, anyhow.

I heard that there was going to be a great meeting near here yesterday afternoon, and I attended it. I think it was a success. If such is any proof, I felt elated as well as satisfied when I came away. Aunt Janet's Second Sight on the subject was comforting, though grim, and in a measure disconcerting. When I was saying good-night she asked me to bend down my head. As I did so, she laid her hands on it and passed them all over it. I heard her say to herself:

"Strange! There's nothing there; yet I could have sworn I saw it!" I asked her to explain, but she would not. For once she was a little obstinate, and refused point blank to even talk of the subject. She was not worried nor unhappy; so I had no cause for concern. I said nothing, but I shall wait and see. Most mysteries become plain or disappear altogether in time. But about the meeting—lest I forget!

When I joined the mountaineers who had assembled, I really think they were glad to see me; though some of them seemed adverse, and others did not seem over well satisfied. However, absolute unity is very seldom to be found. Indeed, it is almost impossible; and in a free community is not altogether to be desired. When it is apparent, the gathering lacks that sense of individual feeling which makes for the real consensus of opinion—which is the real unity of purpose. The meeting was at first, therefore, a little cold and distant. But presently it began to thaw, and after some fiery harangues I was asked to speak. Happily, I had begun to learn the Balkan language as soon as ever Uncle Roger's wishes had been made known to me, and as I have some facility of tongues and a great deal of experience, I soon began to know something of it. Indeed, when I had been here a few weeks, with opportunity of speaking daily with the people themselves, and learned to understand the intonations and vocal inflexions, I felt quite easy in speaking it. I understood every word which had up to then been spoken at the meeting, and when I spoke myself I felt that they understood. That is an experience which every speaker has in a certain way and up to a certain point. He knows by some kind of instinct if his hearers are with him; if they respond, they must certainly have understood. Last night this was marked. I felt it every instant I was talking and when I came to realize that the men were in strict accord with my general views, I took them into confidence with regard to my own personal purpose. It was the beginning of a mutual trust; so for peroration I told them that I had come to the conclusion that what they wanted most for their own protection and the security and consolidation of their nation was arms—

arms of the very latest pattern. Here they interrupted me with wild cheers, which so strung me up that I went farther than I intended, and made a daring venture. "Ay," I repeated, "the security and consolidation of your country—of *our* country, for I have come to live amongst you. Here is my home whilst I live. I am with you heart and soul. I shall live with you, fight shoulder to shoulder with you, and, if need be, shall die with you!" Here the shouting was terrific, and the younger men raised their guns to fire a salute in Blue Mountain fashion. But on the instant the Vladika held up his hands and motioned them to desist. In the immediate silence he spoke, sharply at first, but later ascending to a high pitch of single-minded, lofty eloquence. His words rang in my ears long after the meeting was over and other thoughts had come between them and the present.

"Silence!" he thundered. "Make no echoes in the forest or through the hills at this dire time of stress and threatened danger to our land. Bethink ye of this meeting, held here and in secret, in order that no whisper of it may be heard afar. Have ye all, brave men of the Blue Mountains, come hither through the forest like shadows that some of you, thoughtless, may enlighten your enemies as to our secret purpose? The thunder of your guns would doubtless sound well in the ears of those who wish us ill and try to work us wrong. Fellow-countrymen, know ye not that the Turk is awake once more for our harming? The Bureau of Spies has risen from the torpor which came on it when the purpose against our Teuta roused our mountains to such anger that the frontiers blazed with passion, and were swept with fire and sword. Moreover, there is a traitor somewhere in the land, or else incautious carelessness has served the same base purpose. Something of our needs—our doing, whose secret we have tried to hide, has gone out. The myrmidons of the Turk are close on our borders, and it may be that some of them have passed our guards and are amidst us unknown. So it behoves us doubly to be discreet. Believe me that I share with you, my brothers, our love for the gallant Englishman who has come amongst us to share our sorrows and ambitions—and I trust it may be our joys. We are all united in the wish to do him honour—though not in the way by which danger might be carried on the wings of love. My brothers, our newest brother comes to us from the Great Nation which amongst the nations has been our only friend, and which has ere now helped us in our direst need—that mighty Britain whose hand has ever been raised in the cause of freedom. We of the Blue Mountains know her best as she stands with sword in hand face to face with our foes. And this, her son and now our brother, brings further to our need the hand of a giant and the heart of a lion. Later on, when danger does not ring us round, when silence is no longer our outer guard; we shall bid him welcome in true fashion of our land. But till then he will believe—for he is great-hearted—that our love and thanks and welcome are not to be measured by sound. When the time comes, then shall be sound in his honour—not of rifles alone, but bells and cannon and the mighty voice of a free people shouting as one. But now we must be wise and silent, for the Turk is once again at our gates. Alas! the cause of his former coming may not be, for she whose beauty and nobility and whose place in our nation and in our hearts tempted him to fraud and violence is not with us to share even our anxiety."

Here his voice broke, and there arose from all a deep wailing sound, which rose and rose till the woods around us seemed broken by a mighty and long-sustained sob. The orator saw that his purpose was accomplished, and with a short sentence finished his harangue: "But the need of our nation still remains!" Then, with an eloquent gesture to me to proceed, he merged in the crowd and disappeared.

How could I even attempt to follow such a speaker with any hope of success? I simply told them what I had already done in the way of help, saying:

"As you needed arms, I have got them. My agent sends me word through the code between us that he has procured for me—for us—fifty thousand of the newest-pattern rifles, the French Ingis-Malbron, which has surpassed all others, and sufficient ammunition to last for a year of war. The first section is in hand, and will soon be ready for consignment. There are other war materials, too, which, when they arrive, will enable every man and woman—even the children—of our land to take a part in its defence should such be needed. My brothers, I am with you in all things, for good or ill!"

It made me very proud to hear the mighty shout which arose. I had felt exalted before, but now this personal development almost unmanned me. I was glad of the long-sustained applause to recover my self-control.

I was quite satisfied that the meeting did not want to hear any other speaker, for they began to melt away without any formal notification having been given. I doubt if there will be another meeting soon again. The weather has begun to break, and we are in for another spell of rain. It is disagreeable, of course; but it has its own charm. It was during a spell of wet weather that the Lady of the Shroud came to me. Perhaps the rain may bring her again. I hope so, with all my soul.

Rupert's Journal—*Continued*

April 23, 1907

The rain has continued for four whole days and nights, and the low-lying ground is like a quagmire in places. In the sunlight the whole mountains glisten with running streams and falling water. I feel a strange kind of elation, but from no visible cause. Aunt Janet rather queered it by telling me, as she said good-night, to be very careful of myself, as she had seen in a dream last night a figure in a shroud. I fear she was not pleased that I did not take it with all the seriousness that she did. I would not wound her for the world if I could help it, but the idea of a shroud gets too near the bone to be safe, and I had to fend her off at all hazards. So when I doubted if the Fates regarded the visionary shroud as of necessity appertaining to me, she said, in a way that was, for her, almost sharp:

"Take care, laddie. 'Tis ill jesting wi' the powers o' time Unknown."

Perhaps it was that her talk put the subject in my mind. The woman needed no such aid; she was always there; but when I locked myself into my room that night, I half expected to find her in the room. I was not sleepy, so I took a book of Aunt Janet's and began to read. The title was "On the Powers and Qualities of Disembodied Spirits." "Your grammar," said I to the author, "is hardly attractive, but I may learn something which might apply to her. I shall read your book." Before settling down to it, however, I thought I would have a look at the garden. Since the night of the visit the garden seemed to have a new attractiveness for me: a night seldom passed without my having a last look at it before turning in. So I drew the great curtain and looked out.

The scene was beautiful, but almost entirely desolate. All was ghastly in the raw, hard gleams of moonlight coming fitfully through the masses of flying cloud. The wind was rising, and the air was damp and cold. I looked round the room instinctively, and noticed that the fire was laid ready for lighting, and that there were small-cut logs of wood piled beside the hearth. Ever since that night I have had a fire laid ready. I was tempted to light it, but as I never have a fire unless I sleep in the open, I hesitated to begin. I went back to the window, and, opening the catch, stepped out on the terrace. As I looked down the white walk and let my eyes range over the expanse of the garden, where everything glistened as the moonlight caught the wet, I half expected to see some white figure flitting amongst the shrubs and statues. The whole scene of the former visit came back to me so vividly that I could hardly believe that any time had passed since then. It was the same scene, and again late in the evening. Life in Vissarion was primitive, and early hours prevailed—though not so late as on that night.

As I looked I thought I caught a glimpse of something white far away. It was only a ray of moonlight coming through the rugged edge of a cloud. But all the same it set me in a strange state of perturbation. Somehow I seemed to lose sight of my own identity. It was as though I was hypnotized by the situation or by memory, or perhaps by some occult force. Without thinking of what I was doing, or being conscious of any reason for it, I crossed the room and set light to the fire. Then I blew out the candle and came to the window again. I never thought it might be a foolish thing to do—to stand at a window with a light behind me in this country, where every man carries a gun with him always. I was in my evening clothes, too, with my breast well marked by a white shirt. I opened the window and stepped out on the terrace. There I stood for many minutes, thinking. All the time my eyes kept ranging over the garden. Once I thought I saw a white figure moving, but it was not followed up, so, becoming conscious that it was again beginning to rain, I stepped back into the room, shut the window, and drew the curtain. Then I realized the comforting appearance of the fire, and went over and stood before it.

Hark! Once more there was a gentle tapping at the window. I rushed over to it and drew the curtain.

There, out on the rain-beaten terrace, stood the white shrouded figure, more desolate-appearing than ever. Ghastly pale she looked, as before, but her eyes had an eager look which was new. I took it that she was attracted by the fire, which was by now well ablaze, and was throwing up jets of flame as the dry logs crackled. The leaping flames threw fitful light across the room, and every gleam threw the white-clad figure into prominence, showing the gleam of the black eyes, and fixing the stars that lay in them.

Without a word I threw open the window, and, taking the white hand extended to me, drew into the room the Lady of the Shroud.

As she entered and felt the warmth of the blazing fire, a glad look spread over her face. She made a movement as if to run to it. But she drew back an instant after, looking round with instinctive caution. She closed the window and bolted it, touched the lever which spread the grille across the opening, and pulled close the curtain behind it. Then she went swiftly to the door and tried if it was locked. Satisfied as to this, she came quickly over to the fire, and, kneeling before it, stretched out her numbed hands to the blaze. Almost on the instant her wet shroud began to steam. I stood wondering. The precautions of secrecy in the midst of her suffering—for that she did suffer was only too painfully manifest—must have presupposed some danger. Then and there my mind was made up that there should no harm assail her that I by any means could fend off. Still, the present must be attended to; pneumonia and other ills stalked behind such a chill as must infallibly come on her unless precautions were taken. I took again the dressing-gown which she had worn before and handed it to her, motioning as I did so towards the screen which had made a dressing-room for her on the former occasion. To my surprise she hesitated. I waited. She waited, too, and then laid down the dressing-gown on the edge of the stone fender. So I spoke:

"Won't you change as you did before? Your—your frock can then be dried. Do! It will be so much safer for you to be dry clad when you resume your own dress."

"How can I whilst you are here?"

Her words made me stare, so different were they from her acts of the other visit. I simply bowed—speech on such a subject would be at least inadequate—and walked over to the window. Passing behind the curtain, I opened the window. Before stepping out on to the terrace, I looked into the room and said:

"Take your own time. There is no hurry. I dare say you will find there all you may want. I shall remain on the terrace until you summon me." With that I went out on the terrace, drawing close the glass door behind me.

I stood looking out on the dreary scene for what seemed a very short time, my mind in a whirl. There came a rustle from within, and I saw a dark brown figure steal round the edge of the curtain. A white hand was raised, and beckoned me to come in. I entered, bolting the window behind me. She had passed across the room, and was again kneeling before the fire with her hands outstretched. The shroud was laid in partially opened folds on one side of the hearth, and was steaming heavily. I brought over some cushions and pillows, and made a little pile of them beside her.

"Sit there," I said, "and rest quietly in the heat." It may have been the effect of the glowing heat, but there was a rich colour in her face as she looked at me with shining eyes. Without a word, but with a courteous little bow, she sat down at once. I put a thick rug across her shoulders, and sat down myself on a stool a couple of feet away.

For fully five or six minutes we sat in silence. At last, turning her head towards me she said in a sweet, low voice:

"I had intended coming earlier on purpose to thank you for your very sweet and gracious courtesy to me, but circumstances were such that I could not leave my—my"—she hesitated before saying—"my abode. I am not free, as you and others are, to do what I will. My existence is sadly cold and stern, and full of horrors that appal. But I *do* thank you. For myself I am not sorry for the delay, for every hour shows me more clearly how good and understanding and sympathetic you have been to me. I only hope that some day you may realize how kind you have been, and how much I appreciate it."

"I am only too glad to be of any service," I said, feebly I felt, as I held out my hand. She did not seem to see it. Her eyes were now on the fire, and a warm blush dyed forehead and cheek and neck. The reproof was so gentle that no one could have been offended. It was evident that she was something coy and reticent, and would not allow me to come at present more close to her, even to the touching of her hand. But that her heart was not in the denial was also evident in the glance from her glorious dark starry eyes. These glances—veritable lightning flashes coming through her pronounced reserve—finished entirely any wavering there might be in my own purpose. I was aware now to the full that my heart was quite subjugated. I knew that I was in love—veritably so much in love as to feel that without this woman, be she what she might, by my side my future must be absolutely barren.

It was presently apparent that she did not mean to stay as long on this occasion as on the last. When the castle clock struck midnight she suddenly sprang to her feet with a bound, saying:

"I must go! There is midnight!" I rose at once, the intensity of her speech having instantly obliterated the sleep which, under the influence of rest and warmth, was creeping upon me. Once more she was in a frenzy of haste, so I hurried towards the window, but as I looked back saw her, despite her haste, still standing. I motioned towards the screen, and slipping behind the curtain, opened the window and went out on the terrace. As I was disappearing behind the curtain I saw her with the tail of my eye lifting the shroud, now dry, from the hearth.

She was out through the window in an incredibly short time, now clothed once more in that dreadful wrapping. As she sped past me barefooted on the wet, chilly marble which made her shudder, she whispered:

"Thank you again. You *are* good to me. You can understand."

Once again I stood on the terrace, saw her melt like a shadow down the steps, and disappear behind the nearest shrub. Thence she flitted away from point to point with exceeding haste. The moonlight had now disappeared behind heavy banks of cloud, so there was little light to see by. I could just distinguish a pale gleam here and there as she wended her secret way.

For a long time I stood there alone thinking, as I watched the course she had taken, and wondering where might be her ultimate destination. As she had spoken of her "abode," I knew there was some definitive objective of her flight.

It was no use wondering. I was so entirely ignorant of her surroundings that I had not even a starting-place for speculation. So I went in, leaving the window open. It seemed that this being so made one barrier the less between us. I gathered the cushions and rugs from before the fire, which was no longer leaping, but burning with a steady glow, and put them back in their places. Aunt Janet might come in the morning, as she had done before, and I did not wish to set her thinking. She is much too clever a person to have treading on the heels of a mystery—especially one in which my own affections are engaged. I wonder what she would have said had she seen me kiss the cushion on which my beautiful guest's head had rested?

When I was in bed, and in the dark save for the fading glow of the fire, my thoughts became fixed that whether she came from Earth or Heaven or Hell, my lovely visitor was already more to me than aught else in the world. This time she had, on going, said no word of returning. I had been so much taken up with her presence, and so upset by her abrupt departure, that I had omitted to ask her. And so I am driven, as before, to accept the chance of her returning—a chance which I fear I am or may be unable to control.

Surely enough Aunt Janet did come in the morning, early. I was still asleep when she knocked at my door. With that purely physical subconsciousness which comes with habit I must have realized the cause of the sound, for I woke fully conscious of the fact that Aunt Janet had knocked and was waiting to come in. I jumped from bed, and back again when I had unlocked the door. When Aunt Janet came in she noticed the cold of the room.

"Save us, laddie, but ye'll get your death o' cold in this room." Then, as she looked round and noticed the ashes of the extinct fire in the grate:

"Eh, but ye're no that daft after a'; ye've had the sense to light yer fire. Glad I am that we had the fire laid and a wheen o' dry logs ready to yer hand." She evidently felt the cold air coming from the window, for she went over and drew the curtain. When she saw the open window, she raised her hands in a sort of dismay, which to me, knowing how little base for concern could be within her knowledge, was comic. Hurriedly she shut the window, and then, coming close over to my bed, said:

"Yon has been a fearsome nicht again, laddie, for yer poor auld aunty."

"Dreaming again, Aunt Janet?" I asked—rather flippantly as it seemed to me. She shook her head:

"Not so, Rupert, unless it be that the Lord gies us in dreams what we in our spiritual darkness think are veesions." I roused up at this. When Aunt Janet calls me Rupert, as she always used to do in my dear mother's time, things are serious with her. As I was back in childhood now, recalled by her word, I thought the best thing I could do to cheer her would be to bring her back there too—if I could. So I patted the edge of the bed as I used to do when I was a wee kiddie and wanted her to comfort me, and said:

"Sit down, Aunt Janet, and tell me." She yielded at once, and the look of the happy old days grew over her face as though there had come a gleam of sunshine. She sat down, and I put out my hands as I used to do, and took her hand between them. There was a tear in her eye as she raised my hand and kissed it as in old times. But for the infinite pathos of it, it would have been comic:

Aunt Janet, old and grey-haired, but still retaining her girlish slimness of figure, petite, dainty as a Dresden figure, her face lined with the care of years, but softened and ennobled by the unselfishness of those years, holding up my big hand, which would outweigh her whole arm; sitting dainty as a pretty old fairy beside a recumbent giant—for my bulk never seems so great as when I am near this real little good fairy of my life—seven feet beside four feet seven.

So she began as of old, as though she were about to soothe a frightened child with a fairy tale:

"'Twas a veesion, I think, though a dream it may hae been. But whichever or whatever it was, it concerned my little boy, who has grown to be a big giant, so much that I woke all of a tremble. Laddie dear, I thought that I saw ye being married." This gave me an opening, though a small one, for comforting her, so I took it at once:

"Why, dear, there isn't anything to alarm you in that, is there? It was only the other day when you spoke to me about the need of my getting married, if it was only that you might have children of your boy playing around your knees as their father used to do when he was a helpless wee child himself."

"That is so, laddie," she answered gravely. "But your weddin' was none so merry as I fain would see. True, you seemed to lo'e her wi' all yer hairt. Yer eyes shone that bright that ye might ha' set her afire, for all her black locks and her winsome face. But, laddie, that was not all—no, not though her black een, that had the licht o' all the stars o' nicht in them, shone in yours as though a hairt o' love an' passion, too, dwelt in them. I saw ye join hands, an' heard a strange voice that talked stranger still, but I saw none ither. Your eyes an' her eyes, an' your hand an' hers, were all I saw. For all else was dim, and the darkness was close around ye twa. And when the benison was spoken—I knew that by the voices that sang, and by the gladness of her een, as well as by the pride and glory of yours—the licht began to glow a wee more, an' I could see yer bride. She was in a veil o' wondrous fine lace. And there were orange-flowers in her hair, though there were twigs, too, and there was a crown o' flowers on head wi' a golden band round it. And the heathen candles that stood on the table wi' the Book had some strange effect, for the reflex o' it hung in the air o'er her head like the shadow of a crown. There was a gold ring on her finger and a silver one on yours." Here she paused and trembled, so that, hoping to dispel her fears, I said, as like as I could to the way I used to when I was a child:

"Go on, Aunt Janet."

She did not seem to recognize consciously the likeness between past and present; but the effect was there, for she went on more like her old self, though there was a prophetic gravity in her voice, more marked than I had ever heard from her:

"All this I've told ye was well; but, oh, laddie, there was a dreadful lack o' livin' joy such as I should expect from the woman whom my boy had chosen for his wife—and at the marriage coupling, too! And no wonder, when all is said; for though the marriage veil o' love was fine, an' the garland o' flowers was fresh-gathered, underneath them a' was nane ither than a ghastly shroud. As I looked in my veesion—or maybe dream—I expectit to see the worms crawl round the flagstane at her feet. If 'twas not Death, laddie dear, that stood by ye, it was the shadow o' Death that made the darkness round ye, that neither the light o' candles nor the smoke o' heathen incense could pierce. Oh, laddie, laddie, wae is me that I hae seen sic a veesion—waking or sleeping, it matters not! I was sair distressed—so sair that I woke wi' a shriek on my lips and bathed in cold sweat. I would hae come doon to ye to see if you were hearty or no—or even to listen at your door for any sound o' yer being quick, but that I feared to alarm ye till morn should come. I've counted the hours and the minutes since midnight, when I saw the veesion, till I came hither just the now."

"Quite right, Aunt Janet," I said, "and I thank you for your kind thought for me in the matter, now and always." Then I went on, for I wanted to take precautions against the possibility of her discovery of my secret. I could not bear to think that she might run my precious secret to earth in any well-meant piece of bungling. That would be to me disaster unbearable. She might frighten away altogether my beautiful visitor, even whose name or origin I did not know, and I might never see her again:

"You must never do that, Aunt Janet. You and I are too good friends to have sense of distrust or annoyance come between us—which would surely happen if I had to keep thinking that you or anyone else might be watching me."

Rupert's Journal—*Continued*

April 27, 1907

After a spell of loneliness which has seemed endless I have something to write. When the void in my heart was becoming the receptacle for many devils of suspicion and distrust I set myself a task which might, I thought, keep my thoughts in part, at any rate, occupied—to explore minutely the neighbourhood round the Castle. This might, I hoped, serve as an anodyne to my pain of loneliness, which grew more acute as the days, the hours, wore on, even if it should not ultimately afford me some clue to the whereabouts of the woman whom I had now grown to love so madly.

My exploration soon took a systematic form, as I intended that it should be exhaustive. I would take every day a separate line of advance from the Castle, beginning at the south and working round by the east to the north. The first day only took me to the edge of the creek, which I crossed in a boat, and landed at the base of the cliff opposite. I found the cliffs alone worth a visit. Here and there were openings to caves which I made up my mind to explore later. I managed to climb up the cliff at a spot less beetling than the rest, and continued my journey. It was, though very beautiful, not a specially interesting place. I explored that spoke of the wheel of which Vissarion was the hub, and got back just in time for dinner.

The next day I took a course slightly more to the eastward. I had no difficulty in keeping a straight path, for, once I had rowed across the creek, the old church of St. Sava rose before me in stately gloom. This was the spot where many generations of the noblest of the Land of the Blue Mountains had from time immemorial been laid to rest, amongst them the Vissarions. Again, I found the opposite cliffs pierced here and there with caves, some with wide openings,—others the openings of which were partly above and partly below water. I could, however, find no means of climbing the cliff at this part, and had to make a long detour, following up the line of the creek till further on I found a piece of beach from which ascent was possible. Here I ascended, and found that I was on a line between the Castle and the southern side of the mountains. I saw the church of St. Sava away to my right, and not far from the edge of the cliff. I made my way to it at once, for as yet I had never been near it. Hitherto my excursions had been limited to the Castle and its many gardens and surroundings. It was of a style with which I was not familiar—with four wings to the points of the compass. The great doorway, set in a magnificent frontage of carved stone of manifestly ancient date, faced west, so that, when one entered, he went east. To my surprise—for somehow I expected the contrary—I found the door open. Not wide open, but what is called ajar—manifestly not locked or barred, but not sufficiently open for one to look in. I entered, and after passing through a wide vestibule, more like a section of a corridor than an ostensible entrance, made my way through a spacious doorway into the body of the church. The church itself was almost circular, the openings of the four naves being spacious enough to give the appearance of the interior as a whole, being a huge cross. It was strangely dim, for the window openings were small and high-set, and were, moreover, filled with green or blue glass, each window having a colour to itself. The glass was very old, being of the thirteenth or fourteenth century. Such appointments as there were—for it had a general air of desolation—were of great beauty and richness,—especially so to be in a place—even a church—where the door lay open, and no one was to be seen. It was strangely silent even for an old church on a lonesome headland. There reigned a dismal solemnity which seemed to chill me, accustomed as I have been to strange and weird places. It seemed abandoned, though it had not that air of having been neglected which is so often to be noticed in old churches. There was none of the everlasting accumulation of dust which prevails in places of higher cultivation and larger and more strenuous work.

In the church itself or its appending chambers I could find no clue or suggestion which could guide me in any way in my search for the Lady of the Shroud. Monuments there were in profusion—statues, tablets, and all the customary memorials of the dead. The families and dates represented were simply bewildering. Often the name of Vissarion was given, and the inscription which it held I read through carefully, looking to find some enlightenment of any kind. But all in vain: there was nothing to see in the church itself. So I determined to visit the crypt. I had no lantern or candle with me, so had to go back to the Castle to secure one.

It was strange, coming in from the sunlight, here overwhelming to one so recently accustomed to northern skies, to note the slender gleam of the lantern which I carried, and which I had lit inside the door. At my first entry to the church my mind had been so much taken up with the strangeness of the place, together with the intensity of wish for some sort of clue, that I had really no opportunity of examining detail. But now detail became necessary, as I had to find the entrance to the crypt. My puny light could not dissipate the semi-Cimmerian gloom of the vast edifice; I had to throw the feeble gleam into one after another of the dark corners.

At last I found, behind the great screen, a narrow stone staircase which seemed to wind down into the rock. It was not in any way secret, but being in the narrow space behind the great screen, was not visible except when close to it. I knew I was now close to my objective, and began to descend. Accustomed though I have been to all sorts of mysteries and dangers, I felt awed and almost overwhelmed by a sense of loneliness and desolation as I descended the ancient winding steps. These were many in number, roughly hewn of old in the solid rock on which the church was built.

I met a fresh surprise in finding that the door of the crypt was open. After all, this was different from the church-door being open; for in many places it is a custom to allow all comers at all times to find rest and comfort in the sacred place. But I did expect that at least the final resting-place of the historic dead would be held safe against casual intrusion. Even I, on a quest which was very near my heart, paused with an almost overwhelming sense of decorum before passing through that open door. The crypt was a huge place, strangely lofty for a vault. From its formation, however, I soon came to the conclusion that it was originally a natural cavern altered to its present purpose by the hand of man. I could hear somewhere near the sound of running water, but I could not locate it. Now and again at irregular intervals there was a prolonged booming, which could only come from a wave breaking in a confined place. The recollection then came to me of the proximity of the church to the top of the beetling cliff, and of the half-sunk cavern entrances which pierced it.

With the gleam of my lamp to guide me, I went through and round the whole place. There were many massive tombs, mostly rough-hewn from great slabs or blocks of stone. Some of them were marble, and the cutting of all was ancient. So large and heavy were some of them that it was a wonder to me how they could ever have been brought to this place, to which the only entrance was seemingly the narrow, tortuous stairway by which I had come. At last I saw near one end of the crypt a great chain hanging. Turning the light upward, I found that it depended from a ring set over a wide opening, evidently made artificially. It must have been through this opening that the great sarcophagi had been lowered.

Directly underneath the hanging chain, which did not come closer to the ground than some eight or ten feet, was a huge tomb in the shape of a rectangular coffer or sarcophagus. It was open, save for a huge sheet of thick glass which rested above it on two thick balks of dark oak, cut to exceeding smoothness, which lay across it, one at either end. On the far side from where I stood each of these was joined to another oak plank, also cut smooth, which sloped gently to the rocky floor. Should it be necessary to open the tomb, the glass could be made to slide along the supports and descend by the sloping planks.

Naturally curious to know what might be within such a strange receptacle, I raised the lantern, depressing its lens so that the light might fall within.

Then I started back with a cry, the lantern slipping from my nerveless hand and falling with a ringing sound on the great sheet of thick glass.

Within, pillowed on soft cushions, and covered with a mantle woven of white natural fleece sprigged with tiny sprays of pine wrought in gold, lay the body of a woman—none other than my beautiful visitor. She was marble white, and her long black eyelashes lay on her white cheeks as though she slept.

Without a word or a sound, save the sounds made by my hurrying feet on the stone flooring, I fled up the steep steps, and through the dim expanse of the church, out into the bright sunlight. I found that I had mechanically raised the fallen lamp, and had taken it with me in my flight.

My feet naturally turned towards home. It was all instinctive. The new horror had—for the time, at any rate—drowned my mind in its mystery, deeper than the deepest depths of thought or imagination.

Book IV

UNDER THE FLAGSTAFF

RUPERT'S JOURNAL—*Continued*

May 1, 1907

For some days after the last adventure I was in truth in a half-dazed condition, unable to think sensibly, hardly coherently. Indeed, it was as much as I could do to preserve something of my habitual appearance and manner. However, my first test happily came soon, and when I was once through it I reacquired sufficient self-confidence to go through with my purpose. Gradually the original phase of stupefaction passed, and I was able to look the situation in the face. I knew the worst now, at any rate; and when the lowest point has been reached things must begin to mend. Still, I was wofully sensitive regarding anything which might affect my Lady of the Shroud, or even my opinion of her. I even began to dread Aunt Janet's Second-Sight visions or dreams. These had a fatal habit of coming so near to fact that they always made for a danger of discovery. I had to realize now that the Lady of the Shroud might indeed be a Vampire—one of that horrid race that survives death and carries on a life-in-death existence eternally and only for evil. Indeed, I began to *expect* that Aunt Janet would ere long have some prophetic insight to the matter. She had been so wonderfully correct in her prophetic surmises with regard to both the visits to my room that it was hardly possible that she could fail to take cognizance of this last development.

But my dread was not justified; at any rate, I had no reason to suspect that by any force or exercise of her occult gift she might cause me concern by the discovery of my secret. Only once did I feel that actual danger in that respect was close to me. That was when she came early one morning and rapped at my door. When I called out, "Who is that? What is it?" she said in an agitated way:

"Thank God, laddie, you are all right! Go to sleep again."

Later on, when we met at breakfast, she explained that she had had a nightmare in the grey of the morning. She thought she had seen me in the crypt of a great church close beside a stone coffin; and, knowing that such was an ominous subject to dream about, came as soon as she dared to see if I was all right. Her mind was evidently set on death and burial, for she went on:

"By the way, Rupert, I am told that the great church on time top of the cliff across the creek is St. Sava's, where the great people of the country used to be buried. I want you to take me there some day. We shall go over it, and look at the tombs and monuments together. I really think I should be afraid to go alone, but it will be all right if you are with me." This was getting really dangerous, so I turned it aside:

"Really, Aunt Janet, I'm afraid it won't do. If you go off to weird old churches, and fill yourself up with a fresh supply of horrors, I don't know what will happen. You'll be dreaming dreadful things about me every night and neither you nor I shall get any sleep." It went to my heart to oppose her in any wish; and also this kind of chaffy opposition might pain her. But I had no alternative; the matter was too serious to be allowed to proceed. Should Aunt Janet go to the church, she would surely want to visit the crypt. Should she do so, and there notice the glass-covered tomb—as she could not help doing—the Lord only knew what would happen. She had already Second-Sighted a woman being married to me, and before I myself knew that I had such a hope. What might she not reveal did she know where the woman came from? It may have been that her power of Second Sight had to rest on some basis of knowledge or belief, and that her vision was but some intuitive perception of my own subjective thought. But whatever it was it should be stopped—at all hazards.

This whole episode set me thinking introspectively, and led me gradually but imperatively to self-analysis—not of powers, but of motives. I found myself before long examining myself as to what were my real intentions. I thought at first that this intellectual process was an exercise of pure reason; but soon discarded this as inadequate—even impossible. Reason is a cold manifestation; this feeling which swayed and dominated me is none other than passion, which is quick, hot, and insistent.

As for myself, the self-analysis could lead to but one result—the expression to myself of the reality and definiteness of an already-formed though unconscious intention. I wished to do the woman good—to serve her in some way—to secure her some benefit by any means, no matter how difficult, which might be within my power. I knew that I loved her—loved her most truly and fervently; there was no need for self-analysis to tell me that. And, moreover, no self-analysis, or any other mental process that I knew of, could help my one doubt: whether she was an ordinary woman (or an extraordinary woman, for the matter of that) in some sore and terrible straits; or else one who lay under some dreadful condition, only partially alive, and not mistress of herself or her acts. Whichever her condition might be, there was in my own feeling a superfluity of affection for her. The self-analysis taught me one thing, at any rate—that I had for her, to start with, an infinite pity which had softened towards her my whole being, and had already mastered merely selfish desire. Out of it I began to find excuses for her every act. In the doing so I knew now, though perhaps I did not at the time the process was going on, that my view in its true inwardness was of her as a living woman—the woman I loved.

In the forming of our ideas there are different methods of work, as though the analogy with material life holds good. In the building of a house, for instance, there are many persons employed; men of different trades and occupations—architect, builder, masons, carpenters, plumbers, and a host of others—and all these with the officials of each guild or trade. So in the world of thought and feelings: knowledge and understanding come through various agents, each competent to its task.

How far pity reacted with love I knew not; I only knew that whatever her state might be, were she living or dead, I could find in my heart no blame for the Lady of the Shroud. It could not be that she was dead in the real conventional way; for, after all, the Dead do not walk the earth in corporal substance, even if there be spirits which take the corporal form. This woman was of actual form and weight. How could I doubt that, at all events—I, who had held her in my arms? Might it not be that she was not quite dead, and that it had been given to me to restore her to life again? Ah! that would be, indeed, a privilege well worth the giving my life to accomplish. That such a thing may be is possible. Surely the old myths were not absolute inventions; they must have had a basis somewhere in fact. May not the world-old story of Orpheus and Eurydice have been based on some deep-lying principle or power of human nature? There is not one of us but has wished at some time to bring back the dead. Ay, and who has not felt that in himself or herself was power in the deep love for our dead to make them quick again, did we but know the secret of how it was to be done?

For myself, I have seen such mysteries that I am open to conviction regarding things not yet explained. These have been, of course, amongst savages or those old-world people who have brought unchecked traditions and beliefs—ay, and powers too—down the ages from the dim days when the world was young; when forces were elemental, and Nature's handiwork was experimental rather than completed. Some of these wonders may have been older still than the accepted period of our own period of creation. May we not have to-day other wonders, different only in method, but not more susceptible of belief? Obi-ism and Fantee-ism have been exercised in my own presence, and their results proved by the evidence of my own eyes and other senses. So, too, have stranger rites, with the same object and the same success, in the far Pacific Islands. So, too, in India and China, in Thibet and in the Golden Chersonese. On all and each of these occasions there was, on my own part, enough belief to set in motion the powers of understanding; and there were no moral scruples to stand in the way of realization. Those whose lives are so spent that they achieve the reputation of not fearing man or God or devil are not deterred in their doing or thwarted from a set purpose by things which might deter others not so equipped for adventure. Whatever may be before them—pleasant or painful, bitter or sweet, arduous or facile, enjoyable or terrible, humorous or full of awe and horror—they must accept, taking them in the onward course as a good athlete takes hurdles in his stride. And there must be no hesitating, no looking back. If the explorer or the adventurer has scruples, he had better give up that special branch of effort and come himself to a more level walk in life. Neither must there be regrets. There is no need for such; savage life has this advantage: it begets a certain toleration not to be found in conventional existence.

Rupert's Journal—*Continued*

May 2, 1907

I had heard long ago that Second Sight is a terrible gift, even to its possessor. I am now inclined not only to believe, but to understand it. Aunt Janet has made such a practice of it of late that I go in constant dread of discovery of my secret. She seems to parallel me all the time, whatever I may do. It is like a sort of dual existence to her; for she is her dear old self all the time, and yet some other person with a sort of intellectual kit of telescope and notebook, which are eternally used on me. I know they are *for* me, too—for what she considers my good. But all the same it makes an embarrassment. Happily Second Sight cannot speak as clearly as it sees, or, rather, as it understands. For the translation of the vague beliefs which it inculcates is both nebulous and uncertain—a sort of Delphic oracle which always says things which no one can make out at the time, but which can be afterwards read in any one of several ways. This is all right, for in my case it is a kind of safety; but, then, Aunt Janet is a very clever woman, and some time she herself may be able to understand. Then she may begin to put two and two together. When she does that, it will not be long before she knows more than I do of the facts of the whole affair. And her reading of them and of the Lady of the Shroud, round whom they circle, may not be the same as mine. Well, that will be all right too. Aunt Janet loves me—God knows I have good reason to know that all through these years—and whatever view she may take, her acts will be all I could wish. But I shall come in for a good lot of scolding, I am sure. By the way, I ought to think of that; if Aunt Janet scolds me, it is a pretty good proof that I ought to be scolded. I wonder if I dare tell her all. No! It is too strange. She is only a woman, after all: and if she knew I loved. . . I wish I knew her name, and thought—as I might myself do, only that I resist it—that she is not alive at all. Well, what she would either think or do beats me. I suppose she would want to slipper me as she used to do when I was a wee kiddie—in a different way, of course.

May 3, 1907

I really could not go on seriously last night. The idea of Aunt Janet giving me a licking as in the dear old days made me laugh so much that othing in the world seemed serious then. Oh, Aunt Janet is all right whatever comes. That I am sure of, so I needn't worry over it. A good thing too; there will be plenty to worry about without that. I shall not check her telling me of her visions, however; I may learn something from them.

For the last four-and-twenty hours I have, whilst awake, been looking over Aunt Janet's books, of which I brought a wheen down here. Gee whizz! No wonder the old dear is superstitious, when she is filled up to the back teeth with that sort of stuff! There may be some truth in some of those yarns; those who wrote them may believe in them, or some of them, at all events. But as to coherence or logic, or any sort of reasonable or instructive deduction, they might as well have been written by so many hens! These occult book-makers seem to gather only a lot of bare, bald facts, which they put down in the most uninteresting way possible. They go by quantity only. One story of the kind, well examined and with logical comments, would be more convincing to a third party than a whole hecatomb of them.

RUPERT'S JOURNAL—*Continued*

May 4, 1907

There is evidently something up in the country. The mountaineers are more uneasy than they have been as yet. There is constant going to and fro amongst them, mostly at night and in the grey of the morning. I spend many hours in my room in the eastern tower, from which I can watch the woods, and gather from signs the passing to and fro. But with all this activity no one has said to me a word on the subject. It is undoubtedly a disappointment to me. I had hoped that the mountaineers had come to trust me; that gathering at which they wanted to fire their guns for me gave me strong hopes. But now it is apparent that they do not trust me in full—as yet, at all events. Well, I must not complain. It is all only right and just. As yet I have done nothing to prove to them the love and devotion that I feel to the country. I know that such individuals as I have met trust me, and I believe like me. But the trust of a nation is different. That has to be won and tested; he who would win it must justify, and in a way that only troublous times can allow. No nation will—can—give full meed of honour to a stranger in times of peace. Why should it? I must not forget that I am here a stranger in the land, and that to the great mass of people even my name is unknown. Perhaps they will know me better when Rooke comes back with that store of arms and ammunition that he has bought, and the little warship he has got from South America. When they see that I hand over the whole lot to the nation without a string on them, they may begin to believe. In the meantime all I can do is to wait. It will all come right in time, I have no doubt. And if it doesn't come right, well, we can only die once!

Is that so? What about my Lady of the Shroud? I must not think of that or of her in this gallery. Love and war are separate, and may not mix—cannot mix, if it comes to that. I must be wise in the matter; and if I have got the hump in any degree whatever, must not show it.

But one thing is certain: something is up, and it must be the Turks. From what the Vladika said at that meeting they have some intention of an attack on the Blue Mountains. If that be so, we must be ready; and perhaps I can help there. The forces must be organized; we must have some method of communication. In this country, where are neither roads nor railways nor telegraphs, we must establish a signalling system of some sort. *That* I can begin at once. I can make a code, or adapt one that I have used elsewhere already. I shall rig up a semaphore on the top of the Castle which can be seen for an enormous distance around. I shall train a number of men to be facile in signalling. And then, should need come, I may be able to show the mountaineers that I am fit to live in their hearts. . .

And all this work may prove an anodyne to pain of another kind. It will help, at any rate, to keep my mind occupied whilst I am waiting for another visit from my Lady of the Shroud.

Rupert's Journal—*Continued*

May 18, 1907

The two weeks that have passed have been busy, and may, as time goes on, prove eventful. I really think they have placed me in a different position with the Blue Mountaineers—certainly so far as those in this part of the country are concerned. They are no longer suspicious of me—which is much; though they have not yet received me into their confidence. I suppose this will come in time, but I must not try to hustle them. Already they are willing, so far as I can see, to use me to their own ends. They accepted the signalling idea very readily, and are quite willing to drill as much as I like. This can be (and I think is, in its way) a pleasure to them. They are born soldiers, every man of them; and practice together is only a realization of their own wishes and a further development of their powers. I think I can understand the trend of their thoughts, and what ideas of public policy lie behind them. In all that we have attempted together as yet they are themselves in absolute power. It rests with them to carry out any ideas I may suggest, so they do not fear any assumption of power or governance on my part. Thus, so long as they keep secret from me both their ideas of high policy and their immediate intentions, I am powerless to do them ill, and I *may* be of service should occasion arise. Well, all told, this is much. Already they accept me as an individual, not merely one of the mass. I am pretty sure that they are satisfied of my personal *bona fides*. It is policy and not mistrust that hedges me in. Well, policy is a matter of time. They are a splendid people, but if they knew a little more than they do they would understand that the wisest of all policies is trust—when it can be given. I must hold myself in check, and never be betrayed into a harsh thought towards them. Poor souls! with a thousand years behind them of Turkish aggression, strenuously attempted by both force and fraud, no wonder they are suspicious. Likewise every other nation with whom they have ever come in contact—except one, my own—has deceived or betrayed them. Anyhow, they are fine soldiers, and before long we shall have an army that cannot be ignored. If I can get so that they trust me, I shall ask Sir Colin to come out here. He would be a splendid head for their army. His great military knowledge and tactical skill would come in well. It makes me glow to think of what an army he would turn out of this splendid material, and one especially adapted for the style of fighting which would be necessary in this country.

If a mere amateur like myself, who has only had experience of organizing the wildest kind of savages, has been able to advance or compact their individual style of fighting into systematic effort, a great soldier like MacKelpie will bring them to perfection as a fighting machine. Our Highlanders, when they come out, will foregather with them, as mountaineers always do with each other. Then we shall have a force which can hold its own against any odds. I only hope that Rooke will be returning soon. I want to see those Ingis-Malbron rifles either safely stored in the Castle or, what is better, divided up amongst the mountaineers—a thing which will be done at the very earliest moment that I can accomplish it. I have a conviction that when these men have received their arms and ammunition from me they will understand me better, and not keep any secrets from me.

All this fortnight when I was not drilling or going about amongst the mountaineers, and teaching them the code which I have now got perfected, I was exploring the side of the mountain nearest to here. I could not bear to be still. It is torture to me to be idle in my present condition of mind regarding my Lady of the Shroud. . . Strange I do not mind mentioning the word to myself now. I used to at first; but that bitterness has all gone away.

RUPERT'S JOURNAL—*Continued*

May 19, 1907

I was so restless early this morning that before daylight I was out exploring on the mountain-side. By chance I came across a secret place just as the day was breaking. Indeed, it was by the change of light as the first sun-rays seemed to fall down the mountain-side that my attention was called to an opening shown by a light behind it. It was, indeed, a secret place—so secret that I thought at first I should keep it to myself. In such a place as this either to hide in or to be able to prevent anyone else hiding in might on occasion be an asset of safety.

When, however, I saw indications rather than traces that someone had already used it to camp in, I changed my mind, and thought that whenever I should get an opportunity I would tell the Vladika of it, as he is a man on whose discretion I can rely. If we ever have a war here or any sort of invasion, it is just such places that may be dangerous. Even in my own case it is much too near the Castle to be neglected.

The indications were meagre—only where a fire had been on a little shelf of rock; and it was not possible, through the results of burning vegetation or scorched grass, to tell how long before the fire had been alight. I could only guess. Perhaps the mountaineers might be able to tell or even to guess better than I could. But I am not so sure of this. I am a mountaineer myself, and with larger and more varied experience than any of them. For myself, though I could not be certain, I came to the conclusion that whoever had used the place had done so not many days before. It could not have been quite recently; but it may not have been very long ago. Whoever had used it had covered up his tracks well. Even the ashes had been carefully removed, and the place where they had lain was cleaned or swept in some way, so that there was no trace on the spot. I applied some of my West African experience, and looked on the rough bark of the trees to leeward, to where the agitated air, however directed, must have come, unless it was wanted to call attention to the place by the scattered wood-ashes, however fine. I found traces of it, but they were faint. There had not been rain for several days; so the dust must have been blown there since the rain had fallen, for it was still dry.

The place was a tiny gorge, with but one entrance, which was hidden behind a barren spur of rock—just a sort of long fissure, jagged and curving, in the rock, like a fault in the stratification. I could just struggle through it with considerable effort, holding my breath here and there, so as to reduce my depth of chest. Within it was tree-clad, and full of possibilities of concealment.

As I came away I marked well its direction and approaches, noting any guiding mark which might aid in finding it by day or night. I explored every foot of ground around it—in front, on each side, and above. But from nowhere could I see an indication of its existence. It was a veritable secret chamber wrought by the hand of Nature itself. I did not return home till I was familiar with every detail near and around it. This new knowledge added distinctly to my sense of security.

Later in the day I tried to find the Vladika or any mountaineer of importance, for I thought that such a hiding-place which had been used so recently might be dangerous, and especially at a time when, as I had learned at the meeting where they did *not* fire their guns that there may have been spies about or a traitor in the land.

Even before I came to my own room to-night I had fully made up my mind to go out early in the morning and find some proper person to whom to impart the information, so that a watch might be kept on the place. It is now getting on for midnight, and when I have had my usual last look at the garden I shall turn in. Aunt Janet was uneasy all day, and especially so this evening. I think it must have been my absence at the usual breakfast-hour which got on her nerves; and that unsatisfied mental or psychical irritation increased as the day wore on.

RUPERT'S JOURNAL—*Continued*

May 20, 1907

The clock on the mantelpiece in my room, which chimes on the notes of the clock at St. James's Palace, was striking midnight when I opened the glass door on the terrace. I had put out my lights before I drew the curtain, as I wished to see the full effect of the moonlight. Now that the rainy season is over, the moon is quite as beautiful as it was in the wet, and a great deal more comfortable. I was in evening dress, with a smoking-jacket in lieu of a coat, and I felt the air mild and mellow on the warm side, as I stood on the terrace.

But even in that bright moonlight the further corners of the great garden were full of mysterious shadows. I peered into them as well as I could—and my eyes are pretty good naturally, and are well trained. There was not the least movement. The air was as still as death, the foliage as still as though wrought in stone.

I looked for quite a long time in the hope of seeing something of my Lady. The quarters chimed several times, but I stood on unheeding. At last I thought I saw far off in the very corner of the old defending wall a flicker of white. It was but momentary, and could hardly have accounted in itself for the way my heart beat. I controlled myself, and stood as though I, too, were a graven image. I was rewarded by seeing presently another gleam of white. And then an unspeakable rapture stole over me as I realized that my Lady was coming as she had come before. I would have hurried out to meet her, but that I knew well that this would not be in accord with her wishes. So, thinking to please her, I drew back into the room. I was glad I had done so when, from the dark corner where I stood, I saw her steal up the marble steps and stand timidly looking in at the door. Then, after a long pause, came a whisper as faint and sweet as the music of a distant AEolian harp:

"Are you there? May I come in? Answer me! I am lonely and in fear!" For answer I emerged from my dim corner so swiftly that she was startled. I could hear from the quivering intake of her breath that she was striving—happily with success—to suppress a shriek.

"Come in," I said quietly. "I was waiting for you, for I felt that you would come. I only came in from the terrace when I saw you coming, lest you might fear that anyone might see us. That is not possible, but I thought you wished that I should be careful."

"I did—I do," she answered in a low, sweet voice, but very firmly. "But never avoid precaution. There is nothing that may not happen here. There may be eyes where we least expect—or suspect them." As she spoke the last words solemnly and in a low whisper, she was entering the room. I closed the glass door and bolted it, rolled back the steel grille, and pulled the heavy curtain. Then, when I had lit a candle, I went over and put a light to the fire. In a few seconds the dry wood had caught, and the flames were beginning to rise and crackle. She had not objected to my closing the window and drawing the curtain; neither did she make any comment on my lighting the fire. She simply acquiesced in it, as though it was now a matter of course. When I made the pile of cushions before it as on the occasion of her last visit, she sank down on them, and held out her white, trembling hands to the warmth.

She was different to-night from what she had been on either of the two former visits. From her present bearing I arrived at some gauge of her self-concern, her self-respect. Now that she was dry, and not overmastered by wet and cold, a sweet and gracious dignity seemed to shine from her, enwrapping her, as it were, with a luminous veil. It was not that she was by this made or shown as cold or distant, or in any way harsh or forbidding. On the contrary, protected by this dignity, she seemed much more sweet and genial than before. It was as though she felt that she could afford to stoop now that her loftiness was realized—that her position was recognized and secure. If her inherent dignity made an impenetrable nimbus round her, this was against others; she herself was not bound by it, or to be bound. So marked was this, so entirely and sweetly womanly did she appear, that I caught myself wondering in flashes of thought, which came as sharp periods of doubting judgment between spells of unconscious fascination, how I had ever come to think she was aught but perfect woman. As she rested, half sitting and half lying on the pile of cushions, she was all grace, and beauty, and charm, and sweetness—the veritable perfect woman of the dreams of a man, be he young or old. To have such a woman sit by his hearth and hold her holy of holies in his heart might well be a rapture to any man. Even an hour of such entrancing joy might be well won by a lifetime of pain, by the balance of a long life sacrificed, by the extinction of life itself. Quick behind the record of such thoughts came the answer to the doubt they challenged: if it should turn out that she was not living at all, but one of the doomed and pitiful Un-Dead, then so much more on account of her very sweetness and beauty would be the winning of her back to Life and Heaven—even were it that she might find happiness in the heart and in the arms of another man.

Once, when I leaned over the hearth to put fresh logs on the fire, my face was so close to hers that I felt her breath on my cheek. It thrilled me to feel even the suggestion of that ineffable contact. Her breath was sweet—sweet as the breath of a calf, sweet as the whiff of a summer breeze across beds of mignonette. How could anyone believe for a moment that such sweet breath could come from the lips of the dead—the dead *in esse* or *in posse*—that corruption could send forth fragrance so sweet and pure? It was with satisfied happiness that, as I looked at her from my stool, I saw the dancing of the flames from the beech-logs reflected in her glorious black eyes, and the stars that were hidden in them shine out with new colours and new lustre as they gleamed, rising and falling like hopes and fears. As the light leaped, so did smiles of quiet happiness flit over her beautiful face, the merriment of the joyous flames being reflected in ever-changing dimples.

At first I was a little disconcerted whenever my eyes took note of her shroud, and there came a momentary regret that the weather had not been again bad, so that there might have been compulsion for her putting on another garment—anything lacking the loathsomeness of that pitiful wrapping. Little by little, however, this feeling disappeared, and I found no matter for even dissatisfaction in her wrapping. Indeed, my thoughts found inward voice before the subject was dismissed from my mind:

"One becomes accustomed to anything—even a shroud!" But the thought was followed by a submerging wave of pity that she should have had such a dreadful experience.

By-and-by we seemed both to forget everything—I know I did—except that we were man and woman, and close together. The strangeness of the situation and the circumstances did not seem of moment—not worth even a passing thought. We still sat apart and said little, if anything. I cannot recall a single word that either of us spoke whilst we sat before the fire, but other language than speech came into play; the eyes told their own story, as eyes can do, and more eloquently than lips whilst exercising their function of speech. Question and answer followed each other in this satisfying language, and with an unspeakable rapture I began to realize that my affection was returned. Under these circumstances it was unrealizable that there should be any incongruity in the whole affair. I was not myself in the mood of questioning. I was diffident with that diffidence which comes alone from true love, as though it were a necessary emanation from that delightful and overwhelming and commanding passion. In her presence there seemed to surge up within me that which forbade speech. Speech under present conditions would have seemed to me unnecessary, imperfect, and even vulgarly overt. She, too, was silent. But now that I am alone, and memory is alone with me, I am convinced that she also had been happy. No, not that exactly. "Happiness" is not the word to describe either her feeling or my own. Happiness is more active, a more conscious enjoyment. We had been content. That expresses our condition perfectly; and now that I can analyze my own feeling, and understand what the word implies, I am satisfied of its accuracy. "Content" has both a positive and negative meaning or antecedent condition. It implies an absence of disturbing conditions as well as of wants; also it implies something positive which has been won or achieved, or which has accrued. In our state of mind—for though it may be presumption on my part, I am satisfied that our ideas were mutual—it meant that we had reached an understanding whence all that might come must be for good. God grant that it may be so!

As we sat silent, looking into each other's eyes, and whilst the stars in hers were now full of latent fire, perhaps from the reflection of the flames, she suddenly sprang to her feet, instinctively drawing the

BRAM STOKER

horrible shroud round her as she rose to her full height in a voice full of lingering emotion, as of one who is acting under spiritual compulsion rather than personal will, she said in a whisper:

"I must go at once. I feel the morning drawing nigh. I must be in my place when the light of day comes."

She was so earnest that I felt I must not oppose her wish; so I, too, sprang to my feet and ran towards the window. I pulled the curtain aside sufficiently far for me to press back the grille and reach the glass door, the latch of which I opened. I passed behind the curtain again, and held the edge of it back so that she could go through. For an instant she stopped as she broke the long silence:

"You are a true gentleman, and my friend. You understand all I wish. Out of the depth of my heart I thank you." She held out her beautiful high-bred hand. I took it in both mine as I fell on my knees, and raised it to my lips. Its touch made me quiver. She, too, trembled as she looked down at me with a glance which seemed to search my very soul. The stars in her eyes, now that the firelight was no longer on them, had gone back to their own mysterious silver. Then she drew her hand from mine very, very gently, as though it would fain linger; and she passed out behind the curtain with a gentle, sweet, dignified little bow which left me on my knees.

When I heard the glass door pulled-to gently behind her, I rose from my knees and hurried without the curtain, just in time to watch her pass down the steps. I wanted to see her as long as I could. The grey of morning was just beginning to war with the night gloom, and by the faint uncertain light I could see dimly the white figure flit between shrub and statue till finally it merged in the far darkness.

I stood for a long time on the terrace, sometimes looking into the darkness in front of me, in case I might be blessed with another glimpse of her; sometimes with my eyes closed, so that I might recall and hold in my mind her passage down the steps. For the first time since I had met her she had thrown back at me a glance as she stepped on the white path below the terrace. With the glamour over me of that look, which was all love and enticement, I could have dared all the powers that be.

When the grey dawn was becoming apparent through the lightening of the sky I returned to my room. In a dazed condition—half hypnotized by love—I went to bed, and in dreams continued to think, all happily, of my Lady of the Shroud.

May 27, 1907

A whole week has gone since I saw my Love! There it is; no doubt whatever is left in my mind about it now! Since I saw her my passion has grown and grown by leaps and bounds, as novelists put it. It has now become so vast as to overwhelm me, to wipe out all thought of doubt or difficulty. I suppose it must be what men suffered—suffering need not mean pain—under enchantments in old times. I am but as a straw whirled in the resistless eddies of a whirlpool. I feel that I *must* see her again, even if it be but in her tomb in the crypt. I must, I suppose, prepare myself for the venture, for many things have to be thought of. The visit must not be at night, for in such case I might miss her, did she come to me again here. . .

The morning came and went, but my wish and intention still remained; and so in the full tide of noon, with the sun in all its fiery force, I set out for the old church of St. Sava. I carried with me a lantern with powerful lens. I had wrapped it up secretly, for I had a feeling that I should not like anyone to know that I had such a thing with me.

On this occasion I had no misgivings. On the former visit I had for a moment been overwhelmed at the unexpected sight of the body of the woman I thought I loved—I knew it now—lying in her tomb. But now I knew all, and it was to see this woman, though in her tomb, that I came.

When I had lit my lantern, which I did as soon as I had pushed open the great door, which was once again unlocked, I turned my steps to the steps of the crypt, which lay behind the richly carven wood screen. This I could see, with the better light, was a noble piece of work of priceless beauty and worth. I tried to keep my heart in full courage with thoughts of my Lady, and of the sweetness and dignity of our last meeting; but, despite all, it sank down, down, and turned to water as I passed with uncertain feet down the narrow, tortuous steps. My concern, I am now convinced, was not for myself, but that she whom I adored should have to endure such a fearful place. As anodyne to my own pain I thought what it would be, and how I should feel, when I should have won for her a way out of that horror, at any rate. This thought reassured me somewhat, and restored my courage. It was in something of the same fashion which has hitherto carried me out of tight places as well as into them that at last I pushed open the low, narrow door at the foot of the rock-hewn staircase and entered the crypt.

Without delay I made my way to the glass-covered tomb set beneath the hanging chain. I could see by the flashing of the light around me that my hand which held the lantern trembled. With a great effort I steadied myself, and raising the lantern, turned its light down into the sarcophagus.

Once again the fallen lantern rang on the tingling glass, and I stood alone in the darkness, for an instant almost paralyzed with surprised disappointment.

The tomb was empty! Even the trappings of the dead had been removed.

I knew not what happened till I found myself groping my way up the winding stair. Here, in comparison with the solid darkness of the crypt, it seemed almost light. The dim expanse of the church sent a few straggling rays down the vaulted steps, and as I could see, be it never so dimly, I felt I was not in absolute darkness. With the light came a sense of power and fresh courage, and I groped my way back into the crypt again. There, by now and again lighting matches, I found my way to the tomb and recovered my lantern. Then I took my way slowly—for I wished to prove, if not my own courage, at least such vestiges of self-respect as the venture had left me—through the church, where I extinguished my lantern, and out through the great door into the open sunlight. I seemed to have heard, both in the darkness of the crypt and through the dimness of the church, mysterious sounds as of whispers and suppressed breathing; but the memory of these did not count for much when once I was free. I was only satisfied of my own consciousness and identity when I found myself on the broad rock terrace in front of the church, with the fierce sunlight beating on my upturned face, and, looking downward, saw far below me the rippled blue of the open sea.

Rupert's Journal—*Continued*

June 3, 1907

Another week has elapsed—a week full of movement of many kinds and in many ways—but as yet I have had no tale or tidings of my Lady of the Shroud. I have not had an opportunity of going again in daylight to St. Sava's as I should have liked to have done. I felt that I must not go at night. The night is her time of freedom, and it must be kept for her—or else I may miss her, or perhaps never see her again.

The days have been full of national movement. The mountaineers have evidently been organizing themselves, for some reason which I cannot quite understand, and which they have hesitated to make known to me. I have taken care not to manifest any curiosity, whatever I may have felt. This would certainly arouse suspicion, and might ultimately cause disaster to my hopes of aiding the nation in their struggle to preserve their freedom.

These fierce mountaineers are strangely—almost unduly—suspicious, and the only way to win their confidence is to begin the trusting. A young American attache of the Embassy at Vienna, who had made a ourney through the Land of the Blue Mountains, once put it to me in this form:

"Keep your head shut, and they'll open theirs. If you don't, they'll open it for you—down to the chine!"

It was quite apparent to me that they were completing some fresh arrangements for signalling with a code of their own. This was natural enough, and in no way inconsistent with the measure of friendliness already shown to me. Where there are neither telegraphs, railways, nor roads, any effective form of communication must—can only be purely personal. And so, if they wish to keep any secret amongst themselves, they must preserve the secret of their code. I should have dearly liked to learn their new code and their manner of using it, but as I want to be a helpful friend to them—and as this implies not only trust, but the appearance of it—I had to school myself to patience.

This attitude so far won their confidence that before we parted at our last meeting, after most solemn vows of faith and secrecy, they took me into the secret. This was, however, only to the extent of teaching me the code and method; they still withheld from me rigidly the fact or political secret, or whatever it was that was the mainspring of their united action.

When I got home I wrote down, whilst it was fresh in my memory, all they told me. This script I studied until I had it so thoroughly by heart that I *could* not forget it. Then I burned the paper. However, there is now one gain at least: with my semaphore I can send through the Blue Mountains from side to side, with expedition, secrecy, and exactness, a message comprehensible to all.

June 6, 1907

Last night I had a new experience of my Lady of the Shroud—in so far as form was concerned, at any rate. I was in bed, and just falling asleep, when I heard a queer kind of scratching at the glass door of the terrace. I listened acutely, my heart beating hard. The sound seemed to come from low down, close to the floor. I jumped out of bed, ran to the window, and, pulling aside the heavy curtains, looked out.

The garden looked, as usual, ghostly in the moonlight, but there was not the faintest sign of movement anywhere, and no one was on or near the terrace. I looked eagerly down to where the sound had seemed to come from.

There, just inside the glass door, as though it had been pushed under the door, lay a paper closely folded in several laps. I picked it up and opened it. I was all in a tumult, for my heart told me whence it came. Inside was written in English, in a large, sprawling hand, such as might be from an English child of seven or eight:

"Meet me at the Flagstaff on the Rock!"

I knew the place, of course. On the farthermost point of the rock on which the Castle stands is set a high flagstaff, whereon in old time the banner of the Vissarion family flew. At some far-off time, when the Castle had been liable to attack, this point had been strongly fortified. Indeed, in the days when the bow was a martial weapon it must have been quite impregnable.

A covered gallery, with loopholes for arrows, had been cut in the solid rock, running right round the point, quite surrounding the flagstaff and the great boss of rock on whose centre it was reared. A narrow drawbridge of immense strength had connected—in peaceful times, and still remained—the outer point of rock with an entrance formed in the outer wall, and guarded with flanking towers and a portcullis. Its use was manifestly to guard against surprise. From this point only could be seen the line of the rocks all round the point. Thus, any secret attack by boats could be made impossible.

Having hurriedly dressed myself, and taking with me both hunting-knife and revolver, I went out on the terrace, taking the precaution, unusual to me, of drawing the grille behind me and locking it. Matters around the Castle are in far too disturbed a condition to allow the taking of any foolish chances, either in the way of being unarmed or of leaving the private entrance to the Castle open. I found my way through the rocky passage, and climbed by the Jacob's ladder fixed on the rock—a device of convenience in time of peace—to the foot of the flagstaff.

I was all on fire with expectation, and the time of going seemed exceeding long; so I was additionally disappointed by the contrast when I did not see my Lady there when I arrived. However, my heart beat freely again—perhaps more freely than ever—when I saw her crouching in the shadow of the Castle wall. From where she was she could not be seen from any point save that alone which I occupied; even from there it was only her white shroud that was conspicuous through the deep gloom of the shadow. The moonlight was so bright that the shadows were almost unnaturally black.

I rushed over towards her, and when close was about to say impulsively, "Why did you leave your tomb?" when it suddenly struck me that the question would be malapropos and embarrassing in many ways. So, better judgment prevailing, I said instead:

"It has been so long since I saw you! It has seemed an eternity to me!" Her answer came as quickly as even I could have wished; she spoke impulsively and without thought:

"It has been long to me too! Oh, so long! so long! I have asked you to come out here because I wanted to see you so much that I could not wait any longer. I have been heart-hungry for a sight of you!"

Her words, her eager attitude, the ineffable something which conveys the messages of the heart, the longing expression in her eyes as the full moonlight fell on her face, showing the stars as living gold—for in her eagerness she had stepped out towards me from the shadow—all set me on fire. Without a thought or a word—for it was Nature speaking in the language of Love, which is a silent tongue—I stepped towards her and took her in my arms. She yielded with that sweet unconsciousness which is the perfection of Love, as if it was in obedience to some command uttered before the beginning of the world. Probably without any conscious effort on either side—I know there was none on mine—our mouths met in the first kiss of love.

At the time nothing in the meeting struck me as out of the common. But later in the night, when I was alone and in darkness, whenever I thought of it all—its strangeness and its stranger rapture—I could not but be sensible of the bizarre conditions for a love meeting. The place lonely, the time night, the man young and strong, and full of life and hope and ambition; the woman, beautiful and ardent though she was, a woman seemingly dead, clothed in the shroud in which she had been wrapped when lying in her tomb in the crypt of the old church.

Whilst we were together, anyhow, there was little thought of the kind; no reasoning of any kind on my part. Love has its own laws and its own logic. Under the flagstaff, where the Vissarion banner was wont to flap in the breeze, she was in my arms; her sweet breath was on my face; her heart was beating against my own. What need was there for reason at all? *Inter arma silent leges*—the voice of reason is silent in the stress of passion. Dead she may be, or Un-dead—a Vampire with one foot in Hell and one on earth. But I love her; and come what may, here or hereafter, she is mine. As my mate, we shall fare along together, whatsoever the end may be, or wheresoever our path may lead. If she is indeed to be won from the nethermost Hell, then be mine the task!

But to go back to the record. When I had once started speaking to her in words of passion I could not stop. I did not want to—if I could; and she did not appear to wish it either. Can there be a woman—alive or dead—who would not want to hear the rapture of her lover expressed to her whilst she is enclosed in his arms?

There was no attempt at reticence on my part now; I took it for granted that she knew all that I surmised, and, as she made neither protest nor comment, that she accepted my belief as to her indeterminate existence. Sometimes her eyes would be closed, but even then the rapture of her face was almost beyond belief. Then, when the beautiful eyes would open and gaze on me, the stars that were in them would shine and scintillate as though they were formed of living fire. She said little, very little; but though the words were few, every syllable was fraught with love, and went straight to the very core of my heart.

By-and-by, when our transport had calmed to joy, I asked when I might next see her, and how and where I might find her when I should want to. She did not reply directly, but, holding me close in her arms, whispered in my ear with that breathless softness which is a lover's rapture of speech:

"I have come here under terrible difficulties, not only because I love you—and that would be enough—but because, as well as the joy of seeing you, I wanted to warn you."

"To warn me! Why?" I queried. Her reply came with a bashful hesitation, with something of a struggle in it, as of one who for some ulterior reason had to pick her words:

"There are difficulties and dangers ahead of you. You are beset with them; and they are all the greater because they are, of grim necessity, hidden from you. You cannot go anywhere, look in any direction, do anything, say anything, but it may be a signal for danger. My dear, it lurks everywhere—in the light as well as in the darkness; in the open as well as in the secret places; from friends as well as foes; when you are least prepared; when you may least expect it. Oh, I know it, and what it is to endure; for I share it for you—for your dear sake!"

"My darling!" was all I could say, as I drew her again closer to me and kissed her. After a bit she was calmer; seeing this, I came back to the subject that she had—in part, at all events—come to me to speak about:

"But if difficulty and danger hedge me in so everlastingly, and if I am to have no indication whatever of its kind or purpose, what can I do? God knows I would willingly guard myself—not on my own account, but for your dear sake. I have now a cause to live and be strong, and to keep all my faculties, since it may mean much to you. If you may not tell me details, may you not indicate to me some line of conduct, of action, that would be most in accord with your wishes—or, rather, with your idea of what would be best?"

She looked at me fixedly before speaking—a long, purposeful, loving look which no man born of woman could misunderstand. Then she spoke slowly, deliberately, emphatically:

"Be bold, and fear not. Be true to yourself, to me—it is the same thing. These are the best guards you can use. Your safety does not rest with me. Ah, I wish it did! I wish to God it did!" In my inner heart it thrilled me not merely to hear the expression of her wish, but to hear her use the name of God as she did. I understand now, in the calm of this place and with the sunlight before me, that my belief as to her being all woman—living woman—was not quite dead: but though at the moment my heart did not recognize the doubt, my brain did. And I made up my mind that we should not part this time until she knew that I had seen her, and where; but, despite my own thoughts, my outer ears listened greedily as she went on.

"As for me, you may not find *me*, but *I* shall find *you*, be sure! And now we must say 'Good-night,' my dear, my dear! Tell me once again that you love me, for it is a sweetness that one does not wish to forego— even one who wears such a garment as this—and rests where I must rest." As she spoke she held up part of her cerements for me to see. What could I do but take her once again in my arms and hold her close,

close. God knows it was all in love; but it was passionate love which surged through my every vein as I strained her dear body to mine. But yet this embrace was not selfish; it was not all an expression of my own passion. It was based on pity—the pity which is twin-born with true love. Breathless from our kisses, when presently we released each other, she stood in a glorious rapture, like a white spirit in the moonlight, and as her lovely, starlit eyes seemed to devour me, she spoke in a languorous ecstasy:

"Oh, how you love me! how you love me! It is worth all I have gone through for this, even to wearing this terrible drapery." And again she pointed to her shroud.

Here was my chance to speak of what I knew, and I took it. "I know, I know. Moreover, I know that awful resting-place."

I was interrupted, cut short in the midst of my sentence, not by any word, but by the frightened look in her eyes and the fear-mastered way in which she shrank away from me. I suppose in reality she could not be paler than she looked when the colour-absorbing moonlight fell on her; but on the instant all semblance of living seemed to shrink and fall away, and she looked with eyes of dread as if in I some awful way held in thrall. But for the movement of the pitiful glance, she would have seemed of soulless marble, so deadly cold did she look.

The moments that dragged themselves out whilst I waited for her to speak seemed endless. At length her words came in an awed whisper, so faint that even in that stilly night I could hardly hear it:

"You know—you know my resting-place! How—when was that?" There was nothing to do now but to speak out the truth:

"I was in the crypt of St. Sava. It was all by accident. I was exploring all around the Castle, and I went there in my course. I found the winding stair in the rock behind the screen, and went down. Dear, I loved you well before that awful moment, but then, even as the lantern fell tingling on the glass, my love multiplied itself, with pity as a factor." She was silent for a few seconds. When she spoke, there was a new tone in her voice:

"But were you not shocked?"

"Of course I was," I answered on the spur of the moment, and I now think wisely. "Shocked is hardly the word. I was horrified beyond anything that words can convey that you—*you* should have to so endure! I did not like to return, for I feared lest my doing so might set some barrier between us. But in due time I did return on another day."

"Well?" Her voice was like sweet music.

"I had another shock that time, worse than before, for you were not there. Then indeed it was that I knew to myself how dear you were—how dear you are to me. Whilst I live, you—living or dead—shall always be in my heart." She breathed hard. The elation in her eyes made them outshine the moonlight, but she said no word. I went on:

"My dear, I had come into the crypt full of courage and hope, though I knew what dreadful sight should sear my eyes once again. But we little know what may be in store for us, no matter what we expect. I went out with a heart like water from that dreadful desolation."

"Oh, how you love me, dear!" Cheered by her words, and even more by her tone, I went on with renewed courage. There was no halting, no faltering in my intention now:

"You and I, my dear, were ordained for each other. I cannot help it that you had already suffered before I knew you. It may be that there may be for you still suffering that I may not prevent, endurance that I may not shorten; but what a man can do is yours. Not Hell itself will stop me, if it be possible that I may win through its torments with you in my arms!"

"Will nothing stop you, then?" Her question was breathed as softly as the strain of an ÆEolian harp.

"Nothing!" I said, and I heard my own teeth snap together. There was something speaking within me stronger than I had ever known myself to be. Again came a query, trembling, quavering, quivering, as though the issue was of more than life or death:

"Not this?" She held up a corner of the shroud, and as she saw my face and realized the answer before I spoke, went on: "With all it implies?"

"Not if it were wrought of the cerecloths of the damned!" There was a long pause. Her voice was more resolute when she spoke again. It rang. Moreover, there was in it a joyous note, as of one who feels new hope:

"But do you know what men say? Some of them, that I am dead and buried; others, that I am not only dead and buried, but that I am one of those unhappy beings that may not die the common death of man. Who live on a fearful life-in-death, whereby they are harmful to all. Those unhappy Un-dead whom men call Vampires—who live on the blood of the living, and bring eternal damnation as well as death with the poison of their dreadful kisses!

"I know what men say sometimes," I answered. "But I know also what my own heart says; and I rather choose to obey its calling than all the voices of the living or the dead. Come what may, I am pledged to you. If it be that your old life has to be rewon for you out of the very jaws of Death and Hell, I shall keep the faith I have pledged, and that here I pledge again!" As I finished speaking I sank on my knees at her feet, and, putting my arms round her, drew her close to me. Her tears rained down on my face as she stroked my hair with her soft, strong hand and whispered to me:

"This is indeed to be one. What more holy marriage can God give to any of His creatures?" We were both silent for a time.

I think I was the first to recover my senses. That I did so was manifest by my asking her: "When may we meet again?"—a thing I had never remembered doing at any of our former partings. She answered with a rising and falling of the voice that was just above a whisper, as soft and cooing as the voice of a pigeon:

"That will be soon—as soon as I can manage it, be sure. My dear, my dear!" The last four words of endearment she spoke in a low but prolonged and piercing tone which made me thrill with delight.

"Give me some token," I said, "that I may have always close to me to ease my aching heart till we meet again, and ever after, for love's sake!" Her mind seemed to leap to understanding, and with a purpose all her own. Stooping for an instant, she tore off with swift, strong fingers a fragment of her shroud. This, having kissed it, she handed to me, whispering:

"It is time that we part. You must leave me now. Take this, and keep it for ever. I shall be less unhappy in my terrible loneliness whilst it lasts if I know that this my gift, which for good or ill is a part of me as you know me, is close to you. It may be, my very dear, that some day you may be glad and even proud of this hour, as I am." She kissed me as I took it.

"For life or death, I care not which, so long as I am with you!" I said, as I moved off. Descending the Jacob's ladder, I made my way down the rock-hewn passage.

The last thing I saw was the beautiful face of my Lady of the Shroud as she leaned over the edge of the opening. Her eyes were like glowing stars as her looks followed me. That look shall never fade from my memory.

After a few agitating moments of thought I half mechanically took my way down to the garden. Opening the grille, I entered my lonely room, which looked all the more lonely for the memory of the rapturous moments under the Flagstaff. I went to bed as one in a dream. There I lay till sunrise—awake and thinking.

Book V

A Ritual at Midnight

June 20, 1907

The time has gone as quickly as work can effect since I saw my Lady. As I told the mountaineers, Rooke, whom I had sent on the service, had made a contract for fifty thousand Ingis-Malbron rifles, and as many tons of ammunition as the French experts calculated to be a full supply for a year of warfare. I heard from him by our secret telegraph code that the order had been completed, and that the goods were already on the way. The morning after the meeting at the Flagstaff I had word that at night the vessel—one chartered by Rooke for the purpose—would arrive at Vissarion during the night. We were all expectation. I had always now in the Castle a signalling party, the signals being renewed as fast as the men were sufficiently expert to proceed with their practice alone or in groups. We hoped that every fighting-man in the country would in time become an expert signaller. Beyond these, again, we have always a few priests. The Church of the country is a militant Church; its priests are soldiers, its Bishops commanders. But they all serve wherever the battle most needs them. Naturally they, as men of brains, are quicker at learning than the average mountaineers; with the result that they learnt the code and the signalling almost by instinct. We have now at least one such expert in each community of them, and shortly the priests alone will be able to signal, if need be, for the nation; thus releasing for active service the merely fighting-man. The men at present with me I took into confidence as to the vessel's arrival, and we were all ready for work when the man on the lookout at the Flagstaff sent word that a vessel without lights was creeping in towards shore. We all assembled on the rocky edge of the creek, and saw her steal up the creek and gain the shelter of the harbour. When this had been effected, we ran out the boom which protects the opening, and after that the great armoured sliding-gates which Uncle Roger had himself had made so as to protect the harbour in case of need.

We then came within and assisted in warping the steamer to the side of the dock.

Rooke looked fit, and was full of fire and vigour. His responsibility and the mere thought of warlike action seemed to have renewed his youth.

When we had arranged for the unloading of the cases of arms and ammunition, I took Rooke into the room which we call my "office," where he gave me an account of his doings. He had not only secured the rifles and the ammunition for them, but he had purchased from one of the small American Republics an armoured yacht which had been especially built for war service. He grew quite enthusiastic, even excited, as he told me of her:

"She is the last word in naval construction—a torpedo yacht. A small cruiser, with turbines up to date, oil-fuelled, and fully armed with the latest and most perfect weapons and explosives of all kinds. The fastest boat afloat to-day. Built by Thorneycroft, engined by Parsons, armoured by Armstrong, armed by Crupp. If she ever comes into action, it will be bad for her opponent, for she need not fear to tackle anything less than a *Dreadnought*."

He also told me that from the same Government, whose nation had just established an unlooked-for peace, he had also purchased a whole park of artillery of the very latest patterns, and that for range and accuracy the guns were held to be supreme. These would follow before long, and with them their proper ammunition, with a shipload of the same to follow shortly after.

When he had told me all the rest of his news, and handed me the accounts, we went out to the dock to see the debarkation of the war material. Knowing that it was arriving, I had sent word in the afternoon to the mountaineers to tell them to come and remove it. They had answered the call, and it really seemed to me that the whole of the land must that night have been in motion.

They came as individuals, grouping themselves as they came within the defences of the Castle; some had gathered at fixed points on the way. They went secretly and in silence, stealing through the forests like ghosts, each party when it grouped taking the place of that which had gone on one of the routes radiating round Vissarion. Their coming and going was more than ghostly. It was, indeed, the outward manifestation of an inward spirit—a whole nation dominated by one common purpose.

The men in the steamer were nearly all engineers, mostly British, well conducted, and to be depended upon. Rooke had picked them separately, and in the doing had used well his great experience of both men and adventurous life. These men were to form part of the armoured yacht's crew when she should come into the Mediterranean waters. They and the priests and fighting-men in the Castle worked well together, and with a zeal that was beyond praise. The heavy cases seemed almost of their own accord to leave the holds, so fast came the procession of them along the gangways from deck to dock-wall. It was a part of my design that the arms should be placed in centres ready for local distribution. In such a country as this, without railways or even roads, the distribution of war material in any quantity is a great labour, for it has to be done individually, or at least from centres.

But of this work the great number of mountaineers who were arriving made little account. As fast as the ship's company, with the assistance of the priests and fighting-men, placed the cases on the quay, the engineers opened them and laid the contents ready for portage. The mountaineers seemed to come in a continuous stream; each in turn shouldered his burden and passed out, the captain of his section giving him as he passed his instruction where to go and in what route. The method had been already prepared in my office ready for such a distribution when the arms should arrive, and descriptions and quantities had been noted by the captains. The whole affair was treated by all as a matter of the utmost secrecy. Hardly a word was spoken beyond the necessary directions, and these were given in whispers. All night long the stream of men went and came, and towards dawn the bulk of the imported material was lessened by half. On the following night the remainder was removed, after my own men had stored in the Castle the rifles and ammunition reserved for its defence if necessary. It was advisable to keep a reserve supply in case it should ever be required. The following night Rooke went away secretly in the chartered vessel. He had to bring back with him the purchased cannon and heavy ammunition, which had been in the meantime stored on one of the Greek islands. The second morning, having had secret word that the steamer was on the way, I had given the signal for the assembling of the mountaineers.

A little after dark the vessel, showing no light, stole into the creek. The barrier gates were once again closed, and when a sufficient number of men had arrived to handle the guns, we began to unload. The actual deportation was easy enough, for the dock had all necessary appliances quite up to date, including a pair of shears for gun-lifting which could be raised into position in a very short time.

The guns were well furnished with tackle of all sorts, and before many hours had passed a little procession of them disappeared into the woods in ghostly silence. A number of men surrounded each, and they moved as well as if properly supplied with horses.

In the meantime, and for a week after the arrival of the guns, the drilling went on without pause. The gun-drill was wonderful. In the arduous work necessary for it the great strength and stamina of the mountaineers showed out wonderfully. They did not seem to know fatigue any more than they knew fear.

For a week this went on, till a perfect discipline and management was obtained. They did not practise the shooting, for this would have made secrecy impossible. It was reported all along the Turkish frontier that the Sultan's troops were being massed, and though this was not on a war footing, the movement was more or less dangerous. The reports of our own spies, although vague as to the purpose and extent of the movement, were definite as to something being on foot. And Turkey does not do something without a purpose that bodes ill to someone. Certainly the sound of cannon, which is a far-reaching sound, would have given them warning of our preparations, and would so have sadly minimized their effectiveness.

When the cannon had all been disposed of—except, of course, those destined for defence of the Castle or to be stored there—Rooke went away with the ship and crew. The ship he was to return to the owners; the men would be shipped on the war-yacht, of whose crew they would form a part. The rest of them had been carefully selected by Rooke himself, and were kept in secrecy at Cattaro, ready for service the moment required. They were all good men, and quite capable of whatever work they might be set to. So Rooke told me, and he ought to know. The experience of his young days as a private made him an expert in such a job.

Rupert's Journal—Continued

June 24, 1907

Last night I got from my Lady a similar message to the last, and delivered in a similar way. This time, however, our meeting was to be on the leads of the Keep.

I dressed myself very carefully before going on this adventure, lest by any chance of household concern, any of the servants should see me; for if this should happen, Aunt Janet would be sure to hear of it, which would give rise to endless surmises and questionings—a thing I was far from desiring.

I confess that in thinking the matter over during the time I was making my hurried preparations I was at a loss to understand how any human body, even though it be of the dead, could go or be conveyed to such a place without some sort of assistance, or, at least, collusion, on the part of some of the inmates. At the visit to the Flagstaff circumstances were different. This spot was actually outside the Castle, and in order to reach it I myself had to leave the Castle privately, and from the garden ascend to the ramparts. But here was no such possibility. The Keep was an *imperium in imperio*. It stood within the Castle, though separated from it, and it had its own defences against intrusion. The roof of it was, so far as I knew, as little approachable as the magazine.

The difficulty did not, however, trouble me beyond a mere passing thought. In the joy of the coming meeting and the longing rapture at the mere thought of it, all difficulties disappeared. Love makes its own faith, and I never doubted that my Lady would be waiting for me at the place designated. When I had passed through the little arched passages, and up the doubly-grated stairways contrived in the massiveness of the walls, I let myself out on the leads. It was well that as yet the times were sufficiently peaceful not to necessitate guards or sentries at all such points.

There, in a dim corner where the moonlight and the passing clouds threw deep shadows, I saw her, clothed as ever in her shroud. Why, I know not. I felt somehow that the situation was even more serious than ever. But I was steeled to whatever might come. My mind had been already made up. To carry out my resolve to win the woman I loved I was ready to face death. But now, after we had for a few brief moments held each other in our arms, I was willing to accept death— or more than death. Now, more than before, was she sweet and dear to me. Whatever qualms there might have been at the beginning of our love-making, or during the progress of it, did not now exist. We had exchanged vows and confidences, and acknowledged our loves. What, then, could there be of distrust, or even doubt, that the present might not set at naught? But even had there been such doubts or qualms, they must have disappeared in the ardour of our mutual embrace. I was by now mad for her, and was content to be so mad. When she had breath to speak after the strictness of our embrace, she said:

"I have come to warn you to be more than ever careful." It was, I confess, a pang to me, who thought only of love, to hear that anything else should have been the initiative power of her coming, even though it had been her concern for my own safety. I could not but notice the bitter note of chagrin in my voice as I answered:

"It was for love's sake that I came." She, too, evidently felt the undercurrent of pain, for she said quickly:

"Ah, dearest, I, too, came for love's sake. It is because I love you that I am so anxious about you. What would the world—ay, or heaven—be to me without you?"

There was such earnest truth in her tone that the sense and realization of my own harshness smote me. In the presence of such love as this even a lover's selfishness must become abashed. I could not express myself in words, so simply raised her slim hand in mine and kissed it. As it lay warm in my own I could not but notice, as well as its fineness, its strength and the firmness of its clasp. Its warmth and fervour struck into my heart—and my brain. Thereupon I poured out to her once more my love for her, she listening all afire. When passion had had its say, the calmer emotions had opportunity of expression. When I was satisfied afresh of her affection, I began to value her care for my safety, and so I went back to the subject. Her very insistence, based on personal affection, gave me more solid ground for fear. In the moment of love transports I had forgotten, or did not think, of what wonderful power or knowledge she must have to be able to move in such strange ways as she did. Why, at this very moment she was within my own gates. Locks and bars, even the very seal of death itself, seemed unable to make for her a prison-house. With such freedom of action and movement, going when she would into secret places, what might she not know that was known to others? How could anyone keep secret from such an one even an ill intent? Such thoughts, such surmises, had often flashed through my mind in moments of excitement rather than of reflection, but never long enough to become fixed into belief. But yet the consequences, the convictions, of them were with me, though unconsciously, though the thoughts themselves were perhaps forgotten or withered before development.

"And you?" I asked her earnestly. "What about danger to you?" She smiled, her little pearl-white teeth gleaming in the moonlight, as she spoke:

"There is no danger for me. I am safe. I am the safest person, perhaps the only safe person, in all this land." The full significance of her words did not seem to come to me all at once. Some base for understanding such an assertion seemed to be wanting. It was not that I did not trust or believe her, but that I thought she might be mistaken. I wanted to reassure myself, so in my distress I asked unthinkingly:

"How the safest? What is your protection?" For several moments that spun themselves out endlessly she looked me straight in the face, the stars in her eyes seeming to glow like fire; then, lowering her head, she took a fold of her shroud and held it up to me.

"This!"

The meaning was complete and understandable now. I could not speak at once for the wave of emotion which choked me. I dropped on my knees, and taking her in my arms, held her close to me. She saw that I was moved, and tenderly stroked my hair, and with delicate touch pressed down my head on her bosom, as a mother might have done to comfort a frightened child.

Presently we got back to the realities of life again. I murmured:

"Your safety, your life, your happiness are all-in-all to me. When will you let them be my care?" She trembled in my arms, nestling even closer to me. Her own arms seemed to quiver with delight as she said:

"Would you indeed like me to be always with you? To me it would be a happiness unspeakable; and to you, what would it be?"

I thought that she wished to hear me speak my love to her, and that, woman-like, she had led me to the utterance, and so I spoke again of the passion that now raged in me, she listening eagerly as we strained each other tight in our arms. At last there came a pause, a long, long pause, and our hearts beat consciously in unison as we stood together. Presently she said in a sweet, low, intense whisper, as soft as the sighing of summer wind:

"It shall be as you wish; but oh, my dear, you will have to first go through an ordeal which may try you terribly! Do not ask me anything! You must not ask, because I may not answer, and it would be pain to me to deny you anything. Marriage with such an one as I am has its own ritual, which may not be foregone. It may. . ." I broke passionately into her speaking:

"There is no ritual that I fear, so long as it be that it is for your good, and your lasting happiness. And if the end of it be that I may call you mine, there is no horror in life or death that I shall not gladly face. Dear,

I ask you nothing. I am content to leave myself in your hands. You shall advise me when the time comes, and I shall be satisfied, content to obey. Content! It is but a poor word to express what I long for! I shall shirk nothing which may come to me from this or any other world, so long as it is to make you mine!" Once again her murmured happiness was music to my ears:

"Oh, how you love me! how you love me, dear, dear!" She took me in her arms, and for a few seconds we hung together. Suddenly she tore herself apart from me, and stood drawn up to the full height, with a dignity I cannot describe or express. Her voice had a new dominance, as with firm utterance and in staccato manner she said:

"Rupert Sent Leger, before we go a step further I must say something to you, ask you something, and I charge you, on your most sacred honour and belief, to answer me truly. Do you believe me to be one of those unhappy beings who may not die, but have to live in shameful existence between earth and the nether world, and whose hellish mission is to destroy, body and soul, those who love them till they fall to their level? You are a gentleman, and a brave one. I have found you fearless. Answer me in sternest truth, no matter what the issue may be!"

She stood there in the glamorous moonlight with a commanding dignity which seemed more than human. In that mystic light her white shroud seemed diaphanous, and she appeared like a spirit of power. What was I to say? How could I admit to such a being that I had actually had at moments, if not a belief, a passing doubt? It was a conviction with me that if I spoke wrongly I should lose her for ever. I was in a desperate strait. In such a case there is but one solid ground which one may rest on—the Truth.

I really felt I was between the devil and the deep sea. There was no avoiding the issue, and so, out of this all-embracing, all-compelling conviction of truth, I spoke.

For a fleeting moment I felt that my tone was truculent, and almost hesitated; but as I saw no anger or indignation on my Lady's face, but rather an eager approval, I was reassured. A woman, after all, is glad to see a man strong, for all belief in him must be based on that.

"I shall speak the truth. Remember that I have no wish to hurt your feelings, but as you conjure me by my honour, you must forgive me if I pain. It is true that I had at first—ay, and later, when I came to think matters over after you had gone, when reason came to the aid of impression—a passing belief that you are a Vampire. How can I fail to have, even now, though I love you with all my soul, though I have held you in my arms and kissed you on the mouth, a doubt, when all the evidences seem to point to one thing? Remember that I have only seen you at night, except that bitter moment when, in the broad noonday of the upper world, I saw you, clad as ever in a shroud, lying seemingly dead in a tomb in the crypt of St. Sava's Church. . . But let that pass. Such belief as I have is all in you. Be you woman or Vampire, it is all the same to me. It is *you* whom I love! Should it be that you are—you are not woman, which I cannot believe, then it will be my glory to break your fetters, to open your prison, and set you free. To that I consecrate my life." For a few seconds I stood silent, vibrating with the passion which had been awakened in me. She had by now lost the measure of her haughty isolation, and had softened into womanhood again. It was really like a realization of the old theme of Pygmalion's statue. It was with rather a pleading than a commanding voice that she said:

"And shall you always be true to me?"

"Always—so help me, God!" I answered, and I felt that there could be no lack of conviction in my voice.

Indeed, there was no cause for such lack. She also stood for a little while stone-still, and I was beginning to expand to the rapture which was in store for me when she should take me again in her arms.

But there was no such moment of softness. All at once she started as if she had suddenly wakened from a dream, and on the spur of the moment said:

"Now go, go!" I felt the conviction of necessity to obey, and turned at once. As I moved towards the door by which I had entered, I asked:

"When shall I see you again?"

"Soon!" came her answer. "I shall let you know soon—when and where. Oh, go, go!" She almost pushed me from her.

When I had passed through the low doorway and locked and barred it behind me, I felt a pang that I should have had to shut her out like that; but I feared lest there should arise some embarrassing suspicion if the door should be found open. Later came the comforting thought that, as she had got to the roof though the door had been shut, she would be able to get away by the same means. She had evidently knowledge of some secret way into the Castle. The alternative was that she must have some supernatural quality or faculty which gave her strange powers. I did not wish to pursue that train of thought, and so, after an effort, shut it out from my mind.

When I got back to my room I locked the door behind me, and went to sleep in the dark. I did not want light just then—could not bear it.

This morning I woke, a little later than usual, with a kind of apprehension which I could not at once understand. Presently, however, when my faculties became fully awake and in working order, I realized that I feared, half expected, that Aunt Janet would come to me in a worse state of alarm than ever apropos of some new Second-Sight experience of more than usual ferocity.

But, strange to say, I had no such visit. Later on in the morning, when, after breakfast, we walked together through the garden, I asked her how she had slept, and if she had dreamt. She answered me that she had slept without waking, and if she had had any dreams, they must have been pleasant ones, for she did not remember them. "And you know, Rupert," she added, "that if there be anything bad or fearsome or warning in dreams, I always remember them."

Later still, when I was by myself on the cliff beyond the creek, I could not help commenting on the absence of her power of Second Sight on the occasion. Surely, if ever there was a time when she might have had cause of apprehension, it might well have been when I asked the Lady whom she did not know to marry me—the Lady of whose identity I knew nothing, even whose name I did not know—whom I loved with all my heart and soul—my Lady of the Shroud.

I have lost faith in Second Sight.

RUPERT's JOURNAL—*Continued*

July 1, 1907

Another week gone. I have waited patiently, and I am at last rewarded by another letter. I was preparing for bed a little while ago, when I heard the same mysterious sound at the door as on the last two occasions. I hurried to the glass door, and there found another close-folded letter. But I could see no sign of my Lady, or of any other living being. The letter, which was without direction, ran as follows:

"If you are still of the same mind, and feel no misgivings, meet me at the Church of St. Sava beyond the Creek to-morrow night at a quarter before midnight. If you come, come in secret, and, of course, alone. Do not come at all unless you are prepared for a terrible ordeal. But if you love me, and have neither doubts nor fears, come. Come!"

Needless to say, I did not sleep last night. I tried to, but without success. It was no morbid happiness that kept me awake, no doubting, no fear. I was simply overwhelmed with the idea of the coming rapture when I should call my Lady my very, very own. In this sea of happy expectation all lesser things were submerged. Even sleep, which is an imperative force with me, failed in its usual effectiveness, and I lay still, calm, content.

With the coming of the morning, however, restlessness began. I did not know what to do, how to restrain myself, where to look for an anodyne. Happily the latter came in the shape of Rooke, who turned up shortly after breakfast. He had a satisfactory tale to tell me of the armoured yacht, which had lain off Cattaro on the previous night, and to which he had brought his contingent of crew which had waited for her coming. He did not like to take the risk of going into any port with such a vessel, lest he might be detained or otherwise hampered by forms, and had gone out upon the open sea before daylight. There was on board the yacht a tiny torpedo-boat, for which provision was made both for hoisting on deck and housing there. This last would run into the creek at ten o'clock that evening, at which time it would be dark. The yacht would then run to near Otranto, to which she would send a boat to get any message I might send. This was to be in a code, which we arranged, and would convey instructions as to what night and approximate hour the yacht would come to the creek.

The day was well on before we had made certain arrangements for the future; and not till then did I feel again the pressure of my personal restlessness. Rooke, like a wise commander, took rest whilst he could. Well he knew that for a couple of days and nights at least there would be little, if any, sleep for him.

For myself, the habit of self-control stood to me, and I managed to get through the day somehow without exciting the attention of anyone else. The arrival of the torpedo-boat and the departure of Rooke made for me a welcome break in my uneasiness. An hour ago I said good-night to Aunt Janet, and shut myself up alone here. My watch is on the table before me, so that I may make sure of starting to the moment. I have allowed myself half an hour to reach St. Sava. My skiff is waiting, moored at the foot of the cliff on the hither side, where the zigzag comes close to the water. It is now ten minutes past eleven.

I shall add the odd five minutes to the time for my journey so as to make safe. I go unarmed and without a light.

I shall show no distrust of anyone or anything this night.

BRAM STOKER

July 2, 1907

When I was outside the church, I looked at my watch in the bright moonlight, and found I had one minute to wait. So I stood in the shadow of the doorway and looked out at the scene before me. Not a sign of life was visible around me, either on land or sea. On the broad plateau on which the church stands there was no movement of any kind. The wind, which had been pleasant in the noontide, had fallen completely, and not a leaf was stirring. I could see across the creek and note the hard line where the battlements of the Castle cut the sky, and where the keep towered above the line of black rock, which in the shadow of the land made an ebon frame for the picture. When I had seen the same view on former occasions, the line where the rock rose from the sea was a fringe of white foam. But then, in the daylight, the sea was sapphire blue; now it was an expanse of dark blue—so dark as to seem almost black. It had not even the relief of waves or ripples— simply a dark, cold, lifeless expanse, with no gleam of light anywhere, of lighthouse or ship; neither was there any special sound to be heard that one could distinguish—nothing but the distant hum of the myriad voices of the dark mingling in one ceaseless inarticulate sound. It was well I had not time to dwell on it, or I might have reached some spiritually-disturbing melancholy.

Let me say here that ever since I had received my Lady's message concerning this visit to St. Sava's I had been all on fire—not, perhaps, at every moment consciously or actually so, but always, as it were, prepared to break out into flame. Did I want a simile, I might compare myself to a well-banked furnace, whose present function it is to contain heat rather than to create it; whose crust can at any moment be broken by a force external to itself, and burst into raging, all-compelling heat. No thought of fear really entered my mind. Every other emotion there was, coming and going as occasion excited or lulled, but not fear. Well I knew in the depths of my heart the purpose which that secret quest was to serve. I knew not only from my Lady's words, but from the teachings of my own senses and experiences, that some dreadful ordeal must take place before happiness of any kind could be won. And that ordeal, though method or detail was unknown to me, I was prepared to undertake. This was one of those occasions when a man must undertake, blindfold, ways that may lead to torture or death, or unknown terrors beyond. But, then, a man—if, indeed, he have the heart of a man—can always undertake; he can at least make the first step, though it may turn out that through the weakness of mortality he may be unable to fulfil his own intent, or justify his belief in his own powers. Such, I take it, was the intellectual attitude of the brave souls who of old faced the tortures of the Inquisition.

But though there was no immediate fear, there was a certain doubt. For doubt is one of those mental conditions whose calling we cannot control. The end of the doubting may not be a reality to us, or be accepted as a possibility. These things cannot forego the existence of the doubt. "For even if a man," says Victor Cousin, "doubt everything else, at least he cannot doubt that he doubts." The doubt had at times been on me that my Lady of the Shroud was a Vampire. Much that had happened seemed to point that way, and here, on the very threshold of the Unknown, when, through the door which I was pushing open, my eyes met only an expanse of absolute blackness, all doubts which had ever been seemed to surround me in a legion. I have heard that, when a man is drowning, there comes a time when his whole life passes in review during the space of time which cannot be computed as even a part of a second. So it was to me in the moment of my body passing into the church. In that moment came to my mind all that had been, which bore on the knowledge of my Lady; and the general tendency was to prove or convince that she was indeed a Vampire. Much that had happened, or become known to me, seemed to justify the resolving of doubt into belief. Even my own reading of the books in Aunt Janet's little library, and the dear lady's comments on them, mingled with her own uncanny beliefs, left little opening for doubt. My having to help my Lady over the threshold of my house on her first entry was in accord with Vampire tradition; so, too, her flying at cock-crow from the warmth in which she revelled on that strange first night of our meeting; so, too, her swift departure at midnight on the second. Into the same category came the facts of her constant wearing of her Shroud, even her pledging herself, and me also, on the fragment torn from it, which she had given to me as a souvenir; her lying still in the glass-covered tomb; her coming alone to the most secret places in a fortified Castle where every aperture was secured by unopened locks and bolts; her very movements, though all of grace, as she flitted noiselessly through the gloom of night.

All these things, and a thousand others of lesser import, seemed, for the moment, to have consolidated an initial belief. But then

BRAM STOKER

came the supreme recollections of how she had lain in my arms; of her kisses on my lips; of the beating of her heart against my own; of her sweet words of belief and faith breathed in my ear in intoxicating whispers; of. . . I paused. No! I could not accept belief as to her being other than a living woman of soul and sense, of flesh and blood, of all the sweet and passionate instincts of true and perfect womanhood.

And so, in spite of all—in spite of all beliefs, fixed or transitory, with a mind whirling amid contesting forces and compelling beliefs—I stepped into the church overwhelmed with that most receptive of atmospheres—doubt.

In one thing only was I fixed: here at least was no doubt or misgiving whatever. I intended to go through what I had undertaken. Moreover, I felt that I was strong enough to carry out my intention, whatever might be of the Unknown—however horrible, however terrible.

When I had entered the church and closed the heavy door behind me, the sense of darkness and loneliness in all their horror enfolded me round. The great church seemed a living mystery, and served as an almost terrible background to thoughts and remembrances of unutterable gloom. My adventurous life has had its own schooling to endurance and upholding one's courage in trying times; but it has its contra in fulness of memory.

I felt my way forward with both hands and feet. Every second seemed as if it had brought me at last to a darkness which was actually tangible. All at once, and with no heed of sequence or order, I was conscious of all around me, the knowledge or perception of which— or even speculation on the subject—had never entered my mind. They furnished the darkness with which I was encompassed with all the crowded phases of a dream. I knew that all around me were memorials of the dead—that in the Crypt deep-wrought in the rock below my feet lay the dead themselves. Some of them, perhaps—one of them I knew—had even passed the grim portals of time Unknown, and had, by some mysterious power or agency, come back again to material earth. There was no resting-place for thought when I knew that the very air which I breathed might be full of denizens of the spirit-world. In that impenetrable blackness was a world of imagining whose possibilities of horror were endless.

I almost fancied that I could see with mortal eyes down through that rocky floor to where, in the lonely Crypt, lay, in her tomb of massive stone and under that bewildering coverlet of glass, the woman whom I love. I could see her beautiful face, her long black lashes, her sweet mouth—which I had kissed—relaxed in the sleep of death. I could note the voluminous shroud—a piece of which as a precious souvenir lay even then so close to my heart—the snowy woollen coverlet wrought over in gold with sprigs of pine, the soft dent in the cushion on which her head must for so long have lain. I could see myself—within my eyes the memory of that first visit—coming once again with glad step to renew that dear sight—dear, though it scorched my eyes and harrowed my heart—and finding the greater sorrow, the greater desolation of the empty tomb!

There! I felt that I must think no more of that lest the thought should unnerve me when I should most want all my courage. That way madness lay! The darkness had already sufficient terrors of its own without bringing to it such grim remembrances and imaginings. . . And I had yet to go through some ordeal which, even to her who had passed and repassed the portals of death, was full of fear.

It was a merciful relief to me when, in groping my way forwards through the darkness, I struck against some portion of the furnishing of the church. Fortunately I was all strung up to tension, else I should never have been able to control instinctively, as I did, the shriek which was rising to my lips.

I would have given anything to have been able to light even a match. A single second of light would, I felt, have made me my own man again. But I knew that this would be against the implied condition of my being there at all, and might have had disastrous consequences to her whom I had come to save. It might even frustrate my scheme, and altogether destroy my opportunity. At that moment it was borne upon me more strongly than ever that this was not a mere fight for myself or my own selfish purposes—not merely an adventure or a struggle for only life and death against unknown difficulties and dangers. It was a fight on behalf of her I loved, not merely for her life, but perhaps even for her soul.

And yet this very thinking—understanding—created a new form of terror. For in that grim, shrouding darkness came memories of other moments of terrible stress.

Of wild, mystic rites held in the deep gloom of African forests, when, amid scenes of revolting horror, Obi and the devils of his kind seemed to reveal themselves to reckless worshippers, surfeited with horror, whose lives counted for naught; when even human sacrifice was an episode, and the reek of old deviltries and recent carnage tainted the air, till even I, who was, at the risk of my life, a privileged spectator who had come through dangers without end to behold the scene, rose and fled in horror.

Of scenes of mystery enacted in rock-cut temples beyond the Himalayas, whose fanatic priests, cold as death and as remorseless, in the reaction of their phrenzy of passion, foamed at the mouth and then sank into marble quiet, as with inner eyes they beheld the visions of the hellish powers which they had invoked.

Of wild, fantastic dances of the Devil-worshippers of Madagascar, where even the very semblance of humanity disappeared in the fantastic excesses of their orgies.

Of strange doings of gloom and mystery in the rock-perched monasteries of Thibet.

Of awful sacrifices, all to mystic ends, in the innermost recesses of Cathay.

Of weird movements with masses of poisonous snakes by the medicine-men of the Zuni and Mochi Indians in the far south-west of the Rockies, beyond the great plains.

Of secret gatherings in vast temples of old Mexico, and by dim altars of forgotten cities in the heart of great forests in South America.

Of rites of inconceivable horror in the fastnesses of Patagonia.

Of. . . Here I once more pulled myself up. Such thoughts were no kind of proper preparation for what I might have to endure. My work that night was to be based on love, on hope, on self-sacrifice for the woman who in all the world was the closest to my heart, whose future I was to share, whether that sharing might lead me to Hell or Heaven. The hand which undertook such a task must have no trembling.

Still, those horrible memories had, I am bound to say, a useful part in my preparation for the ordeal. They were of fact which I had seen, of which I had myself been in part a sharer, and which I had survived. With such experiences behind me, could there be aught before me more dreadful? . . .

Moreover, if the coming ordeal was of supernatural or superhuman order, could it transcend in living horror the vilest and most desperate acts of the basest men? . . .

With renewed courage I felt my way before me, till my sense of touch told me that I was at the screen behind which lay the stair to the Crypt.

There I waited, silent, still.

My own part was done, so far as I knew how to do it. Beyond this, what was to come was, so far as I knew, beyond my own control. I had done what I could; the rest must come from others. I had exactly obeyed my instructions, fulfilled my warranty to the utmost in my knowledge and power. There was, therefore, left for me in the present nothing but to wait.

It is a peculiarity of absolute darkness that it creates its own reaction. The eye, wearied of the blackness, begins to imagine forms of light. How far this is effected by imagination pure and simple I know not. It may be that nerves have their own senses that bring thought to the depository common to all the human functions, but, whatever may be the mechanism or the objective, the darkness seems to people itself with luminous entities.

So was it with me as I stood lonely in the dark, silent church. Here and there seemed to flash tiny points of light.

In the same way the silence began to be broken now and again by strange muffled sounds—the suggestion of sounds rather than actual vibrations. These were all at first of the minor importance of movement—rustlings, creakings, faint stirrings, fainter breathings. Presently, when I had somewhat recovered from the sort of hypnotic trance to which the darkness and stillness had during the time of waiting reduced me, I looked around in wonder.

The phantoms of light and sound seemed to have become real. There were most certainly actual little points of light in places—not enough to see details by, but quite sufficient to relieve the utter gloom. I thought—though it may have been a mingling of recollection and imagination—that I could distinguish the outlines of the church; certainly the great altar-screen was dimly visible. Instinctively I looked up—and thrilled. There, hung high above me, was, surely enough, a great Greek Cross, outlined by tiny points of light.

I lost myself in wonder, and stood still, in a purely receptive mood, unantagonistic to aught, willing for whatever might come, ready for all things, in rather a negative than a positive mood—a mood which has an aspect of spiritual meekness. This is the true spirit of the neophyte, and, though I did not think of it at the time, the proper attitude for what is called by the Church in whose temple I stood a "neo-nymph."

As the light grew a little in power, though never increasing enough for distinctness, I saw dimly before me a table on which rested a great open book, whereon were laid two rings—one of sliver, the other of gold—and two crowns wrought of flowers, bound at the joining of their stems with tissue—one of gold, the other of silver. I do not know much of the ritual of the old Greek Church, which is the religion of the Blue Mountains, but the things which I saw before me could be none other than enlightening symbols. Instinctively I knew that I had been brought hither, though in this grim way, to be married. The very idea of it thrilled me to the heart's core. I thought the best thing I could do would be to stay quite still, and not show surprise at anything that might happen; but be sure I was all eyes and ears.

I peered anxiously around me in every direction, but I could see no sign of her whom I had come to meet.

Incidentally, however, I noticed that in the lighting, such as it was, there was no flame, no "living" light. Whatever light there was came muffled, as though through some green translucent stone. The whole effect was terribly weird and disconcerting.

Presently I started, as, seemingly out of the darkness beside me, a man's hand stretched out and took mine. Turning, I found close to me a tall man with shining black eyes and long black hair and beard. He was clad in some kind of gorgeous robe of cloth of gold, rich with variety of adornment. His head was covered with a high, over-hanging hat draped closely with a black scarf, the ends of which formed a long, hanging veil on either side. These veils, falling over the magnificent robes of cloth of gold, had an extraordinarily solemn effect.

I yielded myself to the guiding hand, and shortly found myself, so far as I could see, at one side of the sanctuary.

In the floor close to my feet was a yawning chasm, into which, from so high over my head that in the uncertain light I could not distinguish its origin, hung a chain. At the sight a strange wave of memory swept over me. I could not but remember the chain which hung over the glass-covered tomb in the Crypt, and I had an instinctive feeling that the grim chasm in the floor of the sanctuary was but the other side of the opening in the roof of the crypt from which the chain over the sarcophagus depended.

There was a creaking sound—the groaning of a windlass and the clanking of a chain. There was heavy breathing close to me somewhere. I was so intent on what was going on that I did not see that one by one, seeming to grow out of the surrounding darkness, several black figures in monkish garb appeared with the silence of ghosts. Their faces were shrouded in black cowls, wherein were holes through which I could see dark gleaming eyes. My guide held me tightly by the hand. This gave me a feeling of security in the touch which helped to retain within my breast some semblance of calm.

The strain of the creaking windlass and the clanking chain continued for so long that the suspense became almost unendurable. At last there came into sight an iron ring, from which as a centre depended four lesser chains spreading wide. In a few seconds more I could see that these were fixed to the corners of the great stone tomb with the covering of glass, which was being dragged upward. As it arose it filled closely the whole aperture. When its bottom had reached the level of the floor it stopped, and remained rigid. There was no room for oscillation. It was at once surrounded by a number of black figures, who raised the glass covering and bore it away into the darkness. Then there stepped forward a very tall man, black-bearded, and with head-gear like my guide, but made in triple tiers, he also was gorgeously arrayed in flowing robes of cloth of gold richly embroidered. He raised his hand, and forthwith eight other black-clad figures stepped forward, and bending over the stone coffin, raised from it the rigid form of my Lady, still clad in her Shroud, and laid it gently on the floor of the sanctuary.

I felt it a grace that at that instant the dim lights seemed to grow less, and finally to disappear—all save the tiny points that marked the outline of the great Cross high overhead. These only gave light enough to accentuate the gloom. The hand that held mine now released it, and with a sigh I realized that I was alone. After a few moments more of the groaning of the winch and clanking of the chain there was a sharp sound of stone meeting stone; then there was silence. I listened acutely, but could not hear near me the slightest sound. Even the cautious, restrained breathing around me, of which up to then I had been conscious, had ceased. Not knowing, in the helplessness of my ignorance, what I should do, I remained as I was, still and silent, for a time that seemed endless. At last, overcome by some emotion which I could not at the moment understand, I slowly sank to my knees and bowed my head. Covering my face with my hands, I tried to recall the prayers of my youth. It was not, I am certain, that fear in any form had come upon me, or that I hesitated or faltered in my intention. That much I know now; I knew it even then. It was, I believe, that the prolonged impressive gloom and mystery had at last touched me to the quick. The bending of the knees was but symbolical of the bowing of the spirit to a higher Power. When I had realized that much, I felt more content than I had done since I had entered the church, and with the renewed consciousness of courage, took my hands from my face, and lifted again my bowed head.

Impulsively I sprang to my feet and stood erect—waiting. All seemed to have changed since I had dropped on my knees. The points of light about time church, which had been eclipsed, had come again, and were growing in power to a partial revealing of the dim expanse. Before me was the table with the open book, on which were laid the gold and silver rings and the two crowns of flowers. There were also two tall candles, with tiniest flames of blue—the only living light to be seen.

Out of the darkness stepped the same tall figure in the gorgeous robes and the triple hat. He led by the hand my Lady, still clad in her Shroud; but over it, descending from the crown of her head, was a veil of very old and magnificent lace of astonishing fineness. Even in that dim light I could note the exquisite beauty of the fabric. The veil was fastened with a bunch of tiny sprays of orange-blossom mingled with cypress and laurel—a strange combination. In her hand she carried a great bouquet of the same. Its sweet intoxicating odour floated up to my nostrils. It and the sentiment which its very presence evoked made me quiver.

Yielding to the guiding of the hand which held hers, she stood at my left side before the table. Her guide then took his place behind her. At either end of the table, to right and left of us, stood a long-bearded priest in splendid robes, and wearing the hat with depending veil of black. One of them, who seemed to be the more important of the two, and took the initiative, signed to us to put our right hands on the open book. My Lady, of course, understood the ritual, and knew the words which the priest was speaking, and of her own accord put out her hand. My guide at the same moment directed my hand to the same end. It thrilled me to touch my Lady's hand, even under such mysterious conditions.

After the priest had signed us each thrice on the forehead with the sign of the Cross, he gave to each of us a tiny lighted taper brought to him for the purpose. The lights were welcome, not so much for the solace of the added light, great as that was, but because it allowed us to see a little more of each other's faces. It was rapture to me to see the face of my Bride; and from the expression of her face I was assured that she felt as I did. It gave me an inexpressible pleasure when, as her eyes rested on me, there grew a faint blush over the grey pallor of her cheeks.

The priest then put in solemn voice to each of us in turn, beginning with me, the questions of consent which are common to all such rituals. I answered as well as I could, following the murmured words of my guide. My Lady answered out proudly in a voice which, though given softly, seemed to ring. It was a concern—even a grief—to me that I could not, in the priest's questioning, catch her name, of which, strangely enough,—I was ignorant. But, as I did not know the language, and as the phrases were not in accord literally with our own ritual, I could not make out which word was the name.

After some prayers and blessings, rhythmically spoken or sung by an invisible choir, the priest took the rings from the open book, and, after signing my forehead thrice with the gold one as he repeated the blessing in each case, placed it on my right hand; then he gave my Lady the silver one, with the same ritual thrice repeated. I suppose it was the blessing which is the effective point in making two into one.

After this, those who stood behind us exchanged our rings thrice, taking them from one finger and placing them on the other, so that at the end my wife wore the gold ring and I the silver one.

Then came a chant, during which the priest swung the censer himself, and my wife and I held our tapers. After that he blessed us, the responses coming from the voices of the unseen singers in the darkness.

After a long ritual of prayer and blessing, sung in triplicate, the priest took the crowns of flowers, and put one on the head of each, crowning me first, and with the crown tied with gold. Then he signed and blessed us each thrice. The guides, who stood behind us, exchanged our crowns thrice, as they had exchanged the rings; so that at the last, as I was glad to see, my wife wore the crown of gold, and I that of silver.

Then there came, if it is possible to describe such a thing, a hush over even that stillness, as though some form of added solemnity were to be gone through. I was not surprised, therefore, when the priest took in his hands the great golden chalice. Kneeling, my wife and I partook together thrice.

When we had risen from our knees and stood for a little while, the priest took my left hand in his right, and I, by direction of my guide, gave my right hand to my wife. And so in a line, the priest leading, we circled round the table in rhythmic measure. Those who supported us moved behind us, holding the crowns over our heads, and replacing them when we stopped.

After a hymn, sung through the darkness, the priest took off our crowns. This was evidently the conclusion of the ritual, for the priest placed us in each other's arms to embrace each other. Then he blessed us, who were now man and wife!

The lights went out at once, some as if extinguished, others slowly fading down to blackness.

Left in the dark, my wife and I sought each other's arms again, and stood together for a few moments heart to heart, tightly clasping each other, and kissed each other fervently.

Instinctively we turned to the door of the church, which was slightly open, so that we could see the moonlight stealing in through the aperture. With even steps, she holding me tightly by the left arm— which is the wife's arm, we passed through the old church and out into the free air.

Despite all that the gloom had brought me, it was sweet to be in the open air and together—this quite apart from our new relations to each other. The moon rode high, and the full light, coming after the dimness or darkness in the church, seemed as bright as day. I could now, for the first time, see my wife's face properly. The glamour of the moonlight may have served to enhance its ethereal beauty, but neither moonlight nor sunlight could do justice to that beauty in its living human splendour. As I gloried in her starry eyes I could think of nothing else; but when for a moment my eyes, roving round for the purpose of protection, caught sight of her whole figure, there was a pang to my heart. The brilliant moonlight showed every detail in terrible effect, and I could see that she wore only her Shroud. In the moment of darkness, after the last benediction, before she returned to my arms, she must have removed her bridal veil. This may, of course, have been in accordance with the established ritual of her church; but, all the same, my heart was sore. The glamour of calling her my very own was somewhat obscured by the bridal adornment being shorn. But it made no difference in her sweetness to me. Together we went along the path through the wood, she keeping equal step with me in wifely way.

When we had come through the trees near enough to see the roof of the Castle, now gilded with the moonlight, she stopped, and looking at me with eyes full of love, said:

"Here I must leave you!"

"What?" I was all aghast, and I felt that my chagrin was expressed in the tone of horrified surprise in my voice. She went on quickly:

"Alas! It is impossible that I should go farther—at present!"

"But what is to prevent you?" I queried. "You are now my wife. This is our wedding-night; and surely your place is with me!" The wail in her voice as she answered touched me to the quick:

"Oh, I know, I know! There is no dearer wish in my heart—there can be none—than to share my husband's home. Oh, my dear, my dear, if you only knew what it would be to me to be with you always! But indeed I may not—not yet! I am not free! If you but knew how much that which has happened to-night has cost me—or how much cost to others as well as to myself may be yet to come—you would understand. Rupert"—it was the first time she had ever addressed me by name, and naturally it thrilled me through and through—"Rupert, my husband, only that I trust you with all the faith which is in perfect love—mutual love, I dare not have done what I have done this night. But, dear, I know that you will bear me out; that your wife's honour is your honour, even as your honour is mine. My honour is given to this; and you can help me—the only help I can have at present—by trusting me. Be patient, my beloved, be patient! Oh, be patient for a little longer! It shall not be for long. So soon as ever my soul is freed I shall come to you, my husband; and we shall never part again. Be content for a while! Believe me that I love you with my very soul; and to keep away from your dear side is more bitter for me than even it can be for you! Think, my dear one, I am not as other women are, as some day you shall clearly understand. I am at the present, and shall be for a little longer, constrained by duties and obligations put upon me by others, and for others, and to which I am pledged by the most sacred promises—given not only by myself, but by others—and which I must not forgo. These forbid me to do as I wish. Oh, trust me, my beloved—my husband!"

She held out her hands appealingly. The moonlight, falling through the thinning forest, showed her white cerements. Then the recollection of all she must have suffered—the awful loneliness in that grim tomb in the Crypt, the despairing agony of one who is helpless against the unknown—swept over me in a wave of pity. What could I do but save her from further pain? And this could only be by showing her my faith and trust. If she was to go back to that dreadful charnel-house, she would at least take with her the remembrance that one who loved her and whom she loved—to whom she had been lately bound in the mystery of marriage—trusted her to the full. I loved her more than myself—more than my own soul; and I was moved by pity so great that all possible selfishness was merged in its depths. I bowed my head before her—my Lady and my Wife—as I said:

"So be it, my beloved. I trust you to the full, even as you trust me. And that has been proven this night, even to my own doubting heart. I shall wait; and as I know you wish it, I shall wait as patiently as I can. But till you come to me for good and all, let me see you or hear from you when you can. The time, dear wife, must go heavily with me as I think of you suffering and lonely. So be good to me, and let not too long a time elapse between my glimpses of hope. And, sweetheart, when you *do* come to me, it shall be for ever!" There was something in the intonation of the last sentence—I felt its sincerity myself—some implied yearning for a promise, that made her beautiful eyes swim. The glorious stars in them were blurred as she answered with a fervour which seemed to me as more than earthly:

"For ever! I swear it!"

With one long kiss, and a straining in each others arms, which left me tingling for long after we had lost sight of each other, we parted. I stood and watched her as her white figure, gliding through the deepening gloom, faded as the forest thickened. It surely was no optical delusion or a phantom of the mind that her shrouded arm was raised as though in blessing or farewell before the darkness swallowed her up.

Book VI

The Pursuit in the Forest

July 3, 1907

There is no anodyne but work to pain of the heart; and my pain is all of the heart. I sometimes feel that it is rather hard that with so much to make me happy I cannot know happiness. How can I be happy when my wife, whom I fondly love, and who I know loves me, is suffering in horror and loneliness of a kind which is almost beyond human belief? However, what is my loss is my country's gain, for the Land of the Blue Mountains is my country now, despite the fact that I am still a loyal subject of good King Edward. Uncle Roger took care of that when he said I should have the consent of the Privy Council before I might be naturalized anywhere else.

When I got home yesterday morning I naturally could not sleep. The events of the night and the bitter disappointment that followed my exciting joy made such a thing impossible. When I drew the curtain over the window, the reflection of the sunrise was just beginning to tinge the high-sailing clouds in front of me. I laid down and tried to rest, but without avail. However, I schooled myself to lie still, and at last, if I did not sleep, was at least quiescent.

Disturbed by a gentle tap at the door, I sprang up at once and threw on a dressing gown. Outside, when I opened the door, was Aunt Janet. She was holding a lighted candle in her hand, for though it was getting light in the open, the passages were still dark. When she saw me she seemed to breathe more freely, and asked if she might come in.

Whilst she sat on the edge of my bed, in her old-time way, she said in a hushed voice:

"Oh, laddie, laddie, I trust yer burden is no too heavy to bear."

"My burden! What on earth do you mean, Aunt Janet?" I said in reply. I did not wish to commit myself by a definite answer, for it was evident that she had been dreaming or Second Sighting again. She replied with the grim seriousness usual to her when she touched on occult matters:

"I saw your hairt bleeding, laddie. I kent it was yours, though how I kent it I don't know. It lay on a stone floor in the dark, save for a dim blue light such as corpse-lights are. On it was placed a great book, and close around were scattered many strange things, amongst them two crowns o' flowers—the one bound wi' silver, the other wi' gold. There was also a golden cup, like a chalice, o'erturned. The red wine trickled from it an' mingled wi' yer hairt's bluid; for on the great book was some vast dim weight wrapped up in black, and on it stepped in turn many men all swathed in black. An' as the weight of each came on it the bluid gushed out afresh. And oh, yer puir hairt, my laddie, was quick and leaping, so that at every beat it raised the black-clad weight! An' yet that was not all, for hard by stood a tall imperial shape o' a woman, all arrayed in white, wi' a great veil o' finest lace worn o'er a shroud. An' she was whiter than the snow, an' fairer than the morn for beauty; though a dark woman she was, wi' hair like the raven, an' eyes black as the sea at nicht, an' there was stars in them. An' at each beat o' yer puir bleeding hairt she wrung her white hands, an' the manin' o' her sweet voice rent my hairt in twain. Oh, laddie, laddie! what does it mean?"

I managed to murmur: "I'm sure I don't know, Aunt Janet. I suppose it was all a dream!"

"A dream it was, my dear. A dream or a veesion, whilka matters nane, for a' such are warnin's sent frae God. . ." Suddenly she said in a different voice:

"Laddie, hae ye been fause to any lassie? I'm no blamin' ye. For ye men are different frae us women, an' yer regard on recht and wrang differs from oors. But oh, laddie, a woman's tears fa' heavy when her hairt is for sair wi' the yieldin' to fause words. 'Tis a heavy burden for ony man to carry wi' him as he goes, an' may well cause pain to ithers that he fain would spare." She stopped, and in dead silence waited for me to speak. I thought it would be best to set her poor loving heart at rest, and as I could not divulge my special secret, spoke in general terms:

"Aunt Janet, I am a man, and have led a man's life, such as it is. But I can tell you, who have always loved me and taught me to be true, that in all the world there is no woman who must weep for any falsity of mine. If close there be any who, sleeping or waking, in dreams or visions or in reality, weeps because of me, it is surely not for my doing, but because of something outside me. It may be that her heart is sore because I must suffer, as all men must in some degree; but she does not weep for or through any act of mine."

She sighed happily at my assurance, and looked up through her tears, for she was much moved; and after tenderly kissing my forehead and blessing me, stole away. She was more sweet and tender than I have words to say, and the only regret that I have in all that is gone is that I have not been able to bring my wife to her, and let her share in the love she has for me. But that, too, will come, please God!

In the morning I sent a message to Rooke at Otranto, instructing him by code to bring the yacht to Vissarion in the coming night.

All day I spent in going about amongst the mountaineers, drilling them and looking after their arms. I *could* not stay still. My only chance of peace was to work, my only chance of sleep to tire myself out. Unhappily, I am very strong, so even when I came home at dark I was quite fresh. However, I found a cable message from Rooke that the yacht would arrive at midnight.

There was no need to summon the mountaineers, as the men in the Castle would be sufficient to make preparations for the yacht's coming.

Later

The yacht has come. At half-past eleven the lookout signalled that a steamer without lights was creeping in towards the Creek. I ran out to the Flagstaff, and saw her steal in like a ghost. She is painted a steely blue-grey, and it is almost impossible to see her at any distance. She certainly goes wonderfully. Although there was not enough throb from the engines to mar the absolute stillness, she came on at a fine speed, and within a few minutes was close to the boom. I had only time to run down to give orders to draw back the boom when she glided in and stopped dead at the harbour wall. Rooke steered her himself, and he says he never was on a boat that so well or so quickly answered her helm. She is certainly a beauty, and so far as I can see at night perfect in every detail. I promise myself a few pleasant hours over her in the daylight. The men seem a splendid lot.

But I do not feel sleepy; I despair of sleep to-night. But work demands that I be fit for whatever may come, and so I shall try to sleep—to rest, at any rate.

Rupert's Journal.—*Continued*

July 4, 1907

I was up with the first ray of sunrise, so by the time I had my bath and was dressed there was ample light. I went down to the dock at once, and spent the morning looking over the vessel, which fully justifies Rooke's enthusiasm about her. She is built on lovely lines, and I can quite understand that she is enormously fast. Her armour I can only take on the specifications, but her armament is really wonderful. And there are not only all the very newest devices of aggressive warfare—indeed, she has the newest up-to-date torpedoes and torpedo-guns—but also the old-fashioned rocket-tubes, which in certain occasions are so useful. She has electric guns and the latest Massillon water-guns, and Reinhardt electro-pneumatic "deliverers" for pyroxiline shells. She is even equipped with war-balloons easy of expansion, and with compressible Kitson aeroplanes. I don't suppose that there is anything quite like her in the world.

The crew are worthy of her. I can't imagine where Rooke picked up such a splendid lot of men. They are nearly all man-of-warsmen; of various nationalities, but mostly British. All young men—the oldest of them hasn't got into the forties—and, so far as I can learn, all experts of one kind or another in some special subject of warfare. It will go hard with me, but I shall keep them together.

How I got through the rest of the day I know not. I tried hard not to create any domestic trouble by my manner, lest Aunt Janet should, after her lurid dream or vision of last night, attach some new importance to it. I think I succeeded, for she did not, so far as I could tell, take any special notice of me. We parted as usual at half-past ten, and I came here and made this entry in my journal. I am more restless than ever to-night, and no wonder. I would give anything to be able to pay a visit to St. Sava's, and see my wife again—if it were only sleeping in her tomb. But I dare not do even that, lest she should come to see me here, and I should miss her. So I have done what I can. The glass door to the Terrace is open, so that she can enter at once if she comes. The fire is lit, and the room is warm. There is food ready in case she should care for it. I have plenty of light in the room, so that through the aperture where I have not fully drawn the curtain there may be light to guide her.

Oh, how the time drags! The clock has struck midnight. One, two! Thank goodness, it will shortly be dawn, and the activity of the day may begin! Work may again prove, in a way, to be an anodyne. In the meantime I must write on, lest despair overwhelm me.

Once during the night I thought I heard a footstep outside. I rushed to the window and looked out, but there was nothing to see, no sound to hear. That was a little after one o'clock. I feared to go outside, lest that should alarm her; so I came back to my table. I could not write, but I sat as if writing for a while. But I could not stand it, so rose and walked about the room. As I walked I felt that my Lady—it gives me a pang every time I remember that I do not know even her name—was not quite so far away from me. It made my heart beat to think that it might mean that she was coming to me. Could not I as well as Aunt Janet have a little Second Sight! I went towards the window, and, standing behind the curtain, listened. Far away I thought I heard a cry, and ran out on the Terrace; but there was no sound to be heard, and no sign of any living thing anywhere; so I took it for granted that it was the cry of some night bird, and came back to my room, and wrote at my journal till I was calm. I think my nerves must be getting out of order, when every sound of the night seems to have a special meaning for me.

RUPERT'S JOURNAL—*Continued*

July 7, 1907

When the grey of the morning came, I gave up hope of my wife appearing, and made up my mind that, so soon as I could get away without exciting Aunt Janet's attention, I would go to St. Sava's. I always eat a good breakfast, and did I forgo it altogether, it would be sure to excite her curiosity—a thing I do not wish at present. As there was still time to wait, I lay down on my bed as I was, and—such is the way of Fate— shortly fell asleep.

I was awakened by a terrific clattering at my door. When I opened it I found a little group of servants, very apologetic at awaking me without instructions. The chief of them explained that a young priest had come from the Vladika with a message so urgent that he insisted on seeing me immediately at all hazards. I came out at once, and found him in the hall of the Castle, standing before the great fire, which was always lit in the early morning. He had a letter in his hand, but before giving it to me he said:

"I am sent by the Vladika, who pressed on me that I was not to lose a single instant in seeing you; that time is of golden price—nay, beyond price. This letter, amongst other things, vouches for me. A terrible misfortune has occurred. The daughter of our leader has disappeared during last night—the same, he commanded me to remind you, that he spoke of at the meeting when he would not let the mountaineers fire their guns. No sign of her can be found, and it is believed that she has been carried off by the emissaries of the Sultan of Turkey, who once before brought our nations to the verge of war by demanding her as a wife. I was also to say that the Vladika Plamenac would have come himself, but that it was necessary that he should at once consult with the Archbishop, Stevan Palealogue, as to what step is best to take in this dire calamity. He has sent out a search-party under the Archimandrite of Spazac, Petrof Vlastimir, who is to come on here with any news he can get, as you have command of the signalling, and can best spread the news. He knows that you, Gospodar, are in your great heart one of our compatriots, and that you have already proved your friendship by many efforts to strengthen our hands for war. And as a great compatriot, he calls on you to aid us in our need." He then handed me the letter, and stood by respectfully whilst I broke the seal and read it. It was written in great haste, and signed by the Vladika.

"Come with us now in our nation's peril. Help us to rescue what we most adore, and henceforth we shall hold you in our hearts. You shall learn how the men of the Blue Mountains can love faith and valour. Come!"

This was a task indeed—a duty worthy of any man. It thrilled me to the core to know that the men of the Blue Mountains had called on me in their dire need. It woke all the fighting instinct of my Viking forbears, and I vowed in my heart that they should be satisfied with my work. I called to me the corps of signallers who were in the house, and led them to the Castle roof, taking with me the young messenger-priest.

"Come with me," I said to him, "and see how I answer the Vladika's command."

The National flag was run up—the established signal that the nation was in need. Instantly on every summit near and far was seen the flutter of an answering flag. Quickly followed the signal that commanded the call to arms.

One by one I gave the signallers orders in quick succession, for the plan of search unfolded itself to me as I went on. The arms of the semaphore whirled in a way that made the young priest stare. One by one, as they took their orders, the signallers seemed to catch fire. Instinctively they understood the plan, and worked like demigods. They knew that so widespread a movement had its best chance in rapidity and in unity of action.

From the forest which lay in sight of the Castle came a wild cheering, which seemed to interpret the former stillness of the hills. It was good to feel that those who saw the signals—types of many—were ready. I saw the look of expectation on the face of the messenger-priest, and rejoiced at the glow that came as I turned to him to speak. Of course, he wanted to know something of what was going on. I saw the flashing of my own eyes reflected in his as I spoke:

"Tell the Vladika that within a minute of his message being read the Land of the Blue Mountains was awake. The mountaineers are already marching, and before the sun is high there will be a line of guards within hail of each other round the whole frontier—from Angusa to Ilsin; from Ilsin to Bajana; from Bajana to Ispazar; from Ispazar to Volok; from Volok to Tatra; from Tatra to Domitan; from Domitan to Gravaja; and from Gravaja back to Angusa. The line is double. The old men keep guard on the line, and the young men advance. These will close in at the advancing line, so that nothing can escape them. They will cover mountain-top and forest depth, and will close in finally on the Castle here, which they can behold from afar. My own yacht is here, and will sweep the coast from end to end. It is the fastest boat afloat, and armed against a squadron. Here will all signals come. In an hour where we stand will be a signal bureau, where trained eyes will watch night and day till the lost one has been found and the outrage has been avenged. The robbers are even now within a ring of steel, and cannot escape."

The young priest, all on fire, sprang on the battlements and shouted to the crowd, which was massing round the Castle in the gardens far below. The forest was giving up its units till they seemed like the nucleus of an army. The men cheered lustily, till the sound swung high up to us like the roaring of a winter sea. With bared heads they were crying:

"God and the Blue Mountains! God and the Blue Mountains!"

I ran down to them as quickly as I could, and began to issue their instructions. Within a time to be computed by minutes the whole number, organized by sections, had started to scour the neighbouring mountains. At first they had only understood the call to arms for general safety. But when they learned that the daughter of a chief had been captured, they simply went mad. From something which the messenger first said, but which I could not catch or did not understand, the blow seemed to have for them some sort of personal significance which wrought them to a frenzy.

When the bulk of the men had disappeared, I took with me a few of my own men and several of the mountaineers whom I had asked to remain, and together we went to the hidden ravine which I knew. We found the place empty; but there were unmistakable signs that a party of men had been encamped there for several days. Some of our men, who were skilled in woodcraft and in signs generally, agreed that there must have been some twenty of them. As they could not find any trail either coming to or going from the place, they came to the conclusion that they must have come separately from different directions and gathered there, and that they must have departed in something of the same mysterious way.

However, this was, at any rate, some sort of a beginning, and the men separated, having agreed amongst themselves to make a wide cast round the place in the search for tracks. Whoever should find a trail was to follow with at least one comrade, and when there was any definite news, it was to be signalled to the Castle.

I myself returned at once, and set the signallers to work to spread amongst our own people such news as we had.

When presently such discoveries as had been made were signalled with flags to the Castle, it was found that the marauders had, in their flight, followed a strangely zigzag course. It was evident that, in trying to baffle pursuit, they had tried to avoid places which they thought might be dangerous to them. This may have been simply a method to disconcert pursuit. If so, it was, in a measure, excellent, for none of those immediately following could possibly tell in what direction they were heading. It was only when we worked the course on the great map in the signaller's room (which was the old guard room of the Castle) that we could get an inkling of the general direction of their flight. This gave added trouble to the pursuit; for the men who followed, being ignorant of their general intent, could not ever take chance to head them off, but had to be ready to follow in any or every direction. In this manner the pursuit was altogether a stern chase, and therefore bound to be a long one.

As at present we could not do anything till the intended route was more marked, I left the signalling corps to the task of receiving and giving information to the moving bands, so that, if occasion served, they might head off the marauders. I myself took Rooke, as captain of the yacht, and swept out of the creek. We ran up north to Dalairi, then down south to Olesso, and came back to Vissarion. We saw nothing suspicious except, far off to the extreme southward, one warship which flew no flag. Rooke, however, who seemed to know ships by instinct, said she was a Turk; so on our return we signalled along the whole shore to watch her. Rooke held The Lady—which was the name I had given the armoured yacht—in readiness to dart out in case anything suspicious was reported. He was not to stand on any ceremony, but if necessary to attack. We did not intend to lose a point in this desperate struggle which we had undertaken. We had placed in different likely spots a couple of our own men to look after the signalling.

When I got back I found that the route of the fugitives, who had now joined into one party, had been definitely ascertained. They had gone south, but manifestly taking alarm from the advancing line of guards, had headed up again to the north-east, where the country was broader and the mountains wilder and less inhabited.

Forthwith, leaving the signalling altogether in the hands of the fighting priests, I took a small chosen band of the mountaineers of our own district, and made, with all the speed we could, to cut across the track of the fugitives a little ahead of them. The Archimandrite (Abbot) of Spazac, who had just arrived, came with us. He is a splendid man—a real fighter as well as a holy cleric, as good with his handjar as with his Bible, and a runner to beat the band. The marauders were going at a fearful pace, considering that they were all afoot; so we had to go fast also! Amongst these mountains there is no other means of progressing. Our own men were so aflame with ardour that I could not but notice that they, more than any of the others whom I had seen, had some special cause for concern.

When I mentioned it to the Archimandrite, who moved by my side, he answered:

"All natural enough; they are not only fighting for their country, but for their own!" I did not quite understand his answer, and so began to ask him some questions, to the effect that I soon began to understand a good deal more than he did.

Letter from Archbishop Stevan Palealogue, Head of the Eastern Church of the Blue Mountains, to the Lady Janet MacKelpie, Vissarion.

Written July 9, 1907

Honoured Lady,

As you wish for an understanding regarding the late lamentable occurrence in which so much danger was incurred to this our Land of the Blue Mountains, and one dear to us, I send these words by request of the Gospodar Rupert, beloved of our mountaineers.

When the Voivode Peter Vissarion made his journey to the great nation to whom we looked in our hour of need, it was necessary that he should go in secret. The Turk was at our gates, and full of the malice of baffled greed. Already he had tried to arrange a marriage with the Voivodin, so that in time to come he, as her husband, might have established a claim to the inheritance of the land. Well he knew, as do all men, that the Blue Mountaineers owe allegiance to none that they themselves do not appoint to rulership. This has been the history in the past. But now and again an individual has arisen or come to the front adapted personally for such government as this land requires. And so the Lady Teuta, Voivodin of the Blue Mountains, was put for her proper guarding in the charge of myself as Head of the Eastern Church in the Land of the Blue Mountains, steps being taken in such wise that no capture of her could be effected by unscrupulous enemies of this our Land. This task and guardianship was gladly held as an honour by all concerned. For the Voivodin Teuta of Vissarion must be taken as representing in her own person the glory of the old Serb race, inasmuch as being the only child of the Voivode Vissarion, last male of his princely race—the race which ever, during the ten centuries of our history, unflinchingly gave life and all they held for the protection, safety, and well-being of the Land of the Blue Mountains. Never during those centuries had any one of the race been known to fail in patriotism, or to draw back from any loss or hardship enjoined by high duty or stress of need. Moreover, this was the race of that first Voivode Vissarion, of whom, in legend, it was prophesied that he—once known as "The Sword of Freedom," a giant amongst men—would some day, when the nation had need of him, come forth from his water-tomb in the lost Lake of Reo, and lead once more the men of the Blue Mountains to lasting victory. This noble race, then, had come to be known as the last hope of the Land. So that when the Voivode was away on his country's service, his daughter should be closely guarded. Soon after the Voivode had gone, it was reported that he might be long delayed in his diplomacies, and also in studying the system of Constitutional Monarchy, for which it had been hoped to exchange our imperfect political system. I may say *inter alia* that he was mentioned as to be the first king when the new constitution should have been arranged.

Then a great misfortune came on us; a terrible grief overshadowed the land. After a short illness, the Voivodin Teuta Vissarion died mysteriously of a mysterious ailment. The grief of the mountaineers was so great that it became necessary for the governing Council to warn them not to allow their sorrow to be seen. It was imperatively necessary that the fact of her death should be kept secret. For there were dangers and difficulties of several kinds. In the first place it was advisable that even her father should be kept in ignorance of his terrible loss. It was well known that he held her as the very core of his heart and that if he should hear of her death, he would be too much prostrated to be able to do the intricate and delicate work which he had undertaken. Nay, more: he would never remain afar off, under the sad circumstances, but would straightway return, so as to be in the land where she lay. Then suspicions would crop up, and the truth must shortly be known afield, with the inevitable result that the Land would become the very centre of a war of many nations.

In the second place, if the Turks were to know that the race of Vissarion was becoming extinct, this would encourage them to further aggression, which would become immediate should they find out that the Voivode was himself away. It was well known that they were already only suspending hostilities until a fitting opportunity should arise. Their desire for aggression had become acute after the refusal of the nation, and of the girl herself, that she should become a wife of the Sultan.

The dead girl had been buried in the Crypt of the church of St. Sava, and day after day and night after night, singly and in parties, the sorrowing mountaineers had come to pay devotion and reverence at her tomb. So many had wished to have a last glimpse of her face that the Vladika had, with my own consent as Archbishop, arranged for a glass cover to be put over the stone coffin wherein her body lay.

After a little time, however, there came a belief to all concerned in the guarding of the body—these, of course, being the priests of various degrees of dignity appointed to the task—that the Voivodin was not really dead, but only in a strangely-prolonged trance. Thereupon a new complication arose. Our mountaineers are, as perhaps you know, by nature deeply suspicious—a characteristic of all brave and self-sacrificing people who are jealous of their noble heritage. Having, as they believed, seen the girl dead, they might not be willing to accept the fact of her being alive. They might even imagine that there was on foot some deep, dark plot which was, or might be, a menace, now or hereafter, to their independence. In any case, there would be certain to be two parties on the subject, a dangerous and deplorable thing in the present condition of affairs.

As the trance, or catalepsy, whatever it was, continued for many days, there had been ample time for the leaders of the Council, the Vladika, the priesthood represented by the Archimandrite of Spazac, myself as Archbishop and guardian of the Voivodin in her father's absence, to consult as to a policy to be observed in case of the girl awaking. For in such case the difficulty of the situation would be multiplied indefinitely. In the secret chambers of St. Sava's we had many secret meetings, and were finally converging on agreement when the end of the trance came.

The girl awoke!

She was, of course, terribly frightened when she found herself in a tomb in the Crypt. It was truly fortunate that the great candles around her tomb had been kept lighted, for their light mitigated the horror of the place. Had she waked in darkness, her reason might have become unseated.

She was, however, a very noble girl; brave, with extraordinary will, and resolution, and self-command, and power of endurance. When she had been taken into one of the secret chambers of the church, where she was warmed and cared for, a hurried meeting was held by the Vladika, myself, and the chiefs of the National Council. Word had been at once sent to me of the joyful news of her recovery; and with the utmost haste I came, arriving in time to take a part in the Council.

At the meeting the Voivodin was herself present, and full confidence of the situation was made to her. She herself proposed that the belief in her death should be allowed to prevail until the return of her father, when all could be effectively made clear. To this end she undertook to submit to the terrific strain which such a proceeding would involve. At first we men could not believe that any woman could go through with such a task, and some of us did not hesitate to voice our doubts—our disbelief. But she stood to her guns, and actually down-faced us. At the last we, remembering things that had been done, though long ages ago, by others of her race, came to believe not merely in her self-belief and intention, but even in the feasibility of her plan. She took the most solemn oaths not to betray the secret under any possible stress.

The priesthood undertook through the Vladika and myself to further a ghostly belief amongst the mountaineers which would tend to prevent a too close or too persistent observation. The Vampire legend was spread as a protection against partial discovery by any mischance, and other weird beliefs were set afoot and fostered. Arrangements were made that only on certain days were the mountaineers to be admitted to the Crypt, she agreeing that for these occasions she was to take opiates or carry out any other aid to the preservation of the secret. She was willing, she impressed upon us, to make any personal sacrifice which might be deemed necessary for the carrying out her father's task for the good of the nation.

Of course, she had at first terrible frights lying alone in the horror of the Crypt. But after a time the terrors of the situation, if they did not cease, were mitigated. There are secret caverns off the Crypt, wherein in troublous times the priests and others of high place have found safe retreat. One of these was prepared for the Voivodin, and there she remained, except for such times as she was on show—and certain other times of which I shall tell you. Provision was made for the possibility of any accidental visit to the church. At such times, warned by an automatic signal from the opening door, she was to take her place in the tomb. The mechanism was so arranged that the means to replace the glass cover, and to take the opiate, were there ready to her hand. There was to be always a watch of priests at night in the church, to guard her from ghostly fears as well as from more physical dangers; and if she was actually in her tomb, it was to be visited at certain intervals. Even the draperies which covered her in the sarcophagus were rested on a bridge placed from side to side just above her, so as to hide the rising and falling of her bosom as she slept under the narcotic.

After a while the prolonged strain began to tell so much on her that it was decided that she should take now and again exercise out of doors. This was not difficult, for when the Vampire story which we had spread began to be widely known, her being seen would be accepted as a proof of its truth. Still, as there was a certain danger in her being seen at all, we thought it necessary to exact from her a solemn oath that so long as her sad task lasted she should under no circumstances ever wear any dress but her shroud—this being the only way to insure secrecy and to prevail against accident.

There is a secret way from the Crypt to a sea cavern, whose entrance is at high-tide under the water-line at the base of the cliff on which the church is built. A boat, shaped like a coffin, was provided for her; and in this she was accustomed to pass across the creek whenever she wished to make excursion. It was an excellent device, and most efficacious in disseminating the Vampire belief.

This state of things had now lasted from before the time when the Gospodar Rupert came to Vissarion up to the day of the arrival of the armoured yacht.

That night the priest on duty, on going his round of the Crypt just before dawn, found the tomb empty. He called the others, and they made full search. The boat was gone from the cavern, but on making search they found it on the farther side of the creek, close to the garden stairs. Beyond this they could discover nothing. She seemed to have disappeared without leaving a trace.

Straightway they went to the Vladika, and signalled to me by the fire-signal at the monastery at Astrag, where I then was. I took a band of mountaineers with me, and set out to scour the country. But before going I sent an urgent message to the Gospodar Rupert, asking him, who showed so much interest and love to our Land, to help us in our trouble. He, of course, knew nothing then of all have now told you. Nevertheless, he devoted himself whole-heartedly to our needs—as doubtless you know.

But the time had now come close when the Voivode Vissarion was about to return from his mission; and we of the council of his daughter's guardianship were beginning to arrange matters so that at his return the good news of her being still alive could be made public. With her father present to vouch for her, no question as to truth could arise.

But by some means the Turkish "Bureau of Spies" must have got knowledge of the fact already. To steal a dead body for the purpose of later establishing a fictitious claim would have been an enterprise even more desperate than that already undertaken. We inferred from many signs, made known to us in an investigation, that a daring party of the Sultan's emissaries had made a secret incursion with the object of kidnapping the Voivodin. They must have been bold of heart and strong of resource to enter the Land of the Blue Mountains on any errand, let alone such a desperate one as this. For centuries we have been teaching the Turk through bitter lessons that it is neither a safe task nor an easy one to make incursion here.

How they did it we know not—at present; but enter they did, and, after waiting in some secret hiding-place for a favourable opportunity, secured their prey. We know not even now whether they had found entrance to the Crypt and stole, as they thought, the dead body, or whether, by some dire mischance, they found her abroad—under her disguise as a ghost. At any rate, they had captured her, and through devious ways amongst the mountains were bearing her back to Turkey. It was manifest that when she was on Turkish soil the Sultan would force a marriage on her so as eventually to secure for himself or his successors as against all other nations a claim for the suzerainty or guardianship of the Blue Mountains.

Such was the state of affairs when the Gospodar Rupert threw himself into the pursuit with fiery zeal and the Berserk passion which he inherited from Viking ancestors, whence of old came "The Sword of Freedom" himself.

But at that very time was another possibility which the Gospodar was himself the first to realize. Failing the getting the Voivodin safe to Turkish soil, the ravishers might kill her! This would be entirely in accord with the base traditions and history of the Moslems. So, too, it would accord with Turkish customs and the Sultan's present desires. It would, in its way, benefit the ultimate strategetic ends of Turkey. For were once the Vissarion race at an end, the subjection of the Land of the Blue Mountains might, in their view, be an easier task than it had yet been found to be.

Such, illustrious lady, were the conditions of affairs when the Gospodar Rupert first drew his handjar for the Blue Mountains and what it held most dear.

PALEALOGUE,
Archbishop of the Eastern Church,
in the Land of the Blue Mountains

RUPERT'S JOURNAL—*Continued*

July 8, 1907

I wonder if ever in the long, strange history of the world had there come to any other such glad tidings as came to me—and even then rather inferentially than directly—from the Archimandrite's answers to my questioning. Happily I was able to restrain myself, or I should have created some strange confusion which might have evoked distrust, and would certainly have hampered us in our pursuit. For a little I could hardly accept the truth which wove itself through my brain as the true inwardness of each fact came home to me and took its place in the whole fabric. But even the most welcome truth has to be accepted some time by even a doubting heart. My heart, whatever it may have been, was not then a doubting heart, but a very, very grateful one. It was only the splendid magnitude of the truth which forbade its immediate acceptance. I could have shouted for joy, and only stilled myself by keeping my thoughts fixed on the danger which my wife was in. My wife! My wife! Not a Vampire; not a poor harassed creature doomed to terrible woe, but a splendid woman, brave beyond belief, patriotic in a way which has but few peers even in the wide history of bravery! I began to understand the true meaning of the strange occurrences that have come into my life. Even the origin and purpose of that first strange visit to my room became clear. No wonder that the girl could move about the Castle in so mysterious a manner. She had lived there all her life, and was familiar with the secret ways of entrance and exit. I had always believed that the place must have been honeycombed with secret passages. No wonder that she could find a way to the battlements, mysterious to everybody else. No wonder that she could meet me at the Flagstaff when she so desired.

To say that I was in a tumult would be to but faintly express my condition. I was rapt into a heaven of delight which had no measure in all my adventurous life—the lifting of the veil which showed that my wife—mine—won in all sincerity in the very teeth of appalling difficulties and dangers—was no Vampire, no corpse, no ghost or phantom, but a real woman of flesh and blood, of affection, and love, and passion. Now at last would my love be crowned indeed when, having rescued her from the marauders, I should bear her to my own home, where she would live and reign in peace and comfort and honour, and in love and wifely happiness if I could achieve such a blessing for her—and for myself.

But here a dreadful thought flashed across me, which in an instant turned my joy to despair, my throbbing heart to ice:

"As she is a real woman, she is in greater danger than ever in the hands of Turkish ruffians. To them a woman is in any case no more than a sheep; and if they cannot bring her to the harem of the Sultan, they may deem it the next wisest step to kill her. In that way, too, they might find a better chance of escape. Once rid of her the party could separate, and there might be a chance of some of them finding escape as individuals that would not exist for a party. But even if they did not kill her, to escape with her would be to condemn her to the worst fate of all the harem of the Turk! Lifelong misery and despair—however long that life might be—must be the lot of a Christian woman doomed to such a lot. And to her, just happily wedded, and after she had served her country in such a noble way as she had done, that dreadful life of shameful slavery would be a misery beyond belief.

"She must be rescued—and quickly! The marauders must be caught soon, and suddenly, so that they may have neither time nor opportunity to harm her, as they would be certain to do if they have warning of immediate danger.

"On! on!"

And "on" it was all through that terrible night as well as we could through the forest.

It was a race between the mountaineers and myself as to who should be first. I understood now the feeling that animated them, and which singled them out even from amongst their fiery comrades, when the danger of the Voivodin became known. These men were no mean contestants even in such a race, and, strong as I am, it took my utmost effort to keep ahead of them. They were keen as leopards, and as swift. Their lives had been spent among the mountains, and their hearts and souls on were in the chase. I doubt not that if the death of any one of us could have through any means effected my wife's release, we should, if necessary, have fought amongst ourselves for the honour.

From the nature of the work before us our party had to keep to the top of the hills. We had not only to keep observation on the flying party whom we followed, and to prevent them making discovery of us, but we had to be always in a position to receive and answer signals made to us from the Castle, or sent to us from other eminences.

Letter from Petrof Vlastimir, Archimandrite of Spazac, to the Lady Janet MacKelpie, of Vissarion.

Written July 8, 1907

Great Lady,

I am asked to write by the Vladika, and have permission of the Archbishop. I have the honour of transmitting to you the record of the pursuit of the Turkish spies who carried off the Voivodin Teuta, of the noble House of Vissarion. The pursuit was undertaken by the Gospodar Rupert, who asked that I would come with his party, since what he was so good as to call my "great knowledge of the country and its people" might serve much. It is true that I have had much knowledge of the Land of the Blue Mountains and its people, amongst which and whom my whole life has been passed. But in such a cause no reason was required. There was not a man in the Blue Mountains who would not have given his life for the Voivodin Teuta, and when they heard that she had not been dead, as they thought, but only in a trance, and that it was she whom the marauders had carried off, they were in a frenzy. So why should I—to whom has been given the great trust of the Monastery of Spazac—hesitate at such a time? For myself, I wanted to hurry on, and to come at once to the fight with my country's foes; and well I knew that the Gospodar Rupert, with a lion's heart meet for his giant body, would press on with a matchless speed. We of the Blue Mountains do not lag when our foes are in front of us; most of all do we of the Eastern Church press on when the Crescent wars against the Cross!

We took with us no gear or hamper of any kind; no coverings except what we stood in; no food—nothing but our handjars and our rifles, with a sufficiency of ammunition. Before starting, the Gospodar gave hurried orders by signal from the Castle to have food and ammunition sent to us (as we might signal) by the nearest hamlet.

It was high noon when we started, only ten strong—for our leader would take none but approved runners who could shoot straight and use the handjar as it should be used. So as we went light, we expected to go fast. By this time we knew from the reports signalled to Vissarion that the enemies were chosen men of no despicable prowess.

The Keeper of the Green Flag of Islam is well served, and as though the Turk is an infidel and a dog, he is sometimes brave and strong. Indeed, except when he passes the confines of the Blue Mountains, he has been known to do stirring deeds. But as none who have dared to wander in amongst our hills ever return to their own land, we may not know of how they speak at home of their battles here. Still, these men were evidently not to be despised; and our Gospodar, who is a wise man as well as a valiant, warned us to be prudent, and not to despise our foes over much. We did as he counselled, and in proof we only took ten men, as we had only twenty against us. But then there was at stake much beyond life, and we took no risks. So, as the great clock at Vissarion clanged of noon, the eight fastest runners of the Blue Mountains, together with the Gospodar Rupert and myself, swept out on our journey. It had been signalled to us that the course which the marauders had as yet taken in their flight was a zigzag one, running eccentrically at all sorts of angles in all sorts of directions. But our leader had marked out a course where we might intercept our foes across the main line of their flight; and till we had reached that region we paused not a second, but went as fast as we could all night long. Indeed, it was amongst us a race as was the Olympic race of old Greece, each one vying with his fellows, though not in jealous emulation, but in high spirit, to best serve his country and the Voivodin Teuta. Foremost amongst us went the Gospodar, bearing himself as a Paladin of old, his mighty form pausing for no obstacle. Perpetually did he urge us on. He would not stop or pause for a moment, but often as he and I ran together—for, lady, in my youth I was the fleetest of all in the race, and even that now can head a battalion when duty calls—he would ask me certain questions as to the Lady Teuta and of the strange manner of her reputed death, as it was gradually unfolded in my answers to his questioning. And as each new phase of knowledge came to him, he would rush on as one possessed of fiends: whereat our mountaineers, who seem to respect even fiends for their thoroughness, would strive to keep pace with him till they too seemed worked into diabolic possession. And I myself, left alone in the calmness of sacerdotal office, forgot even that. With surging ears and eyes that saw blood, I rushed along with best of them.

Then truly the spirit of a great captain showed itself in the Gospodar, for when others were charged with fury he began to force himself into calm, so that out of his present self-command and the memory of his exalted position came a worthy strategy and thought for every contingency that might arise. So that when some new direction was required for our guidance, there was no hesitation in its coming. We, nine men of varying kinds, all felt that we had a master; and so, being willing to limit ourselves to strict obedience, we were free to use such thoughts as well as such powers as we had to the best advantage of the doing.

We came across the trail of the flying marauders on the second morning after the abduction, a little before noon. It was easy enough to see, for by this time the miscreants were all together, and our people, who were woodlanders, were able to tell much of the party that passed. These were evidently in a terrified hurry, for they had taken no precautions such as are necessary baffle pursuit, and all of which take time. Our foresters said that two went ahead and two behind. In the centre went the mass, moving close together, as though surrounding their prisoner. We caught not even a single glimpse her—could not have, they encompassed her so closely. But our foresters saw other than the mass; the ground that had been passed was before them. They knew that the prisoner had gone unwillingly—nay, more: one of them said as he rose from his knees, where he had been examining of the ground:

"The misbegotten dogs have been urging her on with their yataghans! There are drops of blood, though there are no blood-marks on her feet."

Whereupon the Gospodar flamed with passion. His teeth ground together, and with a deep-breathed "On, on!" he sprang off again, handjar in hand, on the track.

Before long we saw the party in the distance. They this were far below us in a deep valley, although the track of their going passed away to the right hand. They were making for the base of the great cliff, which rose before us all. Their reason was twofold, as we soon knew. Far off down the valley which they were crossing we saw signs of persons coming in haste, who must be of the search party coming from the north. Though the trees hid them, we could not mistake the signs. I was myself forester enough to have no doubt. Again, it was evident that the young Voivodin could travel no longer at the dreadful pace at which they had been going. Those blood-marks told their own tale! They meant to make a last stand here in case they should be discovered.

Then it was that he, who amongst us all had been most fierce and most bent on rapid pursuit, became the most the calm. Raising his hand for silence—though, God knows, we were and had been silent enough during that long rush through the forest—he said, in a low, keen whisper which cut the silence like a knife:

"My friends, the time is come for action. God be thanked, who has now brought us face to face with our foes! But we must be careful here—not on our own account, for we wish nothing more than to rush on and conquer or die—but for the sake of her whom you love, and whom I, too, love. She is in danger from anything which may give warning to those fiends. If they know or even suspect for an instant that we are near, they will murder her. . ."

Here his voice broke for an instant with the extremity of his passion or the depth of his feeling—I hardly know which; I think both acted on him.

"We know from those blood-marks what they can do— even to her." His teeth ground together again, but he went on without stopping further:

"Let us arrange the battle. Though we are but little distance from them as the crow flies, the way is far to travel. There is, I can see, but one path down to the valley from this side. That they have gone by, and that they will sure to guard—to watch, at any rate. Let us divide, as to surround them. The cliff towards which they make runs far to the left without a break. That to the right we cannot see from this spot; but from the nature of the ground it is not unlikely that it turns round in this direction, making the hither end of the valley like a vast pocket or amphitheatre. As they have studied the ground in other places, they may have done so in this, and have come hither as to a known refuge. Let one man, a marksman, stay here."

As he spoke a man stepped to the front. He was, I knew, an excellent shot.

"Let two others go to the left and try to find a way down the cliff before us. When they have descended to the level of the valley—path or no path—let them advance cautiously and secretly, keeping their guns in readiness. But they must not fire till need. Remember, my brothers," said, turning to those who stepped out a pace or two to the left, "that the first shot gives the warning which will be the signal for the

Voivodin's death. These men will not hesitate. You must judge yourselves of the time to shoot. The others of us will move to the right and try to find a path on that side. If the valley be indeed a pocket between the cliffs, we must find a way down that is not a path!"

As he spoke thus there was a blaze in his eyes that betokened no good to aught that might stand in his way. I ran by his side as we moved to the right.

It was as he surmised about the cliff. When we got a little on our way we saw how the rocky formation trended to our right, till, finally, with a wide curve, it came round to the other side.

It was a fearful valley that, with its narrow girth and its towering walls that seemed to topple over. On the farther side from us the great trees that clothed the slope of the mountain over it grew down to the very edge of the rock, so that their spreading branches hung far over the chasm. And, so far as we could understand, the same condition existed on our own side. Below us the valley was dark even in the daylight. We could best tell the movement of the flying marauders by the flashes of the white shroud of their captive in the midst of them.

From where we were grouped, amid the great tree-trunks on the very brow of the cliff, we could, when our eyes were accustomed to the shadow, see them quite well. In great haste, and half dragging, half carrying the Voivodin, they crossed the open space and took refuge in a little grassy alcove surrounded, save for its tortuous entrance, by undergrowth. From the valley level it was manifestly impossible to see them, though we from our altitude could see over the stunted undergrowth. When within the glade, they took their hands from her. She, shuddering instinctively, withdrew to a remote corner of the dell.

And then, oh, shame on their manhood!—Turks and heathens though they were—we could see that they had submitted her to the indignity of gagging her and binding her hands!

Our Voivodin Teuta bound! To one and all of us it was like lashing us across the face. I heard the Gospodar's teeth grind again. But once more he schooled himself to calmness ere he said:

"It is, perhaps, as well, great though the indignity be. They are seeking their own doom, which is coming quickly. . . Moreover, they are thwarting their own base plans. Now that she is bound they will trust to their binding, so that they will delay their murderous alternative to the very last moment. Such is our chance of rescuing her alive!"

For a few moments he stood as still as a stone, as though revolving something in his mind whilst he watched. I could see that some grim resolution was forming in his mind, for his eyes ranged to the top of the trees above cliff, and down again, very slowly this time, as though measuring and studying the detail of what was in front of him. Then he spoke:

"They are in hopes that the other pursuing party may not come across them. To know that, they are waiting. If those others do not come up the valley, they will proceed on their way. They will return up the path the way they came. There we can wait them, charge into the middle of them when she is opposite, and cut down those around her. Then the others will open fire, and we shall be rid of them!

Whilst he was speaking, two of the men of our party, who I knew to be good sharpshooters, and who had just before lain on their faces and had steadied their rifles to shoot, rose to their feet.

"Command us, Gospodar!" they said simply, as they stood to attention. "Shall we go to the head of the ravine road and there take hiding?" He thought for perhaps a minute, whilst we all stood as silent as images. I could hear our hearts beating. Then he said:

"No, not yet. There is time for that yet. They will not— cannot stir or make plans in any way till they know whether the other party is coming towards them or not. From our height here we can see what course the others are taking long before those villains do. Then we can make our plans and be ready in time."

We waited many minutes, but could see no further signs the other pursuing party. These had evidently adopted greater caution in their movements as they came closer to where they expected to find the enemy. The marauders began to grow anxious. Even at our distance we could gather as much from their attitude and movements.

Presently, when the suspense of their ignorance grew too much for them, they drew to the entrance of the glade, which was the farthest place to which, without exposing themselves to anyone who might come to the valley, they could withdraw from their captive. Here they consulted together. We could follow from their gestures what they were saying, for as they did not wish their prisoner to hear, their gesticulation was enlightening to us as to each other. Our people, like all mountaineers, have good eyes, and the Gospodar is himself an eagle in this as in other ways. Three men stood back from the rest. They stacked their rifles so that they could seize them easily. Then they drew their scimitars, and stood ready, as though on guard.

These were evidently the appointed murderers. Well they knew their work; for though they stood in a desert place with none within long distance except the pursuing party, of whose approach they would have good notice, they stood so close to their prisoner that no marksman in the world—now or that ever had been; not William Tell himself—could have harmed any of them without at least endangering her. Two of them turned the Voivodin round so that her face was towards the precipice—in which position she could not see what was going on—whilst he who was evidently leader of the gang explained, in gesture, that the others were going to spy upon the pursuing party. When they had located them he, or one of his men, would come out of the opening of the wood wherein they had had evidence of them, and hold up his hand.

That was to be the signal for the cutting of the victim's throat—such being the chosen method (villainous even for heathen murderers) of her death. There was not one of our men who did not grind his teeth when we witnessed the grim action, only too expressive, of the Turk as he drew his right hand, clenched as though he held a yataghan in it, across his throat.

At the opening of the glade all the spying party halted whilst the leader appointed to each his place of entry of the wood, the front of which extended in an almost straight across the valley from cliff to cliff.

The men, stooping low when in the open, and taking instant advantage of every little obstacle on the ground, seemed to fade like spectres with incredible swiftness across the level mead, and were swallowed up in the wood.

When they had disappeared the Gospodar Rupert revealed to us the details of the plan of action which he had revolving in his mind. He motioned us to follow him: we threaded a way between the tree-trunks, keeping all the while on the very edge of the cliff, so that the space below was all visible to us. When we had got round the curve sufficiently to see the whole of the wood on the valley level, without losing sight of the Voivodin and her appointed assassins, we halted under his direction. There was an added advantage of this point over the other, for we could see directly the rising of the hill-road, up which farther side ran the continuation of the mountain path which the marauders had followed. It was somewhere on that path that the other pursuing party had hoped to intercept the fugitives. The Gospodar spoke quickly, though in a voice of command which true soldiers love to hear:

"Brothers, the time has come when we can strike a blow for Teuta and the Land. Do you two, marksmen, take position here facing the wood." The two men here lay down and got their rifles ready. "Divide the frontage of the wood between you; arrange between yourselves the limits of your positions. The very instant one of the marauders appears, cover him; drop him before he emerges from the wood. Even then still watch and treat similarly whoever else may take his place. Do this if they come singly till not a man is left. Remember, brothers, that brave hearts alone will not suffice at this grim crisis. In this hour the best safety of the Voivodin is in the calm spirit and the steady eye!" Then he turned to the rest of us, and spoke to me:

"Archimandrite of Plazac, you who are interpreter to God of the prayers of so many souls, my own hour has come. If I do not return, convey my love to my Aunt Janet—Miss MacKelpie, at Vissarion. There is but one thing left to us if we wish to save the Voivodin. Do you, when the time comes, take these men and join the watcher at the top of the ravine road. When the shots are fired, do you out handjar, and rush the ravine and across the valley. Brothers, you may be in time to avenge the Voivodin, if you cannot save her. For me there must be a quicker way, and to it I go. As there is not, and will not be, time to traverse the path, I must take a quicker way. Nature finds me a path that man has made it necessary for me to travel. See that giant beech-tree that towers above the glade where the Voivodin is held? There is my path! When you from here have marked the return of the spies, give me a signal with your hat—do not use a handkerchief, as others might see its white, and take warning. Then rush that ravine. I shall take that as the signal for my descent by the leafy road. If I can do naught else, I can crush the murderers with my falling weight, even if I have to kill her too. At least we shall die together—and free. Lay us together in the tomb at St. Sava's. Farewell, if it be the last!"

He threw down the scabbard in which he carried his handjar, adjusted the naked weapon in his belt behind his back, and was gone!

We who were not watching the wood kept our eyes fixed on the great beech-tree, and with new interest noticed the long trailing branches which hung low, and swayed even in the gentle breeze. For a few minutes, which seemed amazingly long, we saw no sign of him. Then, high up on one of the great branches which stood clear of obscuring leaves, we saw something crawling flat against the bark. He was well out on the branch, hanging far over the precipice. He was looking over at us, and I waved my hand so that he should know we saw him. He was clad in green—his usual forest dress—so that there was not any likelihood of any other eyes noticing him. I took off my hat, and held it ready to signal with when the time should come. I glanced down at the glade and saw the Voivodin standing, still safe, with her guards so close to her as to touch. Then I, too, fixed my eyes on the wood.

Suddenly the man standing beside me seized my arm and pointed. I could just see through the trees, which were lower than elsewhere in the front of the wood, a Turk moving stealthily; so I waved my hat. At the same time a rifle underneath me cracked. A second or two later the spy pitched forward on his face and lay still. At the same instant my eyes sought the beech-tree, and I saw the close-lying figure raise itself and slide forward to a joint of the branch. Then the Gospodar, as he rose, hurled himself forward amid the mass of the trailing branches. He dropped like a stone, and my heart sank.

But an instant later he seemed in poise. He had clutched the thin, trailing branches as he fell; and as he sank a number of leaves which his motion had torn off floated out round him.

Again the rifle below me cracked, and then again, and again, and again. The marauders had taken warning, and were coming out in mass. But my own eyes were fixed on the tree. Almost as a thunderbolt falls fell the giant body of the Gospodar, his size lost in the immensity of his surroundings. He fell in a series of jerks, as he kept clutching the trailing beech-branches whilst they lasted, and then other lesser verdure growing out from the fissures in the rock after the lengthening branches had with all their elasticity reached their last point.

At length—for though this all took place in a very few seconds the gravity of the crisis prolonged them immeasurably—there came a large space of rock some three times his own length. He did not pause, but swung himself to one side, so that he should fall close to the Voivodin and her guards. These men did not seem to notice, for their attention was fixed on the wood whence they expected their messenger to signal. But they raised their yataghans in readiness. The shots had alarmed them; and they meant to do the murder now—messenger or no messenger

But though the men did not see the danger from above, the Voivodin did. She raised her eyes quickly at the first sound, and even from where we were, before we began to run towards the ravine path, I could see the triumphant look in her glorious eyes when she recognized the identity of the man who was seemingly coming straight down from Heaven itself to help her—as, indeed, she, and we too, can very well imagine that he did; for if ever heaven had a hand in a rescue on earth, it was now.

Even during the last drop from the rocky foliage the Gospodar kept his head. As he fell he pulled his handjar free, and almost as he was falling its sweep took off the head of one of the assassins. As he touched ground he stumbled for an instant, but it was towards his enemies. Twice with lightning rapidity the handjar swept the air, and at each sweep a head rolled on the sward.

The Voivodin held up her tied hands. Again the handjar flashed, this time downwards, and the lady was free. Without an instant's pause the Gospodar tore off the gag, and with his left arm round her and handjar in right hand, stood face toward his living foes. The Voivodin stooped suddenly, and then, raising the yataghan which had fallen from the hand of one of the dead marauders, stood armed beside him.

The rifles were now cracking fast, as the marauders— those that were left of them—came rushing out into the open. But well the marksmen knew their work. Well they bore in mind the Gospodar's command regarding calmness. They kept picking off the foremost men only, so that the onward rush never seemed to get more forward.

As we rushed down the ravine we could see clearly all before us. But now, just as we were beginning to fear lest some mischance might allow some of them to reach the glade, there was another cause of surprise—of rejoicing.

From the face of the wood seemed to burst all at once a body of men, all wearing the national cap, so we knew them as our own. They were all armed with the handjar only, and they came like tigers. They swept on the rushing Turks as though, for all their swiftness, they were standing still— literally wiping them out as a child wipes a lesson from its slate.

A few seconds later these were followed by a tall figure with long hair and beard of black mingled with grey. Instinctively we all, as did those in the valley, shouted with joy. For this was the Vladika Milosh Plamenac himself.

I confess that, knowing what I knew, I was for a short space of time anxious lest, in the terrific excitement in which we were all lapped, someone might say or do something which might make for trouble later on. The Gospodar's splendid achievement, which was worthy of any hero of old romance, had set us all on fire. He himself must have been wrought to a high pitch of excitement to dare such an act; and it is not at such a time that discretion must be expected from any man. Most of all did I fear danger from the womanhood of the Voivodin. Had I not assisted at her marriage, I might not have understood then what it must have been to her to be saved from such a doom at such a time by such a man, who was so much to her, and in such a way. It would have been only natural if at such a moment of gratitude and triumph she had proclaimed the secret which we of the Council of the Nation and her father's Commissioners had so religiously kept. But none of us knew then either the Voivodin or the Gospodar Rupert as we do now. It was well that they were as they are, for the jealousy and suspicion of our mountaineers might, even at such a moment, and even whilst they throbbed at such a deed, have so manifested themselves as to have left a legacy of distrust. The Vladika and I, who of all (save the two immediately concerned) alone knew, looked at each other apprehensively. But at that instant the Voivodin, with a swift glance at her husband, laid a finger on her lip; and he, with quick understanding, gave assurance by a similar sign. Then she sank before him on one knee, and, raising his hand to her lips, kissed it, and spoke:

"Gospodar Rupert, I owe you all that a woman may owe, except to God. You have given me life and honour! I cannot thank you adequately for what you have done; my father will try to do so when he returns. But I am right sure that the men of the Blue Mountains, who so value honour, and freedom, and liberty, and bravery, will hold you in their hearts for ever!"

This was so sweetly spoken, with lips that trembled and eyes that swam in tears, so truly womanly and so in accord with the custom of our nation regarding the reverence that women owe to men, that the hearts of our mountaineers were touched to the quick. Their noble simplicity found expression in tears. But if the gallant Gospodar could have for a moment thought that so to weep was unmanly, his error would have had instant correction. When the Voivodin had risen to her feet, which she did with queenly dignity, the men around closed in on the Gospodar like a wave of the sea, and in a second held him above their heads, tossing on their lifted hands as if on stormy breakers. It was as though the old Vikings of whom we have heard, and whose blood flows in Rupert's veins, were choosing a chief in old fashion. I was myself glad that the men were so taken up with the Gospodar that they did not see the glory of the moment in the Voivodin's starry eyes; for else they might have guessed the secret. I knew from the Vladika's look that he shared my own satisfaction, even as he had shared my anxiety.

As the Gospodar Rupert was tossed high on the lifted hands of the mountaineers, their shouts rose to such a sudden volume that around us, as far as I could see, the frightened birds rose from the forest, and their noisy alarm swelled the tumult.

The Gospodar, ever thoughtful for others, was the first to calm himself.

"Come, brothers," he said, "let us gain the hilltop, where we can signal to the Castle. It is right that the whole nation should share in the glad tidings that the Voivodin Teuta of Vissarion is free. But before we go, let us remove the arms and clothing of these carrion marauders. We may have use for them later on."

The mountaineers set him down, gently enough. And he, taking the Voivodin by the hand, and calling the Vladika and myself close to them, led the way up the ravine path which the marauders had descended, and thence through the forest to the top of the hill that dominated the valley. Here we could, from an opening amongst the trees, catch a glimpse far off of the battlements of Vissarion. Forthwith the Gospodar signalled; and on the moment a reply of their awaiting was given. Then the Gospodar signalled the glad news. It was received with manifest rejoicing. We could not hear any sound so far away, but we could see the movement of lifted faces and waving hands, and knew that it was well. But an instant after came a calm so dread that we knew before the semaphore had begun to work that there was bad news in store for us. When the news did come, a bitter wailing arose amongst us; for the news that was signalled ran:

"The Voivode has been captured by the Turks on his return, and is held by them at Ilsin."

In an instant the temper of the mountaineers changed. It was as though by a flash summer had changed to winter, as though the yellow glory of the standing corn had been obliterated by the dreary waste of snow. Nay, more: it was as when one beholds the track of the whirlwind when the giants of the forest are levelled with the sward. For a few seconds there was silence; and then, with an angry roar, as when God speaks in the thunder, came the fierce determination of the men of the Blue Mountains:

"To Ilsin! To Ilsin!" and a stampede in the direction of the south began. For, Illustrious Lady, you, perhaps, who have been for so short a time at Vissarion, may not know that at the extreme southern point of the Land of the Blue Mountains lies the little port of Ilsin, which long ago we wrested from the Turk.

The stampede was checked by the command, "Halt!" spoken in a thunderous voice by the Gospodar. Instinctively all stopped. The Gospodar Rupert spoke again:

"Had we not better know a little more before we start on our journey? I shall get by semaphore what details are known. Do you all proceed in silence and as swiftly as possible. The Vladika and I will wait here till we have received the news and have sent some instructions, when we shall follow, and, if we can, overtake you. One thing: be absolutely silent on what has been. Be secret of every detail—even as to the rescue of the Voivodin—except what I send."

Without a word—thus showing immeasurable trust—the whole body—not a very large one, it is true—moved on, and the Gospodar began signalling. As I was myself expert in the code, I did not require any explanation, but followed question and answer on either side. The first words the Gospodar Rupert signalled were:

"Silence, absolute and profound, as to everything which has been." Then he asked for details of the capture of the Voivode. The answer ran:

"He was followed from Flushing, and his enemies advised by the spies all along the route. At Ragusa quite a number of strangers—travellers seemingly—went on board the packet. When he got out, the strangers debarked too, and evidently followed him, though, as yet, we have no details. He disappeared at Ilsin from the Hotel Reo, whither he had gone. All possible steps are being taken to trace his movements, and strictest silence and secrecy are observed."

His answer was:

"Good! Keep silent and secret. Am hurrying back. Signal request to Archbishop and all members of National Council to come to Gadaar with all speed. There the yacht will meet him. Tell Rooke take yacht all speed to Gadaar; there meet Archbishop and Council—give him list of names—and return full speed. Have ready plenty arms, six flying artillery. Two hundred men, provisions three days. Silence, silence. All depends on that. All to go on as usual at Castle, except to those in secret."

When the receipt of his message had been signalled, we three—for, of course, the Voivodin was with us; she had refused to leave the Gospodar—set out hot-foot after our comrades. But by the time we had descended the hill it was evident that the Voivodin could not keep up the terrific pace at which we were going. She struggled heroically, but the long journey she had already taken, and the hardship and anxiety she had suffered, had told on her. The Gospodar stopped, and said that it would be better that he should press on—it was, perhaps, her father's life—and said he would carry her.

"No, no!" she answered. "Go on! I shall follow with the Vladika. And then you can have things ready to get on soon after the Archbishop and Council arrive." They kissed each other after, on her part, a shy glance at me; and he went on the track of our comrades at a great pace. I could see him shortly after catch them up,—though they, too, were going fast. For a few minutes they ran together, he speaking—I could note it from the way they kept turning their heads towards him. Then he broke away from them hurriedly. He went like a stag breaking covert, and was soon out of sight. They halted a moment or two. Then some few ran on, and all the rest came back towards us. Quickly they improvised a litter with cords and branches, and insisted that the Voivodin should use it. In an incredibly short time we were under way again, and proceeding with great rapidity towards Vissarion. The men took it in turns to help with the litter; I had the honour of taking a hand in the work myself.

About a third of the way out from Vissarion a number of our people met us. They were fresh, and as they carried the litter, we who were relieved were free for speed. So we soon arrived at the Castle.

Here we found all humming like a hive of bees. The yacht, which Captain Rooke had kept fired ever since the pursuing party under the Gospodar had left Vissarion, was already away, and tearing up the coast at a fearful rate. The rifles and ammunition were stacked on the quay. The field-guns, too, were equipped, and the cases of ammunition ready to ship. The men, two hundred of them, were paraded in full kit, ready to start at a moment's notice. The provision for three days was all ready to put aboard, and barrels of fresh water to trundle aboard when the yacht should return. At one end of the quay, ready to lift on board, stood also the Gospodar's aeroplane, fully equipped, and ready, if need were, for immediate flight.

I was glad to see that the Voivodin seemed none the worse for her terrible experience. She still wore her shroud; but no one seemed to notice it as anything strange. The whisper had evidently gone round of what had been. But discretion ruled the day. She and the Gospodar met as two who had served and suffered in common; but I was glad to notice that both kept themselves under such control that none of those not already in the secret even suspected that there was any love between them, let alone marriage.

We all waited with what patience we could till word was signalled from the Castle tower that the yacht had appeared over the northern horizon, and was coming down fast, keeping inshore as she came.

When she arrived, we heard to our joy that all concerned had done their work well. The Archbishop was aboard, and of the National Council not one was missing. The Gospodar hurried them all into the great hall of the Castle, which had in the meantime been got ready. I, too, went with him, but the Voivodin remained without.

When all were seated, he rose and said:

"My Lord Archbishop, Vladika, and Lords of the Council all, I have dared to summon you in this way because time presses, and the life of one you all love—the Voivode Vissarion—is at stake. This audacious attempt of the Turk is the old aggression under a new form. It is a new and more daring step than ever to try to capture your chief and his daughter, the Voivodin, whom you love. Happily, the latter part of the scheme is frustrated. The Voivodin is safe and amongst us. But the Voivode is held prisoner—if, indeed, he be still alive. He must be somewhere near Ilsin—but where exactly we know not as yet. We have an expedition ready to start the moment we receive your sanction—your commands. We shall obey your wishes with our lives. But as the matter is instant, I would venture to ask one question, and one only: 'Shall we rescue the Voivode at any cost that may present itself?' I ask this, for the matter has now become an international one, and, if our enemies are as earnest as we are, the issue is war!"

Having so spoken, and with a dignity and force which is inexpressible, he withdrew; and the Council, having appointed a scribe—the monk Cristoferos, whom I had suggested—began its work.

The Archbishop spoke:

"Lords of the Council of the Blue Mountains, I venture to ask you that the answer to the Gospodar Rupert be an instant 'Yes!' together with thanks and honour to that gallant Englisher, who has made our cause his own, and who has so valiantly rescued our beloved Voivodin from the ruthless hands of our enemies." Forthwith the oldest member of the

Council—Nicolos of Volok—rose, and, after throwing a searching look round the faces of all, and seeing grave nods of assent—for not a word was spoken—said to him who held the door: "Summon the Gospodar Rupert forthwith!" When Rupert entered, he spoke to him:

"Gospodar Rupert, the Council of the Blue Mountains has only one answer to give: Proceed! Rescue the Voivode Vissarion, whatever the cost may be! You hold henceforth in your hand the handjar of our nation, as already, for what you have done in your valiant rescue of our beloved Voivodin, your breast holds the heart of our people. Proceed at once! We give you, I fear, little time; but we know that such is your own wish. Later, we shall issue formal authorization, so that if war may ensue, our allies may understand that you have acted for the nation, and also such letters credential as may be required by you in this exceptional service. These shall follow you within an hour. For our enemies we take no account. See, we draw the handjar that we offer you." As one man all in the hall drew their handjars, which flashed as a blaze of lightning.

There did not seem to be an instant's delay. The Council broke up, and its members, mingling with the people without, took active part in the preparations. Not many minutes had elapsed when the yacht, manned and armed and stored as arranged, was rushing out of the creek. On the bridge, beside Captain Rooke, stood the Gospodar Rupert and the still-shrouded form of the Voivodin Teuta. I myself was on the lower deck with the soldiers, explaining to certain of them the special duties which they might be called on to fulfil. I held the list which the Gospodar Rupert had prepared whilst we were waiting for the yacht to arrive from Gadaar.

PETROF VLASTIMIR

FROM RUPERT'S JOURNAL—*Continued*

July 9, 1907

We went at a terrific pace down the coast, keeping well inshore so as to avoid, if possible, being seen from the south. Just north of Ilsin a rocky headland juts out, and that was our cover. On the north of the peninsula is a small land-locked bay, with deep water. It is large enough to take the yacht, though a much larger vessel could not safely enter. We ran in, and anchored close to the shore, which has a rocky frontage—a natural shelf of rock, which is practically the same as a quay. Here we met the men who had come from Ilsin and the neighbourhood in answer to our signalling earlier in the day. They gave us the latest information regarding the kidnapping of the Voivode, and informed us that every man in that section of the country was simply aflame about it. They assured us that we could rely on them, not merely to fight to the death, but to keep silence absolutely. Whilst the seamen, under the direction of Rooke, took the aeroplane on shore and found a suitable place for it, where it was hidden from casual view, but from which it could be easily launched, the Vladika and I—and, of course, my wife—were hearing such details as were known of the disappearance of her father.

It seems that he travelled secretly in order to avoid just such a possibility as has happened. No one knew of his coming till he came to Fiume, whence he sent a guarded message to the Archbishop, which the latter alone would understand. But this Turkish agents were evidently on his track all the time, and doubtless the Bureau of Spies was kept well advised. He landed at Ilsin from a coasting steamer from Ragusa to the Levant.

For two days before his coming there had been quite an unusual number of arrivals at the little port, at which arrivals are rare. And it turned out that the little hotel—the only fairly good one in Ilsin—was almost filled up. Indeed, only one room was left, which the Voivode took for the night. The innkeeper did not know the Voivode in his disguise, but suspected who it was from the description. He dined quietly, and went to bed. His room was at the back, on the ground-floor, looking out on the bank of the little River Silva, which here runs into the harbour. No disturbance was heard in the night. Late in the morning, when the elderly stranger had not made his appearance, inquiry was made at his door. He did not answer, so presently the landlord forced the door, and found the room empty. His luggage was seemingly intact, only the clothes which he had worn were gone. A strange thing was that, though the bed had been slept in and his clothes were gone, his night-clothes were not to be found, from which it was argued by the local authorities, when they came to make inquiry, that he had gone or been taken from the room in his night-gear, and that his clothes had been taken with him. There was evidently some grim suspicion on the part of the authorities, for they had commanded absolute silence on all in the house. When they came to make inquiry as to the other guests, it was found that one and all had gone in the course of the morning, after paying their bills. None of them had any heavy luggage, and there was nothing remaining by which they might be traced or which would afford any clue to their identity. The authorities, having sent a confidential report to the seat of government, continued their inquiries, and even now all available hands were at work on the investigation. When I had signalled to Vissarion, before my arrival there, word had been sent through the priesthood to enlist in the investigation the services of all good men, so that every foot of ground in that section of the Blue Mountains was being investigated. The port-master was assured by his watchmen that no vessel, large or small, had heft the harbour during the night. The inference, therefore, was that the Voivode's captors had made inland with him—if, indeed, they were not already secreted in or near the town.

Whilst we were receiving the various reports, a hurried message came that it was now believed that the whole party were in the Silent Tower. This was a well-chosen place for such an enterprise. It was a massive tower of immense strength, built as a memorial—and also as a "keep"—after one of the massacres of the invading Turks.

It stood on the summit of a rocky knoll some ten miles inland from the Port of Ilsin. It was a place shunned as a rule, and the country all around it was so arid and desolate that there were no residents near it. As it was kept for state use, and might be serviceable in time of war, it was closed with massive iron doors, which were kept locked except upon certain occasions. The keys were at the seat of government at Plazac. If, therefore, it had been possible to the Turkish marauders to gain entrance and exit, it might be a difficult as well as a dangerous task to try to cut the Voivode out. His presence with them was a dangerous menace to any force attacking them, for they would hold his life as a threat.

I consulted with the Vladika at once as to what was best to be done. And we decided that, though we should put a cordon of guards around it at a safe distance to prevent them receiving warning, we should at present make no attack.

We made further inquiry as to whether there had been any vessel seen in the neighbourhood during the past few days, and were informed that once or twice a warship had been seen on the near side of the southern horizon. This was evidently the ship which Rooke had seen on his rush down the coast after the abduction of the Voivodin, and which he had identified as a Turkish vessel. The glimpses of her which had been had were all in full daylight—there was no proof that she had not stolen up during the night-time without lights. But the Vladika and I were satisfied that the Turkish vessel was watching—was in league with both parties of marauders—and was intended to take off any of the strangers, or their prey, who might reach Ilsin undetected. It was evidently with this view that the kidnappers of Teuta had, in the first instance, made with all speed for the south. It was only when disappointed there that they headed up north, seeking in desperation for some chance of crossing the border. That ring of steel had so far well served its purpose.

I sent for Rooke, and put the matter before him. He had thought it out for himself to the same end as we had. His deduction was:

"Let us keep the cordon, and watch for any signal from the Silent Tower. The Turks will tire before we shall. I undertake to watch the Turkish warship. During the night I shall run down south, without lights, and have a look at her, even if I have to wait till the grey of the dawn to do so. She may see us; but if she does I shall crawl away at such pace that she shall not get any idea of our speed. She will certainly come nearer before a day is over, for be sure the bureau of spies is kept advised, and they know that when the country is awake each day increases the hazard of them and their plans being discovered. From their caution I gather that they do not court discovery; and from that that they do not wish for an open declaration of war. If this be so, why should we not come out to them and force an issue if need be?"

When Teuta and I got a chance to be alone, we discussed the situation in every phase. The poor girl was in a dreadful state of anxiety regarding her father's safety. At first she was hardly able to speak, or even to think, coherently. Her utterance was choked, and her reasoning palsied with indignation. But presently the fighting blood of her race restored her faculties, and then her woman's quick wit was worth the reasoning of a camp full of men. Seeing that she was all on fire with the subject, I sat still and waited, taking care not to interrupt her. For quite a long time she sat still, whilst the coming night thickened. When she spoke, the whole plan of action, based on subtle thinking, had mapped itself out in her mind:

"We must act quickly. Every hour increases the risk to my father." Here her voice broke for an instant; but she recovered herself and went on:

"If you go to the ship, I must not go with you. It would not do for me to be seen. The Captain doubtless knows of both attempts: that to carry me off as well as that against my father. As yet he is in ignorance of what has happened. You and your party of brave, loyal men did their work so well that no news could go forth. So long, therefore, as the naval Captain is ignorant, he must delay till the last. But if he saw me he would know that *that* branch of the venture had miscarried. He would gather from our being here that we had news of my father's capture, and as he would know that the marauders would fail unless they were relieved by force, he would order the captive to be slain."

"Yes, dear, to-morrow you had, perhaps, better see the Captain, but to-night we must try to rescue my father. Here I think I see a way. You have your aeroplane. Please take me with you into the Silent Tower."

"Not for a world of chrysolite!" said I, horrified. She took my hand and held it tight whilst she went on:

"Dear, I know, I know! Be satisfied. But it is the only way. You can, I know, get there, and in the dark. But if you were to go in it, it would give warning to the enemies, and besides, my father would not understand. Remember, he does not know you; he has never seen you, and does not, I suppose, even know as yet of your existence. But he would know me at once, and in any dress. You can manage to lower me into the Tower by a rope from the aeroplane. The Turks as yet do not know of our pursuit, and doubtless rely, at all events in part, on the strength and security of the Tower. Therefore their guard will be less active than it would at first or later on. I shall post father in all details, and we shall be ready quickly. Now, dear, let us think out the scheme together. Let your man's wit and experience help my ignorance, and we shall save my father!"

How could I have resisted such pleading—even had it not seemed wise? But wise it was; and I, who knew what the aeroplane could do under my own guidance, saw at once the practicalities of the scheme. Of course there was a dreadful risk in case anything should go wrong. But we are at present living in a world of risks—and her father's life was at stake. So I took my dear wife in my arms, and told her that my mind was hers for this, as my soul and body already were. And I cheered her by saying that I thought it might be done.

I sent for Rooke, and told him of the new adventure, and he quite agreed with me in the wisdom of it. I then told him that he would have to go and interview the Captain of the Turkish warship in the morning, if I did not turn up. "I am going to see the Vladika," I said. "He will lead our own troops in the attack on the Silent Tower. But it will rest with you to deal with the warship. Ask the Captain to whom or what nation the ship belongs. He is sure to refuse to tell. In such case mention to him that if he flies no nation's flag, his vessel is a pirate ship, and that you, who are in command of the navy of the Blue Mountains, will deal with him as a pirate is dealt with—no quarter, no mercy. He will temporize, and perhaps try a bluff; but when things get serious with him he will land a force, or try to, and may even prepare to shell the town. He will threaten to, at any rate. In such case deal with him as you think best, or as near to it as you can." He answered:

"I shall carry out your wishes with my life. It is a righteous task. Not that anything of that sort would ever stand in my way. If he attacks our nation, either as a Turk or a pirate, I shall wipe him out. We shall see what our own little packet can do. Moreover, any of the marauders who have entered the Blue Mountains, from sea or otherwise, shall never get out by sea! I take it that we of my contingent shall cover the attacking party. It will be a sorry time for us all if that happens without our seeing you and the Voivodin; for in such case we shall understand the worst!" Iron as he was, the man trembled.

"That is so, Rooke," I said. "We are taking a desperate chance, we know. But the case is desperate! But we all have our duty to do, whatever happens. Ours and yours is stern; but when we have done it, the result will be that life will be easier for others—for those that are left."

Before he left, I asked him to send up to me three suits of the Masterman bullet-proof clothes of which we had a supply on the yacht.

"Two are for the Voivodin and myself," I said; "the third is for the Voivode to put on. The Voivodin will take it with her when she descends from the aeroplane into the Tower."

Whilst any daylight was left I went out to survey the ground. My wife wanted to come with me, but I would not let her. "No," said I; "you will have at the best a fearful tax on your strength and your nerves. You will want to be as fresh as is possible when you get on the aeroplane." Like a good wife, she obeyed, and lay down to rest in the little tent provided for her.

I took with me a local man who knew the ground, and who was trusted to be silent. We made a long detour when we had got as near the Silent Tower as we could without being noticed. I made notes from my compass as to directions, and took good notice of anything that could possibly serve as a landmark. By the time we got home I was pretty well satisfied that if all should go well I could easily sail over the Tower in the dark. Then I had a talk with my wife, and gave her full instructions:

"When we arrive over the Tower," I said, "I shall lower you with a long rope. You will have a parcel of food and spirit for your father in case he is fatigued or faint; and, of course, the bullet-proof suit, which he must put on at once. You will also have a short rope with a belt at either end—one for your father, the other for you. When I turn the aeroplane and come back again, you will have ready the ring which lies midway between the belts. This you will catch into the hook at the end of the lowered rope. When all is secure, and I have pulled you both up by the windlass so as to clear the top, I shall throw out ballast which we shall carry on purpose, and away we go! I am sorry it must be so uncomfortable for you both, but there is no other way. When we get well clear of the Tower, I shall take you both up on the platform. If necessary, I shall descend to do it—and then we shall steer for Ilsin."

"When all is safe, our men will attack the Tower. We must let them do it, for they expect it. A few men in the clothes and arms which we took from your captors will be pursued by some of ours. It is all arranged. They will ask the Turks to admit them, and if the latter have not learned of your father's escape, perhaps they will do so. Once in, our men will try to open the gate. The chances are against them, poor fellows! but they are all volunteers, and will die fighting. If they win out, great glory will be theirs."

"The moon does not rise to-night till just before midnight, so we have plenty of time. We shall start from here at ten. If all be well, I shall place you in the Tower with your father in less than a quarter-hour from that. A few minutes will suffice to clothe him in bullet-proof and get on his belt. I shall not be away from the Tower more than a very few minutes, and, please God, long before eleven we shall be safe. Then the Tower can be won in an attack by our mountaineers. Perhaps, when the guns are heard on the ship of war—for there is sure to be firing—the Captain may try to land a shore party. But Rooke will stand in the way, and if I know the man and *The Lady*, we shall not be troubled with many Turks to-night. By midnight you and your father can be on the way to Vissarion. I can interview the naval Captain in the morning."

My wife's marvellous courage and self-possession stood to her. At half an hour before the time fixed she was ready for our adventure. She had improved the scheme in one detail. She had put on her own belt and coiled the rope round her waist, so the only delay would be in bringing her father's belt. She would keep the bullet-proof dress intended to be his strapped in a packet on her back, so that if occasion should be favourable he would not want to put it on till he and she should have reached the platform of the aeroplane. In such case, I should not steer away from the Tower at all, but would pass slowly across it and take up the captive and his brave daughter before leaving. I had learned from local sources that the Tower was in several stories. Entrance was by the foot, where the great iron-clad door was; then came living-rooms and storage, and an open space at the top. This would probably be thought the best place for the prisoner, for it was deep-sunk within the massive walls, wherein was no loophole of any kind. This, if it should so happen, would be the disposition of things best for our plan. The guards would at this time be all inside the Tower—probably resting, most of them— so that it was possible that no one might notice the coming of the airship. I was afraid to think that all might turn out so well, for in such case our task would be a simple enough one, and would in all human probability be crowned with success.

At ten o'clock we started. Teuta did not show the smallest sign of fear or even uneasiness, though this was the first time she had even seen an aeroplane at work. She proved to be an admirable passenger for an airship. She stayed quite still, holding herself rigidly in the position arranged, by the cords which I had fixed for her.

When I had trued my course by the landmarks and with the compass lit by the Tiny my electric light in the dark box, I had time to look about me. All seemed quite dark wherever I looked—to land, or sea, or sky. But darkness is relative, and though each quarter and spot looked dark in turn, there was not such absolute darkness as a whole. I could tell the difference, for instance, between land and sea, no matter how far off we might be from either. Looking upward, the sky was dark; yet there was light enough to see, and even distinguish broad effects. I had no difficulty in distinguishing the Tower towards which we were moving, and that, after all, was the main thing. We drifted slowly, very slowly, as the air was still, and I only used the minimum pressure necessary for the engine. I think I now understood for the first time the extraordinary value of the engine with which my Kitson was equipped. It was noiseless, it was practically of no weight, and it allowed the machine to progress as easily as the old-fashioned balloon used to drift before a breeze. Teuta, who had naturally very fine sight, seemed to see even better than I did, for as we drew nearer to the Tower, and its round, open top began to articulate itself, she commenced to prepare for her part of the task. She it was who uncoiled the long drag-rope ready for her lowering. We were proceeding so gently that she as well as I had hopes that I might be able to actually balance the machine on the top of the curving wall—a thing manifestly impossible on a straight surface, though it might have been possible on an angle.

On we crept—on, and on! There was no sign of light about the Tower, and not the faintest sound to be heard till we were almost close to the line of the rising wall; then we heard a sound of something like mirth, but muffled by distance and thick walls. From it we took fresh heart, for it told us that our enemies were gathered in the lower chambers. If only the Voivode should be on the upper stage, all would be well.

Slowly, almost inch by inch, and with a suspense that was agonizing, we crossed some twenty or thirty feet above the top of the wall. I could see as we came near the jagged line of white patches where the heads of the massacred Turks placed there on spikes in old days seemed to give still their grim warning. Seeing that they made in themselves a difficulty of landing on the wall, I deflected the plane so that, as we crept over the wall, we might, if they became displaced, brush them to the outside of the wall. A few seconds more, and I was able to bring the machine to rest with the front of the platform jutting out beyond the Tower wall. Here I anchored her fore and aft with clamps which had been already prepared.

Whilst I was doing so Teuta had leaned over the inner edge of the platform, and whispered as softly as the sigh of a gentle breeze:

"Hist! hist!" The answer came in a similar sound from some twenty feet below us, and we knew that the prisoner was alone. Forthwith, having fixed the hook of the rope in the ring to which was attached her belt, I lowered my wife. Her father evidently knew her whisper, and was ready. The hollow Tower—a smooth cylinder within—sent up the voices from it faint as were the whispers:

"Father, it is I—Teuta!"

"My child, my brave daughter!"

"Quick, father; strap the belt round you. See that it is secure. We have to be lifted into the air if necessary. Hold together. It will be easier for Rupert to lift us to the airship."

"Rupert?"

"Yes; I shall explain later. Quick, quick! There is not a moment to lose. He is enormously strong, and can lift us together; but we must help him by being still, so he won't have to use the windlass, which might creak." As she spoke she jerked slightly at the rope, which was our preconcerted signal that I was to lift. I was afraid the windlass might creak, and her thoughtful hint decided me. I bent my back to the task, and in a few seconds they were on the platform on which they, at Teuta's suggestion, lay flat, one at each side of my seat, so as to keep the best balance possible.

I took off the clamps, lifted the bags of ballast to the top of the wall, so that there should be no sound of falling, and started the engine. The machine moved forward a few inches, so that it tilted towards the outside of the wall. I threw my weight on the front part of the platform, and we commenced our downward fall at a sharp angle. A second enlarged the angle, and without further ado we slid away into the darkness. Then, ascending as we went, when the engine began to work at its strength, we turned, and presently made straight for Ilsin.

The journey was short—not many minutes. It almost seemed as if no time whatever had elapsed till we saw below us the gleam of lights, and by them saw a great body of men gathered in military array. We slackened and descended. The crowd kept deathly silence, but when we were amongst them we needed no telling that it was not due to lack of heart or absence of joy. The pressure of their hands as they surrounded us, and the devotion with which they kissed the hands and feet of both the Voivode and his daughter, were evidence enough for me, even had I not had my own share of their grateful rejoicing.

In the midst of it all the low, stern voice of Rooke, who had burst a way to the front beside the Vladika, said:

"Now is the time to attack the Tower. Forward, brothers, but in silence. Let there not be a sound till you are near the gate; then play your little comedy of the escaping marauders. And 'twill be no comedy for them in the Tower. The yacht is all ready for the morning, Mr. Sent Leger, in case I do not come out of the scrimmage if the bluejackets arrive. In such case you will have to handle her yourself. God keep you, my Lady; and you, too, Voivode! Forward!"

In a ghostly silence the grim little army moved forwards. Rooke and the men with him disappeared into the darkness in the direction of the harbour of Ilsin.

July 7, 1907

I had little idea, when I started on my homeward journey, that it would have such a strange termination. Even I, who ever since my boyhood have lived in a whirl of adventure, intrigue, or diplomacy—whichever it may be called—statecraft, and war, had reason to be surprised. I certainly thought that when I locked myself into my room in the hotel at Ilsin that I would have at last a spell, however short, of quiet. All the time of my prolonged negotiations with the various nationalities I had to be at tension; so, too, on my homeward journey, lest something at the last moment should happen adversely to my mission. But when I was safe on my own Land of the Blue Mountains, and laid my head on my pillow, where only friends could be around me, I thought I might forget care.

But to wake with a rude hand over my mouth, and to feel myself grasped tight by so many hands that I could not move a limb, was a dreadful shock. All after that was like a dreadful dream. I was rolled in a great rug so tightly that I could hardly breathe, let alone cry out. Lifted by many hands through the window, which I could hear was softly opened and shut for the purpose, and carried to a boat. Again lifted into some sort of litter, on which I was borne a long distance, but with considerable rapidity. Again lifted out and dragged through a doorway opened on purpose—I could hear the clang as it was shut behind me. Then the rug was removed, and I found myself, still in my night-gear, in the midst of a ring of men. There were two score of them, all Turks, all strong-looking, resolute men, armed to the teeth. My clothes, which had been taken from my room, were thrown down beside me, and I was told to dress. As the Turks were going from the room—shaped like a vault—where we then were, the last of them, who seemed to be some sort of officer, said:

"If you cry out or make any noise whatever whilst you are in this Tower, you shall die before your time!" Presently some food and water were brought me, and a couple of blankets. I wrapped myself up and slept till early in the morning. Breakfast was brought, and the same men filed in. In the presence of them all the same officer said:

"I have given instructions that if you make any noise or betray your presence to anyone outside this Tower, the nearest man is to restore you to immediate quiet with his yataghan. It you promise me that you will remain quiet whilst you are within the Tower, I can enlarge your liberties somewhat. Do you promise?" I promised as he wished; there was no need to make necessary any stricter measure of confinement. Any chance of escape lay in having the utmost freedom allowed to me. Although I had been taken away with such secrecy, I knew that before long there would be pursuit. So I waited with what patience I could. I was allowed to go on the upper platform—a consideration due, I am convinced, to my captors' wish for their own comfort rather than for mine.

It was not very cheering, for during the daytime I had satisfied myself that it would be quite impossible for even a younger and more active man than I am to climb the walls. They were built for prison purposes, and a cat could not find entry for its claws between the stones. I resigned myself to my fate as well as I could. Wrapping my blanket round me, I lay down and looked up at the sky. I wished to see it whilst I could. I was just dropping to sleep—the unutterable silence of the place broken only now and again by some remark by my captors in the rooms below me—when there was a strange appearance just over me—an appearance so strange that I sat up, and gazed with distended eyes.

Across the top of the tower, some height above, drifted, slowly and silently, a great platform. Although the night was dark, it was so much darker where I was within the hollow of the Tower that I could actually see what was above me. I knew it was an aeroplane—one of which I had seen in Washington. A man was seated in the centre, steering; and beside him was a silent figure of a woman all wrapped in white. It made my heart beat to see her, for she was figured something like my Teuta, but broader, less shapely. She leaned over, and a whispered "Ssh!" crept down to me. I answered in similar way. Whereupon she rose, and the man lowered her down into the Tower. Then I saw that it was my dear daughter who had come in this wonderful way to save me. With infinite haste she helped me to fasten round my waist a belt attached to a rope, which was coiled round her; and then the man, who was a giant in strength as well as stature, raised us both to the platform of the aeroplane, which he set in motion without an instant's delay.

Within a few seconds, and without any discovery being made of my escape, we were speeding towards the sea. The lights of Ilsin were in front of us. Before reaching the town, however, we descended in the midst of a little army of my own people, who were gathered ready to advance upon the Silent Tower, there to effect, if necessary, my rescue by force. Small chance would there have been of my life in case of such a struggle. Happily, however, the devotion and courage of my dear daughter and of her gallant companion prevented such a necessity. It was strange to me to find such joyous reception amongst my friends expressed in such a whispered silence. There was no time for comment or understanding or the asking of questions—I was fain to take things as they stood, and wait for fuller explanation.

This came later, when my daughter and I were able to converse alone.

When the expedition went out against the Silent Tower, Teuta and I went to her tent, and with us came her gigantic companion, who seemed not wearied, but almost overcome with sleep. When we came into the tent, over which at a little distance a cordon of our mountaineers stood on guard, he said to me:

"May I ask you, sir, to pardon me for a time, and allow the Voivodin to explain matters to you? She will, I know, so far assist me, for there is so much work still to be done before we are free of the present peril. For myself, I am almost overcome with sleep. For three nights I have had no sleep, but all during that time much labour and more anxiety. I could hold on longer; but at daybreak I must go out to the Turkish warship that lies in the offing. She is a Turk, though she does not confess to it; and she it is who has brought hither the marauders who captured both your daughter and yourself. It is needful that I go, for I hold a personal authority from the National Council to take whatever step may be necessary for our protection. And when I go I should be clear-headed, for war may rest on that meeting. I shall be in the adjoining tent, and shall come at once if I am summoned, in case you wish for me before dawn." Here my daughter struck in:

"Father, ask him to remain here. We shall not disturb him, I am sure, in our talking. And, moreover, if you knew how much I owe to him—to his own bravery and his strength—you would understand how much safer I feel when he is close to me, though we are surrounded by an army of our brave mountaineers."

"But, my daughter," I said, for I was as yet all in ignorance, "there are confidences between father and daughter which none other may share. Some of what has been I know, but I want to know all, and it might be better that no stranger—however valiant he may be, or no matter in what measure we are bound to him—should be present." To my astonishment, she who had always been amenable to my lightest wish actually argued with me:

"Father, there are other confidences which have to be respected in like wise. Bear with me, dear, till I have told you all, and I am right sure that you will agree with me. I ask it, father."

That settled the matter, and as I could see that the gallant gentleman who had rescued me was swaying on his feet as he waited respectfully, I said to him:

"Rest with us, sir. We shall watch over your sleep."

Then I had to help him, for almost on the instant he sank down, and I had to guide him to the rugs spread on the ground. In a few seconds he was in a deep sleep. As I stood looking at him, till I had realized that he vas really asleep, I could not help marvelling at the bounty of Nature that could uphold even such a man as this to the last moment of work to be done, and then allow so swift a collapse when all was over, and he could rest peacefully.

He was certainly a splendid fellow. I think I never saw so fine a man physically in my life. And if the lesson of his physiognomy be true, he is as sterling inwardly as his external is fair. "Now," said I to Teuta, "we are to all intents quite alone. Tell me all that has been, so that I may understand."

Whereupon my daughter, making me sit down, knelt beside me, and told me from end to end the most marvellous story I had ever heard or read of. Something of it I had already known from the Archbishop Paleologue's later letters, but of all else I was ignorant. Far away in the great West beyond the Atlantic, and again on the fringe of the Eastern seas, I had been thrilled to my heart's core by the heroic devotion and fortitude of my daughter in yielding herself for her country's sake to that fearful ordeal of the Crypt; of the grief of the nation at her reported death, news of which was so mercifully and wisely withheld from me as long as possible; of the supernatural rumours that took root so deep; but no word or hint had come to me of a man who had come across the orbit of her life, much less of all that has resulted from it. Neither had I known of her being carried off, or of the thrice gallant rescue of her by Rupert. Little wonder that I thought so highly of him even at the first moment I had a clear view of him when he sank down to sleep before me. Why, the man must be a marvel. Even our mountaineers could not match such endurance as his. In the course of her narrative my daughter told me of how, being wearied with her long waiting in the tomb, and waking to find herself alone when the floods were out, and even the Crypt submerged, she sought safety and warmth elsewhere; and how she came to the Castle in the night, and found the strange man alone. I said: "That was dangerous, daughter, if not wrong. The man, brave and devoted as he is, must answer me—your father." At that she was greatly upset, and before going on with her narrative, drew me close in her arms, and whispered to me:

"Be gentle to me, father, for I have had much to bear. And be good to him, for he holds my heart in his breast!" I reassured her with a gentle pressure—there was no need to speak. She then went on to tell me about her marriage, and how her husband, who had fallen into the belief that she was a Vampire, had determined to give even his soul for her; and how she had on the night of the marriage left him and gone back to the tomb to play to the end the grim comedy which she had undertaken to perform till my return; and how, on the second night after her marriage, as she was in the garden of the Castle—going, as she shyly told me, to see if all was well with her husband—she was seized secretly, muffled up, bound, and carried off. Here she made a pause and a digression. Evidently some fear lest her husband and myself should quarrel assailed her, for she said:

"Do understand, father, that Rupert's marriage to me was in all ways regular, and quite in accord with our customs. Before we were married I told the Archbishop of my wish. He, as your representative during your absence, consented himself, and brought the matter to the notice of the Vladika and the Archimandrites. All these concurred, having exacted from me—very properly, I think—a sacred promise to adhere to my self-appointed task. The marriage itself was orthodox in all ways—though so far unusual that it was held at night, and in darkness, save for the lights appointed by the ritual. As to that, the Archbishop himself, or the Archimandrite of Spazac, who assisted him, or the Vladika, who acted as Paranymph, will, all or any of them, give you full details. Your representative made all inquiries as to Rupert Sent Leger, who lived in Vissarion, though he did not know who I was, or from his point of view who I had been. But I must tell you of my rescue."

And so she went on to tell me of that unavailing journey south by her captors; of their bafflement by the cordon which Rupert had established at the first word of danger to "the daughter of our leader," though he little knew who the "leader" was, or who was his "daughter"; of how the brutal marauders tortured her to speed with their daggers; and how her wounds left blood-marks on the ground as she passed along; then of the halt in the valley, when the marauders came to know that their road north was menaced, if not already blocked; of the choosing of the murderers, and their keeping ward over her whilst their companions went to survey the situation; and of her gallant rescue by that noble fellow, her husband—my son I shall call him henceforth, and thank God that I may have that happiness and that honour!

Then my daughter went on to tell me of the race back to Vissarion, when Rupert went ahead of all—as a leader should do; of the summoning of the Archbishop and the National Council; and of their placing the nation's handjar in Rupert's hand; of the journey to Ilsin, and the flight of my daughter—and my son—on the aeroplane.

The rest I knew.

As she finished, the sleeping man stirred and woke—broad awake in a second—sure sign of a man accustomed to campaign and adventure. At a glance he recalled everything that had been, and sprang to his feet. He stood respectfully before me for a few seconds before speaking. Then he said, with an open, engaging smile:

"I see, sir, you know all. Am I forgiven—for Teuta's sake as well as my own?" By this time I was also on my feet. A man like that walks straight into my heart. My daughter, too, had risen, and stood by my side. I put out my hand and grasped his, which seemed to leap to meet me—as only the hand of a swordsman can do.

"I am glad you are my son!" I said. It was all I could say, and I meant it and all it implied. We shook hands warmly. Teuta was pleased; she kissed me, and then stood holding my arm with one hand, whilst she linked her other hand in the arm of her husband.

He summoned one of the sentries without, and told him to ask Captain Rooke to come to him. The latter had been ready for a call, and came at once. When through the open flap of the tent we saw him coming, Rupert—as I must call him now, because Teuta wishes it; and I like to do it myself—said:

"I must be off to board the Turkish vessel before it comes inshore. Good-bye, sir, in case we do not meet again." He said the last few words in so low a voice that I only could hear them. Then he kissed his wife, and told her he expected to be back in time for breakfast, and was gone. He met Rooke—I am hardly accustomed to call him Captain as yet, though, indeed, he well deserves it—at the edge of the cordon of sentries, and they went quickly together towards the port, where the yacht was lying with steam up.

Book VII

The Empire of the Air

From the Report of Cristoferos, War-Scribe to the National Council

July 7, 1907

When the Gospodar Rupert and Captain Rooke came within hailing distance of the strange ship, the former hailed her, using one after another the languages of England, Germany, France, Russia, Turkey, Greece, Spain, Portugal, and another which I did not know; I think it must have been American. By this time the whole line of the bulwark was covered by a row of Turkish faces. When, in Turkish, the Gospodar asked for the Captain, the latter came to the gangway, which had been opened, and stood there. His uniform was that of the Turkish navy—of that I am prepared to swear—but he made signs of not understanding what had been said; whereupon the Gospodar spoke again, but in French this time. I append the exact conversation which took place, none other joining in it. I took down in shorthand the words of both as they were spoken:

THE GOSPODAR: "Are you the Captain of this ship?"

THE CAPTAIN: "I am."

GOSPODAR: "To what nationality do you belong?"

CAPTAIN: "It matters not. I am Captain of this ship."

GOSPODAR: "I alluded to your ship. What national flag is she under?"

CAPTAIN (*throwing his eye over the top-hamper*): "I do not see that any flag is flying."

GOSPODAR: "I take it that, as commander, you can allow me on board with my two companions?"

CAPTAIN: "I can, upon proper request being made!"

GOSPODAR (*taking off his cap*): "I ask your courtesy, Captain. I am the representative and accredited officer of the National Council of the Land of the Blue Mountains, in whose waters you now are; and on their account I ask for a formal interview on urgent matters."

The Turk, who was, I am bound to say, in manner most courteous as yet, gave some command to his officers, whereupon the companion-ladders and stage were lowered and the gangway manned, as is usual for the reception on a ship of war of an honoured guest.

CAPTAIN: "You are welcome, sir—you and your two companions—
as you request."

The Gospodar bowed. Our companion-ladder was rigged on the instant, and a launch lowered. The Gospodar and Captain Rooke—taking me with them—entered, and rowed to the warship, where we were all honourably received. There were an immense number of men on board, soldiers as well as seamen. It looked more like a warlike expedition than a fighting-ship in time of peace. As we stepped on the deck, the seamen and marines, who were all armed as at drill, presented arms. The Gospodar went first towards the Captain, and Captain Rooke and I followed close behind him. The Gospodar spoke:

"I am Rupert Sent Leger, a subject of his Britannic Majesty, presently residing at Vissarion, in the Land of the Blue Mountains. I am at present empowered to act for the National Council in all matters. Here is my credential!" As he spoke he handed to the Captain a letter. It was written in five different languages—Balkan, Turkish, Greek, English, and French. The Captain read it carefully all through, forgetful for the moment that he had seemingly been unable to understand the Gospodar's question spoken in the Turkish tongue. Then he answered:

"I see the document is complete. May I ask on what subject you wish to see me?"

GOSPODAR: "You are here in a ship of war in Blue Mountain waters, yet you fly no flag of any nation. You have sent armed men ashore in your boats, thus committing an act of war. The National Council of the Land of the Blue Mountains requires to know what nation you serve, and why the obligations of international law are thus broken."

The Captain seemed to wait for further speech, but the Gospodar remained silent; whereupon the former spoke.

CAPTAIN: "I am responsible to my own—chiefs. I refuse to answer your question."

The Gospodar spoke at once in reply.

GOSPODAR: "Then, sir, you, as commander of a ship—and especially a ship of war—must know that in thus violating national and maritime laws you, and all on board this ship, are guilty of an act of piracy. This is not even piracy on the high seas. You are not merely within territorial waters, but you have invaded a national port. As you refuse to disclose the nationality of your ship, I accept, as you seem to do, your status as that of a pirate, and shall in due season act accordingly."

CAPTAIN (*with manifest hostility*): "I accept the responsibility of my own acts. Without admitting your contention, I tell you now that whatever action you take shall be at your own peril and that of your National Council. Moreover, I have reason to believe that my men who were sent ashore on special service have been beleaguered in a tower which can be seen from the ship. Before dawn this morning firing was heard from that direction, from which I gather that attack was made on them. They, being only a small party, may have been murdered. If such be so, I tell you that you and your miserable little nation, as you call it, shall pay such blood-money as you never thought of. I am responsible for this, and, by Allah! there shall be a great revenge. You have not in all your navy—if navy you have at all—power to cope with even one ship like this, which is but one of many. My guns shall be trained on Ilsin, to which end I have come inshore. You and your companions have free conduct back to port; such is due to the white flag which you fly. Fifteen minutes will bring you back whence you came. Go! And remember that whatever you may do amongst your mountain defiles, at sea you cannot even defend yourselves."

GOSPODAR (*slowly and in a ringing voice*): "The Land of the Blue Mountains has its own defences on sea and land. Its people know how to defend themselves."

CAPTAIN (*taking out his watch*): "It is now close on five bells. At the first stroke of six bells our guns shall open fire."

GOSPODAR (*calmly*): "It is my last duty to warn you, sir—and to warn all on this ship—that much may happen before even the first stroke of six bells. Be warned in time, and give over this piratical attack, the very threat of which may be the cause of much bloodshed."

CAPTAIN (*violently*): "Do you dare to threaten me, and, moreover, my ship's company? We are one, I tell you, in this ship; and the last man shall perish like the first ere this enterprise fail. Go!"

With a bow, the Gospodar turned and went down the ladder, we following him. In a couple of minutes the yacht was on her way to the port.

FROM RUPERT'S JOURNAL

July 10, 1907

When we turned shoreward after my stormy interview with the pirate Captain—I can call him nothing else at present, Rooke gave orders to a quartermaster on the bridge, and *The Lady* began to make to a little northward of Ilsin port. Rooke himself went aft to the wheel-house, taking several men with him.

When we were quite near the rocks—the water is so deep here that there is no danger—we slowed down, merely drifting along southwards towards the port. I was myself on the bridge, and could see all over the decks. I could also see preparations going on upon the warship. Ports were opened, and the great guns on the turrets were lowered for action. When we were starboard broadside on to the warship, I saw the port side of the steering-house open, and Rooke's men sliding out what looked like a huge grey crab, which by tackle from within the wheel-house was lowered softly into the sea. The position of the yacht hid the operation from sight of the warship. The doors were shut again, and the yacht's pace began to quicken. We ran into the port. I had a vague idea that Rooke had some desperate project on hand. Not for nothing had he kept the wheel-house locked on that mysterious crab.

All along the frontage was a great crowd of eager men. But they had considerately left the little mole at the southern entrance, whereon was a little tower, on whose round top a signal-gun was placed, free for my own use. When I was landed on this pier I went along to the end, and, climbing the narrow stair within, went out on the sloping roof. I stood up, for I was determined to show the Turks that I was not afraid for myself, as they would understand when the bombardment should begin. It was now but a very few minutes before the fatal hour—six bells. But all the same I was almost in a state of despair. It was terrible to think of all those poor souls in the town who had done nothing wrong, and who were to be wiped out in the coming blood-thirsty, wanton attack. I raised my glasses to see how preparations were going on upon the warship.

As I looked I had a momentary fear that my eyesight was giving way. At one moment I had the deck of the warship focussed with my glasses, and could see every detail as the gunners waited for the word to begin the bombardment with the great guns of the barbettes. The next I saw nothing but the empty sea. Then in another instant there was the ship as before, but the details were blurred. I steadied myself against the signal-gun, and looked again. Not more than two, or at the most three, seconds had elapsed. The ship was, for the moment, full in view. As I looked, she gave a queer kind of quick shiver, prow and stern, and then sideways. It was for all the world like a rat shaken in the mouth of a skilled terrier. Then she remained still, the one placid thing to be seen, for all around her the sea seemed to shiver in little independent eddies, as when water is broken without a current to guide it.

I continued to look, and when the deck was, or seemed, quite still—for the shivering water round the ship kept catching my eyes through the outer rays of the lenses—I noticed that nothing was stirring. The men who had been at the guns were all lying down; the men in the fighting-tops had leaned forward or backward, and their arms hung down helplessly. Everywhere was desolation—in so far as life was concerned. Even a little brown bear, which had been seated on the cannon which was being put into range position, had jumped or fallen on deck, and lay there stretched out—and still. It was evident that some terrible shock had been given to the mighty war-vessel. Without a doubt or a thought why I did so, I turned my eyes towards where *The Lady* lay, port broadside now to the inside, in the harbour mouth. I had the key now to the mystery of Rooke's proceedings with the great grey crab.

As I looked I saw just outside the harbour a thin line of cleaving water. This became more marked each instant, till a steel disc with glass eyes that shone in the light of the sun rose above the water. It was about the size of a beehive, and was shaped like one. It made a straight line for the aft of the yacht. At the same moment, in obedience to some command, given so quietly that I did not hear it, the men went below— all save some few, who began to open out doors in the port side of the wheel-house. The tackle was run out through an opened gangway on that side, and a man stood on the great hook at the lower end, balancing himself by hanging on the chain. In a few seconds he came up again. The chain tightened and the great grey crab rose over the edge of the deck, and was drawn into the wheel-house, the doors of which were closed, shutting in a few only of the men.

I waited, quite quiet. After a space of a few minutes, Captain Rooke in his uniform walked out of the wheel-house. He entered a small boat, which had been in the meantime lowered for the purpose, and was rowed to the steps on the mole. Ascending these, he came directly towards the signal-tower. When he had ascended and stood beside me, he saluted.

"Well?" I asked.

"All well, sir," he answered. "We shan't have any more trouble with that lot, I think. You warned that pirate—I wish he had been in truth a clean, honest, straightforward pirate, instead of the measly Turkish swab he was—that something might occur before the first stroke of six bells. Well, something has occurred, and for him and all his crew that six bells will never sound. So the Lord fights for the Cross against the Crescent! Bismillah. Amen!" He said this in a manifestly formal way, as though declaiming a ritual. The next instant he went on in the thoroughly practical conventional way which was usual to him:

"May I ask a favour, Mr. Sent Leger?"

"A thousand, my dear Rooke," I said. "You can't ask me anything which I shall not freely grant. And I speak within my brief from the National Council. You have saved Ilsin this day, and the Council will thank you for it in due time."

"Me, sir?" he said, with a look of surprise on his face which seemed quite genuine. "If you think that, I am well out of it. I was afraid, when I woke, that you might court-martial me!"

"Court-martial you! What for?" I asked, surprised in my turn.

"For going to sleep on duty, sir! And the fact is, I was worn out in the attack on the Silent Tower last night, and when you had your interview with the pirate—all good pirates forgive me for the blasphemy! Amen!—and I knew that everything was going smoothly, I went into the wheel-house and took forty winks." He said all this without moving so much as an eyelid, from which I gathered that he wished absolute silence to be observed on my part. Whilst I was revolving this in my mind he went on:

"Touching that request, sir. When I have left you and the Voivode—and the Voivodin, of course—at Vissarion, together with such others as you may choose to bring there with you, may I bring the yacht back here for a spell? I rather think that there is a good deal of cleaning up to be done, and the crew of *The Lady* with myself are the men to do it. We shall be back by nightfall at the creek."

"Do as you think best, Admiral Rooke," I said.

"Admiral?"

"Yes, Admiral. At present I can only say that tentatively, but by to-morrow I am sure the National Council will have confirmed it. I am afraid, old friend, that your squadron will be only your flagship for the present; but later we may do better."

"So long as I am Admiral, your honour, I shall have no other flagship than *The Lady*. I am not a young man, but, young or old, my pennon shall float over no other deck. Now, one other favour, Mr. Sent Leger? It is a corollary of the first, so I do not hesitate to ask. May I appoint Lieutenant Desmond, my present First Officer, to the command of the battleship? Of course, he will at first only command the prize crew; but in such case he will fairly expect the confirmation of his rank later. I had better, perhaps, tell you, sir, that he is a very capable seaman, learned in all the sciences that pertain to a battleship, and bred in the first navy in the world."

"By all means, Admiral. Your nomination shall, I think I may promise you, be confirmed."

Not another word we spoke. I returned with him in his boat to *The Lady*, which was brought to the dock wall, where we were received with tumultuous cheering.

I hurried off to my Wife and the Voivode. Rooke, calling Desmond to him, went on the bridge of *The Lady*, which turned, and went out at terrific speed to the battleship, which was already drifting up northward on the tide.

July 8, 1907

The meeting of the National Council, July 6, was but a continuation of that held before the rescue of the Voivodin Vissarion, the members of the Council having been during the intervening night housed in the Castle of Vissarion. When, in the early morning, they met, all were jubilant; for late at night the fire-signal had flamed up from Ilsin with the glad news that the Voivode Peter Vissarion was safe, having been rescued with great daring on an aeroplane by his daughter and the Gospodar Rupert, as the people call him—Mister Rupert Sent Leger, as he is in his British name and degree.

Whilst the Council was sitting, word came that a great peril to the town of Ilsin had been averted. A war-vessel acknowledging to no nationality, and therefore to be deemed a pirate, had threatened to bombard the town; but just before the time fixed for the fulfilment of her threat, she was shaken to such an extent by some sub-aqueous means that, though she herself was seemingly uninjured, nothing was left alive on board. Thus the Lord preserves His own! The consideration of this, as well as the other incident, was postponed until the coming Voivode and the Gospodar Rupert, together with who were already on their way hither.

THE SAME (LATER IN THE SAME DAY)

The Council resumed its sitting at four o'clock. The Voivode Peter Vissarion and the Voivodin Teuta had arrived with the "Gospodar Rupert," as the mountaineers call him (Mr. Rupert Sent Leger) on the armoured yacht he calls *The Lady*. The National Council showed great pleasure when the Voivode entered the hall in which the Council met. He seemed much gratified by the reception given to him. Mr. Rupert Sent Leger, by the express desire of the Council, was asked to be present at the meeting. He took a seat at the bottom of the hall, and seemed to prefer to remain there, though asked by the President of the Council to sit at the top of the table with himself and the Voivode.

When the formalities of such Councils had been completed, the Voivode handed to the President a memorandum of his report on his secret mission to foreign Courts on behalf of the National Council. He then explained at length, for the benefit of the various members of the Council, the broad results of his mission. The result was, he said, absolutely satisfactory. Everywhere he had been received with distinguished courtesy, and given a sympathetic hearing. Several of the Powers consulted had made delay in giving final answers, but this, he explained, was necessarily due to new considerations arising from the international complications which were universally dealt with throughout the world as "the Balkan Crisis." In time, however (the Voivode went on), these matters became so far declared as to allow the waiting Powers to form definite judgment—which, of course, they did not declare to him—as to their own ultimate action. The final result—if at this initial stage such tentative setting forth of their own attitude in each case can be so named—was that he returned full of hope (founded, he might say, upon a justifiable personal belief) that the Great Powers throughout the world—North, South, East, and West— were in thorough sympathy with the Land of the Blue Mountains in its aspirations for the continuance of its freedom. "I also am honoured," he continued, "to bring to you, the Great Council of the nation, the assurance of protection against unworthy aggression on the part of neighbouring nations of present greater strength."

Whilst he was speaking, the Gospodar Rupert was writing a few words on a strip of paper, which he sent up to the President. When the Voivode had finished speaking, there was a prolonged silence. The President rose, and in a hush said that the Council would like to hear Mr. Rupert Sent Leger, who had a communication to make regarding certain recent events.

Mr. Rupert Sent Leger rose, and reported how, since he had been entrusted by the Council with the rescue of the Voivode Peter of Vissarion, he had, by aid of the Voivodin, effected the escape of the Voivode from the Silent Tower; also that, following this happy event, the mountaineers, who had made a great cordon round the Tower so soon as it was known that the Voivode had been imprisoned within it, had stormed it in the night. As a determined resistance was offered by the marauders, who had used it as a place of refuge, none of these escaped. He then went on to tell how he sought interview with the Captain of the strange warship, which, without flying any flag, invaded our waters. He asked the President to call on me to read the report of that meeting. This, in obedience to his direction, I did. The acquiescent murmuring of the Council showed how thoroughly they endorsed Mr. Sent Leger's words and acts.

When I resumed my seat, Mr. Sent Leger described how, just before the time fixed by the "pirate Captain"—so he designated him, as did every speaker thereafter—the warship met with some under-sea accident, which had a destructive effect on all on board her. Then he added certain words, which I give verbatim, as I am sure that others will some time wish to remember them in their exactness:

"By the way, President and Lords of the Council, I trust I may ask you to confirm Captain Rooke, of the armoured yacht *The Lady*, to be Admiral of the Squadron of the Land of the Blue Mountains, and also Captain (tentatively) Desmond, late First-Lieutenant of *The Lady*, to the command of the second warship of our fleet—the as yet unnamed vessel, whose former Captain threatened to bombard Ilsin. My Lords, Admiral Rooke has done great service to the Land of the Blue Mountains, and deserves well at your hands. You will have in him, I am sure, a great official. One who will till his last breath give you good and loyal service."

He had sat down, the President put to the Council resolutions, which were passed by acclamation. Admiral Rooke was given command of the navy, and Captain Desmond confirmed in his appointment to the captaincy of the new ship, which was, by a further resolution, named *The Gospodar Rupert*.

In thanking the Council for acceding to his request, and for the great honour done him in the naming of the ship, Mr. Sent Leger said:

"May I ask that the armoured yacht *The Lady* be accepted by you, the National Council, on behalf of the nation, as a gift on behalf of the cause of freedom from the Voivodin Teuta?"

In response to the mighty cheer of the Council with which the splendid gift was accepted the Gospodar Rupert—Mr. Sent Leger— bowed, and went quietly out of the room.

As no agenda of the meeting had been prepared, there was for a time, not silence, but much individual conversation. In the midst of it the Voivode rose up, whereupon there was a strict silence. All listened with an intensity of eagerness whilst he spoke.

"President and Lords of the Council, Archbishop, and Vladika, I should but ill show my respect did I hesitate to tell you at this the first opportunity I have had of certain matters personal primarily to myself, but which, in the progress of recent events, have come to impinge on the affairs of the nation. Until I have done so, I shall not feel that I have done a duty, long due to you or your predecessors in office, and which I hope you will allow me to say that I have only kept back for purposes of statecraft. May I ask that you will come back with me in memory to the year 1890, when our struggle against Ottoman aggression, later on so successfully brought to a close, was begun. We were then in a desperate condition. Our finances had run so low that we could not purchase even the bread which we required. Nay, more, we could not procure through the National Exchequer what we wanted more than bread—arms of modern effectiveness; for men may endure hunger and yet fight well, as the glorious past of our country has proved again and again and again. But when our foes are better armed than we are, the penalty is dreadful to a nation small as our own is in number, no matter how brave their hearts. In this strait I myself had to secretly raise a sufficient sum of money to procure the weapons we needed. To this end I sought the assistance of a great merchant-prince, to whom our nation as well as myself was known. He met me in the same generous spirit which he had shown to other struggling nationalities throughout a long and honourable career. When I pledged to him as security my own estates, he wished to tear up the bond, and only under pressure would he meet my wishes in this respect. Lords of the Council, it was his money, thus generously advanced, which procured for us the arms with which we hewed out our freedom.

"Not long ago that noble merchant—and here I trust you will pardon me that I am so moved as to perhaps appear to suffer in want of respect to this great Council—this noble merchant passed to his account— leaving to a near kinsman of his own the royal fortune which he had amassed. Only a few hours ago that worthy kinsman of the benefactor of our nation made it known to me that in his last will he had bequeathed to me, by secret trust, the whole of those estates which long ago I had forfeited by effluxion of time, inasmuch as I had been unable to fulfil the terms of my voluntary bond. It grieves me to think that I have had to keep you so long in ignorance of the good thought and wishes and acts of this great man.

"But it was by his wise counsel, fortified by my own judgment, that I was silent; for, indeed, I feared, as he did, lest in our troublous times some doubting spirit without our boundaries, or even within it, might mistrust the honesty of my purposes for public good, because I was no longer one whose whole fortune was invested within our confines. This prince-merchant, the great English Roger Melton—let his name be for ever graven on the hearts of our people!—kept silent during his own life, and enjoined on others to come after him to keep secret from the men of the Blue Mountains that secret loan made to me on their behalf, lest in their eyes I, who had striven to be their friend and helper, should suffer wrong repute. But, happily, he has left me free to clear myself in your eyes. Moreover, by arranging to have—under certain contingencies, which have come to pass—the estates which were originally my own retransferred to me, I have no longer the honour of having given what I could to the national cause. All such now belongs to him; for it was his money—and his only—which purchased our national armament.

"His worthy kinsman you already know, for he has not only been amongst you for many months, but has already done you good service in his own person. He it was who, as a mighty warrior, answered the summons of the Vladika when misfortune came upon my house in the capture by enemies of my dear daughter, the Voivodin Teuta, whom you hold in your hearts; who, with a chosen band of our brothers, pursued the marauders, and himself, by a deed of daring and prowess, of which poets shall hereafter sing, saved her, when hope itself seemed to be dead, from their ruthless hands, and brought her back to us; who administered condign punishment to the miscreants who had dared to so wrong her. He it was who later took me, your servant, out of the prison wherein another band of Turkish miscreants held me captive; rescued me, with the help of my dear daughter, whom he had already freed, whilst I had on my person the documents of international secrecy of which I have already advised you—rescued me whilst I had been as yet unsubjected to the indignity of search.

"Beyond this you know now that of which I was in partial ignorance: how he had, through the skill and devotion of your new Admiral, wrought destruction on a hecatomb of our malignant foes. You who have received for the nation the splendid gift of the little warship, which already represents a new era in naval armament, can understand the great-souled generosity of the man who has restored the vast possessions of my House. On our way hither from Ilsin, Rupert Sent Leger made known to me the terms of the trust of his noble uncle, Roger Melton, and—believe me that he did so generously, with a joy that transcended my own—restored to the last male of the Vissarion race the whole inheritance of a noble line.

"And now, my Lords of the Council, I come to another matter, in which I find myself in something of a difficulty, for I am aware that in certain ways you actually know more of it than even I myself do. It is regarding the marriage of my daughter to Rupert Sent Leger. It is known to me that the matter has been brought before you by the Archbishop, who, as guardian of my daughter during my absence on the service of the nation, wished to obtain your sanction, as till my return he held her safety in trust. This was so, not from any merit of mine, but because she, in her own person, had undertaken for the service of our nation a task of almost incredible difficulty. My Lords, were she child of another father, I should extol to the skies her bravery, her self-devotion, her loyalty to the land she loves. Why, then, should I hesitate to speak of her deeds in fitting terms, since it is my duty, my glory, to hold them in higher honour than can any in this land? I shall not shame her—or even myself—by being silent when such a duty urges me to speak, as Voivode, as trusted envoy of our nation, as father. Ages hence loyal men and women of our Land of the Blue Mountains will sing her deeds in song and tell them in story. Her name, Teuta, already sacred in these regions, where it was held by a great Queen, and honoured by all men, will hereafter be held as a symbol and type of woman's devotion. Oh, my Lords, we pass along the path of life, the best of us but a little time marching in the sunlight between gloom and gloom, and it is during that march that we must be judged for the future. This brave woman has won knightly spurs as well as any Paladin of old. So is it meet that ere she might mate with one worthy of her you, who hold in your hands the safety and honour of the State, should give your approval. To you was it given to sit in judgment on the worth of this gallant Englisher, now my son. You judged him then, before you had seen his valour, his strength, and skill exercised on behalf of a national cause. You judged wisely, oh, my brothers, and out of a grateful heart I thank you one and all for it. Well has he justified your trust by his later acts. When, in obedience to the summons of the Vladika, he put the nation in a blaze and ranged our boundaries with a ring of steel, he did so unknowing that what was dearest to him in the world was at stake. He saved my daughter's honour and happiness, and won her safety by an act of valour that outvies any told in history. He took my daughter with him to bring me out from the Silent Tower on the wings of the air, when earth had for me no possibility of freedom—I, that had even then in my possession the documents involving other nations which the Soldan would fain have purchased with the half of his empire.

"Henceforth to me, Lords of the Council, this brave man must ever be as a son of my heart, and I trust that in his name grandsons of my own may keep in bright honour the name which in glorious days of old my fathers made illustrious. Did I know how adequately to thank you for your interest in my child, I would yield up to you my very soul in thanks."

The speech of the Voivode was received with the honour of the Blue Mountains—the drawing and raising of handjars.

From Rupert's Journal

July 14, 1907

For nearly a week we waited for some message from Constantinople, fully expecting either a declaration of war, or else some inquiry so couched as to make war an inevitable result. The National Council remained on at Vissarion as the guests of the Voivode, to whom, in accordance with my uncle's will, I had prepared to re-transfer all his estates. He was, by the way, unwilling at first to accept, and it was only when I showed him Uncle Roger's letter, and made him read the Deed of Transfer prepared in anticipation by Mr. Trent, that he allowed me to persuade him. Finally he said:

"As you, my good friends, have so arranged, I must accept, be it only in honour to the wishes of the dead. But remember, I only do so but for the present, reserving to myself the freedom to withdraw later if I so desire."

But Constantinople was silent. The whole nefarious scheme was one of the "put-up jobs" which are part of the dirty work of a certain order of statecraft—to be accepted if successful; to be denied in case of failure.

The matter stood thus: Turkey had thrown the dice—and lost. Her men were dead; her ship was forfeit. It was only some ten days after the warship was left derelict with every living thing—that is, everything that had been living—with its neck broken, as Rooke informed me, when he brought the ship down the creek, and housed it in the dock behind the armoured gates—that we saw an item in *The Roma* copied from *The Constantinople Journal* of July 9:

"Loss of an Ottoman Ironclad with all Hands

"News has been received at Constantinople of the total loss, with all hands, of one of the newest and finest warships in the Turkish fleet—*The Mahmoud*, Captain Ali Ali—which foundered in a storm on the night of July 5, some distance off Cabrera, in the Balearic

Isles. There were no survivors, and no wreckage was discovered by the ships which went in relief—the *Pera* and the *Mustapha*—or reported from anywhere along the shores of the islands, of which exhaustive search was made. *The Mahmoud* was double-manned, as she carried a full extra crew sent on an educational cruise on the most perfectly scientifically equipped warship on service in the Mediterranean waters."

When the Voivode and I talked over the matter, he said:

"After all, Turkey is a shrewd Power. She certainly seems to know when she is beaten, and does not intend to make a bad thing seem worse in the eyes of the world."

Well, 'tis a bad wind that blows good to nobody. As *The Mahmoud* was lost off the Balearics, it cannot have been her that put the marauders on shore and trained her big guns on Ilsin. We take it, therefore, that the latter must have been a pirate, and as we have taken her derelict in our waters, she is now ours in all ways. Anyhow, she is ours, and is the first ship of her class in the navy of the Blue Mountains. I am inclined to think that even if she was—or is still—a Turkish ship, Admiral Rooke would not be inclined to let her go. As for Captain Desmond, I think he would go straight out of his mind if such a thing was to be even suggested to him.

It will be a pity if we have any more trouble, for life here is very happy with us all now. The Voivode is, I think, like a man in a dream. Teuta is ideally happy, and the real affection which sprang up between them when she and Aunt Janet met is a joy to think of. I had posted Teuta about her, so that when they should meet my wife might not, by any inadvertence, receive or cause any pain. But the moment Teuta saw her she ran straight over to her and lifted her in her strong young arms, and, raising her up as one would lift a child, kissed her. Then, when she had put her sitting in the chair from which she had arisen when we entered the room, she knelt down before her, and put her face down in her lap. Aunt Janet's face was a study; I myself could hardly say whether at the first moment surprise or joy predominated. But there could be no doubt about it the instant after. She seemed to beam with happiness. When Teuta knelt to her, she could only say:

"My dear, my dear, I am glad! Rupert's wife, you and I must love each other very much." Seeing that they were laughing and crying in each other's arms, I thought it best to come away and leave them alone. And I didn't feel a bit lonely either when I was out of sight of them. I knew that where those two dear women were there was a place for my own heart.

When I came back, Teuta was sitting on Aunt Janet's knee. It seemed rather stupendous for the old lady, for Teuta is such a splendid creature that even when she sits on my own knee and I catch a glimpse of us in some mirror, I cannot but notice what a nobly-built girl she is.

My wife was jumping up as soon as I was seen, but Aunt Janet held her tight to her, and said:

"Don't stir, dear. It is such happiness to me to have you there. Rupert has always been my 'little boy,' and, in spite of all his being such a giant, he is so still. And so you, that he loves, must be my little girl—in spite of all your beauty and your strength—and sit on my knee, till you can place there a little one that shall be dear to us all, and that shall let me feel my youth again. When first I saw you I was surprised, for, somehow, though I had never seen you nor even heard of you, I seemed to know your face. Sit where you are, dear. It is only Rupert—and we both love him."

Teuta looked at me, flushing rosily; but she sat quiet, and drew the old lady's white head on her young breast.

Janet Mackelpie's Notes

July 8, 1907

I used to think that whenever Rupert should get married or start on the way to it by getting engaged—I would meet his future wife with something of the same affection that I have always had for himself. But I know now that what was really in my mind was *jealousy*, and that I was really fighting against my own instincts, and pretending to myself that I was not jealous. Had I ever had the faintest idea that she would be anything the least like Teuta, that sort of feeling should never have had even a foothold. No wonder my dear boy is in love with her, for, truth to tell, I am in love with her myself. I don't think I ever met a creature—a woman creature, of course, I mean—with so many splendid qualities. I almost fear to say it, lest it should seem to myself wrong; but I think she is as good as a woman as Rupert is as a man. And what more than that can I say? I thought I loved her and trusted her, and knew her all I could, until this morning.

I was in my own room, as it is still called. For, though Rupert tells me in confidence that under his uncle's will the whole estate of

Vissarion, Castle and all, really belongs to the Voivode, and though the Voivode has been persuaded to accept the position, he (the Voivode) will not allow anything to be changed. He will not even hear a word of my going, or changing my room, or anything. And Rupert backs him up in it, and Teuta too. So what am I to do but let the dears have their way?

Well, this morning, when Rupert was with the Voivode at a meeting of the National Council in the Great Hall, Teuta came to me, and (after closing the door and bolting it, which surprised me a little) came and knelt down beside me, and put her face in my lap. I stroked her beautiful black hair, and said:

"What is it, Teuta darling? Is there any trouble? And why did you bolt the door? Has anything happened to Rupert?" When she looked up I saw that her beautiful black eyes, with the stars in them, were overflowing with tears not yet shed. But she smiled through them, and the tears did not fall. When I saw her smile my heart was eased, and I said without thinking: "Thank God, darling, Rupert is all right."

"I thank God, too, dear Aunt Janet!" she said softly; and I took her in my arms and laid her head on my breast.

"Go on, dear," I said; "tell me what it is that troubles you?" This time I saw the tears drop, as she lowered her head and hid her face from me.

"I'm afraid I have deceived you, Aunt Janet, and that you will not—cannot—forgive me."

"Lord save you, child!" I said, "there's nothing that you could do that I could not and would not forgive. Not that you would ever do anything base, for that is the only thing that is hard to forgive. Tell me now what troubles you."

She looked up in my eyes fearlessly, this time with only the signs of tears that had been, and said proudly:

"Nothing base, Aunt Janet. My father's daughter would not willingly be base. I do not think she could. Moreover, had I ever done anything base I should not be here, for—for—I should never have been Rupert's wife!"

"Then what is it? Tell your old Aunt Janet, dearie." She answered me with another question:

"Aunt Janet, do you know who I am, and how I first met Rupert?"

"You are the Voivodin Teuta Vissarion—the daughter of the Voivode—Or, rather, you were; you are now Mrs. Rupert Sent Leger. For he is still an Englishman, and a good subject of our noble King."

"Yes, Aunt Janet," she said, "I am that, and proud to be it—prouder than I would be were I my namesake, who was Queen in the old days. But how and where did I see Rupert first?" I did not know, and frankly told her so. So she answered her question herself:

"I saw him first in his own room at night." I knew in my heart that in whatever she did had been nothing wrong, so I sat silent waiting for her to go on:

"I was in danger, and in deadly fear. I was afraid I might die—not that I fear death—and I wanted help and warmth. I was not dressed as I am now!"

On the instant it came to me how I knew her face, even the first time I had seen it. I wished to help her out of the embarrassing part of her confidence, so I said:

"Dearie, I think I know. Tell me, child, will you put on the frock. . . the dress. . . costume you wore that night, and let me see you in it? It is not mere idle curiosity, my child, but something far, far above such idle folly."

"Wait for me a minute, Aunt Janet," she said, as she rose up; "I shall not be long." Then she left the room.

In a very few minutes she was back. Her appearance might have frightened some people, for she was clad only in a shroud. Her feet were bare, and she walked across the room with the gait of an empress, and stood before me with her eyes modestly cast down. But when presently she looked up and caught my eyes, a smile rippled over her face. She threw herself once more before me on her knees, and embraced me as she said:

"I was afraid I might frighten you, dear." I knew I could truthfully reassure her as to that, so I proceeded to do so:

"Do not worry yourself, my dear. I am not by nature timid. I come of a fighting stock which has sent out heroes, and I belong to a family wherein is the gift of Second Sight. Why should we fear? We know! Moreover, I saw you in that dress before. Teuta, I saw you and Rupert married!" This time she herself it was that seemed disconcerted.

"Saw us married! How on earth did you manage to be there?"

"I was not there. My Seeing was long before! Tell me, dear, what day, or rather what night, was it that you first saw Rupert?" She answered sadly:

"I do not know. Alas! I lost count of the days as I lay in the tomb in that dreary Crypt."

"Was your—your clothing wet that night?" I asked.

"Yes. I had to leave the Crypt, for a great flood was out, and the church was flooded. I had to seek help—warmth—for I feared I might die. Oh, I was not, as I have told you, afraid of death. But I had undertaken a terrible task to which I had pledged myself. It was for my father's sake, and the sake of the Land, and I felt that it was a part of my duty to live. And so I lived on, when death would have been relief. It was to tell you all about this that I came to your room to-day. But how did you see me—us—married?"

"Ah, my child!" I answered, "that was before the marriage took place. The morn after the night that you came in the wet, when, having been troubled in uncanny dreaming, I came to see if Rupert was a'richt, I lost remembrance o' my dreaming, for the floor was all wet, and that took off my attention. But later, the morn after Rupert used his fire in his room for the first time, I told him what I had dreamt; for, lassie, my dear, I saw ye as bride at that weddin' in fine lace o'er yer shrood, and orange-flowers and ithers in yer black hair; an' I saw the stars in yer bonny een—the een I love. But oh, my dear, when I saw the shrood, and kent what it might mean, I expeckit to see the worms crawl round yer feet. But do ye ask yer man to tell ye what I tell't him that morn. 'Twill interest ye to know how the hairt o' men can learn by dreams. Has he ever tellt ye aught o' this?"

"No, dear," she said simply. "I think that perhaps he was afraid that one or other of us, if not both, might be upset by it if he did. You see, he did not tell you anything at all of our meeting, though I am sure that he will be glad when he knows that we both know all about it, and have told each other everything."

That was very sweet of her, and very thoughtful in all ways, so I said that which I thought would please her best—that is, the truth:

"Ah, lassie, that is what a wife should be—what a wife should do. Rupert is blessed and happy to have his heart in your keeping."

I knew from the added warmth of her kiss what I had said had pleased her.

Letter from Ernest Roger Halbard Melton, Humcroft, Salop, to Rupert Sent Leger, Vissarion, Land of the Blue Mountains.

July 29, 1907

MY DEAR COUSIN RUPERT,

We have heard such glowing accounts of Vissarion that I am coming out to see you. As you are yourself now a landowner, you will understand that my coming is not altogether a pleasure. Indeed, it is a duty first. When my father dies I shall be head of the family—the family of which Uncle Roger, to whom we were related, was a member. It is therefore meet and fitting that I should know something of our family branches and of their Seats. I am not giving you time for much warning, so am coming on immediately—in fact, I shall arrive almost as soon as this letter. But I want to catch you in the middle of your tricks. I hear that the Blue Mountaineer girls are peaches, so don't send them *all* away when you hear I'm coming!

Do send a yacht up to Fiume to meet me. I hear you have all sorts of craft at Vissarion. The MacSkelpie, I hear, said you received her as a Queen; so I hope you will do the decent by one of your own flesh and blood, and the future Head of the House at that. I shan't bring much of a retinue with me. *I* wasn't made a billionaire by old Roger, so can only take my modest "man Friday"—whose name is Jenkinson, and a Cockney at that. So don't have too much gold lace and diamond-hilted scimitars about, like a good chap, or else he'll want the very worst—his wyges ryzed. That old image Rooke that came over for Miss McS., and whom by chance I saw at the attorney man's, might pilot me down from Fiume. The old gentleman-by-Act-of-Parliament Mr. Bingham Trent (I suppose he has hyphened it by this time) told me that Miss McS. said he "did her proud" when she went over under his charge. I shall be at Fiume on the evening of Wednesday, and shall stay at the Europa, which is, I am told, the least indecent hotel in the place. So you know where to find me, or any of your attendant demons can know, in case I am to suffer "substituted service."

Your affectionate Cousin,
ERNEST ROGER HALBARD MELTON

Letter from Admiral Rooke to the Gospodar Rupert.

August 1, 1907

SIR,

In obedience to your explicit direction that I should meet Mr. Ernest R. H. Melton at Fiume, and report to you exactly what occurred, "without keeping anything back,"—as you will remember you said, I beg to report.

I brought the steam-yacht *Trent* to Fiume, arriving there on the morning of Thursday. At 11.30 P.M. I went to meet the train from St. Peter, due 11.40. It was something late, arriving just as the clock was beginning to strike midnight. Mr. Melton was on board, and with him his valet Jenkinson. I am bound to say that he did not seem very pleased with his journey, and expressed much disappointment at not seeing Your Honour awaiting him. I explained, as you directed, that you had to attend with the Voivode Vissarion and the Vladika the National Council, which met at Plazac, or that otherwise you would have done yourself the pleasure of coming to meet him. I had, of course, reserved rooms (the Prince of Wales's suite), for him at the Re d'Ungheria, and had waiting the carriage which the proprietor had provided for the Prince of Wales when he stayed there. Mr. Melton took his valet with him (on the box-seat), and I followed in a *Stadtwagen* with the luggage. When I arrived, I found the *maitre d'hotel* in a stupor of concern. The English nobleman, he said, had found fault with everything, and used to him language to which he was not accustomed. I quieted him, telling him that the stranger was probably unused to foreign ways, and assuring him that Your Honour had every faith in him. He announced himself satisfied and happy at the assurance. But I noticed that he promptly put everything in the hands of the headwaiter, telling him to satisfy the milor at any cost, and then went away to some urgent business in Vienna. Clever man!

I took Mr. Melton's orders for our journey in the morning, and asked if there was anything for which he wished. He simply said to me:

"Everything is rotten. Go to hell, and shut the door after you!" His man, who seems a very decent little fellow, though he is as vain as a peacock, and speaks with a Cockney accent which is simply terrible, came down the passage after me, and explained "on his own," as he expressed it, that his master, "Mr. Ernest," was upset by the long journey, and that I was not to mind. I did not wish to make him uncomfortable, so

I explained that I minded nothing except what Your Honour wished; that the steam-yacht would be ready at 7 A.M.; and that I should be waiting in the hotel from that time on till Mr. Melton cared to start, to bring him aboard.

In the morning I waited till the man Jenkinson came and told me that Mr. Ernest would start at ten. I asked if he would breakfast on board; he answered that he would take his *cafe-complet* at the hotel, but breakfast on board.

We left at ten, and took the electric pinnace out to the *Trent*, which lay, with steam up, in the roads. Breakfast was served on board, by his orders, and presently he came up on the bridge, where I was in command. He brought his man Jenkinson with him. Seeing me there, and not (I suppose) understanding that I was in command, he unceremoniously ordered me to go on the deck. Indeed, he named a place much lower. I made a sign of silence to the quartermaster at the wheel, who had released the spokes, and was going, I feared, to make some impertinent remark. Jenkinson joined me presently, and said, as some sort of explanation of his master's discourtesy (of which he was manifestly ashamed), if not as an amende:

"The governor is in a hell of a wax this morning."

When we got in sight of Meleda, Mr. Melton sent for me and asked me where we were to land. I told him that, unless he wished to the contrary, we were to run to Vissarion; but that my instructions were to land at whatever port he wished. Whereupon he told me that he wished to stay the night at some place where he might be able to see some "life." He was pleased to add something, which I presume he thought jocular, about my being able to "coach" him in such matters, as doubtless even "an old has-been like you" had still some sort of an eye for a pretty girl. I told him as respectfully as I could that I had no knowledge whatever on such subjects, which were possibly of some interest to younger men, but of none to me. He said no more; so after waiting for further orders, but without receiving any, I said:

"I suppose, sir, we shall run to Vissarion?"

"Run to the devil, if you like!" was his reply, as he turned away. When we arrived in the creek at Vissarion, he seemed much milder—less aggressive in his manner; but when he heard that you were detained at Plazac, he got rather "fresh"—I use the American term—again. I greatly feared there would be a serious misfortune before we got into the Castle, for on the dock was Julia, the wife of Michael, the Master of the Wine, who is, as you know, very beautiful. Mr. Melton seemed much taken with her; and she, being flattered by the attention of a strange gentleman and Your Honour's kinsman, put aside the stand-offishness of most of the Blue Mountain women. Whereupon Mr. Melton, forgetting himself, took her in his arms and kissed her. Instantly there was a hubbub. The mountaineers present drew their handjars, and almost on the instant sudden death appeared to be amongst us. Happily the men waited as Michael, who had just arrived on the quay-wall as the outrage took place, ran forward, wheeling his handjar round his head, and manifestly intending to decapitate Mr. Melton. On the instant—I am sorry to say it, for it created a terribly bad effect—Mr. Melton dropped on his knees in a state of panic. There was just this good use in it—that there was a pause of a few seconds. During that time the little Cockney valet, who has the heart of a man in him, literally burst his way forward, and stood in front of his master in boxing attitude, calling out:

"'Ere, come on, the 'ole lot of ye! 'E ain't done no 'arm. He honly kissed the gal, as any man would. If ye want to cut off somebody's 'ed, cut off mine. I ain't afride!" There was such genuine pluck in this, and it formed so fine a contrast to the other's craven attitude (forgive me, Your Honour; but you want the truth!), that I was glad he was an Englishman, too. The mountaineers recognized his spirit, and saluted with their handjars, even Michael amongst the number. Half turning his head, the little man said in a fierce whisper:

"Buck up, guv'nor! Get up, or they'll slice ye! 'Ere's Mr. Rooke; 'e'll see ye through it."

By this time the men were amenable to reason, and when I reminded them that Mr. Melton was Your Honour's cousin, they put aside their handjars and went about their work. I asked Mr. Melton to follow, and led the way to the Castle.

When we got close to the great entrance within the walled courtyard, we found a large number of the servants gathered, and with them many of the mountaineers, who have kept an organized guard all round the Castle ever since the abducting of the Voivodin. As both Your Honour and the Voivode were away at Plazac, the guard had for the time been doubled. When the steward came and stood in the doorway, the servants stood off somewhat, and the mountaineers drew back to the farther sides and angles of the courtyard. The Voivodin had, of course, been informed of the guest's (your cousin) coming, and came to meet him in the old custom of the Blue Mountains. As Your Honour only came to the Blue Mountains recently, and as no occasion has been since then of illustrating the custom since the Voivode was away, and the Voivodin then believed to be dead, perhaps I, who have lived here so long, may explain:

When to an old Blue Mountain house a guest comes whom it is wished to do honour, the Lady, as in the vernacular the mistress of the house is called, comes herself to meet the guest at the door—or, rather, *outside* the door—so that she can herself conduct him within. It is a pretty ceremony, and it is said that of old in kingly days the monarch always set much store by it. The custom is that, when she approaches the honoured guest (he need not be royal), she bends—or more properly kneels—before him and kisses his hand. It has been explained by historians that the symbolism is that the woman, showing obedience to her husband, as the married woman of the Blue Mountains always does, emphasizes that obedience to her husband's guest. The custom is always observed in its largest formality when a young wife receives for the first time a guest, and especially one whom her husband wishes to honour. The Voivodin was, of course, aware that Mr. Melton was your kinsman, and naturally wished to make the ceremony of honour as marked as possible, so as to show overtly her sense of her husband's worth.

When we came into the courtyard, I held back, of course, for the honour is entirely individual, and is never extended to any other, no matter how worthy he may be. Naturally

Mr. Melton did not know the etiquette of the situation, and so for that is not to be blamed. He took his valet with him when, seeing someone coming to the door, he went forward. I thought he was going to rush to his welcomer. Such, though not in the ritual, would have been natural in a young kinsman wishing to do honour to the bride of his host, and would to anyone have been both understandable and forgivable. It did not occur to me at the time, but I have since thought that perhaps he had not then heard of Your Honour's marriage, which I trust you will, in justice to the young gentleman, bear in mind when considering the matter. Unhappily, however, he did not show any such eagerness. On the contrary, he seemed to make a point of showing indifference. It seemed to me myself that he, seeing somebody wishing to make much of him, took what he considered a safe opportunity of restoring to himself his own good opinion, which must have been considerably lowered in the episode of the Wine Master's wife.

The Voivodin, thinking, doubtless, Your Honour, to add a fresh lustre to her welcome, had donned the costume which all her nation has now come to love and to accept as a dress of ceremonial honour. She wore her shroud. It moved the hearts of all of us who looked on to see it, and we appreciated its being worn for such a cause. But Mr. Melton did not seem to care. As he had been approaching she had begun to kneel, and was already on her knees whilst he was several yards away. There he stopped and turned to speak to his valet, put a glass in his eye, and looked all round him and up and down—indeed, everywhere except at the Great Lady, who was on her knees before him, waiting to bid him welcome. I could see in the eyes of such of the mountaineers as were within my range of vision a growing animosity; so, hoping to keep down any such expression, which I knew would cause harm to Your Honour and the Voivodin, I looked all round them straight in their faces with a fixed frown, which, indeed, they seemed to understand, for they regained, and for the time maintained, their usual dignified calm. The Voivodin, may I say, bore the trial wonderfully. No human being could see that she was in any degree pained or even surprised. Mr. Melton stood looking round him so long that I had full time to regain my own attitude of calm. At last he seemed to come back to the knowledge that someone was waiting for him, and sauntered leisurely forward. There was so much insolence—mind you, not insolence that was intended to appear as such—in his movement that the mountaineers began to steal forward. When he was close up to the Voivodin, and she put out her hand to take his, he put forward *one finger*! I could hear the intake of the breath of the men, now close around, for I had moved forward, too. I thought it would be as well to be close to your guest, lest something should happen to him. The Voivodin still kept her splendid self-control. Raising the finger put forward by the guest with the same deference as though it had been the hand of a King, she bent her head down and kissed it. Her duty of courtesy now done, she was preparing to rise, when he put his hand into his pocket, and, pulling out a sovereign, offered it to her. His valet moved his hand forward, as if to pull back his arm, but it was too late. I am sure, Your Honour, that no affront was intended. He doubtless thought that he was doing a kindness of the sort usual in England when one "tips" a housekeeper. But all the same, to one in her position, it was an affront, an insult, open and unmistakable. So it was received by the mountaineers, whose handjars flashed out as one. For a second it was so received even by the Voivodin, who, with face flushing scarlet, and the stars in her eves flaming red, sprang to her feet. But in that second she had regained herself, and to all appearances her righteous anger passed away. Stooping, she took the hand of her guest and raised it—you know how strong she is—and, holding it in hers, led him into the doorway, saying:

"You are welcome, kinsman of my husband, to the house of my father, which is presently my husband's also. Both are grieved that, duty having called them away for the time, they are unable to be here to help me to greet you."

I tell you, Your Honour, that it was a lesson in self-respect which anyone who saw it can never forget. As to me, it makes my flesh quiver, old as I am, with delight, and my heart leap.

May I, as a faithful servant who has had many years of experience, suggest that Your Honour should seem—for the present, at any rate—not to know any of these things which I have reported, as you wished me to do. Be sure that the Voivodin will tell you her gracious self aught that she would wish you to know. And such reticence on your part must make for her happiness, even if it did not for your own.

So that you may know all, as you desired, and that you may have time to school yourself to whatever attitude you think best to adopt, I send this off to you at once by fleet messenger. Were the aeroplane here, I should take it myself. I leave here shortly to await the arrival of Sir Colin at Otranto.

Your Honour's faithful servant,
ROOKE

JANET MACKELPIE'S NOTES

August 9, 1907

To me it seems very providential that Rupert was not at home when that dreadful young man Ernest Melton arrived, though it is possible that if Rupert had been present he would not have dared to conduct himself so badly. Of course, I heard all about it from the maids; Teuta never opened her lips to me on the subject. It was bad enough and stupid enough for him to try to kiss a decent young woman like Julia, who is really as good as gold and as modest as one of our own Highland lassies; but to think of him insulting Teuta! The little beast! One would think that a champion idiot out of an Equatorial asylum would know better! If Michael, the Wine Master, wanted to kill him, I wonder what my Rupert and hers would have done? I am truly thankful that he was not present. And I am thankful, too, that I was not present either, for I should have made an exhibition of myself, and Rupert would not have liked that. He—the little beast! might have seen from the very dress that the dear girl wore that there was something exceptional about her. But on one account I should have liked to see her. They tell me that she was, in her true dignity, like a Queen, and that her humility in receiving her husband's kinsman was a lesson to every woman in the Land. I must be careful not to let Rupert know that I have heard of the incident. Later on, when it is all blown over and the young man has been got safely away, I shall tell him of it. Mr. Rooke—Lord High Admiral Rooke, I should say—must be a really wonderful man to have so held himself in check; for, from what I have heard of him, he must in his younger days have been worse than Old

Morgan of Panama. Mr. Ernest Roger Halbard Melton, of Humcroft, Salop, little knows how near he was to being "cleft to the chine" also.

Fortunately, I had heard of his meeting with Teuta before he came to see me, for I did not get back from my walk till after he had arrived. Teuta's noble example was before me, and I determined that I, too, would show good manners under any circumstances. But I didn't know how mean he is. Think of his saying to me that Rupert's position here must be a great source of pride to me, who had been his nursery governess. He said "nursemaid" first, but then stumbled in his words, seeming to remember something. I did not turn a hair, I am glad to say. It is a mercy Uncle Colin was not here, for I honestly believe that, if he had been, he would have done the "cleaving to the chine" himself. It has been a narrow escape for Master Ernest, for only this morning Rupert had a message, sent on from Gibraltar, saying that he was arriving with his clansmen, and that they would not be far behind his letter. He would call at Otranto in case someone should come across to pilot him to Vissarion. Uncle told me all about that young cad having offered him one finger in Mr. Trent's office, though, of course, he didn't let the cad see that he noticed it. I have no doubt that, when he does arrive, that young man, if he is here still, will find that he will have to behave himself, if it be only on Sir Colin's account alone.

The Same (Later)

I had hardly finished writing when the lookout on the tower announced that the *Teuta*, as Rupert calls his aeroplane, was sighted crossing the mountains from Plazac. I hurried up to see him arrive, for I had not as yet seen him on his "aero." Mr. Ernest Melton came up, too. Teuta was, of course, before any of us. She seems to know by instinct when Rupert is coming.

It was certainly a wonderful sight to see the little aeroplane, with outspread wings like a bird in flight, come sailing high over the mountains. There was a head-wind, and they were beating against it; otherwise we should not have had time to get to the tower before the arrival.

When once the "aero" had begun to drop on the near side of the mountains, however, and had got a measure of shelter from them, her pace was extraordinary. We could not tell, of course, what sort of pace she came at from looking at herself. But we gathered some idea from the rate at which the mountains and hills seemed to slide away from under her. When she got over the foot-hills, which are about ten miles away, she came on at a swift glide that seemed to throw the distance behind her. When quite close, she rose up a little till she was something higher than the Tower, to which she came as straight as an arrow from the bow, and glided to her moorings, stopping dead as Rupert pulled a lever, which seemed to turn a barrier to the wind. The Voivode sat beside Rupert, but I must say that he seemed to hold on to the bar in front of him even more firmly than Rupert held to his steering-gear.

When they had alighted, Rupert greeted his cousin with the utmost kindness, and bade him welcome to Vissarion.

"I see," he said, "you have met Teuta. Now you may congratulate me, if you wish."

Mr. Melton made a long rodomontade about her beauty, but presently, stumbling about in his speech, said something regarding it being unlucky to appear in grave-clothes. Rupert laughed, and clapped him on the shoulder as he answered:

"That pattern of frock is likely to become a national dress for loyal women of the Blue Mountains. When you know something of what that dress means to us all at present you will understand. In the meantime, take it that there is not a soul in the nation that does not love it and honour her for wearing it." To which the cad replied:

"Oh, indeed! I thought it was some preparation for a fancy-dress ball." Rupert's comment on this ill-natured speech was (for him) quite grumpily given:

"I should not advise you to think such things whilst you are in this part of the world, Ernest. They bury men here for much less."

The cad seemed struck with something—either what Rupert had said or his manner of saying it—for he was silent for several seconds before he spoke.

"I'm very tired with that long journey, Rupert. Would you and Mrs. Sent Leger mind if I go to my own room and turn in? My man can ask for a cup of tea and a sandwich for me."

Rupert's Journal

August 10, 1907

When Ernest said he wished to retire it was about the wisest thing he could have said or done, and it suited Teuta and me down to the ground.

I could see that the dear girl was agitated about something, so thought it would be best for her to be quiet, and not worried with being civil to the Bounder. Though he is my cousin, I can't think of him as anything else. The Voivode and I had certain matters to attend to arising out of the meeting of the Council, and when we were through the night was closing in. When I saw Teuta in our own rooms she said at once:

"Do you mind, dear, if I stay with Aunt Janet to-night? She is very upset and nervous, and when I offered to come to her she clung to me and cried with relief."

So when I had had some supper, which I took with the Voivode, I came down to my old quarters in the Garden Room, and turned in early.

I was awakened a little before dawn by the coming of the fighting monk Theophrastos, a notable runner, who had an urgent message for me. This was the letter to me given to him by Rooke. He had been cautioned to give it into no other hand, but to find me wherever I might be, and convey it personally. When he had arrived at Plazac I had left on the aeroplane, so he had turned back to Vissarion.

When I read Rooke's report of Ernest Melton's abominable conduct I was more angry with him than I can say. Indeed, I did not think before that that I could be angry with him, for I have always despised him. But this was too much. However, I realized the wisdom of Rooke's advice, and went away by myself to get over my anger and reacquire my self-mastery. The aeroplane *Teuta* was still housed on the tower, so I went up alone and took it out.

When I had had a spin of about a hundred miles I felt better. The bracing of the wind and the quick, exhilarating motion restored me to myself, and I felt able to cope with Master Ernest, or whatever else chagrinable might come along, without giving myself away. As Teuta had thought it better to keep silence as to Ernest's affront, I felt I must not acknowledge it; but, all the same, I determined to get rid of him before the day was much older.

When I had had my breakfast I sent word to him by a servant that I was coming to his rooms, and followed not long behind the messenger.

He was in a suit of silk pyjamas, such as not even Solomon in all his glory was arrayed in. I closed the door behind me before I began to speak. He listened, at first amazed, then disconcerted, then angry, and then cowering down like a whipped hound. I felt that it was a case for speaking out. A bumptious ass like him, who deliberately insulted everyone he came across—for if all or any of his efforts in that way were due to mere elemental ignorance he was not fit to live, but should be silenced on sight as a modern Caliban—deserved neither pity nor mercy. To extend to him fine feeling, tolerance, and such-like gentlenesses would be to deprive the world of them without benefit to any. So well as I can remember, what I said was something like this:

"Ernest, as you say, you've got to go, and to go quick, you understand. I dare say you look on this as a land of barbarians, and think that any of your high-toned refinements are thrown away on people here. Well, perhaps it is so. Undoubtedly, the structure of the country is rough; the mountains may only represent the glacial epoch; but so far as I can gather from some of your exploits—for I have only learned a small part as yet—you represent a period a good deal farther back. You seem to have given our folk here an exhibition of the playfulness of the hooligan of the Saurian stage of development; but the Blue Mountains, rough as they are, have come up out of the primeval slime, and even now the people aim at better manners. They may be rough, primitive, barbarian, elemental, if you will, but they are not low down enough to tolerate either your ethics or your taste. My dear cousin, your life is not safe here! I am told that yesterday, only for the restraint exercised by certain offended mountaineers on other grounds than your own worth, you would have been abbreviated by the head. Another day of your fascinating presence would do away with this restraint, and then we should have a scandal. I am a new-comer here myself—too new a comer to be able to afford a scandal of that kind—and so I shall not delay your going. Believe me, my dear cousin, Ernest Roger Halbard Melton, of Humcroft, Salop, that I am inconsolable about your resolution of immediate departure, but I cannot shut my eyes to its wisdom. At present the matter is altogether amongst ourselves, and when you have gone—if it be immediately—silence will be observed on all hands for the sake of the house wherein you are a guest; but if there be time for scandal to spread, you will be made, whether you be alive or dead, a European laughing-stock. Accordingly, I have anticipated your wishes, and have ordered a fast steam yacht to take you to Ancona, or to whatever other port you may desire. The yacht will be under the command of Captain Desmond, of one of our battleships—a most determined officer, who will carry out any directions which may be given to him. This will insure your safety so far as Italian territory. Some of his officials will arrange a special carriage for you up to Flushing, and a cabin on the steamer to Queenboro'. A man of mine will travel on the train and steamer with you, and will see that whatever you may wish in the way of food or comfort will be provided. Of course, you understand, my dear cousin, that you are my guest until you arrive in London. I have not asked Rooke to accompany you, as when he went to meet you, it was a mistake. Indeed, there might have been a danger to you which I never contemplated—a quite unnecessary danger, I assure you. But happily Admiral Rooke, though a man of strong passions, has wonderful self-control."

"Admiral Rooke?" he queried. "Admiral?"

"Admiral, certainly," I replied, "but not an ordinary Admiral—one of many. He is *the* Admiral—the Lord High Admiral of the Land of the Blue Mountains, with sole control of its expanding navy. When such a man is treated as a valet, there may be. . . But why go into this? It is all over. I only mention it lest anything of a similar kind should occur with Captain Desmond, who is a younger man, and therefore with probably less self-repression."

I saw that he had learned his lesson, and so said no more on the subject.

There was another reason for his going which I did not speak of. Sir Colin MacKelpie was coming with his clansmen, and I knew he did not like Ernest Melton. I well remembered that episode of his offering one finger to the old gentleman in Mr. Trent's office, and, moreover, I had my suspicions that Aunt Janet's being upset was probably in some measure due to some rudeness of his that she did not wish to speak about. He is really an impossible young man, and is far better out of this country than in it. If he remained here, there would be some sort of a tragedy for certain.

I must say that it was with a feeling of considerable relief that I saw the yacht steam out of the creek, with Captain Desmond on the bridge and my cousin beside him.

Quite other were my feelings when, an hour after, *The Lady* came flying into the creek with the Lord High Admiral on the bridge, and beside him, more splendid and soldier-like than ever, Sir Colin MacKelpie. Mr. Bingham Trent was also on the bridge.

The General was full of enthusiasm regarding his regiment, for in all, those he brought with him and those finishing their training at home, the force is near the number of a full regiment. When we were alone he explained to me that all was arranged regarding the non-commissioned officers, but that he had held over the question of officers until we should have had a suitable opportunity of talking the matter over together. He explained to me his reasons, which were certainly simple and cogent. Officers, according to him, are a different class, and accustomed to a different standard altogether of life and living, of duties and pleasures. They are harder to deal with and more difficult to obtain. "There was no use," he said, "in getting a lot of failures, with old-crusted ways of their own importance. We must have young men for our purpose—that is, men not old, but with some experience—men, of course, who know how to behave themselves, or else, from what little I have seen of the Blue Mountaineers, they wouldn't last long here if they went on as some of them do elsewhere. I shall start things here as you wish me to, for I am here, my dear boy, to stay with you and Janet, and we shall, if it be given to us by the Almighty, help to build up together a new 'nation'—an ally of Britain, who will stand at least as an outpost of our own nation, and a guardian of our eastern road. When things are organized here on the military side, and are going strong, I shall, if you can spare me, run back to London for a few weeks. Whilst I am there I shall pick up a lot of the sort of officers we want. I know that there are loads of them to be had. I shall go slowly, however, and carefully, too, and every man I bring back will be recommended to me by some old soldier whom I know, and who knows the man he recommends, and has seen him work. We shall have, I dare say, an army for its size second to none in the world, and the day may come when your old country will be proud of your new one. Now I'm off to see that all is ready for my people—your people now."

I had had arrangements made for the comfort of the clansmen and the women, but I knew that the good old soldier would see for himself that his men were to be comfortable. It was not for nothing that he was—is—looked on as perhaps the General most beloved by his men in the whole British Army.

When he had gone, and I was alone, Mr. Trent, who had evidently been waiting for the opportunity, came to me. When we had spoken of my marriage and of Teuta, who seems to have made an immense impression on him, he said suddenly:

"I suppose we are quite alone, and that we shall not be interrupted?" I summoned the man outside—there is always a sentry on guard outside my door or near me, wherever I may be—and gave orders that I was not to be disturbed until I gave fresh orders. "If," I said, "there be anything pressing or important, let the Voivodin or Miss MacKelpie know. If either of them brings anyone to me, it will be all right."

When we were quite alone Mr. Trent took a slip of paper and some documents from the bag which was beside him. He then read out items from the slip, placing as he did so the documents so checked over before him.

1. New Will made on marriage, to be signed presently.
2. Copy of the Re-conveyance of Vissarion estates to Peter Vissarion, as directed by Will of Roger Melton.
3. Report of Correspondence with Privy Council, and proceedings following.

Taking up the last named, he untied the red tape, and, holding the bundle in his hand, went on:

"As you may, later on, wish to examine the details of the Proceedings, I have copied out the various letters, the originals of which are put safely away in my strong-room where, of course, they are always available in case you may want them. For your present information I shall give you a rough synopsis of the Proceedings, referring where advisable to this paper.

"On receipt of your letter of instructions regarding the Consent of the Privy Council to your changing your nationality in accordance with the terms of Roger Melton's Will, I put myself in communication with the Clerk of the Privy Council, informing him of your wish to be naturalized in due time to the Land of the Blue Mountains. After some letters between us, I got a summons to attend a meeting of the Council.

"I attended, as required, taking with me all necessary documents, and such as I conceived might be advisable to produce, if wanted.

"The Lord President informed me that the present meeting of the Council was specially summoned in obedience to the suggestion of the King, who had been consulted as to his personal wishes on the subject—should he have any. The President then proceeded to inform me officially that all Proceedings of the Privy Council were altogether confidential, and were not to be made public under any circumstances. He was gracious enough to add:

"'The circumstances of this case, however, are unique; and as you act for another, we have thought it advisable to enlarge your permission in the matter, so as to allow you to communicate freely with your principal. As that gentleman is settling himself in a part of the world which has been in the past, and may be again, united to this nation by some common interest, His Majesty wishes Mr. Sent Leger to feel assured of the good-will of Great Britain to the Land of the Blue Mountains, and even of his own personal satisfaction that a gentleman of so distinguished a lineage and such approved personal character is about to be—within his own scope—a connecting-link between the nations. To which end he has graciously announced that, should the Privy Council acquiesce in the request of Denaturalization, he will himself sign the Patent therefor.

"'The Privy Council has therefore held private session, at which the matter has been discussed in its many bearings; and it is content that the change can do no harm, but may be of some service to the two nations. We have, therefore, agreed to grant the prayer of the Applicant; and the officials of the Council have the matter of the form of Grant in hand. So you, sir, may rest satisfied that as soon as the formalities—which will, of course, require the formal signing of certain documents by the Applicant—can be complied with, the Grant and Patent will obtain.'"

Having made this statement in formal style, my old friend went on in more familiar way:

"And so, my dear Rupert, all is in hand; and before very long you will have the freedom required under the Will, and will be at liberty to take whatever steps may be necessary to be naturalized in your new country.

"I may tell you, by the way, that several members of the Council made very complimentary remarks regarding you. I am forbidden to give names, but I may tell you facts. One old Field-Marshal, whose name is familiar to the whole world, said that he had served in many places with your father, who was a very valiant soldier, and that he was glad that Great Britain was to have in the future the benefit of your father's son in a friendly land now beyond the outposts of our Empire, but which had been one with her in the past, and might be again.

"So much for the Privy Council. We can do no more at present until you sign and have attested the documents which I have brought with me.

"We can now formally complete the settlement of the Vissarion estates, which must be done whilst you are a British citizen. So, too, with the Will, the more formal and complete document, which is to take the place of that short one which you forwarded to me the day after your marriage. It may be, perhaps, necessary or advisable that, later on, when you are naturalized here, you shall make a new Will in strictest accordance with local law."

August 19, 1907

We had a journey to-day that was simply glorious. We had been waiting to take it for more than a week. Rupert not only wanted the weather suitable, but he had to wait till the new aeroplane came home. It is more than twice as big as our biggest up to now. None of the others could take all the party which Rupert wanted to go. When he heard that the aero was coming from Whitby, where it was sent from Leeds, he directed by cable that it should be unshipped at Otranto, whence he took it here all by himself. I wanted to come with him, but he thought it better not. He says that Brindisi is too busy a place to keep anything quiet—if not secret—and he wants to be very dark indeed about this, as it is worked by the new radium engine. Ever since they found radium in our own hills he has been obsessed by the idea of an aerial navy for our protection. And after to-day's experiences I think he is right. As he wanted to survey the whole country at a glimpse, so that the general scheme of defence might be put in hand, we had to have an aero big enough to take the party as well as fast enough to do it rapidly, and all at once. We had, in addition to Rupert, my father, and myself, Sir Colin and Lord High Admiral Rooke (I do like to give that splendid old fellow his full title!). The military and naval experts had with them scientific apparatus of various kinds, also cameras and range-finders, so that they could mark their maps as they required. Rupert, of course, drove, and I acted as his assistant. Father, who has not yet become accustomed to aerial travel, took a seat in the centre (which Rupert had thoughtfully prepared for him), where there is very little motion. I must say I was amazed to see the way that splendid old soldier Sir Colin bore himself. He had never been on an aeroplane before, but, all the same, he was as calm as if he was on a rock. Height or motion did not trouble him. Indeed, he seemed to *enjoy* himself all the time. The Admiral is himself almost an expert, but in any case I am sure he would have been unconcerned, just as he was in the *Crab* as Rupert has told me.

We left just after daylight, and ran down south. When we got to the east of Ilsin, we kept slightly within the border-line, and went north or east as it ran, making occasional loops inland over the mountains and back again. When we got up to our farthest point north, we began to go much slower. Sir Colin explained that for the rest all would be comparatively plain-sailing in the way of defence; but that as any foreign Power other than the Turk must attack from seaward, he would like to examine the seaboard very carefully in conjunction with the Admiral, whose advice as to sea defence would be invaluable.

Rupert was fine. No one could help admiring him as he sat working his lever and making the great machine obey every touch. He was wrapped up in his work. I don't believe that whilst he was working he ever thought of even me. He *is* splendid!

We got back just as the sun was dropping down over the Calabrian Mountains. It is quite wonderful how the horizon changes when you are sailing away up high on an aeroplane. Rupert is going to teach me how to manage one all by myself, and when I am fit he will give me one, which he is to have specially built for me.

I think I, too, have done some good work—at least, I have got some good ideas—from our journey to-day. Mine are not of war, but of peace, and I think I see a way by which we shall be able to develop our country in a wonderful way. I shall talk the idea over with Rupert to-night, when we are alone. In the meantime Sir Colin and Admiral Rooke will think their plans over individually, and to-morrow morning together. Then the next day they, too, are to go over their idea with Rupert and my father, and something may be decided then.

Rupert's Journal—*Continued*

August 21, 190

Our meeting on the subject of National Defence, held this afternoon, went off well. We were five in all, for with permission of the Voivode and the two fighting-men, naval and military, I brought Teuta with me. She sat beside me quite quietly, and never made a remark of any kind till the Defence business had been gone through. Both Sir Colin and Admiral Rooke were in perfect agreement as to the immediate steps to be taken for defence. In the first instance, the seaboard was to be properly fortified in the necessary places, and the navy largely strengthened. When we had got thus far I asked Rooke to tell of the navy increase already in hand. Whereupon he explained that, as we had found the small battleship *The Lady* of an excellent type for coast defence, acting only in home waters, and of a size to take cover where necessary at many places on our own shores, we had ordered nine others of the same pattern. Of these the first four were already in hand, and were proceeding with the greatest expedition. The General then supplemented this by saying that big guns could be used from points judiciously chosen on the seaboard, which was in all so short a length that no very great quantity of armament would be required.

"We can have," he said, "the biggest guns of the most perfect kind yet accomplished, and use them from land batteries of the most up-to-date pattern. The one serious proposition we have to deal with is the defence of the harbour—as yet quite undeveloped—which is known as the 'Blue Mouth.' Since our aerial journey I have been to it by sea with Admiral Rooke in *The Lady*, and then on land with the Vladika, who was born on its shores, and who knows every inch of it.

"It is worth fortifying—and fortifying well, for as a port it is peerless in Mediterranean seas. The navies of the world might ride in it, land-locked, and even hidden from view seawards. The mountains which enclose it are in themselves absolute protection. In addition, these can only be assailed from our own territory. Of course, Voivode, you understand when I say 'our' I mean the Land of the Blue Mountains, for whose safety and well-being I am alone concerned. Any ship anchoring in the roads of the Blue Mouth would have only one need—sufficient length of cable for its magnificent depth.

"When proper guns are properly placed on the steep cliffs to north and south of the entrance, and when the rock islet between has been armoured and armed as will be necessary, the Mouth will be impregnable. But we should not depend on the aiming of the entrance alone. At certain salient points—which I have marked upon this map—armour-plated sunken forts within earthworks should be established. There should be covering forts on the hillsides, and, of course, the final summits protected. Thus we could resist attack on any side or all sides—from sea or land. That port will yet mean the wealth as well as the strength of this nation, so it will be well to have it properly protected. This should be done soon, and the utmost secrecy observed in the doing of it, lest the so doing should become a matter of international concern."

Here Rooke smote the table hard.

"By God, that is true! It has been the dream of my own life for this many a year."

In the silence which followed the sweet, gentle voice of Teuta came clear as a bell:

"May I say a word? I am emboldened to, as Sir Colin has spoken so splendidly, and as the Lord High Admiral has not hesitated to mention his dreaming. I, too, have had a dream—a day-dream—which came in a flash, but no less a dream, for all that. It was when we hung on the aeroplane over the Blue Mouth. It seemed to me in an instant that I saw that beautiful spot as it will some time be—typical, as Sir Colin said, of the wealth as well as the strength of this nation; a mart for the world whence will come for barter some of the great wealth of the Blue Mountains. That wealth is as yet undeveloped. But the day is at hand when we may begin to use it, and through that very port. Our mountains and their valleys are clad with trees of splendid growth, virgin forests of priceless worth; hard woods of all kinds, which have no superior throughout the world. In the rocks, though hidden as yet, is vast mineral wealth of many kinds. I have been looking through the reports of the geological exports of the Commission of Investigation which my husband organized soon after he came to live here, and, according to them, our whole mountain ranges simply teem with vast quantities of minerals, almost more precious for industry than gold and silver are for commerce—though, indeed, gold is not altogether lacking as a mineral. When once our work on the harbour is done, and the place has been made secure against any attempt at foreign aggression, we must try to find a way to bring this wealth of woods and ores down to the sea.

"And then, perhaps, may begin the great prosperity of our Land, of which we have all dreamt."

She stopped, all vibrating, almost choked with emotion. We were all moved. For myself, I was thrilled to the core. Her enthusiasm was all-sweeping, and under its influence I found my own imagination expanding. Out of its experiences I spoke:

"And there is a way. I can see it. Whilst our dear Voivodin was speaking, the way seemed to clear. I saw at the back of the Blue Mouth, where it goes deepest into the heart of the cliffs, the opening of a great tunnel, which ran upward over a steep slope till it debouched on the first plateau beyond the range of the encompassing cliffs. Thither came by various rails of steep gradient, by timber-shoots and cable-rails, by aerial cables and precipitating tubes, wealth from over ground and under it; for as our Land is all mountains, and as these tower up to the clouds, transport to the sea shall be easy and of little cost when once the machinery is established. As everything of much weight goes downward, the cars of the main tunnel of the port shall return upward without cost. We can have from the mountains a head of water under good control, which will allow of endless hydraulic power, so that the whole port and the mechanism of the town to which it will grow can be worked by it.

"This work can be put in hand at once. So soon as the place shall be perfectly surveyed and the engineering plans got ready, we can start on the main tunnel, working from the sea-level up, so that the cost of the transport of material will be almost nil. This work can go on whilst the forts are building; no time need be lost.

"Moreover, may I add a word on National Defence? We are, though old in honour, a young nation as to our place amongst Great Powers. And so we must show the courage and energy of a young nation. The Empire of the Air is not yet won. Why should not we make a bid for it? As our mountains are lofty, so shall we have initial power of attack or defence. We can have, in chosen spots amongst the clouds, depots of war aeroplanes, with which we can descend and smite our enemies quickly on land or sea. We shall hope to live for Peace; but woe to those who drive us to War!"

There is no doubt that the Vissarions are a warlike race. As I spoke, Teuta took one of my hands and held it hard. The old Voivode, his eyes blazing, rose and stood beside me and took the other. The two old fighting-men of the land and the sea stood up and saluted.

This was the beginning of what ultimately became "The National Committee of Defence and Development."

I had other, and perhaps greater, plans for the future in my mind; but the time had not come for their utterance.

To me it seems not only advisable, but necessary, that the utmost discretion be observed by all our little group, at all events for the present. There seems to be some new uneasiness in the Blue Mountains. There are constant meetings of members of the Council, but no formal meeting of the Council, as such, since the last one at which I was present. There is constant coming and going amongst the mountaineers, always in groups, small or large. Teuta and I, who have been about very much on the aeroplane, have both noticed it. But somehow we—that is, the Voivode and myself—are left out of everything; but we have not said as yet a word on the subject to any of the others. The Voivode notices, but he says nothing; so I am silent, and Teuta does whatever I ask. Sir Colin does not notice anything except the work he is engaged on—the planning the defences of the Blue Mouth. His old scientific training as an engineer, and his enormous experience of wars and sieges—for he was for nearly fifty years sent as military representative to all the great wars—seem to have become directed on that point. He is certainly planning it all out in a wonderful way. He consults Rooke almost hourly on the maritime side of the question. The Lord High Admiral has been a watcher all his life, and very few important points have ever escaped him, so that he can add greatly to the wisdom of the defensive construction. He notices, I think, that something is going on outside ourselves; but he keeps a resolute silence.

What the movement going on is I cannot guess. It is not like the uneasiness that went before the abduction of Teuta and the Voivode, but it is even more pronounced. That was an uneasiness founded on some suspicion. This is a positive thing, and has definite meaning—of some sort. We shall, I suppose, know all about it in good time. In the meantime we go on with our work. Happily the whole Blue Mouth and the mountains round it are on my own property, the portion acquired long ago by Uncle Roger, exclusive of the Vissarion estate. I asked the Voivode to allow me to transfer it to him, but he sternly refused and forbade me, quite peremptorily, to ever open the subject to him again. "You have done enough already," he said. "Were I to allow you to go further, I should feel mean. And I do not think you would like your wife's father to suffer that feeling after a long life, which he has tried to live in honour."

I bowed, and said no more. So there the matter rests, and I have to take my own course. I have had a survey made, and on the head of it the Tunnel to the harbour is begun.

Book VIII

The Flashing of the Handjar

Private Memorandum of the Meeting of Various Members of the National Council, Held at the State House of the Blue Mountains at Plazac on Monday, August 26, 1907.

(Written by Cristoferos, Scribe of the Council, by instruction of those present)

When the private meeting of various Members of the National Council had assembled in the Council Hall of the State House at Plazac, it was as a preliminary decided unanimously that now or hereafter no names of those present were to be mentioned, and that officials appointed for the purposes of this meeting should be designated by office only, the names of all being withheld.

The proceedings assumed the shape of a general conversation, quite informal, and therefore not to be recorded. The nett outcome was the unanimous expression of an opinion that the time, long contemplated by very many persons throughout the nation, had now come when the Constitution and machinery of the State should be changed; that the present form of ruling by an Irregular Council was not sufficient, and that a method more in accord with the spirit of the times should be adopted. To this end Constitutional Monarchy, such as that holding in Great Britain, seemed best adapted. Finally, it was decided that each Member of the Council should make a personal canvass of his district, talk over the matter with his electors, and bring back to another meeting—or, rather, as it was amended, to this meeting postponed for a week, until September 2nd—the opinions and wishes received. Before separating, the individual to be appointed King, in case the new idea should prove grateful to the nation, was discussed. The consensus of opinion was entirely to the effect that the Voivode Peter Vissarion should, if he would accept the high office, be appointed. It was urged that, as his daughter, the Voivodin Teuta, was now married to the Englishman, Rupert

Sent Leger—called generally by the mountaineers "the Gospodar Rupert"—a successor to follow the Voivode when God should call him would be at hand—a successor worthy in every way to succeed to so illustrious a post. It was urged by several speakers, with general acquiescence, that already Mr. Sent Leger's services to the State were such that he would be in himself a worthy person to begin the new Dynasty; but that, as he was now allied to the Voivode Peter Vissarion, it was becoming that the elder, born of the nation, should receive the first honour.

The Same—*Continued*

The adjourned meeting of certain members of the National Council was resumed in the Hall of the State House at Plazac on Monday, September 2nd, 1907. By motion the same chairman was appointed, and the rule regarding the record renewed.

Reports were made by the various members of the Council in turn, according to the State Roll. Every district was represented. The reports were unanimously in favour of the New Constitution, and it was reported by each and all of the Councillors that the utmost enthusiasm marked in every case the suggestion of the Voivode Peter Vissarion as the first King to be crowned under the new Constitution, and that remainder should be settled on the Gospodar Rupert (the mountaineers would only receive his lawful name as an alternative; one and all said that he would be "Rupert" to them and to the nation—for ever).

The above matter having been satisfactorily settled, it was decided that a formal meeting of the National Council should be held at the State House, Plazac, in one week from to-day, and that the Voivode Peter Vissarion should be asked to be in the State House in readiness to attend. It was also decided that instruction should be given to the High Court of National Law to prepare and have ready, in skeleton form, a rescript of the New Constitution to be adopted, the same to be founded on the Constitution and Procedure of Great Britain, so far as the same may be applicable to the traditional ideas of free Government in the Land of the Blue Mountains.

By unanimous vote this private and irregular meeting of "Various National Councillors" was then dissolved.

RECORD OF THE FIRST MEETING OF THE NATIONAL
COUNCIL OF THE LAND OF THE BLUE MOUNTAINS, HELD AT
PLAZAC ON MONDAY, SEPTEMBER 9TH, 1907, TO CONSIDER
THE ADOPTION OF A NEW CONSTITUTION, AND TO GIVE
PERMANENT EFFECT TO THE SAME IF, AND WHEN,
DECIDED UPON

(Kept by the Monk Cristoferos, Scribe to the National Council)

The adjourned meeting duly took place as arranged. There was a full attendance of Members of the Council, together with the Vladika, the Archbishop, the Archimandrites of Spazac, of Ispazar, of Domitan, and Astrag; the Chancellor; the Lord of the Exchequer; the President of the High Court of National Law; the President of the Council of Justice; and such other high officials as it is customary to summon to meetings of the National Council on occasions of great importance. The names of all present will be found in the full report, wherein are given the ipsissima verba of the various utterances made during the consideration of the questions discussed, the same having been taken down in shorthand by the humble scribe of this precis, which has been made for the convenience of Members of the Council and others.

The Voivode Peter Vissarion, obedient to the request of the Council, was in attendance at the State House, waiting in the "Chamber of the High Officers" until such time as he should be asked to come before the Council.

The President put before the National Council the matter of the new Constitution, outlining the headings of it as drawn up by the High Court of National Law, and the Constitution having been formally accepted *nem. con.* by the National Council on behalf of the people, he proposed that the Crown should be offered to the Voivode Peter Vissarion, with remainder to the "Gospodar Rupert" (legally, Rupert Sent Leger), husband of his only child, the Voivodin Teuta. This also was received with enthusiasm, and passed *nem. con.*

Thereupon the President of Council, the Archbishop, and the Vladika, acting together as a deputation, went to pray the attention of the Voivode Peter Vassarion.

When the Voivode entered, the whole Council and officials stood up, and for a few seconds waited in respectful silence with heads bowed down. Then, as if by a common impulse—for no word was spoken nor any signal given—they all drew their handjars, and stood to attention—with points raised and edges of the handjars to the front.

The Voivode stood very still. He seemed much moved, but controlled himself admirably. The only time when be seemed to lose his self-control was when, once again with a strange simultaneity, all present raised their handjars on high, and shouted: "Hail, Peter, King!" Then lowering their points till these almost touched the ground, they once again stood with bowed heads.

When he had quite mastered himself, the Voivode Peter Vissarion spoke:

"How can I, my brothers, sufficiently thank you, and, through you, the people of the Blue Mountains, for the honour done to me this day? In very truth it is not possible, and therefore I pray you to consider it as done, measuring my gratitude in the greatness of your own hearts. Such honour as you offer to me is not contemplated by any man in whose mind a wholesome sanity rules, nor is it even the dream of fervent imagination. So great is it, that I pray you, men with hearts and minds like my own, to extend to me, as a further measure of your generosity, a little time to think it over. I shall not want long, for even already, with the blaze of honour fresh upon me, I see the cool shadow of Duty, though his substance is yet hardly visible. Give me but an hour of solitude—an hour at most—if it do not prolong this your session unduly. It may be that a lesser time will serve, but in any case I promise you that, when I can see a just and fitting issue to my thought, I shall at once return."

The President of the Council looked around him, and, seeing everywhere the bowing heads of acquiescence, spoke with a reverent gravity:

"We shall wait in patience whatsoever time you will, and may the God who rules all worthy hearts guide you to His Will!"

And so in silence the Voivode passed out of the hall.

From my seat near a window I could watch him go, as with measured steps he passed up the hill which rises behind the State House, and disappeared into the shadow of the forest. Then my work claimed me, for I wished to record the proceedings so far whilst all was fresh in my mind. In silence, as of the dead, the Council waited, no man challenging opinion of his neighbour even by a glance.

Almost a full hour had elapsed when the Voivode came again to the Council, moving with slow and stately gravity, as has always been his wont since age began to hamper the movement which in youth had been so notable. The Members of the Council all stood up uncovered, and so remained while he made announcement of his conclusion. He spoke slowly; and as his answer was to be a valued record of this Land and its Race, I wrote down every word as uttered, leaving here and there space for description or comment, which spaces I have since then filled in.

"Lords of the National Council, Archbishop, Vladika, Lords of the Council of Justice and of National Law, Archimandrites, and my brothers all, I have, since I left you, held in the solitude of the forest counsel with myself—and with God; and He, in His gracious wisdom, has led my thinking to that conclusion which was from the first moment of knowledge of your intent presaged in my heart. Brothers, you know—or else a long life has been spent in vain—that my heart and mind are all for the nation—my experience, my life, my handjar. And when all is for her, why should I shrink to exercise on her behalf my riper judgment though the same should have to combat my own ambition? For ten centuries my race has not failed in its duty. Ages ago the men of that time trusted in the hands of my ancestors the Kingship, even as now you, their children, trust me. But to me it would be base to betray that trust, even by the smallest tittle. That would I do were I to take the honour of the crown which you have tendered to me, so long as there is another more worthy to wear it. Were there none other, I should place myself in your hands, and yield myself over to blind obedience of your desires. But such an one there is; dear to you already by his own deeds, now doubly dear to me, since he is my son by my daughter's love. He is young, whereas I am old. He is strong and brave and true; but my days of the usefulness of strength and bravery are over. For myself, I have long contemplated as the crown of my later years a quiet life in one of our monasteries, where I can still watch the whirl of the world around us on your behalf, and be a counsellor of younger men of more active minds. Brothers, we are entering on stirring times. I can see the signs of their coming all around us. North and South—the Old Order and the New, are about to clash, and we lie between the opposing forces. True it is that the Turk, after warring for a thousand years, is fading into insignificance. But from the North where conquests spring, have crept towards our Balkans the men of a mightier composite Power. Their march has been steady; and as they came, they fortified every step of the way. Now they are hard upon us, and are already beginning to swallow up the regions that we have helped to win from the dominion of Mahound. The Austrian is at our very gates. Beaten back by the Irredentists of Italy, she has so enmeshed herself with the Great Powers of Europe that she seems for the moment to be impregnable to a foe of our stature. There is but one hope for us—the uniting of the Balkan forces to turn a masterly front to North and West as well as to South and East. Is that a task for old hands to undertake? No; the hands must be young and supple; and the brain subtle, as well as the heart be strong, of whomsoever would dare such an accomplishment. Should I accept the crown, it would only postpone the doing of that which must ultimately be done. What avail would it be if, when the darkness closes over me, my daughter should be Queen Consort to the first King of a new dynasty? You know this man, and from your record I learn that you are already willing to have him as King to follow me. Why not begin with him? He comes of a great nation, wherein the principle of freedom is a vital principle that quickens all things. That nation has more than once shown to us its friendliness; and doubtless the very fact that an Englishman would become our King, and could carry into our Government the spirit and customs which have made his own country great, would do much to restore the old friendship, and even to create a new one, which would in times of trouble bring British fleets to our waters, and British bayonets to support our own handjars. It is within my own knowledge, though as yet unannounced to you, that Rupert Sent Leger has already obtained a patent, signed by the King of England himself, allowing him to be denaturalized in England, so that he can at once apply for naturalization here. I know also that he has brought hither a vast fortune, by aid of which he is beginning to strengthen our hands for war, in case that sad eventuality should arise. Witness his late ordering to be built nine other warships of the class that has already done such effective service in overthrowing the Turk— or the pirate, whichever he may have been. He has undertaken the defence of the Blue Mouth at his own cost in a way which will make it stronger than Gibraltar, and secure us against whatever use to which the Austrian may apply the vast forces already gathered in the Bocche di Cattaro. He is already founding aerial stations on our highest peaks for use of the war aeroplanes which are being built for him. It is such a man as this who makes a nation great; and right sure I am that in his hands this splendid land and our noble, freedom-loving people will flourish and become a power in the world. Then, brothers, let me, as one to whom this nation and its history and its future are dear, ask you to give to the husband of my daughter the honour which you would confer on me. For her I can speak as well as for myself. She shall suffer nothing in dignity either. Were I indeed King, she, as my daughter, would be a Princess of the world. As it will be, she shall be companion and Queen of a great King, and her race, which is mine, shall flourish in all the lustre of the new Dynasty.

"Therefore on all accounts, my brothers, for the sake of our dear Land of the Blue Mountains, make the Gospodar Rupert, who has so proved himself, your King. And make me happy in my retirement to the cloister."

When the Voivode ceased to speak, all still remained silent and standing. But there was no mistaking their acquiescence in his most generous prayer. The President of the Council well interpreted the general wish when he said:

"Lords of the National Council, Archbishop, Vladika, Lords of the Councils of Justice and National Law, Archimandrites, and all who are present, is it agreed that we prepare at leisure a fitting reply to the Voivode Peter of the historic House of Vissarion, stating our agreement with his wish?"

To which there was a unanimous answer:

"It is." He went on:

"Further. Shall we ask the Gospodar Rupert of the House of Sent Leger, allied through his marriage to the Voivodin Teuta, daughter and only child of the Voivode Peter of Vissarion, to come hither to-morrow? And that, when he is amongst us, we confer on him the Crown and Kingship of the Land of the Blue Mountains?"

Again came the answer: "It is."

But this time it rang out like the sound of a gigantic trumpet, and the handjars flashed.

Whereupon the session was adjourned for the space of a day.

THE SAME—*Continued*

September 10, 1907

When the National Council met to-day the Voivode Peter Vissarion sat with them, but well back, so that at first his presence was hardly noticeable. After the necessary preliminaries had been gone through, they requested the presence of the Gospodar Rupert—Mr. Rupert Sent

Leger—who was reported as waiting in the "Chamber of the High Officers." He at once accompanied back to the Hall the deputation sent to conduct him. As he made his appearance in the doorway the Councillors stood up. There was a burst of enthusiasm, and the handjars flashed. For an instant he stood silent, with lifted hand, as though indicating that he wished to speak. So soon as this was recognized, silence fell on the assembly, and he spoke:

"I pray you, may the Voivodin Teuta of Vissarion, who has accompanied me hither, appear with me to hear your wishes?" There was an immediate and enthusiastic acquiescence, and, after bowing his thanks, he retired to conduct her.

Her appearance was received with an ovation similar to that given to Gospodar Rupert, to which she bowed with dignified sweetness. She, with her husband, was conducted to the top of the Hall by the President, who came down to escort them. In the meantime another chair had been placed beside that prepared for the Gospodar, and these two sat.

The President then made the formal statement conveying to the "Gospodar Rupert" the wishes of the Council, on behalf of the nation, to offer to him the Crown and Kingship of the Land of the Blue Mountains. The message was couched in almost the same words as had been used the previous day in making the offer to the Voivode Peter Vissarion, only differing to meet the special circumstances. The Gospodar Rupert listened in grave silence. The whole thing was manifestly quite new to him, but he preserved a self-control wonderful under the circumstances. When, having been made aware of the previous offer to the Voivode and the declared wish of the latter, he rose to speak, there was stillness in the Hall. He commenced with a few broken words of thanks; then he grew suddenly and strangely calm as he went on:

"But before I can even attempt to make a fitting reply, I should know if it is contemplated to join with me in this great honour my dear wife the Voivodin Teuta of Vissarion, who has so splendidly proved her worthiness to hold any place in the government of the Land. I fain would. . ."

He was interrupted by the Voivodin, who, standing up beside him and holding his left arm, said:

"Do not, President, and Lords all, think me wanting in that respect of a wife for husband which in the Blue Mountains we hold so dear, if I venture to interrupt my lord. I am here, not merely as a wife, but as

Voivodin of Vissarion, and by the memory of all the noble women of that noble line I feel constrained to a great duty. We women of Vissarion, in all the history of centuries, have never put ourselves forward in rivalry of our lords. Well I know that my own dear lord will forgive me as wife if I err; but I speak to you, the Council of the nation, from another ground and with another tongue. My lord does not, I fear, know as you do, and as I do too, that of old, in the history of this Land, when Kingship was existent, that it was ruled by that law of masculine supremacy which, centuries after, became known as the *Lex Salica*. Lords of the Council of the Blue Mountains, I am a wife of the Blue Mountains—as a wife young as yet, but with the blood of forty generations of loyal women in my veins. And it would ill become me, whom my husband honours—wife to the man whom you would honour—to take a part in changing the ancient custom which has been held in honour for all the thousand years, which is the glory of Blue Mountain womanhood. What an example such would be in an age when self-seeking women of other nations seek to forget their womanhood in the struggle to vie in equality with men! Men of the Blue Mountains, I speak for our women when I say that we hold of greatest price the glory of our men. To be their companions is our happiness; to be their wives is the completion of our lives; to be mothers of their children is our share of the glory that is theirs.

"Therefore, I pray you, men of the Blue Mountains, let me but be as any other wife in our land, equal to them in domestic happiness, which is our woman's sphere; and if that priceless honour may be vouchsafed to me, and I be worthy and able to bear it, an exemplar of woman's rectitude." With a low, modest, graceful bow, she sat down.

There was no doubt as to the reception of her renunciation of Queenly dignity. There was more honour to her in the quick, fierce shout which arose, and the unanimous upward swing of the handjars, than in the wearing of any crown which could adorn the head of woman.

The spontaneous action of the Gospodar Rupert was another source of joy to all—a fitting corollary to what had gone before. He rose to his feet, and, taking his wife in his arms, kissed her before all. Then they sat down, with their chairs close, bashfully holding hands like a pair of lovers.

Then Rupert arose—he is Rupert now; no lesser name is on the lips of his people henceforth. With an intense earnestness which seemed to glow in his face, he said simply:

"What can I say except that I am in all ways, now and for ever, obedient to your wishes?" Then, raising his handjar and holding it before him, he kissed the hilt, saying:

"Hereby I swear to be honest and just—to be, God helping me, such a King as you would wish—in so far as the strength is given me. Amen."

This ended the business of the Session, and the Council showed unmeasured delight. Again and again the handjars flashed, as the cheers rose "three times three" in British fashion.

When Rupert—I am told I must not write him down as "King Rupert" until after the formal crowning, which is ordained for Wednesday, October 16th,—and Teuta had withdrawn, the Voivode Peter Vissarion, the President and Council conferred in committee with the Presidents of the High Courts of National Law and of Justice as to the formalities to be observed in the crowning of the King, and of the formal notification to be given to foreign Powers. These proceedings kept them far into the night.

From "*The London Messenger*"

CORONATION FESTIVITIES OF THE BLUE MOUNTAINS.
(*From our Special Correspondent*)

PLAZAC,
October 14, 1907

As I sat down to a poorly-equipped luncheon-table on board the Austro-Orient liner *Franz Joseph*, I mourned in my heart (and I may say incidentally in other portions of my internal economy) the comfort and gastronomic luxury of the King and Emperor Hotel at Trieste. A brief comparison between the menus of to-day's lunch and yesterday's will afford to the reader a striking object-lesson:

Trieste	*Steamer*
Eggs a la cocotte	Scrambled eggs on toast
Stewed chicken, with paprika	Cold chicken
Devilled slices of Westphalian ham (boiled in wine)	Cold ham
Tunny fish, pickled	Bismarck herrings
Rice, burst in cream	Stewed apples
Guava jelly	Swiss cheese

Consequence: Yesterday I was well and happy, and looked forward to a good night's sleep, which came off. To-day I am dull and heavy, also restless, and I am convinced that at sleeping-time my liver will have it all its own way.

The journey to Ragusa, and thence to Plazac, is writ large with a pigment of misery on at least one human heart. Let a silence fall upon it! In such wise only can Justice and Mercy join hands.

Plazac is a miserable place. There is not a decent hotel in it. It was perhaps on this account that the new King, Rupert, had erected for the alleged convenience of his guests of the Press a series of large temporary hotels, such as were in evidence at the St. Louis Exposition. Here each guest was given a room to himself, somewhat after the nature of the cribs in a Rowton house. From my first night in it I am able to speak from experience of the sufferings of a prisoner of the third class. I am, however, bound to say that the dining and reception rooms were, though uncomfortably plain, adequate for temporary use. Happily we shall not have to endure many more meals here, as to-morrow we all dine with the King in the State House; and as the cuisine is under the control of that *cordon bleu*, Gaston de Faux Pas, who so long controlled the gastronomic (we might almost say Gastonomic) destinies of the Rois des Diamants in the Place Vendome, we may, I think, look forward to not going to bed hungry. Indeed, the anticipations formed from a survey of our meagre sleeping accommodation were not realized at dinnertime to-night. To our intense astonishment, an excellent dinner was served, though, to be sure, the cold dishes predominated (a thing I always find bad for one's liver). Just as we were finishing, the King (nominated) came amongst us in quite an informal way, and, having bidden us a hearty welcome, asked that we should drink a glass of wine together. This we did in an excellent (if rather sweet) glass of Cliquot '93. King Rupert (nominated) then asked us to resume our seats. He walked between the tables, now and again recognizing some journalistic friend whom he had met early in life in his days of adventure. The men spoken to seemed vastly pleased—with themselves probably. Pretty bad form of them, I call it! For myself, I was glad I had not previously met him in the same casual way, as it saved me from what I should have felt a humiliation—the being patronized in that public way by a prospective King who had not (in a Court sense) been born. The writer, who is by profession a barrister-at-law, is satisfied at being himself a county gentleman and heir to an historic estate in the ancient county of

Salop, which can boast a larger population than the Land of the Blue Mountains.

EDITORIAL NOTE.—WE MUST ASK OUR readers to pardon the report in yesterday's paper sent from Plazac. The writer was not on our regular staff, but asked to be allowed to write the report, as he was a kinsman of King Rupert of the Blue Mountains, and would therefore be in a position to obtain special information and facilities of description "from inside," as he puts it. On reading the paper, we cabled his recall; we cabled also, in case he did not obey, to have his ejectment effected forthwith.

We have also cabled Mr. Mordred Booth, the well-known correspondent, who was, to our knowledge, in Plazac for his own purposes, to send us full (and proper) details. We take it our readers will prefer a graphic account of the ceremony to a farrago of cheap menus, comments on his own liver, and a belittling of an Englishman of such noble character and achievements that a rising nation has chosen him for their King, and one whom our own nation loves to honour. We shall not, of course, mention our abortive correspondent's name, unless compelled thereto by any future utterance of his.

FROM "*The London Messenger*"

THE CORONATION OF KING RUPERT OF THE BLUE MOUNTAINS.
(*By our Special Correspondent, Mordred Booth*)

PLAZAC,
October 17, 1907

Plazac does not boast of a cathedral or any church of sufficient dimensions for a coronation ceremony on an adequate scale. It was therefore decided by the National Council, with the consent of the King, that it should be held at the old church of St. Sava at Vissarion—the former home of the Queen. Accordingly, arrangements had been made to bring thither on the warships on the morning of the coronation the whole of the nation's guests. In St. Sava's the religious ceremony would take place, after which there would be a banquet in the Castle of Vissarion. The guests would then return on the warships to Plazac, where would be held what is called here the "National Coronation."

In the Land of the Blue Mountains it was customary in the old days, when there were Kings, to have two ceremonies—one carried out by the official head of the national Church, the Greek Church; the other by the people in a ritual adopted by themselves, on much the same basis as the Germanic Folk-Moot. The Blue Mountains is a nation of strangely loyal tendencies. What was a thousand years ago is to be to-day—so far, of course, as is possible under the altered condition of things.

The church of St. Sava is very old and very beautiful, built in the manner of old Greek churches, full of monuments of bygone worthies of the Blue Mountains. But, of course, neither it nor the ceremony held in it to-day can compare in splendour with certain other ceremonials—for instance, the coronation of the penultimate Czar in Moscow, of Alfonso XII in Madrid, of Carlos I in Lisbon.

The church was arranged much after the fashion of Westminster Abbey for the coronation of King Edward VII, though, of course, not so many persons present, nor so much individual splendour. Indeed, the number of those present, outside those officially concerned and the Press of the world, was very few.

The most striking figure present—next to King Rupert, who is seven feet high and a magnificent man—was the Queen Consort, Teuta. She sat in front of a small gallery erected for the purpose just opposite the throne. She is a strikingly beautiful woman, tall and finely-formed, with jet-black hair and eyes like black diamonds, but with the unique quality that there are stars in them which seem to take varied colour according to each strong emotion. But it was not even her beauty or the stars in her eyes which drew the first glance of all. These details showed on scrutiny, but from afar off the attractive point was her dress. Surely never before did woman, be she Queen or peasant, wear such a costume on a festive occasion.

She was dressed in a white *Shroud*, and in that only. I had heard something of the story which goes behind that strange costume, and shall later on send it to you.

When the procession entered the church through the great western door, the national song of the Blue Mountains, "Guide our feet through darkness, O Jehovah," was sung by an unseen choir, in which the organ, supplemented by martial instruments, joined. The Archbishop was robed in readiness before the altar, and close around him stood the Archimandrites of the four great monasteries. The Vladika stood in front of the Members of the National Council. A little to one side of this body was a group of high officials, Presidents of the Councils of National Law and Justice, the Chancellor, etc.—all in splendid robes of great antiquity—the High Marshall of the Forces and the Lord high Admiral.

When all was ready for the ceremonial act of coronation, the Archbishop raised his hand, whereupon the music ceased. Turning around, so that he faced the Queen, who thereon stood up, the King drew his handjar and saluted her in Blue Mountain fashion—the point raised as high possible, and then dropped down till it almost touches the ground. Every man in the church, ecclesiastics and all, wear the handjar, and, following the King by the interval of a second, their weapons flashed out. There was something symbolic, as well as touching, in this truly royal salute, led by the King. His handjar is a mighty blade, and held high in the hands of a man of his stature, it overtowered everything in the church. It was an inspiriting sight. No one who saw will ever forget that noble flashing of blades in the thousand-year-old salute. . .

The coronation was short, simple, and impressive. Rupert knelt whilst the Archbishop, after a short, fervent prayer, placed on his head the bronze crown of the first King of the Blue Mountains, Peter. This was handed to him by the Vladika, to whom it was brought from the National Treasury by a procession of the high officers. A blessing of the new King and his Queen Teuta concluded the ceremony. Rupert's first act on rising from his knees was to draw his handjar and salute his people.

After the ceremony in St. Sava, the procession was reformed, and took its way to the Castle of Vissarion, which is some distance off across a picturesque creek, bounded on either side by noble cliffs of vast height. The King led the way, the Queen walking with him and holding his hand. . . The Castle of Vissarion is of great antiquity, and picturesque beyond belief. I am sending later on, as a special article, a description of it. . .

The "Coronation Feast," as it was called on the menu, was held in the Great Hall, which is of noble proportions. I enclose copy of the menu, as our readers may wish to know something of the details of such a feast in this part of the world.

One feature of the banquet was specially noticeable. As the National Officials were guests of the King and Queen, they were waited on and served by the King and Queen in person. The rest of the guests, including us of the Press, were served by the King's household, not the servants—none of that cult were visible—but by the ladies and gentlemen of the Court.

There was only one toast, and that was given by the King, all standing: "The Land of the Blue Mountains, and may we all do our duty to the Land we love!" Before drinking, his mighty handjar flashed out again, and in an instant every table at which the Blue Mountaineers sat was ringed with flashing steel. I may add parenthetically that the handjar is essentially the national weapon. I do not know if the Blue Mountaineers take it to bed with them, but they certainly wear it everywhere else. Its drawing seems to emphasize everything in national life. . .

We embarked again on the warships—one a huge, steel-plated Dreadnought, up to date in every particular, the other an armoured yacht most complete in every way, and of unique speed. The King and Queen, the Lords of the Council, together with the various high ecclesiastics and great officials, went on the yacht, which the Lord High Admiral, a man of remarkably masterful physiognomy, himself steered. The rest of those present at the Coronation came on the warship. The latter went fast, but the yacht showed her heels all the way. However, the King's party waited in the dock in the Blue Mouth. From this a new cable-line took us all to the State House at Plazac. Here the procession was reformed, and wound its way to a bare hill in the immediate vicinity. The King and Queen—the King still wearing the ancient bronze crown with which the Archbishop had invested him at St. Sava's—the Archbishop, the Vladika, and the four Archimandrites stood together at the top of the hill, the King and Queen being, of course, in the front. A courteous young gentleman, to whom I had been accredited at the beginning of the day—all guests were so attended—explained to me that, as this was the national as opposed to the religious ceremony, the Vladika, who is the official representative of the laity, took command here. The ecclesiastics were put prominently forward, simply out of courtesy, in obedience to the wish of the people, by whom they were all greatly beloved.

Then commenced another unique ceremony, which, indeed, might well find a place in our Western countries. As far as ever we could see were masses of men roughly grouped, not in any uniform, but all in national costume, and armed only with the handjar. In the front of each of these groups or bodies stood the National Councillor for that district, distinguishable by his official robe and chain. There were in all seventeen of these bodies. These were unequal in numbers, some of them predominating enormously over others, as, indeed, might be expected in so mountainous a country. In all there were present, I was told, over a hundred thousand men. So far as I can judge from long experience of looking at great bodies of men, the estimate was a just one. I was a little surprised to see so many, for the population of the Blue Mountains is never accredited in books of geography as a large one. When I made inquiry as to how the frontier guard was being for the time maintained, I was told:

"By the women mainly. But, all the same, we have also a male guard which covers the whole frontier except that to seaward. Each man has with him six women, so that the whole line is unbroken. Moreover, sir, you must bear in mind that in the Blue Mountains our women are trained to arms as well as our men—ay, and they could give a good account of themselves, too, against any foe that should assail us. Our history shows what women can do in defence. I tell you, the Turkish population would be bigger to-day but for the women who on our frontier fought of old for defence of their homes!"

"No wonder this nation has kept her freedom for a thousand years!" I said.

At a signal given by the President of the National Council one of the Divisions moved forwards. It was not an ordinary movement, but an intense rush made with all the *elan* and vigour of hardy and highly-trained men. They came on, not merely at the double, but as if delivering an attack. Handjar in hand, they rushed forward. I can only compare their rush to an artillery charge or to an attack of massed cavalry battalions. It was my fortune to see the former at Magenta and the latter at Sadowa, so that I know what such illustration means. I may also say that I saw the relief column which Roberts organized rush through a town on its way to relieve Mafeking; and no one who had the delight of seeing that inspiring progress of a flying army on their way to relieve their comrades needs to be told what a rush of armed men can be. With speed which was simply desperate they ran up the hill, and, circling to the left, made a ring round the topmost plateau, where stood the King. When the ring was complete, the stream went on lapping round and round till the whole tally was exhausted. In the meantime another Division had followed, its leader joining close behind the end of the first. Then came another and another. An unbroken line circled and circled round the hill in seeming endless array, till the whole slopes were massed with moving men, dark in colour, and with countless glittering points everywhere. When the whole of the Divisions had thus surrounded the King, there was a moment's hush—a silence so still that it almost seemed as if Nature stood still also. We who looked on were almost afraid to breathe.

Then suddenly, without, so far as I could see, any fugleman or word of command, the handjars of all that mighty array of men flashed upward as one, and like thunder pealed the National cry:

"The Blue Mountains and Duty!"

After the cry there was a strange subsidence which made the onlooker rub his eyes. It seemed as though the whole mass of fighting men had partially sunk into the ground. Then the splendid truth burst upon us—the whole nation was kneeling at the feet of their chosen King, who stood upright.

Another moment of silence, as King Rupert, taking off his crown, held it up in his left hand, and, holding his great handjar high in his right, cried in a voice so strong that it came ringing over that serried mass like a trumpet:

"To Freedom of our Nation, and to Freedom within it, I dedicate these and myself. I swear!"

So saying, he, too, sank on his knees, whilst we all instinctively uncovered.

The silence which followed lasted several seconds; then, without a sign, as though one and all acted instinctively, the whole body stood up. Thereupon was executed a movement which, with all my experience of soldiers and war, I never saw equalled—not with the Russian Royal Guard saluting the Czar at his Coronation, not with an impi of Cetewayo's Zulus whirling through the opening of a kraal.

For a second or two the whole mass seemed to writhe or shudder, and then, lo! the whole District Divisions were massed again in completeness, its Councillors next the King, and the Divisions radiating outwards down the hill like wedges.

This completed the ceremony, and everything broke up into units. Later, I was told by my official friend that the King's last movement—the oath as he sank to his knees—was an innovation of his own. All I can say is, if, in the future, and for all time, it is not taken for a precedent, and made an important part of the Patriotic Coronation ceremony, the Blue Mountaineers will prove themselves to be a much more stupid people than they seem at present to be.

The conclusion of the Coronation festivities was a time of unalloyed joy. It was the banquet given to the King and Queen by the nation; the guests of the nation were included in the royal party. It was a unique ceremony. Fancy a picnic-party of a hundred thousand persons, nearly all men. There must have been made beforehand vast and elaborate preparations, ramifying through the whole nation. Each section had brought provisions sufficient for their own consumption in addition to several special dishes for the guest-tables; but the contribution of each section was not consumed by its own members.

It was evidently a part of the scheme that all should derive from a common stock, so that the feeling of brotherhood and common property should be preserved in this monumental fashion.

The guest-tables were the only tables to be seen. The bulk of the feasters sat on the ground. The tables were brought forward by the men themselves—no such thing as domestic service was known on this day—from a wood close at hand, where they and the chairs had been placed in readiness. The linen and crockery used had been sent for the purpose from the households of every town and village. The flowers were plucked in the mountains early that morning by the children, and the gold and silver plate used for adornment were supplied from the churches. Each dish at the guest-tables was served by the men of each section in turn.

Over the whole array seemed to be spread an atmosphere of joyousness, of peace, of brotherhood. It would be impossible to adequately describe that amazing scene, a whole nation of splendid men surrounding their new King and Queen, loving to honour and serve them. Scattered about through that vast crowd were groups of musicians, chosen from amongst themselves. The space covered by this titanic picnic was so vast that there were few spots from which you could hear music proceeding from different quarters.

After dinner we all sat and smoked; the music became rather vocal than instrumental—indeed, presently we did not hear the sound of any instrument at all. Only knowing a few words of Balkan, I could not follow the meanings of the songs, but I gathered that they were all legendary or historical. To those who could understand, as I was informed by my tutelary young friend, who stayed beside me the whole of this memorable day, we were listening to the history of the Land of the Blue Mountains in ballad form. Somewhere or other throughout that vast concourse each notable record of ten centuries was being told to eager ears.

It was now late in the day. Slowly the sun had been dropping down over the Calabrian Mountains, and the glamorous twilight was stealing over the immediate scene. No one seemed to notice the coming of the dark, which stole down on us with an unspeakable mystery. For long we sat still, the clatter of many tongues becoming stilled into the witchery of the scene. Lower the sun sank, till only the ruddiness of the afterglow lit the expanse with rosy light; then this failed in turn, and the night shut down quickly.

At last, when we could just discern the faces close to us, a simultaneous movement began. Lights began to flash out in places all over the hillside. At first these seemed as tiny as glow-worms seen in a summer wood, but by degrees they grew till the space was set with little circles of light. These in turn grew and grew in both number and strength. Flames began to leap out from piles of wood, torches were lighted and held high. Then the music began again, softly at first, but then louder as the musicians began to gather to the centre, where sat the King and Queen. The music was wild and semi-barbaric, but full of sweet melody. It somehow seemed to bring before us a distant past; one and all, according to the strength of our imagination and the volume of our knowledge, saw episodes and phases of bygone history come before us. There was a wonderful rhythmic, almost choric, force in the time kept, which made it almost impossible to sit still. It was an invitation to the dance such as I had never before heard in any nation or at any time. Then the lights began to gather round. Once more the mountaineers took something of the same formation as at the crowning. Where the royal party sat was a level mead, with crisp, short grass, and round it what one might well call the Ring of the Nation was formed.

The music grew louder. Each mountaineer who had not a lit torch already lighted one, and the whole rising hillside was a glory of light. The Queen rose, and the King an instant after. As they rose men stepped forward and carried away their chairs, or rather thrones. The Queen gave the King her hand—this is, it seems, the privilege of the wife as distinguished from any other woman. Their feet took the time of the music, and they moved into the centre of the ring.

That dance was another thing to remember, won from the haunting memories of that strange day. At first the King and Queen danced all alone. They began with stately movement, but as the music quickened their feet kept time, and the swing of their bodies with movements kept growing more and more ecstatic at every beat till, in true Balkan fashion, the dance became a very agony of passionate movement.

At this point the music slowed down again, and the mountaineers began to join in the dance. At first slowly, one by one, they joined in, the Vladika and the higher priests leading; then everywhere the whole vast crowd began to dance, till the earth around us seemed to shake. The lights quivered, flickered, blazed out again, and rose and fell as that hundred thousand men, each holding a torch, rose and fell with the rhythm of the dance. Quicker, quicker grew the music, faster grew the rushing and pounding of the feet, till the whole nation seemed now in an ecstasy.

I stood near the Vladika, and in the midst of this final wildness I saw him draw from his belt a short, thin flute; then he put it to his lips and blew a single note—a fierce, sharp note, which pierced the volume of sound more surely than would the thunder of a cannon-shot. On the instant everywhere each man put his torch under his foot.

There was complete and immediate darkness, for the fires, which had by now fallen low, had evidently been trodden out in the measure of the dance. The music still kept in its rhythmic beat, but slower than it had yet been. Little by little this beat was pointed and emphasized by the clapping of hands—at first only a few, but spreading till everyone present was beating hands to the slow music in the darkness. This lasted a little while, during which, looking round, I noticed a faint light beginning to steal up behind the hills. The moon was rising.

Again there came a note from the Vladika's flute—a single note, sweet and subtle, which I can only compare with a note from a nightingale, vastly increased in powers. It, too, won through the thunder of the hand-claps, and on the second the sound ceased. The sudden stillness, together with the darkness, was so impressive that we could almost hear our hearts beating. And then came through the darkness the most beautiful and impressive sound heard yet. That mighty concourse, without fugleman of any sort, began, in low, fervent voice, to sing the National Anthem. At first it was of so low tone as to convey the idea of a mighty assembly of violinists playing with the mutes on. But it gradually rose till the air above us seemed to throb and quiver. Each syllable—each word—spoken in unison by the vast throng was as clearly enunciated as though spoken by a single voice:

"Guide our feet through darkness, O Jehovah."

This anthem, sung out of full hearts, remains on our minds as the last perfection of a perfect day. For myself, I am not ashamed to own that it made me weep like a child. Indeed, I cannot write of it now as I would; it unmans me so!

In the early morning, whilst the mountains were still rather grey than blue, the cable-line took us to the Blue Mouth, where we embarked in the King's yacht, *The Lady*, which took us across the Adriatic at a pace which I had hitherto considered impossible. The King and Queen came to the landing to see us off. They stood together at the right-hand side of the red-carpeted gangway, and shook hands with each guest as he went on board. The instant the last passenger had stepped on deck the gangway was withdrawn. The Lord High Admiral, who stood on the bridge, raised his hand, and we swept towards the mouth of the gulf. Of course, all hats were off, and we cheered frantically. I can truly say that if King Rupert and Queen Teuta should ever wish to found in the Blue Mountains a colony of diplomatists and journalists, those who were their guests on this great occasion will volunteer to a man. I think old Hempetch, who is the doyen of English-speaking journalists, voiced our sentiments when he said:

"May God bless them and theirs with every grace and happiness, and send prosperity to the Land and the rule!" I think the King and Queen heard us cheer, they turned to look at our flying ship again.

Book IX

Balka

February 10, 1908

It is so long since I even thought of this journal that I hardly know where to begin. I always heard that a married man is a pretty busy man; but since I became one, though it is a new life to me, and of a happiness undreamt of, I *know* what that life is. But I had no idea that this King business was anything like what it is. Why, it never leaves me a moment at all to myself—or, what is worse, to Teuta. If people who condemn Kings had only a single month of my life in that capacity, they would form an opinion different from that which they hold. It might be useful to have a Professor of Kingship in the Anarchists' College—whenever it is founded!

Everything has gone on well with us, I am glad to say. Teuta is in splendid health, though she has—but only very lately—practically given up going on her own aeroplane. It was, I know, a great sacrifice to make, just as she had become an expert at it. They say here that she is one of the best drivers in the Blue Mountains—and that is in the world, for we have made that form of movement our own. Ever since we found the pitch-blende pockets in the Great Tunnel, and discovered the simple process of extracting the radium from it, we have gone on by leaps and bounds. When first Teuta told me she would "aero" no more for a while, I thought she was wise, and backed her up in it: for driving an aeroplane is trying work and hard on the nerves. I only learned then the reason for her caution—the usual one of a young wife. That was three months ago, and only this morning she told me she would not go sailing in the air, even with me, till she could do so "without risk"—she did not mean risk to herself. Aunt Janet knew what she meant, and counselled her strongly to stick to her resolution. So for the next few months I am to do my air-sailing alone.

The public works which we began immediately after the Coronation are going strong. We began at the very beginning on an elaborate system. The first thing was to adequately fortify the Blue Mouth. Whilst the fortifications were being constructed we kept all the warships in the gulf. But when the point of safety was reached, we made the ships do sentry-go along the coast, whilst we trained men for service at sea. It is our plan to take by degrees all the young men and teach them this wise, so that at the end the whole population shall be trained for sea as well as for land. And as we are teaching them the airship service, too, they will be at home in all the elements—except fire, of course, though if that should become a necessity, we shall tackle it too!

We started the Great Tunnel at the farthest inland point of the Blue Mouth, and ran it due east at an angle of 45 degrees, so that, when complete, it would go right through the first line of hills, coming out on the plateau Plazac. The plateau is not very wide—half a mile at most—and the second tunnel begins on the eastern side of it. This new tunnel is at a smaller angle, as it has to pierce the second hill—a mountain this time. When it comes out on the east side of that, it will tap the real productive belt. Here it is that our hardwood-trees are finest, and where the greatest mineral deposits are found. This plateau is of enormous length, and runs north arid south round the great bulk of the central mountain, so that in time, when we put up a circular railway, we can bring, at a merely nominal cost, all sorts of material up or down. It is on this level that we have built the great factories for war material. We are tunnelling into the mountains, where are the great deposits of coal. We run the trucks in and out on the level, and can get perfect ventilation with little cost or labour. Already we are mining all the coal which we consume within our own confines, and we can, if we wish, within a year export largely. The great slopes of these tunnels give us the necessary aid of specific gravity, and as we carry an endless water-supply in great tubes that way also, we can do whatever we wish by hydraulic power. As one by one the European and Asiatic nations began to reduce their war preparations, we took over their disbanded workmen though our agents, so that already we have a productive staff of skilled workmen larger than anywhere else in the world. I think myself that we were fortunate in being able to get ahead so fast with our preparations for war manufacture, for if some of the "Great Powers," as they call themselves, knew the measure of our present production, they would immediately try to take active measures against us. In such case we should have to fight them, which would delay us. But if we can have another year untroubled, we shall, so far as war material is concerned, be able to defy any nation in the world. And if the time may only come peacefully till we have our buildings and machinery complete, we can prepare war-stores and implements for the whole Balkan nations. And then—But that is a dream. We shall know in good time.

In the meantime all goes well. The cannon foundries are built and active. We are already beginning to turn out finished work. Of course, our first guns are not very large, but they are good. The big guns, and especially siege-guns, will come later. And when the great extensions are complete, and the boring and wire-winding machines are in working order, we can go merrily on. I suppose that by that time the whole of the upper plateau will be like a manufacturing town—at any rate, we have plenty of raw material to hand. The haematite mines seem to be inexhaustible, and as the raising of the ore is cheap and easy by means of our extraordinary water-power, and as coal comes down to the plateau by its own gravity on the cable-line, we have natural advantages which exist hardly anywhere else in the world—certainly not all together, as here. That bird's eye view of the Blue Mouth which we had from the aeroplane when Teuta saw that vision of the future has not been in vain. The aeroplane works are having a splendid output. The aeroplane is a large and visible product; there is no mistaking when it is there! We have already a large and respectable aerial fleet. The factories for explosives are, of course, far away in bare valleys, where accidental effects are minimized. So, too, are the radium works, wherein unknown dangers may lurk. The turbines in the tunnel give us all the power we want at present, and, later on, when the new tunnel, which we call the "water tunnel," which is already begun, is complete, the available power will be immense. All these works are bringing up our shipping, and we are in great hopes for the future.

So much for our material prosperity. But with it comes a larger life and greater hopes. The stress of organizing and founding these great works is practically over. As they are not only self-supporting, but largely productive, all anxiety in the way of national expenditure is minimized. And, more than all, I am able to give my unhampered attention to those matters of even more than national importance on which the ultimate development, if not the immediate strength, of our country must depend.

I am well into the subject of a great Balkan Federation. This, it turns out, has for long been the dream of Teuta's life, as also that of the present Archimandrite of Plazac, her father, who, since I last touched this journal, having taken on himself a Holy Life, was, by will of the

Church, the Monks, and the People, appointed to that great office on the retirement of Petrof Vlastimir.

Such a Federation had long been in the air. For myself, I had seen its inevitableness from the first. The modern aggressions of the Dual Nation, interpreted by her past history with regard to Italy, pointed towards the necessity of such a protective measure. And now, when Servia and Bulgaria were used as blinds to cover her real movements to incorporate with herself as established the provinces, once Turkish, which had been entrusted to her temporary protection by the Treaty of Berlin; when it would seem that Montenegro was to be deprived for all time of the hope of regaining the Bocche di Cattaro, which she had a century ago won, and held at the point of the sword, until a Great Power had, under a wrong conviction, handed it over to her neighbouring Goliath; when the Sandjack of Novi-Bazar was threatened with the fate which seemed to have already overtaken Bosnia and Herzegovina; when gallant little Montenegro was already shut out from the sea by the octopus-like grip of Dalmatia crouching along her western shore; when Turkey was dwindling down to almost ineptitude; when Greece was almost a byword, and when Albania as a nation—though still nominally subject—was of such unimpaired virility that there were great possibilities of her future, it was imperative that something must happen if the Balkan race was not to be devoured piecemeal by her northern neighbours. To the end of ultimate protection I found most of them willing to make defensive alliance.

And as the true defence consists in judicious attack, I have no doubt that an alliance so based must ultimately become one for all purposes. Albania was the most difficult to win to the scheme, as her own complications with her suzerain, combined with the pride and suspiciousness of her people, made approach a matter of extreme caution. It was only possible when I could induce her rulers to see that, no matter how great her pride and valour, the magnitude of northern advance, if unchecked, must ultimately overwhelm her.

I own that this map-making was nervous work, for I could not shut my eyes to the fact that German lust of enlargement lay behind Austria's advance. At and before that time expansion was the dominant idea of the three Great Powers of Central Europe. Russia went eastward, hoping to gather to herself the rich north-eastern provinces of China, till ultimately she should dominate the whole of Northern Europe and Asia from the Gulf of Finland to the Yellow Sea. Germany wished to link the North Sea to the Mediterranean by her own territory, and thus stand as a flawless barrier across Europe from north to south.

When Nature should have terminated the headship of the Empire-Kingdom, she, as natural heir, would creep southward through the German-speaking provinces. Thus Austria, of course kept in ignorance of her neighbour's ultimate aims, had to extend towards the south. She had been barred in her western movement by the rise of the Irredentist party in Italy, and consequently had to withdraw behind the frontiers of Carinthia, Carniola, and Istria.

My own dream of the new map was to make "Balka"—the Balkan Federation—take in ultimately all south of a line drawn from the Isle of Serpents to Aquileia. There would—must—be difficulties in the carrying out of such a scheme. Of course, it involved Austria giving up Dalmatia, Istria, and Sclavonia, as well as a part of Croatia and the Hungarian Banat. On the contrary, she might look for centuries of peace in the south. But it would make for peace so strongly that each of the States impinging on it would find it worth while to make a considerable sacrifice to have it effected. To its own integers it would offer a lasting settlement of interests which at present conflicted, and a share in a new world-power. Each of these integers would be absolutely self-governing and independent, being only united for purposes of mutual good. I did not despair that even Turkey and Greece, recognizing that benefit and safety would ensue without the destruction or even minimizing of individuality, would, sooner or later, come into the Federation. The matter is already so far advanced that within a month the various rulers of the States involved are to have a secret and informal meeting. Doubtless some larger plan and further action will be then evolved. It will be an anxious time for all in this zone—and outside it—till this matter is all settled. In any case, the manufacture of war material will go on until it is settled, one way or another.

RUPERT'S JOURNAL—*Continued*

March 6, 1908

I breathe more freely. The meeting has taken place here at Vissarion. Nominal cause of meeting: a hunting-party in the Blue Mountains. Not any formal affair. Not a Chancellor or Secretary of State or Diplomatist of any sort present. All headquarters. It was, after all, a real hunting-party. Good sportsmen, plenty of game, lots of beaters, everything organized properly, and an effective tally of results. I think we all enjoyed ourselves in the matter of sport; and as the political result was absolute unanimity of purpose and intention, there could be no possible cause of complaint.

So it is all decided. Everything is pacific. There is not a suggestion even of war, revolt, or conflicting purpose of any kind. We all go on exactly as we are doing for another year, pursuing our own individual objects, just as at present. But we are all to see that in our own households order prevails. All that is supposed to be effective is to be kept in good working order, and whatever is, at present, not adequate to possibilities is to be made so. This is all simply protective and defensive. We understand each other. But if any hulking stranger should undertake to interfere in our domestic concerns, we shall all unite on the instant to keep things as we wish them to remain. We shall be ready. Alfred's maxim of Peace shall be once more exemplified. In the meantime the factories shall work overtime in our own mountains, and the output shall be for the general good of our special community—the bill to be settled afterwards amicably. There can hardly be any difference of opinion about that, as the others will be the consumers of our surplus products. We are the producers, who produce for ourselves first, and then for the limited market of those within the Ring. As we undertake to guard our own frontiers—sea and land—and are able to do so, the goods are to be warehoused in the Blue Mountains until required—if at all—for participation in the markets of the world, and especially in the European market. If all goes well and the markets are inactive, the goods shall be duly delivered to the purchasers as arranged.

So much for the purely mercantile aspect.

The Voivodin Janet Mackelpie's Notes

May 21, 1908

As Rupert began to neglect his Journal when he was made a King, so, too, I find in myself a tendency to leave writing to other people. But one thing I shall not be content to leave to others—little Rupert. The baby of Rupert and Teuta is much too precious a thing to be spoken of except with love, quite independent of the fact that he will be, in natural course, a King! So I have promised Teuta that whatever shall be put into this record of the first King of the Sent Leger Dynasty relating to His Royal Highness the Crown Prince shall only appear in either her hand or my own. And she has deputed the matter to me.

Our dear little Prince arrived punctually and in perfect condition. The angels that carried him evidently took the greatest care of him, and before they left him they gave him dower of all their best. He is a dear! Like both his father and his mother, and that says everything. My own private opinion is that he is a born King! He does not know what fear is, and he thinks more of everyone else than he does of his dear little self. And if those things do not show a truly royal nature, I do not know what does. . .

Teuta has read this. She held up a warning finger, and said:

"Aunt Janet dear, that is all true. He is a dear, and a King, and an angel! But we mustn't have too much about him just yet. This book is to be about Rupert. So our little man can only be what we shall call a corollary." And so it is.

I should mention here that the book is Teuta's idea. Before little Rupert came she controlled herself wonderfully, doing only what was thought best for her under the circumstances. As I could see that it would be a help for her to have some quiet occupation which would interest her without tiring her, I looked up (with his permission, of course) all Rupert's old letters and diaries, and journals and reports—all that I had kept for him during his absences on his adventures. At first I was a little afraid they might harm her, for at times she got so excited over some things that I had to caution her. Here again came in her wonderful self-control. I think the most soothing argument I used with her was to point out that the dear boy had come through all the dangers safely, and was actually with us, stronger and nobler than ever.

After we had read over together the whole matter several times—for it was practically new to me too, and I got nearly as excited as she was, though I have known him so much longer—we came to the conclusion that this particular volume would have to be of selected matter. There is enough of Rupert's work to make a lot of volumes and we have an ambitious literary project of some day publishing an *edition de luxe* of his whole collected works. It will be a rare showing amongst the works of Kings. But this is to be all about himself, so that in the future it may serve as a sort of backbone of his personal history.

By-and-by we came to a part when we had to ask him questions; and he was so interested in Teuta's work—he is really bound up body and soul in his beautiful wife, and no wonder—that we had to take him into full confidence. He promised he would help us all he could by giving us the use of his later journals, and such letters and papers as he had kept privately. He said he would make one condition—I use his own words: "As you two dear women are to be my editors, you must promise to put in everything exactly as I wrote it. It will not do to have any fake about this. I do not wish anything foolish or egotistical toned down out of affection for me. It was all written in sincerity, and if I had faults, they must not be hidden. If it is to be history, it must be true history, even if it gives you and me or any of us away."

So we promised.

He also said that, as Sir Edward Bingham Trent, Bart.—as he is now—was sure to have some matter which we should like, he would write and ask him to send such to us. He also said that Mr. Ernest Roger Halbard Melton, of Humcroft, Salop (he always gives this name and address in full, which is his way of showing contempt), would be sure to have some relevant matter, and that he would have him written to on the subject. This he did. The Chancellor wrote him in his most grandiloquent style. Mr. E. R. H. Melton, of H., S., replied by return post. His letter is a document which speaks for itself:

Humcroft, Salop,
May 30, 1908

My Dear Cousin King Rupert,

I am honoured by the request made on your behalf by the Lord High Chancellor of your kingdom that I should make a literary contribution to the volume which my cousin, Queen Teuta, is, with the help of your former governess, Miss MacKelpie, compiling. I am willing to do so, as you naturally wish to have in that work some contemporary record made by the Head of the House of Melton, with which you are connected, though only on the distaff side. It is a natural ambition enough, even on the part of a barbarian—or perhaps semi-barbarian—King, and far be it from me, as Head of the House, to deny you such a coveted privilege. Perhaps you may not know that I am now Head of the House; my father died three days ago. I offered my mother the use of the Dower House—to the incumbency of which, indeed, she is entitled by her marriage settlement. But she preferred to go to live at her seat, Carfax, in Kent. She went this morning after the funeral. In letting you have the use of my manuscript I make only one stipulation, but that I expect to be rigidly adhered to. It is that all that I have written be put in the book *in extenso*. I do not wish any record of mine to be garbled to suit other ends than those ostensible, or whatever may be to the honour of myself or my House to be burked. I dare say you have noticed, my dear Rupert, that the compilers of family histories often, through jealousy, alter matter that they are allowed to use so as to suit their own purpose or minister to their own vanity. I think it right to tell you that I have had a certified copy made by Petter and Galpin, the law stationers, so that I shall be able to verify whether my stipulation has been honourably observed. I am having the book, which is naturally valuable, carefully packed, and shall have it forwarded to Sir Edward Bingham Trent, Baronet (which he now is—Heaven save the mark!), the Attorney. Please see that he returns it to me, and in proper order. He is not to publish for himself anything in it about him. A man of that class is apt to advertise the fact of anyone of distinction taking any notice of him. I would bring out the Ms. to you myself, and stay for a while with you for some sport, only your lot—subjects I suppose you call them!—are such bounders that a gentleman's life is hardly safe amongst them. I never met anyone who had so poor an appreciation of a joke as they have. By the way, how is Teuta? She is one of them. I heard all about the hatching business. I hope the kid is all right. This is only a word in your ear, so don't get cocky, old son. I am open to a godfathership. Think of that, Hedda! Of course, if the other godfather and the godmother are up to the mark; I don't want to have to boost up the whole lot! Savvy? Kiss Teuta and the kid for me. I must have the boy over here for a bit later on—when he is presentable, and has learned not to be a nuisance. It will be good for him to see something of a real first-class English country house like Humcroft. To a person only accustomed to rough ways and meagre living its luxury will make a memory which will serve in time as an example to be aimed at. I shall write again soon. Don't hesitate to ask any favour which I may be able to confer on you. So long!

Your affectionate cousin,
Ernest Roger Halbard Melton

Extract from Letter from E. Bingham Trent to Queen Teuta of the Blue Mountains.

. . . So I thought the best way to serve that appalling cad would be to take him at his word, and put in his literary contribution in full. I have had made and attested a copy of his "Record," as he calls it, so as to save you trouble. But I send the book itself, because I am afraid that unless you see his words in his own writing, you will not believe that he or anyone else ever penned seriously a document so incriminating. I am sure he must have forgotten what he had written, for even such a dull dog as he is could never have made public such a thing knowingly. . . Such a nature has its revenges on itself. In this case the officers of revenge are his *ipsissima verba*.

RUPERT'S JOURNAL—*Continued*

February 1, 1909

All is now well in train. When the Czar of Russia, on being asked by the Sclavs (as was meet) to be the referee in the "Balkan Settlement," declined on the ground that he was himself by inference an interested party, it was unanimously agreed by the Balkan rulers that the Western King should be asked to arbitrate, as all concerned had perfect confidence in his wisdom, as well as his justice. To their wish he graciously assented. The matter has now been for more than six months in his hands, and he has taken endless trouble to obtain full information. He has now informed us through his Chancellor that his decision is almost ready, and will be communicated as soon as possible.

We have another hunting-party at Vissarion next week. Teuta is looking forward to it with extraordinary interest. She hopes then to present to our brothers of the Balkans our little son, and she is eager to know if they endorse her mother-approval of him.

RUPERT'S JOURNAL—*Continued*

April 15, 1909

The arbitrator's decision has been communicated to us through the Chancellor of the Western King, who brought it to us himself as a special act of friendliness. It met with the enthusiastic approval of all. The Premier remained with us during the progress of the hunting-party, which was one of the most joyous occasions ever known. We are all of good heart, for the future of the Balkan races is now assured. The strife—internal and external—of a thousand years has ceased, and we look with hope for a long and happy time. The Chancellor brought messages of grace and courtliness and friendliness to all. And when I, as spokesman of the party, asked him if we might convey a request of His Majesty that he would honour us by attending the ceremony of making known formally the Balkan Settlement, he answered that the King had authorized him to say that he would, if such were wished by us, gladly come; and that if he should come, he would attend with a fleet as an escort. The Chancellor also told me from himself that it might be possible to have other nationalities represented on such a great occasion by Ambassadors and even fleets, though the monarchs themselves might not be able to attend. He hinted that it might be well if I put the matter in train. (He evidently took it for granted that, though I was only one of several, the matter rested with me—possibly he chose me as the one to whom to make the confidence, as I was born a stranger.) As we talked it over, he grew more enthusiastic, and finally said that, as the King was taking the lead, doubtless all the nations of the earth friendly to him would like to take a part in the ceremony. So it is likely to turn out practically an international ceremony of a unique kind. Teuta will love it, and we shall all do what we can.

Janet Mackelpie's Notes

June 1, 1909

Our dear Teuta is full of the forthcoming celebration of the Balkan Federation, which is to take place this day month, although I must say, for myself, that the ceremony is attaining to such dimensions that I am beginning to have a sort of vague fear of some kind. It almost seems uncanny. Rupert is working unceasingly—has been for some time. For weeks past he seems to have been out day and night on his aeroplane, going through and round over the country arranging matters, and seeing for himself that what has been arranged is being done. Uncle Colin is always about, too, and so is Admiral Rooke. But now Teuta is beginning to go with Rupert. That girl is simply fearless—just like Rupert. And they both seem anxious that little Rupert shall be the same. Indeed, he is the same. A few mornings ago Rupert and Teuta were about to start just after dawn from the top of the Castle. Little Rupert was there—he is always awake early and as bright as a bee. I was holding him in my arms, and when his mother leant over to kiss him good-bye, he held out his arms to her in a way that said as plainly as if he had spoken, "Take me with you."

She looked appealingly at Rupert, who nodded, and said: "All right. Take him, darling. He will have to learn some day, and the sooner the better." The baby, looking eagerly from one to the other with the same questioning in his eyes as there is sometimes in the eyes of a kitten or a puppy—but, of course, with an eager soul behind it—saw that he was going, and almost leaped into his mother's arms. I think she had expected him to come, for she took a little leather dress from Margareta, his nurse, and, flushing with pride, began to wrap him in it. When Teuta, holding him in her arms, stepped on the aeroplane, and took her place in the centre behind Rupert, the young men of the Crown Prince's Guard raised a cheer, amid which Rupert pulled the levers, and they glided off into the dawn.

The Crown Prince's Guard was established by the mountaineers themselves the day of his birth. Ten of the biggest and most powerful and cleverest young men of the nation were chosen, and were sworn in with a very impressive ceremony to guard the young Prince. They were to so arrange and order themselves and matters generally that two at least of them should always have him, or the place in which he was, within their sight. They all vowed that the last of their lives should go before harm came to him. Of course, Teuta understood, and so did Rupert. And these young men are the persons most privileged in the whole Castle. They are dear boys, every one of them, and we are all fond of them and respect them. They simply idolize the baby.

Ever since that morning little Rupert has, unless it is at a time appointed for his sleeping, gone in his mother's arms. I think in any other place there would be some State remonstrance at the whole royal family being at once and together in a dangerous position, but in the Blue Mountains danger and fear are not thought of—indeed, they can hardly be in their terminology. And I really think the child enjoys it even more than his parents. He is just like a little bird that has found the use of his wings. Bless him!

I find that even I have to study Court ritual a little. So many nationalities are to be represented at the ceremony of the "Balkan Settlement," and so many Kings and Princes and notabilities of all kinds are coming, that we must all take care not to make any mistakes.

The Press alone would drive anyone silly. Rupert and Teuta come and sit with me sometimes in the evening when we are all too tired to work, and they rest themselves by talking matters over. Rupert says that there will be over five hundred reporters, and that the applications for permission are coming in so fast that there may be a thousand when the day comes. Last night he stopped in the middle of speaking of it, and said:

"I have an inspiration! Fancy a thousand journalists,—each wanting to get ahead of the rest, and all willing to invoke the Powers of Evil for exclusive information! The only man to look after this department is Rooke. He knows how to deal with men, and as we have already a large staff to look after the journalistic guests, he can be at the head, and appoint his own deputies to act for him. Somewhere and sometime the keeping the peace will be a matter of nerve and resolution, and Rooke is the man for the job."

We were all concerned about one thing, naturally important in the eyes of a woman: What robes was Teuta to wear? In the old days, when there were Kings and Queens, they doubtless wore something gorgeous or impressive; but whatever it was that they wore has gone to dust centuries ago, and there were no illustrated papers in those primitive days. Teuta was talking to me eagerly, with her dear beautiful brows all wrinkled, when Rupert who was reading a bulky document of some kind, looked up and said:

"Of course, darling, you will wear your Shroud?"

"Capital!" she said, clapping her hands like a joyous child. "The very thing, and our people will like it."

I own that for a moment I was dismayed. It was a horrible test of a woman's love and devotion. At a time when she was entertaining Kings and notabilities in her own house—and be sure they would all be decked in their finery—to have to appear in such a garment! A plain thing with nothing even pretty, let alone gorgeous, about it! I expressed my views to Rupert, for I feared that Teuta might be disappointed, though she might not care to say so; but before he could say a word Teuta answered:

"Oh, thank you so much, dear! I should love that above everything, but I did not like to suggest it, lest you should think me arrogant or presuming; for, indeed, Rupert, I am very proud of it, and of the way our people look on it."

"Why not?" said Rupert, in his direct way. "It is a thing for us all to be proud of; the nation has already adopted it as a national emblem—our emblem of courage and devotion and patriotism, which will always, I hope, be treasured beyond price by the men and women of our Dynasty, the Nation, that is—of the Nation that is to be."

Later on in the evening we had a strange endorsement of the national will. A "People's Deputation" of mountaineers, without any official notice or introduction, arrived at the Castle late in the evening in the manner established by Rupert's "Proclamation of Freedom," wherein all citizens were entitled to send a deputation to the King, at will and in private, on any subject of State importance. This deputation was composed of seventeen men, one selected from each political section, so that the body as a whole represented the entire nation. They were of all sorts of social rank and all degrees of fortune, but they were mainly "of the people." They spoke hesitatingly—possibly because Teuta, or even because I, was present—but with a manifest earnestness. They made but one request—that the Queen should, on the great occasion of the Balkan Federation, wear as robes of State the Shroud that they loved to see her in. The spokesman, addressing the Queen, said in tones of rugged eloquence:

"This is a matter, Your Majesty, that the women naturally have a say in, so we have, of course, consulted them. They have discussed the matter by themselves, and then with us, and they are agreed without a flaw that it will be good for the Nation and for Womankind that you do this thing. You have shown to them, and to the world at large, what women should do, what they can do, and they want to make, in memory of your great act, the Shroud a garment of pride and honour for women who have deserved well of their country. In the future it can be a garment to be worn only by privileged women who have earned the right. But they hope, and we hope with them, that on this occasion of our Nation taking the lead before the eyes of the world, all our women may wear it on that day as a means of showing overtly their willingness to do their duty, even to the death. And so"—here he turned to the King—"Rupert, we trust that Her Majesty Queen Teuta will understand that in doing as the women of the Blue Mountains wish, she will bind afresh to the Queen the loyal devotion which she won from them as Voivodin. Henceforth and for all time the Shroud shall be a dress of honour in our Land."

Teuta looked all ablaze with love and pride and devotion. Stars in her eyes shone like white fire as she assured them of the granting of their request. She finished her little speech:

"I feared that if I carried out my own wish, it might look arrogant, but Rupert has expressed the same wish, and now I feel that I am free to wear that dress which brought me to you and to Rupert"—here she beamed on him, and took his hand—"fortified as I am by your wishes and the command of my lord the King."

Rupert took her in his arms and kissed her fondly before them all, saying:

"Tell your wives, my brothers, and the rest of the Blue Mountain women, that that is the answer of the husband who loves and honours his wife. All the world shall see at the ceremony of the Federation of Balka that we men love and honour the women who are loyal and can die for duty. And, men of the Blue Mountains, some day before long we shall organize that great idea, and make it a permanent thing—that the Order of the Shroud is the highest guerdon that a noble-hearted woman can wear."

Teuta disappeared for a few moments, and came back with the Crown Prince in her arms. Everyone present asked to be allowed to kiss him, which they did kneeling.

The Federation Balka

By the Correspondents of "Free America."

The Editors of *Free America* have thought it well to put in consecutive order the reports and descriptions of their Special Correspondents, of whom there were present no less than eight. Not a word they wrote is omitted, but the various parts of their reports are placed in different order, so that, whilst nothing which any of them recorded is left out, the reader may be able to follow the proceedings from the various points of view of the writers who had the most favourable opportunity of moment. In so large an assemblage of journalists—there were present over a thousand—they could not all be present in one place; so our men, in consultation amongst themselves, arranged to scatter, so as to cover the whole proceeding from the various "coigns of vantage," using their skill and experience in selecting these points. One was situated on the summit of the steel-clad tower in the entrance to the Blue Mouth; another on the "Press-boat," which was moored alongside King Rupert's armoured yacht, *The Lady*, whereon were gathered the various Kings and rulers of the Balkan States, all of whom were in the Federation; another was in a swift torpedo-boat, with a roving commission to cruise round the harbour as desired; another took his place on the top of the great mountain which overlooks Plazac, and so had a bird's-eye view of the whole scene of operations; two others were on the forts to right and left of the Blue Mouth; another was posted at the entrance to the Great Tunnel which runs from the water level right up through the mountains to the plateau, where the mines and factories are situate; another had the privilege of a place on an aeroplane, which went everywhere and saw everything. This aeroplane was driven by an old Special Correspondent of *Free America*, who had been a chum of our Special in the Japanese and Russian War, and who has taken service on the Blue Mountain *Official Gazette*.

PLAZAC,
June 30, 1909

Two days before the time appointed for the ceremony the guests of the Land of the Blue Mountains began to arrive. The earlier comers were mostly the journalists who had come from almost over the whole inhabited world. King Rupert, who does things well, had made a camp for their exclusive use. There was a separate tent for each—of course, a small one, as there were over a thousand journalists—but there were big tents for general use scattered about—refectories, reading and writing rooms, a library, idle rooms for rest, etc. In the rooms for reading and writing, which were the work-rooms for general use, were newspapers, the latest attainable from all over the world, Blue-Books, guides, directories, and all such aids to work as forethought could arrange. There was for this special service a body of some hundreds of capable servants in special dress and bearing identification numbers—in fact, King Rupert "did us fine," to use a slang phrase of pregnant meaning.

There were other camps for special service, all of them well arranged, and with plenty of facility for transport. Each of the Federating Monarchs had a camp of his own, in which he had erected a magnificent pavilion. For the Western King, who had acted as Arbitrator in the matter of the Federation, a veritable palace had been built by King Rupert—a sort of Aladdin's palace it must have been, for only a few weeks ago the place it occupied was, I was told, only primeval wilderness. King Rupert and his Queen, Teuta, had a pavilion like the rest of the Federators of Balka, but infinitely more modest, both in size and adornments.

Everywhere were guards of the Blue Mountains, armed only with the "handjar," which is the national weapon. They wore the national dress, but so arranged in colour and accoutrement that the general air of uniformity took the place of a rigid uniform. There must have been at least seventy or eighty thousand of them.

The first day was one of investigation of details by the visitors. During the second day the retinues of the great Federators came. Some of these retinues were vast. For instance, the Soldan (though only just become a Federator) sent of one kind or another more than a thousand men. A brave show they made, for they are fine men, and drilled to perfection. As they swaggered along, singly or in mass, with their gay jackets and baggy trousers, their helmets surmounted by the golden crescent, they looked a foe not to be despised. Landreck Martin, the Nestor of journalists, said to me, as we stood together looking at them:

"To-day we witness a new departure in Blue Mountain history. This is the first occasion for a thousand years that so large a Turkish body has entered the Blue Mountains with a reasonable prospect of ever getting out again."

July 1, 1909

To-day, the day appointed for the ceremony, was auspiciously fine, even for the Blue Mountains, where at this time of year the weather is nearly always fine. They are early folk in the Blue Mountains, but to-day things began to hum before daybreak. There were bugle-calls all over the place—everything here is arranged by calls of musical instruments—trumpets, or bugles, or drums (if, indeed, the drum can be called a musical instrument)—or by lights, if it be after dark. We journalists were all ready; coffee and bread-and-butter had been thoughtfully served early in our sleeping-tents, and an elaborate breakfast was going on all the time in the refectory pavilions. We had a preliminary look round, and then there was a sort of general pause for breakfast. We took advantage of it, and attacked the sumptuous—indeed, memorable—meal which was served for us.

The ceremony was to commence at noon, but at ten o'clock the whole place was astir—not merely beginning to move, but actually moving; everybody taking their places for the great ceremony. As noon drew near, the excitement was intense and prolonged. One by one the various signatories to the Federation began to assemble. They all came by sea; such of them as had sea-boards of their own having their fleets around them. Such as had no fleets of their own were attended by at least one of the Blue Mountain ironclads. And I am bound to say that I never in my life saw more dangerous craft than these little warships of King Rupert of the Blue Mountains. As they entered the Blue Mouth each ship took her appointed station, those which carried the signatories being close together in an isolated group in a little bay almost surrounded by high cliffs in the farthest recesses of the mighty harbour. King Rupert's armoured yacht all the time lay close inshore, hard by the mouth of the Great Tunnel which runs straight into the mountain from a wide plateau, partly natural rock, partly built up with mighty blocks of stone. Here it is, I am told, that the inland products are brought down to the modern town of Plazac. Just as the clocks were chiming the half-hour before noon this yacht glided out into the expanse of the "Mouth." Behind her came twelve great barges, royally decked, and draped each in the colour of the signatory nation. On each of these the ruler entered with his guard, and was carried to Rupert's yacht, he going on the bridge, whilst his suite remained on the lower deck. In the meantime whole fleets had been appearing on the southern horizon; the nations were sending their maritime quota to the christening of "Balka"! In such wonderful order as can only be seen with squadrons of fighting ships, the mighty throng swept into the Blue Mouth, and took up their stations in groups. The only armament of a Great Power now missing was that of the Western King. But there was time. Indeed, as the crowd everywhere began to look at their watches a long line of ships began to spread up northward from the Italian coast. They came at great speed—nearly twenty knots. It was a really wonderful sight—fifty of the finest ships in the world; the very latest expression of naval giants, each seemingly typical of its class—Dreadnoughts, cruisers, destroyers. They came in a wedge, with the King's yacht flying the Royal Standard the apex. Every ship of the squadron bore a red ensign long enough to float from the masthead to the water. From the armoured tower in the waterway one could see the myriad of faces—white stars on both land and sea—for the great harbour was now alive with ships and each and all of them alive with men.

Suddenly, without any direct cause, the white masses became eclipsed—everyone had turned round, and was looking the other way. I looked across the bay and up the mountain behind—a mighty mountain, whose slopes run up to the very sky, ridge after ridge seeming like itself a mountain. Far away on the very top the standard of the Blue Mountains was run up on a mighty Flagstaff which seemed like a shaft of light. It was two hundred feet high, and painted white, and as at the distance the steel stays were invisible, it towered up in lonely grandeur. At its foot was a dark mass grouped behind a white space, which I could not make out till I used my field-glasses.

Then I knew it was King Rupert and the Queen in the midst of a group of mountaineers. They were on the aero station behind the platform of the aero, which seemed to shine—shine, not glitter—as though it were overlaid with plates of gold.

Again the faces looked west. The Western Squadron was drawing near to the entrance of the Blue Mouth. On the bridge of the yacht stood the Western King in uniform of an Admiral, and by him his Queen in a dress of royal purple, splendid with gold. Another glance at the mountain-top showed that it had seemed to become alive. A whole park of artillery seemed to have suddenly sprung to life, round each its crew ready for action. Amongst the group at the foot of the Flagstaff we could distinguish King Rupert; his vast height and bulk stood out from and above all round him. Close to him was a patch of white, which we understood to be Queen Teuta, whom the Blue Mountaineers simply adore.

By this time the armoured yacht, bearing all the signatories to "Balka" (excepting King Rupert), had moved out towards the entrance, and lay still and silent, waiting the coming of the Royal Arbitrator, whose whole squadron simultaneously slowed down, and hardly drifted in the seething water of their backing engines.

When the flag which was in the yacht's prow was almost opposite the armoured fort, the Western King held up a roll of vellum handed to him by one of his officers. We onlookers held our breath, for in an instant was such a scene as we can never hope to see again.

At the raising of the Western King's hand, a gun was fired away on the top of the mountain where rose the mighty Flagstaff with the standard of the Blue Mountains. Then came the thunder of salute from the guns, bright flashes and reports, which echoed down the hillsides in never-ending sequence. At the first gun, by some trick of signalling, the flag of the Federated "Balka" floated out from the top of the Flagstaff, which had been mysteriously raised, and flew above that of the Blue Mountains.

At the same moment the figures of Rupert and Teuta sank; they were taking their places on the aeroplane. An instant after, like a great golden bird, it seemed to shoot out into the air, and then, dipping its head, dropped downward at an obtuse angle. We could see the King and Queen from time waist upwards—the King in Blue Mountain dress of green; the Queen, wrapped in her white Shroud, holding her baby on her breast. When far out from the mountain-top and over the Blue Mouth, the wings and tail of the great bird-like machine went up, and the aero dropped like a stone, till it was only some few hundred feet over the water. Then the wings and tail went down, but with diminishing speed. Below the expanse of the plane the King and Queen were now seen seated together on the tiny steering platform, which seemed to have been lowered; she sat behind her husband, after the manner of matrons of the Blue Mountains. That coming of that aeroplane was the most striking episode of all this wonderful day.

After floating for a few seconds, the engines began to work, whilst the planes moved back to their normal with beautiful simultaneity. There was a golden aero finding its safety in gliding movement. At the same time the steering platform was rising, so that once more the occupants were not far below, but above the plane. They were now only about a hundred feet above the water, moving from the far end of the Blue Mouth towards the entrance in the open space between the two lines of the fighting ships of the various nationalities, all of which had by now their yards manned—a manoeuvre which had begun at the firing of the first gun on the mountain-top. As the aero passed along, all the seamen began to cheer—a cheering which they kept up till the King and Queen had come so close to the Western King's vessel that the two Kings and Queens could greet each other. The wind was now beginning to blow westward from the mountain-top, and it took the sounds towards the armoured fort, so that at moments we could distinguish the cheers of the various nationalities, amongst which, more keen than the others, came the soft "Ban Zai!" of the Japanese.

King Rupert, holding his steering levers, sat like a man of marble. Behind him his beautiful wife, clad in her Shroud, and holding in her arms the young Crown Prince, seemed like a veritable statue.

The aero, guided by Rupert's unerring hand, lit softly on the after-deck of the Western King's yacht; and King Rupert, stepping on deck, lifted from her seat Queen Teuta with her baby in her arms. It was only when the Blue Mountain King stood amongst other men that one could realize his enormous stature. He stood literally head and shoulders over every other man present.

Whilst the aeroplane was giving up its burden, the Western King and his Queen were descending from the bridge. The host and hostess, hand in hand—after their usual fashion, as it seems—hurried forward to greet their guests. The meeting was touching in its simplicity. The two monarchs shook hands, and their consorts, representatives of the foremost types of national beauty of the North and South, instinctively drew close and kissed each other. Then the hostess Queen, moving towards the Western King, kneeled before him with the gracious obeisance of a Blue Mountain hostess, and kissed his hand.

Her words of greeting were:

"You are welcome, sire, to the Blue Mountains. We are grateful to you for all you have done for Balka, and to you and Her Majesty for giving us the honour of your presence."

The King seemed moved. Accustomed as he was to the ritual of great occasions, the warmth and sincerity, together with the gracious humility of this old Eastern custom, touched him, monarch though he was of a great land and many races in the Far East. Impulsively he broke through Court ritual, and did a thing which, I have since been told, won for him for ever a holy place in the warm hearts of the Blue Mountaineers. Sinking on his knee before the beautiful shroud-clad Queen, he raised her hand and kissed it. The act was seen by all in and around the Blue Mouth, and a mighty cheering rose, which seemed to rise and swell as it ran far and wide up the hillsides, till it faded away on the far-off mountain-top, where rose majestically the mighty Flagstaff bearing the standard of the Balkan Federation.

For myself, I can never forget that wonderful scene of a nation's enthusiasm, and the core of it is engraven on my memory. That spotless deck, typical of all that is perfect in naval use; the King and Queen of the greatest nation of the earth received by the newest King and Queen—a King and Queen who won empire for themselves, so that the former subject of another King received him as a brother-monarch on a history-making occasion, when a new world-power was, under his tutelage, springing into existence. The fair Northern Queen in the arms of the dark Southern Queen with the starry eyes. The simple splendour of Northern dress arrayed against that of almost peasant plainness of the giant King of the South. But all were eclipsed—even the thousand years of royal lineage of the Western King, Rupert's natural dower of stature, and the other Queen's bearing of royal dignity and sweetness—by the elemental simplicity of Teuta's Shroud. Not one of all that mighty throng but knew something of her wonderful story; and not one but felt glad and proud that such a noble woman had won an empire through her own bravery, even in the jaws of the grave.

The armoured yacht, with the remainder of the signatories to the Balkan Federation, drew close, and the rulers stepped on board to greet the Western King, the Arbitrator, Rupert leaving his task as personal host and joining them. He took his part modestly in the rear of the group, and made a fresh obeisance in his new capacity.

Presently another warship, *The Balka*, drew close. It contained the ambassadors of Foreign Powers, and the Chancellors and high officials of the Balkan nations. It was followed by a fleet of warships, each one representing a Balkan Power. The great Western fleet lay at their moorings, but with the exception of manning their yards, took no immediate part in the proceedings.

On the deck of the new-comer the Balkan monarchs took their places, the officials of each State grading themselves behind their monarch. The Ambassadors formed a foremost group by themselves.

Last came the Western King, quite alone (save for the two Queens), bearing in his hand the vellum scroll, the record of his arbitration. This he proceeded to read, a polyglot copy of it having been already supplied to every Monarch, Ambassador, and official present. It was a long statement, but the occasion was so stupendous—so intense—that the time flew by quickly. The cheering had ceased the moment the Arbitrator opened the scroll, and a veritable silence of the grave abounded.

When the reading was concluded Rupert raised his hand, and on the instant came a terrific salvo of cannon-shots from not only the ships in the port, but seemingly all up and over the hillsides away to the very summit.

When the cheering which followed the salute had somewhat toned down, those on board talked together, and presentations were made. Then the barges took the whole company to the armour-clad fort in the entrance-way to the Blue Mouth. Here, in front, had been arranged for the occasion, platforms for the starting of aeroplanes. Behind them were the various thrones of state for the Western King and Queen, and the various rulers of "Balka"—as the new and completed Balkan Federation had become—*de jure* as well as *de facto*. Behind were seats for the rest of the company. All was a blaze of crimson and gold. We of the Press were all expectant, for some ceremony had manifestly been arranged, but of all details of it we had been kept in ignorance. So far as I could tell from the faces, those present were at best but partially informed. They were certainly ignorant of all details, and even of the entire programme of the day. There is a certain kind of expectation which is not concerned in the mere execution of fore-ordered things.

The aero on which the King and Queen had come down from the mountain now arrived on the platform in the charge of a tall young mountaineer, who stepped from the steering-platform at once. King Rupert, having handed his Queen (who still carried her baby) into her seat, took his place, and pulled a lever. The aero went forward, and seemed to fall head foremost off the fort. It was but a dip, however, such as a skilful diver takes from a height into shallow water, for the plane made an upward curve, and in a few seconds was skimming upwards towards the Flagstaff. Despite the wind, it arrived there in an incredibly short time. Immediately after his flight another aero, a big one this time, glided to the platform. To this immediately stepped a body of ten tall, fine-looking young men. The driver pulled his levers, and the plane glided out on the track of the King. The Western King, who was noticing, said to the Lord High Admiral, who had been himself in command of the ship of war, and now stood close behind him:

"Who are those men, Admiral?"

"The Guard of the Crown Prince, Your Majesty. They are appointed by the Nation."

"Tell me, Admiral, have they any special duties?"

"Yes, Your Majesty," came the answer: "to die, if need be, for the young Prince!"

"Quite right! That is fine service. But how if any of them should die?"

"Your Majesty, if one of them should die, there are ten thousand eager to take his place."

"Fine, fine! It is good to have even one man eager to give his life for duty. But ten thousand! That is what makes a nation!"

When King Rupert reached the platform by the Flagstaff, the Royal Standard of the Blue Mountains was hauled up under it. Rupert stood up and raised his hand. In a second a cannon beside him was fired; then, quick as thought, others were fired in sequence, as though by one prolonged lightning-flash. The roar was incessant, but getting less in detonating sound as the distance and the hills subdued it. But in the general silence which prevailed round us we could hear the sound as though passing in a distant circle, till finally the line which had gone northward came back by the south, stopping at the last gun to south'ard of the Flagstaff.

"What was that wonderful circle?" asked the King of the Lord High Admiral.

"That, Your Majesty, is the line of the frontier of the Blue Mountains. Rupert has ten thousand cannon in line."

"And who fires them? I thought all the army must be here."

"The women, Your Majesty. They are on frontier duty to-day, so that the men can come here."

Just at that moment one of the Crown Prince's Guards brought to the side of the King's aero something like a rubber ball on the end of a string. The Queen held it out to the baby in her arms, who grabbed at it. The guard drew back. Pressing that ball must have given some signal, for on the instant a cannon, elevated to perpendicular, was fired. A shell went straight up an enormous distance. The shell burst, and sent out both a light so bright that it could be seen in the daylight, and a red smoke, which might have been seen from the heights of the Calabrian Mountains over in Italy.

As the shell burst, the King's aero seemed once more to spring from the platform out into mid-air, dipped as before, and glided out over the Blue Mouth with a rapidity which, to look at, took one's breath away.

As it came, followed by the aero of the Crown Prince's Guard and a group of other aeros, the whole mountain-sides seemed to become alive. From everywhere, right away up to the farthest visible mountain-tops, darted aeroplanes, till a host of them were rushing with dreadful speed in the wake of the King. The King turned to Queen Teuta, and evidently said something, for she beckoned to the Captain of the Crown Prince's Guard, who was steering the plane. He swerved away to the right, and instead of following above the open track between the lines of warships, went high over the outer line. One of those on board began to drop something, which, fluttering down, landed on every occasion on the bridge of the ship high over which they then were.

The Western King said again to the Gospodar Rooke (the Lord High Admiral):

"It must need some skill to drop a letter with such accuracy."

With imperturbable face the Admiral replied:

"It is easier to drop bombs, Your Majesty."

The flight of aeroplanes was a memorable sight. It helped to make history. Henceforth no nation with an eye for either defence or attack can hope for success without the mastery of the air.

In the meantime—and after that time, too—God help the nation that attacks "Balka" or any part of it, so long as Rupert and Teuta live in the hearts of that people, and bind them into an irresistible unity.

A Note About the Author

Bram Stoker (1847–1912) was an Irish novelist. Born in Dublin, Stoker suffered from an unknown illness as a young boy before entering school at the age of seven. He would later remark that the time he spent bedridden enabled him to cultivate his imagination, contributing to his later success as a writer. He attended Trinity College, Dublin from 1864, graduating with a BA before returning to obtain an MA in 1875. After university, he worked as a theatre critic, writing a positive review of acclaimed Victorian actor Henry Irving's production of *Hamlet* that would spark a lifelong friendship and working relationship between them. In 1878, Stoker married Florence Balcombe before moving to London, where he would work for the next 27 years as business manager of Irving's influential Lyceum Theatre. Between his work in London and travels abroad with Irving, Stoker befriended such artists as Oscar Wilde, Walt Whitman, Hall Caine, James Abbott McNeill Whistler, and Sir Arthur Conan Doyle. In 1895, having published several works of fiction and nonfiction, Stoker began writing his masterpiece *Dracula* (1897) while vacationing at the Kilmarnock Arms Hotel in Cruden Bay, Scotland. Stoker continued to write fiction for the rest of his life, achieving moderate success as a novelist. Known more for his association with London theatre during his life, his reputation as an artist has grown since his death, aided in part by film and television adaptations of *Dracula*, the enduring popularity of the horror genre, and abundant interest in his work from readers and scholars around the world.

A Note from the Publisher

Spanning many genres, from non-fiction essays to literature classics to children's books and lyric poetry, Mint Edition books showcase the master works of our time in a modern new package. The text is freshly typeset, is clean and easy to read, and features a new note about the author in each volume. Many books also include exclusive new introductory material. Every book boasts a striking new cover, which makes it as appropriate for collecting as it is for gift giving. Mint Edition books are only printed when a reader orders them, so natural resources are not wasted. We're proud that our books are never manufactured in exce
quantity they need to be read and enjoyed.

Discover more of your favorite classics with Bookfinity™.

- Track your reading with custom book lists.
- Get great book recommendations for your personalized Reader Type.
- Add reviews for your favorite books.
- AND MUCH MORE!

Visit **bookfinity.com** and take the fun Reader Type quiz to get started.

Enjoy our classic and modern companion pairings!

Printed in the USA
CPSIA information can be obtained
at www.ICGtesting.com
JSHW022212140824
68134JS00018B/1001